James Douglas was born in Belfast in 1947, though he grew up in Aberdeen. He moved to Australia in 1965 and worked on a wildcat oil rig in Bass Strait. He has also been a publican and now lives in Melbourne with his wife and five children. He divides his time between the UK and Australia.

JAMES DOUGLAS

THE CLAN

PENGUIN BOOKS

PENGUIN BOOKS

Published by the Penguin Group
Penguin Books Ltd, 27 Wrights Lane, London W8 5TZ, England
Penguin Putnam Inc., 375 Hudson Street, New York, New York 10014, USA
Penguin Books Australia Ltd, Ringwood, Victoria, Australia
Penguin Books Canada Ltd, 10 Alcorn Avenue, Toronto, Ontario, Canada M4V 3B2
Penguin Books (NZ) Ltd, 182–190 Wairau Road, Auckland 10, New Zealand

Penguin Books Ltd, Registered Offices: Harmondsworth, Middlesex, England

First published in Australia as *Kin* in Penguin Books 1996
First published in Great Britain as *The Clan* in Penguin Books 1997
1 3 5 7 9 10 8 6 4 2

Copyright © James Douglas, 1996
All rights reserved

The moral right of the author has been asserted

Printed in England by Clays Ltd, St Ives plc

Except in the United States of America, this book is sold subject
to the condition that it shall not, by way of trade or otherwise, be lent,
re-sold, hired out, or otherwise circulated without the publisher's
prior consent in any form of binding or cover other than that in
which it is published and without a similar condition including this
condition being imposed on the subsequent purchaser

To my wife Linda and my children, Julieanne, Jacqui, James, Richard and Kara, with love.

PROLOGUE

Steve Munro glanced over his shoulder at the clock in the tower of the old Dearborn Station and turned left into Dearborn Street, bracing himself against the chill by burying his face as far as he could into the raised collar of his ancient blue Burberry.

Kasey's Bar, a hundred or so yards from the corner in this old redbrick section of downtown Chicago was all but deserted, save for Kascy himself and an old regular customer perched up at the bar. Both looked up when a biting wind barged in ahead of Munro.

'I think we're in for a bit of snow.' Munro rubbed his gloved hands together and backed up to the radiator sandwiched between the coat-stand and the wall-mounted jukebox that nobody played at this time of the day.

'It wouldn't surprise me.' Kasey glanced out the cluttered store-front window with a practised measure of concern and placed on the polished mahogany bar-top a napkin, a glass and a bottle of Coors Light, in that order.

Munro liked Kasey's. It was comfortable and old and original, a lot like his worn old coat. A case of 'everything old will be new again', he thought, knowing that Kasey hadn't planned it that way. His resistance to change had done it for him.

'You early tonight Munro, or has that clock stopped again?'

Munro wished Kasey hadn't reminded him. He knew he should have gone back to the office. Doubly so, when Kasey answered the phone and looked directly at him, with his hand clamped firmly over the mouthpiece. 'Are you here?' Kasey whispered.

'Who is it?'

'It's himself,' Kasey answered, in that Chicago–Irish brogue of his.

'Tell him I just walked in,' Munro said, wondering if it would've been a better idea to tell him that he had just walked out.

Kasey nodded. 'I can just see him walking up the sidewalk. Do you want me to go get him, in case he walks on by, Walter?'

'Kasey.'

'Yes, Walter?'

'Just put him on, will you? Better still, tell him to get his ass over here right away. Tell him it's important.'

Munro was already at the coat-stand with his scarf around his neck when Kasey delivered the message.

He was in a Yellow Cab and gone before Kasey had a chance to clear away his empty glass.

'Keep the change,' he told the Nigerian driver, pulling into the kerb in front of the Chicago *Post*. On his way to the editor's office he exchanged quips with several colleagues, ignored others and fired two quick blasts from a breath purifier directly to the back of his throat.

'Come in,' he heard, before he had time to knock on the frosted glass pane in the editor's door.

'Walter, I know what you're thinking, but –'

The editor, an overweight, moon-faced man with a constantly flushed complexion extending to the back of his bald head, held his hand up to silence him. 'Steve, I know you're going through a rough patch, but man, let me tell you, you look like a piece of shit.'

Munro looked up from the carpet, the same carpet he had found himself staring at with increasing regularity over the past few months.

'Take your coat off and sit down, Steve.' Walter Caldwell motioned to the chair, his tone significantly mellowed.

Munro looked down at his clothes and retorted, 'So when did you join the fashion police?' Munro sat heavily in the chair opposite Caldwell.

The editor glanced up momentarily from the paperwork he was needlessly rearranging and said, 'Don't be a smartass Steve. I don't want to see your attitude slip as low as your self-esteem.' He then shook his head and cast an eye over the man he had once considered fit to take over the *Post* when he stepped down. It saddened him that Steve Munro, looking decidedly older than his fifty-three years, was now fighting to keep his job, not to mention his dignity.

'I've got something here that might interest you,' he continued, heartened when Munro leaned forward with one elbow on the desk, displaying more interest than he'd done in a long time. Caldwell noted that despite the dark circles below his friend's bloodshot hazel eyes, he hadn't completely gone to seed, yet. If anything his recent gaunt appearance accentuated his high cheekbones and granted a subtle prominence to his once beefy jaw line.

'Are you looking after yourself, Steve?' Caldwell realised that his friend's weight loss was due more to his irregular eating habits than any conscious attempt to stay in shape.

'Walter . . .' Munro waited for his boss to make eye contact.

Caldwell found the piece of paper he was looking for and placed it on top of the bundle before he looked up, his silence inviting Munro to continue.

Standing, Munro hastily brushed a hand over his unkempt, greying brown hair and leaned across the desk as far as he could, taking his weight on the knuckles of his free hand. 'Did you drag me all the way up here just to ridicule me, because, if you did, you can shove your job right up your ass, Walter.' Munro lingered long enough to gauge his boss's reaction before he turned on his heel and walked towards the door. Before he was halfway there the satisfaction of responding to the rising tide of anger at what he considered an overt attempt, by a lifelong friend, to humiliate him, had turned to regret. He knew that if he walked out of the door, his chances of picking up the pieces, keeping his job, would be next to none. At least I've proved that I've still got some dignity, he thought.

Caldwell waited until Munro's hand was on the doorknob. 'Now that you've got that off your chest would you mind listening to what I've got to say before you leave?' He was loath to admit it, but he was secretly pleased. Munro, it seemed, still had some spark left in him.

Munro allowed five agonising seconds to pass then slowly relaxed his grip on the knob and turned to face his boss. He too was pleased, now that the chest-beating contest had ended in a draw. At least in his eyes.

'Sit down, Steve.' Caldwell smiled and once again motioned to the chair. 'Your pal Hewson down in Classifieds brought this to my attention. He tells me you're not returning his calls. He said he didn't want to leave this with your answering service.' Caldwell slid across his desk a sheet of paper, in the centre of which was a business-card size copy of an advertisement Hewson had been running.

Squinting, Munro flipped the paper to face him and read:

> **A MATTER OF LIFE AND DEATH**
> A substantial reward is offered for information leading to the location of Thomas Edgely Gilfeather or any of his living relatives. Contact PO Box 1739, South Lambeth Road, London SW8, UK.

Caldwell leaned back in his swivel chair and knitted his fingers in a platform under his chin. 'If this isn't the break you've been looking for, I don't know what is.' Both men broke into a smile simultaneously.

'When do I leave?'

Caldwell took an envelope from the top drawer of his desk and handed it over to Munro. 'I took the liberty of booking you a ticket. You can pay me back later. You're flying out tonight. It was the first available flight. You can take a couple of weeks' vacation. No more. Oh, and by the way, the only contact you can make with whoever placed the advertisement is by way of that PO box in London. I checked.'

After peeking at the plane ticket in the manila envelope Munro reached across the desk, extended his hand and said, 'Thanks.'

'Don't thank me,' Caldwell grinned, 'I'm looking on this as an investment. If you can get your life back in order, I might get what was my best reporter to return to normal.'

'I won't let you down.'

The editor smiled to himself as he watched Munro saunter towards the door, deep in thought. 'Before you go, Steve ... It looks like you're not the only one looking for Tommy. Presuming it's one and the same person.'

'Gilfeather's an extremely rare name in this country. In any country, for that matter. Add up all the Gilfeathers in the world and I wonder how many Tommys you'll find? And whoever placed the advertisement knows enough about him to look for him here. That's too much of a coincidence. Mind you, much as I'd hate to disappoint them, if Tommy *was* here I know I would have found him by now.' Munro waited to field the next question.

When Caldwell responded with a delicate nod of his head Munro waved the envelope in an improvised salute and turned to leave the room. He was clear of the door when Caldwell shouted after him. Stopping, he waited for the monologue he thought he had escaped this time. 'I know you don't want to talk about it Steve, but it's time to get on with your life, whether you find him or not.'

In silence Munro hesitated, nodded slowly and continued on his way, leaving the door open behind him.

Caldwell called after him once more. 'If you need anything, you know where to reach me. Keep in touch.' Munro caught a cab to his apartment overlooking the South branch of the Chicago River and packed in a hurry. He then poured himself a drink and telephoned the limo service, informing them that he was ready any time they were. Settling down to wait he contemplated his future, rationalising firstly that, of late, he hadn't exactly been setting the world on fire. Blaming himself for the reasons behind Tom Gilfeather's disappearance he had succumbed to the comfort of the bottle and had gradually become even more dependent on it. The steady decline, first of his appearance, then the work ethic he had once held sacred, was obvious to all long before it reached a level where he was forced to acknowledge the depths to which he had sunk. His future, or lack thereof, he determined, was intrinsically dependent upon him finding Tom Gilfeather.

ONE

Donna Macintyre entered the post office right on opening time, retrieved her mail from Box 1739 and shuffled through the handful of envelopes, needlessly checking that they all bore a Chicago postmark. On her way to the exit, and oblivious to those she forced to negotiate a path around her, she stopped, opened the first envelope and read eagerly, disappointment registering in her eyes before she was halfway down the page. She followed her usual procedure and slotted the envelopes into her over-the-shoulder leather bag and left the post office, hurried past the laundromat and into Stan's Cafe, next to the Pakistani deli on the corner of Tradescant Road.

'One tea please,' she ordered from the smiling Stan.

'Take a seat, love, and I'll bring it over to you.'

She found a table well away from the window and began reading, unaware of the cup and saucer being placed in front of her, or the smile and kind word from Stan. When she finished and the tea had gone cold, a blink released the wells of tears to track down her cheeks until a single wipe with the back of her hand dismissed them. Once again she had laboured to read correspondence that dwelled mainly on the reward while offering nothing other than the same two names taken straight out of the Chicago telephone directory. Names she had already checked up on.

Steve Munro slipped into the cafe behind her and seated himself at the only available table, the one directly in line with the ankle-numbing draught blowing in under the door. After settling, he dipped the corner of the *Daily Telegraph* he was lurking behind, hoping to get a closer look at the woman he'd been keeping an eye on for the past few days. He saw the black, chin-level hair cut in a bob, and the troubled, green eyes set wide of a naturally slender nose. High cheekbones being dabbed by a powder puff and full, well-proportioned lips receiving a maintenance coat of flame-red lipstick stamped her as a woman of considerable beauty. But what puzzled Munro was the reason such a stunning woman, one so elegantly dressed in an expensive, tailored black coat, lived in the hovel across the road.

As he watched Donna get to her feet, wedge the letters deep into the bottom of her bag and leave without paying for the tea that remained untouched, or returning Stan's cordial, 'See ya later Donna,' curiosity nearly got the better of Munro. Had the need for caution not been foremost on his mind – based on the fear of driving Gilfeather further underground should he become aware of the added interest in him – he would have approached her on the spot.

His intentions had always been to allow this stranger to lead him to Gilfeather, but with each passing day and the regular trips to the post office, the likelihood of that seemed to be becoming more remote. This was despite the fact that at his request the *Post* had run her advertisement continuously, at no cost and without her knowledge, long after her commissioned time had expired. It worried him that if something didn't break soon he would be forced to liaise with the woman, or head back to Chicago emptyhanded. With neither option particularly appealing, he made the same decision he had made the day before, and the day before that: to return tomorrow and give it one more try.

On leaving the comparative warmth of Stan's Cafe, and being greeted by a freezing wind and a persistent light rain, Donna lowered her head and stayed close to the deli window on her way around the corner to the taxi rank in Tradescant Road. When she was out of the wind she glanced at her watch to confirm that she was still on schedule.

She climbed into the back of the black cab, plopped herself down and forced a smile when she made eye contact with the familiar face of the driver via the rear-view mirror. The driver raised his eyebrows and returned the smile. 'Where to, Donna?'

'Pentonville,' she answered.

'Umm, your old man getting out then?' the driver said, thinking that the time must be about due and doubting that there could be any other possible explanation for his regular passenger making the trip to Pentonville Prison at this hour of the morning. If he was right, and he was pretty sure he was, he was glad that he would be the first to spread the news.

'Not before time,' Donna confirmed, her longing to have her husband home at complete odds with her desire, and frantic attempts, to find Tom Gilfeather before he got out. 'You know he didn't get one day off for good behaviour.'

'Is that a fact?'

'Not one solitary day. Not one.'

'Away you go?'

'I'm telling you.'

'Well, when you come to think of it, it stands to reason, don't it? I mean, no offence, Donna, but it's not exactly his cup of tea, is it? Know what I mean?'

'That's my Jimmy,' Donna grinned, her slight Northern accent contrasting sharply with that of the Londoner.

'Yeah, how would it look, the likes of your Jimmy behaving he'self? I mean, it's not altogether what we've come to expect, is it? Doesn't go with the territory, does it?' Fearing that he might have created the wrong impression, the driver quickly added, 'Don't get me wrong, Donna. I'm not talking about as far as us punters are concerned, ordinary people the likes of me. I'm talking about the bleeding authorities. As far as I'm concerned, your Jimmy is a thorough gentleman, a real toff, and I'll have no hesitation in telling him that to his face. A thorough gentleman.'

Yeah, join the queue, Donna thought, waiting until the cab had merged with the traffic on South Lambeth Road before she reached into her handbag for a cigarette. 'Hope you don't mind?' she said, blowing the smoke directly at the open sliding window that separated her from the driver. As she expected, the driver said 'Not at all,' and slid the window shut, leaving her alone with her thoughts. She was nervous enough at the prospect of confronting her husband and the last thing she needed was a trip across town listening to the cabbie's incessant chatter.

She was thinking that the days were gone when the prestige of being married to the most feared enforcer in London was compensation for the price she had to pay: an impost her husband flippantly referred to as an 'occupational hazard', the stretches where he spent more time in than out of prison. Prolonged periods where she was deprived of her husband and Corrie, their nine-year-old son, his father. 'You've got to take the good with the bad,' she could hear him say. Well, not any more. This time, one way or the other, she would get the message across, give him an ultimatum. If he returned to his old ways he would have no family to come home to.

On the approach to the main gates of Pentonville the driver was first to spot Jimmy Macintyre leaving the prison by the side door next to the main gates. 'There he is now,' he proclaimed, sliding the window open behind him and appearing almost as excited as Donna, minus the apprehension.

In his mid-thirties, and a touch under six feet, Jimmy Macintyre had never looked better. Two years spent with little else to do than maintain his body in peak physical condition had done him no harm. He was dressed in a single-breasted blue serge suit with collar and tie, his dark, almost black hair, with its unintentionally fashionable short back and sides prison haircut, was combed back off his forehead. In a certain light his often intense brown eyes looked black; like his heavyset jaw and prominent cheekbones, they were a trait inherited from his grandfather on his mother's side. A nose slightly flattened in the middle did nothing to detract from his rugged good looks.

Donna forgot all thoughts of the impending confrontation the moment she set eyes on him. Even before the vehicle came to a stop she had the door open ready to jump out, and sprinted towards him as fast as her high heels would carry her. Flinging her arms around his neck she nearly knocked him backwards over the leather carry-all he'd placed on the ground behind him.

'Steady on,' he laughed in a Glasgow accent still strong despite the ten and more years he'd spent in England.

Donna clung to his neck and lifted her heels clear

of the ground behind her when Jimmy, after steadying himself, gripped her by the waist and spun her in a full circle. The driver, loitering for an acknowledgment from Jimmy, turned and looked away when the couple locked in a long passionate embrace. After holding Donna at arm's length Jimmy instinctively looked over her shoulder, hoping to see his son.

'You didn't bring Corrie?' he said, half-expecting him to jump out from somewhere.

A frown came over Donna's face. 'He was still asleep when I was ready to leave the house and I decided not to wake him. The less he sees of this place the better, and anyway, I thought you'd be seeing him soon enough.'

'Aye, fair enough, I suppose. How is he anyway? All right?'

Donna hesitated for a moment, forcing a smile before she answered. 'Well, he hasn't gotten any worse, so I suppose we can be thankful for that.'

'Ach, he'll be all right. No danger.' Jimmy said, in keeping with his habit of burying his head in the sand when things didn't suit him. He was reluctant to pursue the point in case he heard something that might mar the elation of his first day out. For the same reason Donna decided not to elaborate.

'Don't forget your bag,' the driver said, swooping on the carry-all when Jimmy put his arm around Donna's waist and steered her towards the cab.

'Thanks, pal.'

'Welcome to the outside world,' the driver gushed,

glad at last to be getting a bit of attention.

'Aye, ta mate, it's good to be out.' Jimmy answered, ducking into the taxi.

After five minutes of excited, one-sided conversation Jimmy sensed a certain reticence in his wife, a brooding silence punctuated by weak smiles and half-hearted replies. 'You're a wee bit on the quiet side there, doll. I thought you might've managed to get yourself a wee bit more excited, seeing that this's my first day out. There's nothing the matter, is there? You said our Corrie was going to be all right, didn't you?'

Donna leaned forward and pushed the sliding window all the way shut. Dwelling on the reality of having her husband home before she found Tom Gilfeather had proved to be more harrowing than she had anticipated. 'Jimmy,' she began resolutely, pressing on with the prepared speech designed to keep him out of prison, 'I didn't want to bring this up so soon, you know, on account of this being your first day out and all that, but, um, I suppose now's as good a time as any.'

Jimmy's heart sank. He was sure she was about to tell him that there was somebody else. The fate of many a released prisoner. 'Fire away,' he gulped.

'I've given this a lot of thought Jimmy . . .'

When Donna paused to choose her words Jimmy had to stop himself from saying, For Christsake, mean what?

'I've made a decision. I'm going to take our Corrie and

move back to Yorkshire until you decide what comes first, your family or spending half your life in jail.'

'Is that what's up with you? Come on, doll, it's me you're talking to.' Jimmy forced a nervous smile and glanced over to make sure that the driver wasn't listening. He was more than relieved to learn that she wasn't about to confess to having another man in her life.

'No, Jimmy, I love you and all that, but I've made up my mind this time. I spend half *my* life waiting for you to get out and the other half waiting for the knock at the door that'll put you back inside. Nope, I'm afraid I've got no intentions of hanging around waiting for you to be sent back to jail. Enough's enough.'

'Even though it's our livelihood we're talking about here, eh? What am I supposed to do to make a living? Going the demand is the only thing I know.'

'Livelihood!' Donna scoffed. 'Who do you think keeps us when you're inside? It's not that family of yours, I can tell you. Quite the opposite. If it wasn't for me the only money coming into the house would be from the Social Security.'

Jimmy shook his head and slowly let out his breath. 'For Christsake, Donna, I told you to watch them. You don't need me to tell you what they're like. Christ, you've known them long enough.'

'Don't you Christsake me, Jimmy Macintyre. It was your idea for me to move in with them while you were inside. I don't know which one of us got the worst sentence.'

'Apart from giving you the chance to save a wee bit of money it was supposed to be so's our Corrie'd have a bit of company and somebody to look after him while you were at your work.'

'It would've been a sight cheaper hiring a nanny, aye and a whole lot easier. I don't know why I let you talk me into it. We were all right where we were.'

'What brought this on? I can't believe it. I haven't been out five bloody minutes.' Jimmy shook his head and looked out the window to his left.

'This has been building up, Jimmy. For two years as a matter of fact. And I'm not just talking about that disfu –, whatever it is you call it, family of yours.' Donna wanted to take him in her arms, but she was well aware that, as usual, he wasn't taking her all that seriously.

'I could look for a new line of work, I suppose. If that's what you're talking about. Anyway, it's about time. I'm getting too old for this caper. Too many young bucks out there trying to make a name for themselves.'

Donna looked at him out of the corner of her eye and shook her head slowly. 'Young bucks? Who do you think you're kidding?' she scoffed. 'Anyway, the penny might drop when you see me packing my bags the minute we walk in the door.'

Time to be a bit more convincing, Jimmy thought, realising that his wife appeared to be much more determined than she had been on similar occasions in the past. 'Hey, giv'us a bit of credit, doll, will you?

I've been giving this a bit of thought myself lately. You know, taking stock and all that, the future and that type of thing, and guess what? I've come to the exact same conclusion as yourself. No shit. I swear on my granny's life.'

Donna, recognising his superficial tone, answered, 'Jimmy, if you mean it, never mind swearing on your granny's life. Swear on our Corrie's life. Swear that you're done with jail and all that standover stuff.'

'If you can keep us until I get on my feet, I'll tell you one thing, Donna, you won't see me setting foot back inside. No chance. Like you said, enough's enough.'

'Swear Jimmy. Let me hear you say it.'

'I swear. What else can I say? I can't put it any simpler than that.'

'Swear on our Corrie's life,' she urged, tiring of the continued resistance.

'I swear on our Corrie's life. There, are you happy now?'

Staring directly into his eyes Donna swallowed and rested her head on his shoulder. Several moments later she raised her head and stressed, 'If you go back on your word this time, I *swear* on our Corrie's life that we won't be around when you get out.' Although she believed he was being sincere at the moment she knew that he put more stock in her oath than she did in his.

'Ach, it's my own stupid, bloody fault, so it is. And eh, see me, I'm the first to admit I deserve everything

I get. But I've got the message this time. All right, Donna doll?' Jimmy placed his hand on top of her head and gently eased it towards his lap.

'Jimmy,' Donna withdrew her head and glanced up at the back of the driver's head.

'What's up. I said I got the message, didn't I?'

'Yeah, I suppose. But Jimmy –'

'Donna, I told you I got the message, Christsake.'

'As long as you're well aware,' Donna said, determined to have the last word. 'Oh, and you'll just have to content yourself till we get home, mister.'

On Jimmy's instruction the driver took the scenic route along the Victoria Embankment and crossed the Thames back into South London by way of Westminster Bridge. To disguise his ulterior motive he told Donna that there was something about the activity on the river that heightened his sense of freedom: the frenzied skirl of seagulls, and the smell of diesel-contaminated water rippling in the wake of an assortment of tugs, barges and a lone pleasure boat.

The detour, as planned, lined him up with St George's Road, on the way to the New Kent Road, and a car yard situated near the Elephant and Castle. No chance of mending my ways until this is out of the road, he told himself.

'While we're this close,' he said, addressing Donna before he tapped on the driver's window to inform of the change of plan. 'Go straight ahead, driver, on up to the Elephant and Castle and I'll show you where to go when we get there. If you know what I mean?'

'What's this, Jimmy?' Donna said, making no attempt to hide her exasperation. 'Corrie's at home waiting for us.'

'I'll only be a minute,' Jimmy said, tapping the window again and pointing up ahead to the used car yard on the other side of the New Kent Road.

'Won't be long, pet,' Jimmy said and stepped out onto the pavement under a garish sign festooned with red, white and blue bunting fluttering furiously in the wind. The sign proclaimed YOU'LL DO ALL RIGHT WITH BERT WRIGHT.

The proprietor, surveying his yard from the doorway of a portable office, smiled at what he took to be the arrival of a potential customer. He was a stocky, balding man in his late thirties, immaculately dressed in a two-piece Armani suit that served only to emphasise his hardened features and his unmistakable working-class accent. His apprehension was visible through the smile when he realised that his caller was no potential customer. 'Well, if it ain't Jimmy Macintyre,' he said nervously, adjusting his tie and offering his hand.

'How's it going, Bert, all right?' Jimmy sneered.

Though the car dealer was loath to present an image other than that of absolute prosperity caution determined his answer. 'Oh, you know how it is, Jimmy. Times are tough.'

Jimmy reached out and took the lapels of the Armani suit between his thumb and forefinger, feeling the quality of the cloth. A wry smile informed the dealer that his answer lacked credibility.

'When did you get out, Jimmy?'

'This morning,' Jimmy answered, and began walking towards a line of cars.

'This morning? Christ, come into the office and have a snort. This calls for a celebration.' He was looking for any excuse to steer Jimmy away from his stock.

'Haven't got time. Donna's out the front waiting for me,' Jimmy said, stopping beside an almost new black Vauxhall Cavalier, the car he judged to be the pick of the bunch.

The car dealer switched to selling mode. He was thinking that, as Jimmy Macintyre hadn't mentioned the money owing to him, he intended using it as a deposit on a car. 'Nice motor this one, Jim. If I wasn't in such dire need of the readies I'd keep it for myself. On my life.'

'I'll take it,' Jimmy said, getting into the driver's seat and taking hold of the steering wheel.

'Don't you want to know how much it is, Jimmy? Or is money no object?' Bert laughed.

'I didn't say I was going to buy it, Berty. I said I was going to *take* it. Now on you go and toddle off to that wee office of yours and get me the keys. I'm in a bit of a hurry.'

'Awh, come on, Jimmy,' Bert protested meekly, screwing up his face and displaying his open palms. 'I only owe you a couple of hundred quid. This motor's worth –'

'Plus two years interest, yeh cunt. Me and you'd still be friends if you'd done what I told you and sent the money round to Donna.' At the mention of his wife's name Jimmy glanced over at the parked cab. 'Now see, if I hav'to get out of this motor –'

The car dealer stepped back from the vehicle and raised his hands chest-high. 'Stay where you are,' he pleaded, and backed towards his office, returning two minutes later with the keys and the blank paperwork for Jimmy to sign. 'Don't get me wrong here Jimmy, whatever you do, but eh, I don't think Anton's going to be too pleased about this. He more or less took over this patch when you went back inside. Know what I mean. He's been collecting the weekly contributions.'

Jimmy laughed. 'Do I look like a fucken mirage to you, eh?'

'No, Jimmy.'

'Good. In that case you can expect to see me every ... let me see, what day's this, as if I could forget? Aye, you have the fifty quid ready each and every Friday, starting today, or me and you are going to fall out something chronic.'

'What about Anton?' Bert replied, extracting a fifty pound note from his pocket without revealing the wad.

'Hey listen, mister,' Jimmy snapped, again glancing towards Donna, who was now standing on the pavement beside the parked cab, 'you tell Anton he can go and fuck himself. Aye, and open your yapper once more and I'll ... I'll charge you for two years' arrears.'

'There'll be no need for that, Jimmy.'

'OK then. Nice to do business with you, Bert.' Jimmy winked, and drove out of the car yard and around to where the cab was parked.

Donna had already spotted him and was standing, hands on hips, waiting for an explanation. 'This better be good,' she told him, opening the passenger side door of the Cavalier and leaning in.

'What are you talking about? We'll be needing something to run around in, surely to Christ?'

'How much did you pay for this? Here's me trying to save every penny I can for our Corrie's –'

'Donna, hold on a wee minute, will yeh doll?' Jimmy said, exasperation showing in his voice. 'Yer man Bert was kind enough to give me a wee lend of it. So don't start.'

Donna remained silent, her narrowed eyes flitting over the car.

'I'll take it back if you don't want it.' Jimmy offered.

'How long have you got the lend of it for, then?'

'Until I get sick of it.'

Bert Wright hurried into his office, pulled his swivel chair away from the window and positioned himself for a clear view of Jimmy Macintyre. As soon as he saw him drive away he grabbed for the phone and punched in the numbers. 'We've got trouble, Anton,' he said, dispensing with the usual pleasantries.

'Yeah. What's up Bert? Those kids been at it again? Why don't you just –'

'Jimmy Macintyre just paid me a visit,' Bert cut in. The line went quiet, prompting Bert to say, 'Are you there Anton?'

'What did he say? I hope you gave him the message.'

'*Me* give him the message? I thought that was your job, Anton.'

'Don't be a smart arse, Bert, you know what I mean. Did you tell him there'd been a few changes since he's been away?'

'I did.'

'Did you mention my name?'

'That as well.'

'And?'

'He said to tell you to go fuck yourself.' Bert Wright was beside himself with glee. Relaying the message was every bit as enjoyable, and a sight safer, than if he'd been speaking for himself.

'Did he now? Well, we'll just have to see about that.'

TWO

'Christ,' Jimmy said, alighting from the car and joining Donna on the pavement outside the once-grand row of three-storey Victorian houses. 'It's amazing what goes on in your napper when you're in the nick, you know. You wouldn't credit it, but I pictured this joint as if it was a palace. Look at the state of it! Your auld nut must play tricks on you. You know, tizzie things up a bit.'

'Your life's one big tizzie-up,' Donna reminded him.

Jimmy could see that those houses not already condemned were in an even more advanced state of disrepair and neglect than when he'd last sighted them, and that No. 38 South Lambeth Road, the end house next to Mawbey Street, was no exception. 'We're out of here as soon as I get on my feet, doll,' he promised, taking Donna by the elbow and negotiating the wet steps that a low parapet wall separated from a drop into the limited space in front of the basement flat.

The confined, open courtyard of the flat, which was more than two yards below street level, directly under the bay window of the front room, was fenced by ornate and rusting cast-iron spikes, many of which were missing.

'Don't forget your belongings,' Donna reminded him.

'Aye Christ,' Jimmy said, and returned to the car to fetch his bag.

No. 38 was a boarding-house of sorts, run but not owned by Donna's mother-in-law, Agnes Macintyre. With the exception of the top floor, which was rendered useless by the leaking roof, the remaining rooms were taken up by the Macintyres themselves. Donna's status as a breadwinner earned her and Corrie a comparative palace of two adjoining rooms on the first floor. A communal toilet, down a flight of stairs, shared the landing with a tiny, grime-encrusted bathroom that the Macintyres seldom ventured into. Especially Old Davey, who, with his wife Agnes, used the only other inhabitable room on the first floor as a bedroom. William Macintyre, Jimmy's younger brother by two years, and Mick, the youngest by five years, used the basement flat for sleeping purposes only. Most of the time the family congregated in the front room.

The Macintyres had come down from Glasgow as a unit, ten or more years ago. They were bred from a long line of unskilled and unemployed labourers. With the exception of William, who packed children's books for Heinemann in Greycoat Lane, Victoria, the thought of work was both offensive and foreign to their natures.

At the sound of the creaking front door Agnes Macintyre appeared from behind the curtain separating the front parlour from the tiny kitchenette that overlooked the back garden. 'Oh, it's you, Donna, hen,' Agnes said, squinting from the smoke wafting up from the half-smoked cigarette lodged at the corner of her mouth. 'Is our Jimmy with you? He was supposed to be getting out the day, wasn't he?'

'He just ran up the stairs to get Corrie. He said he'll be down in a minute.'

'Would youse like a bite to eat, pet? I could round youse up a nice plate of beans on toast or something. What about a plate of bubble and squeak? Sure Auld Davey only poked at the good dinner I cooked for him last night. He said his auld guts were playing up again. I told him if he wasn't so fond of the bloody drink his health would improve.'

'Actually, I was just making sure that Corrie wasn't in here. I thought it would save me going up the stairs.'

Agnes rubbed her hands down the front of her floral apron. 'You mustn't have mentioned that his da was getting out the day because, if I'm not mistaken, I saw him going off to school the same as usual. And you know me, hen, I didn't like to say anything in case I got my days mixed up. That's right, isn't it, Davey?'

Her husband of thirty or so years was asleep in an easy chair that, along with the rest of the furniture, had seen better days. With his tongue lolling from his open mouth he woke with a start when he heard the question repeated and smeared the dribble running down his chin with the back of his hand. 'Wha, wha,' he shouted, and looked around bewildered.

Casting her eyes to the ceiling Agnes said, 'Never mind.'

'I've been sitting here asleep, yeh edjit yeh! A man can't get a minute's bloody peace around here, so he can't.'

'Pay no attention to him, Donna hen. He's nothing but a crabbit old git when he wakes up. Do you hear me, mister. You're nothing but a crabbit old git.'

'Is that you, Donna? Why didn't you tell me Donna was standing there, for Christsake?' Davey rose to his full five feet two inches and patted down the greasy grey hairs that fringed his shiny bald head.

'I was just looking for Corrie,' Donna said and started backing from the parlour, her nose twitching at the enduring and sweetly pungent stink that never seemed to leave the room.

'Before you go pet,' they said in unison, each looking daggers at the other when they realised what was going on. Old Davey got in first. 'You couldn't slip me a lazy tenner, could you pet? I've got a terrible thirst on me, so I have,' he said, massaging his throat and making smacking noises with his lips.

'No, she can not.' Jimmy's voice could be heard

from the landing at the foot of the stairs.

'Christ, our Jimmy. If it's not the man himself.' Old Davey opened his arms, ready to give his son a hug as soon as he walked into the room.

Jimmy smiled and returned the gesture, stopping short of taking his father in his arms. 'Phew, when was the last time you had a bath, mister? It must've been before I went inside, was it?'

'Try the time before that,' Agnes grinned.

'Away and shite the lot of you. Your noses are too close to your arses. That's your problem, you know that, don't you?'

Jimmy shook his father's hand, kissed his mother on the cheek and said, 'I don't see any sign of our Corrie. He's not out the back with the pigeons, is he?'

'Apparently he got up and took himself off to school,' Donna answered, shrugging her shoulders. 'He goes in if he's feeling OK. That's the arrangement.'

'What are you talking about, Donna? Didn't you tell him I was coming home today?'

'Sorry Jimmy. I don't know what I must've been thinking, what with one thing and another. I must've thought today was Saturday or something.'

'Sure you know they always liberate you on a Friday, Donna. Come on, Christ.'

Old Davey saw an opportunity. 'Ach, sure he'll be home soon enough. Why don't me and you nip around to the Wheatsheaf for a welcome-home pint? A nice wee bevie.'

'There'll be plenty of time for that, da.' Jimmy winked at Donna and nodded towards the door. He had just realised that they would have the flat to themselves and was growing hard at the thought.

'Christ, don't tell me you haven't got time to spend an hour or two with your auld man,' Davey protested, reluctant to let the opportunity for a free drink pass without a fight.

'Behave yourself mister. Have you no bloody sense at all?' Agnes scolded.

'Oh aye. Right. Nay bother. On you go,' Old Davey stammered, adding, 'Don't worry about me.'

Jimmy shook his head. 'You're nothing but a pest, so you are, do you know that? Here's me hardly out of the nick five bloody minutes and you're in to my liberation money already. Here, don't spend it all at once.'

Alone with his wife, old Davey held up the ten pound note and kissed it. 'Where's that cap of mine, Aggie. I'm away out for a bevie.'

'See you, mister. I should've let you lay there asleep. I was bloody well going to snip Jimmy myself.' Agnes feigned a back-hander and made a face.

Old Davey baulked and threw a playful punch of his own. 'It's the last thing you'd ever do, yeh old bag,' he grinned and closed the door behind him.

'Don't come back,' Agnes shouted, trying not to laugh.

'I'm away to get myself a fancy woman, one that'll give me a minute's bloody peace.'

Agnes went to the bay window just as a passing No. 8, red double-decker bus sent a spray of water from the road over her man. She saw Davey react like a fighting cockerel, shaking his fist and shouting abuse. Now in his early sixties, she saw, as if for the first time, that he had taken on an almost skeletal look. His once clear blue eyes had lost their sparkle, except at the mention of a drink. Christ, she thought, and went straight to the cracked mirror above the fireplace, leaning in with her mouth and eyes wide open, trying to eradicate the wrinkles. Unlike her husband, her face had filled out over the years, except for her lips, which had thinned considerably. She reached for the handbag containing her make-up and dabbed her eyelids with bright blue eyeshadow, creating an odd alliance with her own brown eyes. When she had applied a coat of pink lipstick and run a comb through her wiry, dyed black hair, she tilted her head upwards in what she assumed was an elegant pose and rolled her lips together. 'That's better,' she said aloud.

Upstairs, as soon as he shut the door to the small, two-room flat Jimmy took off his suit jacket and threw it over the back of a chair. He discarded his shirt and tie on the floor and approached Donna from behind, kissing her on the side of the neck. Donna looked over her shoulder at him when she felt his arms go around her. Smiling, she led him to the bedroom.

Lying awake Jimmy heard the key turning in the latch and jumped out of bed, fumbling for his pants in the fading light. Donna woke from a nap and switched on the bedside light ahead of Corrie bursting into the bedroom.

'Dad's home, dad's home. My dad's home,' Corrie sang and clutched Jimmy around the waist.

Jimmy put his hands under his son's arms and hoisted him chest-high, the action knocking the baseball cap from the boy's head. Startled at the sight of the shiny bald head he said, 'Giv'us a good look at you, wee son. Geez, look at the size of you. You're going to be a big man like your dad. That's right, isn't it, Donna?'

Donna acknowledged him with a warm smile. It was the first time for more than a year Jimmy had seen Corrie without a hat, and if she hadn't known better she would have suspected her husband was choking back tears. It had been a year and a half since blood tests and a bone-marrow biopsy had diagnosed Corrie as having acute myeloid leukaemia. A year and a half when Jimmy had missed the full impact of his son's illness. The initial month in hospital with its administration of chemotherapy had reduced Corrie to a vomiting, lethargic and anaemic wreck.

Though Donna's description of events had been vivid enough Jimmy now realised that he had been once removed from the trauma. He could only imagine Corrie's return to hospital, after a brief spell at home, when the consolidational chemotherapy had resulted in the loss of his hair and had afflicted Corrie with the same physical symptoms.

Donna's account of the subsequent remission and the year of maintenance chemotherapy that had seen Corrie practically return to normal was something he had always taken for granted, based on what she had been prepared to tell him. He hadn't faced the facts until recently when Donna tearfully had told him of the relapse and, in the absence of an available compatible donor, the ongoing and fruitless attempts of the Bone Marrow Donor Registry to locate one. Now, at the sight of his boy grinning up at him, his big blue eyes all the bigger for the absence of any facial hair, he felt the same despair that his wife had lived with since the relapse.

'Come on out here while your mum gets dressed and tell me what you've been up to.'

Corrie grinned. 'How come you and mum were in bed at this time of the day, dad? It's only four o'clock, you know.'

'Aye well, eh, me and your mum were just having a wee lie down, like.'

'Uh, I thought you might've been trying to make a baby.'

'Who told you about that? Not that daft Mick I hope?'

'Nah, one of the big kids at school told us.'

'Hey Donna,' Jimmy called out, 'what kind of school did you send this boy to? You should hear what he just come out with.'

Donna came out of the bedroom tying the sash of her long pink dressing gown, her eyes questioning.

'He thinks we've been making babies,' Jimmy smiled.

'Does he now? And who's been putting ideas like that in your head, our Corrie?'

'Uhh, I think I'll go and feed the pigeons, mum. Coming dad?'

'Aye, you go on son, and I'll be down in a wee minute.'

Jimmy's smile vanished with the sound of Corrie's footsteps descending the linoleum-covered stairs. 'What's the word on this bone-marrow donor lark? Any luck yet?'

Donna appeared as if she was about to say something, then simply shook her head.

'What the fuck's wrong with these people? Surely to Christ it's a simple enough thing. There must be thousands of donors out there. I'll bet you they could come up with one if it was for some rich cunt.'

'Jimmy, I think Dr Cullen's doing the best he can.'

'Aye, I suppose – but do you see if I thought for one minute . . .' Jimmy shook his head and sighed.

'Listen, love, I was thinking of going into work for a couple of hours. You don't mind, do you? I know this is your first day out and all that.' The look on Jimmy's face told her that her timing could have been better.

'Please yourself, but I thought we'd go out for a bevie, me and you. You know, for a wee celebration.'

'I don't want to spoil it for you, but William and Mick have organised a bit of a welcome-home do at the Wheatsheaf. And you know me, I can't stand the place. All those creeps.'

'Fuck the Wheatsheaf. Me and you'll go somewhere else. Just the two of us.'

'It's all organised and paid for, Jimmy. A big surprise. But if things aren't too busy at work I'll try and get away early. You know I don't like missing a night. It's money you never recover, and we need every penny we can get.'

'Aye, well make sure you do. I don't want folk thinking we've split up, or anything like that.'

'If I can manage,' Donna replied, heading towards the bedroom.

Through the open door Jimmy watched his wife go to a white-painted chest of drawers and take a black suspender belt and a pair of sheer black stockings from the top drawer. If she was aware that he was watching her sitting on the edge of the bed putting them on, she gave no indication of it. Nor did she show any reaction to him as she lavishly applied her make-up.

'Are you taking a cab, or do you want me to give you a lift?' he inquired tentatively, having no wish to do battle with the heavy traffic heading for the West End at this time of the night.

'No. If it's all the same to you I'd prefer to take a cab.' Donna stopped short of telling him that his driving was still as woeful as ever.

'Sure? It'd be no trouble,' he said, watching her pull the curtains aside to check that there was a taxi waiting at the rank across the street.

Ready to leave for work she brushed her hand down the front of her tight black skirt, stepped into a pair of black patent leather stilettos and selected an expensive, black, full-length coat from the wardrobe. At a mirror next to the door she clenched her teeth and curled back her lips, checking for wayward lipstick. She pouted at Jimmy, offering him a kiss goodbye. As he responded, she turned her face, permitting him to kiss her on the cheek only. 'See you later,' she said, easing on a pair of skintight, black leather gloves.

'How are you holding, doll?'

Donna reached into the handbag slung over her shoulder and handed him two crisp twenty pound notes. 'Give Corrie a big kiss for me and tell him it's time he was in the house.'

Going to the sink at the window Jimmy watched Donna cross the road and climb into the cab at the head of the rank in Tradescant Street. As the cab pulled away he hurried downstairs to the front room. 'What's for tea?' he asked, rubbing his hands together.

'The bold Jimmy,' greeted Mick, getting to his feet and rushing to throw his arms around his brother. 'I was wondering when you were going to surface, big man,' he added, smiling mischievously. 'And in answer to your question, Jimbo,' Mick continued, breaking from the embrace, 'if I'm right in thinking that it's Friday, then it's sausage, egg and chips. The same as it was two years ago, if you remember rightly?'

A voice carried from the other side of the curtain separating the living-room from the kitchenette. 'I'm just waiting for our William to come in from his work before I stick the sausages on the pan. He shouldn't be long now.' Agnes poked her head through a gap in the curtain and grinned.

'Do me a favour, ma. Stick your head out the window and tell Corrie it was time he was in the house. If I go out the back now I'll get captured, and I'm bloody starving.'

'What about my da? Is he not back from the boozer yet?' Mick wanted to know.

'Oh, you'll probably see him when the tenner our Jimmy gave him runs out. Unless he puts the bite on somebody round at the pub. You know what he's like, once he gets the taste. A bloody nightmare, that's what he is. Never been any different since the day I first clapped eyes on him. I don't know why I put up with him.'

'That sounds like Corrie now, ma. Save your breath.' Jimmy informed her.

'Are you ready for your tea, wee son?' Agnes greeted the boy.

'Hey Jimbo,' Mick cut in, 'what was it like this time? Did you hav'to batter anybody? Give somebody a doing?'

'Ask me later,' Jimmy said, nodding towards his son.

'Awh go on, dad, tell us,' Corrie grinned.

'What have you been telling this boy?' Jimmy accused, glad of the distraction when his mother, responding to the sound of the front door clattering open, announced, 'That'll be our William now.'

William Macintyre entered the living room, his face lighting up when he saw his older brother. 'Hey big man,' he said, clutching Jimmy in his arms. Except that he was stouter and a good three inches taller than Mick, like his younger brother William closely resembled his father. Even the same sandy coloured hair was beginning to thin.

Jimmy stood back and admired the new arrival. 'What're you all dolled up for, Willie? Have you been to a funeral or something?'

Interrupting, Agnes came through from the back, bringing the sound of sizzling sausages with her. 'And where have you been to this hour, anyway? Sure everybody's starving.'

'I was away getting married. A wee lassie from work.'

'Not again, surely to Christ?' Mick said, voicing the opinion of the others. 'How much did you get this time?'

'You have to allow for inflation in my line of work, so I charged her fourteen hundred quid and the right to pay her a wee visit every now and again. Not bad, eh?' William announced proudly. 'I couldn't let the poor lassie get deported.'

'That was very civic-minded of you, William. But

eh, you're up for the bevie tonight, seeing as you're holding.' Mick smirked.

'I'm sorry I opened my big mouth,' William moaned.

Agnes ferried the plates to the table, placing Corrie's meal beside his father's. 'Youse needn't think youse are going anywhere without me,' she declared.

Jimmy gave her a puzzled look and said, 'What about Corrie? Who's going to look after him?'

'I'm nine and a half, dad. I don't need a babysitter.'

By the look on Jimmy's face Agnes could tell that he was far from pleased. 'I'll only stay for an hour, son,' she promised.

'I'll be all right dad, honest.'

'Are you sure?' Jimmy leaned in to whisper, 'It's just that eh, it's just that the boys have organised a wee surprise celebration for me. Know what I mean?'

Corrie returned his father's wink.

At that moment Donna was standing in a doorway in Archer Street, a narrow lane just off Shaftesbury Avenue in the heart of Soho's red light district. She was watching out for tourists and theatre goers and other people of the night. Potential customers who, inadvertently or otherwise, had ventured off the beaten track. At the appropriate moment, when someone approached, she made eye contact with him and stepped back into the doorway. Opening her coat like a flasher she revealed her body, naked except for the black suspenders and stockings. When the man hesitated and looked around tentatively she lured him into the doorway by repeating the exercise and adding her most disarming smile. Once inside the darkened doorway she took him by the hand and led him up a flight of stairs to a dimly lit room, bare except for a chair either side of a king-sized bed.

'Why don't you take your clothes off and tell me what you want, sweetie.' Donna took off her coat, placed it on one of the chairs and stood smiling with her hands on her hips. 'There's no need to be shy,' she encouraged, sensing that it was the punter's first time by his awkward shuffling and his reluctance to focus on the full view of the goods on offer.

Stealing fleeting glimpses Steve Munro didn't know which way to look, the alluring sight of a beautiful woman stripped to her underwear winning out over the embarrassment that was forcing him to avert his eyes.

After several attempts, on consecutive nights, he had succeeded in tracking Donna from South Lambeth Road to the building where she worked in Archer Street. He had been watching the building for ten minutes, intent on learning all he could about Donna, when her sudden appearance at the door had prompted him to make his approach. Now he wished he was elsewhere.

'I think there's been a mistake,' he said backing towards the door. 'I just wanted to talk.'

Donna quickly placed herself between Munro and

the door, saying, 'It's your money, sweetie. You can do what ever you want with the time. It's fifty pounds for half an hour.' It was all the same to her what the punters wanted. As far as she was concerned it was only two pieces of skin rubbing together. Strictly business, just like any other. And with as much emotional input from her as peeling potatoes.

'I, eh, I don't think you understand,' Munro stammered. 'I – I hadn't intended to ... Look, I don't think I should be here. I'm only after some information.'

Donna reacted instinctively as her years of experience warned of a punter wasting her time, of the likelihood of a non-profitmaking transaction. 'Look,' she snapped, raising her voice and reaching for her coat, 'if you're here to fart around, you can just piss off or I'll have you thrown out.'

Oh God, Munro thought, regretting having set foot in the place and picturing some burly bouncer throwing him headfirst into the street. 'I don't mind paying for your time,' he blurted out, reaching for his wallet.

Clutching the money Donna placed her hands deep into the pockets of her coat, drawing it tight about her. 'Fire away,' she smiled, getting back to business.

In the less than wholesome circumstances he found himself in Munro was having second thoughts about declaring his hand. Since his arrival from the States less than a week ago experience and common sense had told him to proceed with caution until he'd tested the lie of the land. Now, looking around him, a sixth sense, his reporter's intuition, warned him that the situation could be dangerous. If not for himself, then certainly for the man he was looking for, Tom Gilfeather. Time to back off, he thought.

'Look eh, miss. I'm sorry if I've wasted your time, but I've just remembered a prior appointment. The money's yours.' Munro gave a weak smile as he backed out of the door.

Punters, Donna thought, shaking her head and reaching for her cigarettes. There's no figuring them out, especially the Yanks. It had been an easy fifty quid, but there was something about the American that unsettled her. It made her all the more determined to give the game away soon. For Corrie's sake, not one more trick after she'd reached her targeted savings. She had it all worked out. Corrie would get well and Jimmy would go straight. After that, when there was enough money saved, they would buy a little shop somewhere, probably in the country, and live happily ever after.

THREE

Shane was nervous. After all the effort she had put into convincing the landlord of the Wheatsheaf to hire her, including an audition, she was having second thoughts. She wanted to become part of that particular pub scene, and had thought about just rolling up, but experience told her that people in her situation took longer than normal to be accepted, and were seldom taken seriously. A cross they had to bear.

In the Wheatsheaf, a long banner proclaiming WELCOME HOME JIMMY was stretched across the bulkhead above the bar. Clusters of coloured balloons adorned the available wall space at hand height and strings of Christmas decorations criss-crossed the ceiling. Mick, at the head of the Macintyre entourage, clapped his hands together and shouted to Jimmy above the din, 'It's straw hats and trumpets time, big man.'

Word spread quickly through the haze of trapped cigarette smoke that Jimmy Macintyre had made an appearance. By reputation he was a big fish in a big pond, of which this was only one small corner. It was common knowledge that his lack of ambition, coupled with his reluctance to play in a team, had stamped him a maverick in the criminal world he could very well have been running. On his way to a reserved table close to the portable stage he ran a gauntlet of back-slappers and well-wishers offering to buy him a drink.

The Wheatsheaf itself had resisted change. Old black and white photographs of bloodied boxers in action dominated the faded, burgundy flock wallpaper. The high, ornate ceilings, like the fake chandeliers, were covered in nicotine and fly droppings. A tarnished brass foot-rail ran the length of the oak panelled bar. Above it was a matching gantry where faded paper remnants of previous Christmases, still stuck with drawing pins, were visible beside this year's decorations.

William took on an air of authority and thought that paying for the drinks entitled him to sit in the seat with the best view of the stage. A look from Jimmy convinced him otherwise. In the past nobody had sat at Jimmy's table unless they were invited, and nobody, but nobody, sat in his chair. He saw no need for change.

'Right, get the bevie up, our William,' Mick said, again clapping his hands. William responded by handing Mick a twenty pound note.

Jimmy, dressed in his favourite blue suit, and ever

mindful of his image, adjusted his tie and told Mick to sit down. If he wasn't mistaken the drinks would soon be arriving on the table.

'Look at the state of your father,' Agnes said, pointing out her husband at the far end of the lounge, barely able to keep his head from crashing onto the table.

'Mick, go and take the stupid old prick home before he gives us a showing up,' Jimmy ordered, without taking his eyes off the contents he was swilling around in his glass.

When Mick returned ten minutes later it was more than obvious that he had been running. 'That was some job. I told him there was plenty of bevie in the house, just to get him out the door. He was all right till the air hit him, then he nearly woke the dead with his singing. Fucken hopeless.' Mick was even more breathless after he attempted to drink a pint of lager straight down. 'Ahh, that's better,' he announced and belched loudly.

'Ach, he'll not remember a bloody thing in the morning. Youse are all the bloody same,' Agnes reminded them and placed her empty glass on the table in front of Jimmy. 'The next one that asks you if you want a drink, Jimmy, tell them your ma would like one of them Orgasms, or whatever it is you call them. There's a good boy.'

The publican was a rotund Cockney with wavy fair hair and bloodshot greyish-blue eyes. As usual he was dressed in a shabby dinner suit and stood at the flap which, when raised, permitted entry behind the bar. He took a long draw on his cigarette and drained his glass before he made his way through the crowded tables to the small stage in the far corner of his lounge. Smiling nervously at the three-man combo waiting in position he tapped the microphone and said, 'A bit of shush, ladies and gentlemen.' He then took another draw on the cigarette that, between drags, he saw fit to conceal behind his back.

'Now I know you don't want to see me up here yabbering all night, you have got better things to do. But in case you are not already aware, ladies and gentlemen, this is a very special occasion. Tonight for the first time in two years, I think it is, we have Mr Jimmy Macintyre gracing us with his presence. What about a big Wheatsheaf welcome for the man himself?' He stopped there to permit a round of whistling, calling out and applause, holding up his hand when he wished to continue. 'What about a few words, Jimmy?'

'Aye, get the bevie up,' Jimmy shouted, the crowd, with the exception of one, responding with a laugh.

The one refusing to laugh was Nigel Paterson, a hard man originally from Manchester, an enforcer who had filled the vacancy created by Anton when he stepped up a rung. His instructions were simple. Sort out Jimmy Macintyre for thinking he could pick up where he left off. Give him the message good and proper.

'Fair enough Jimmy,' the publican agreed. 'Your

money's no good in here tonight. But are you sure you don't want to say a few words?'

Jimmy stood, glass in hand, and turned to face the crowd. 'There's a party back at my place after the pub shuts. Youse are all welcome.'

The publican couldn't get the microphone to his lips quickly enough. 'Don't forget, he said *after* the pub shuts. So there's no need to rush off because we've got a full night's entertainment lined up for you. Speaking of which, ladies and gentlemen, as you know we've had some shocking acts here in the past. Well, tonight's going to be no different.' After a pause, in which time he grinned and waited for the laughter to die down, he said, 'Ladies and gentlemen, kindly put your hands together for another great performance by our regular Thursday, Friday and Saturday night artiste. Ladies and gentlemen, back by popular demand, I give you the lovely *Shane*. You can work the rest out for yourself.'

'Oh,' he added, holding up his hand to defer the applause that would beckon Shane to the stage, 'it's good to see Jimmy's lovely mother Agnes and the rest of the Macintyre family is with us again tonight. Put your hands together for the Macintyres, ladies and gentlemen.'

No one noticed Nigel Paterson refusing to clap. Sipping his mineral water he had received the announcement of the party with interest. The more Scotch Jimmy Macintyre managed to consume, the easier his job would be. It was just a question of picking his time.

Shane burst on stage to a round of tumultuous applause, realising that she was sharing the limelight with the Macintyres. Regardless, she bid the crowd welcome and opened with her signature tune. 'Pack up all your cares and woe, swinging low. Bye, bye blackbird,' she sang, needlessly inviting the crowd to join in. Impersonating other artists was her specialty, a talent that extended to accents and enabled her to talk to the crowd in their own vernacular. At the end of the song she thanked the band playing behind her and peered out over the crowd, scanning for the Macintyre table. Much to Jimmy's embarrassment, and the delight of the crowd, she left the stage and gazed into Jimmy's eyes, doing her impression of Shirley Bassey's, 'I who have nothing'. At the end of the set, which included Judy Garland, Liza Minnelli, Barbra Streisand and many more, she thanked the audience and the resident trio and left the stage to hover near the Macintyre table, waiting for the invite to join them.

Mick and William were keen for her to sit down, but they waited to see if Jimmy would give the word. Jimmy remained silent. He just nodded at the table and Shane sat down as bid.

'Did you enjoy the act, Jimmy?' she gushed, taking a compact from her purse and freshening her make-up, finishing with a lavish coat of bright red lipstick.

Though he was loath to admit that he was enjoying her attention, Jimmy was too protective of his image to appear anything other than reserved in the company of the stunningly convincing transvestite, who, for some reason reminded him a bit of Donna. The same dark eyes, fine features and full lips. But he wasn't to know that, unlike Donna, Shane's face, with the cheek and lip implants, was the work of the surgeon who had supplied her with the silicon breasts.

'I enjoyed it, Shane,' Mick blurted out, making no apologies for sneaking a long look at the expanse of stockinged leg exposed by Shane when her tight sequined frock rode up as she sat down. Shane didn't mind. In fact she quite enjoyed it, taking it as a compliment.

At closing time, after Shane had performed two more sets and the embattled bar staff were busy clearing the tables of litter and overflowing ashtrays, those heading for the party, including Nigel Paterson, spilled out of the pub and filed along the streets. Many had more carry-out than they could possibly consume, the price of entry to No. 38. Corrie, laying wide awake in the bed-settee above the front room, listened to the noisy first arrivals and started scheming, trying to think of an excuse that would permit him downstairs.

The parlour was abuzz with a good-sized crowd. Old Davey lay sprawled unconscious in his chair until several enthusiastic shakes from Agnes stirred him. 'He's from Mars,' she informed all and sundry, shaking her head and screwing up her face. 'Not a good communicator.'

She raised the lid of an old varnished radiogram

and vied with her husband for the right to feed it with a selection of scratched and worn 45s, the nostalgia of which inevitably reduced the pair of them to tears. After 'Red sails in the sunset' by Slim Whitman a sustained barrage of abuse forced them to liven things up a bit.

Shane had changed back into her casual clothes – a tailored, black suit with a tight, knee-length skirt and matching black patent leather stilettos. The bobbed black wig she wore was, by coincidence, similar to Donna's current hairstyle.

Out of the corner of his eye Jimmy noticed Nigel Paterson, a stranger to him, running his eyes approvingly over Shane. He noted the look of disgust in his eyes when one of the locals leaned in and whispered something in his ear. Shane, who had appreciated the attention, saw it too, and looked the other way. Jimmy could smell trouble a mile away and made a mental note to keep an eye on things.

By 12.30 the party was in full swing and the various groups previously capable of coherent conversation had degenerated into the usual rounds of conflicting sing-a-longs. Agnes was in the kitchen transferring the take-away curry onto an odd assortment of plates and Shane was drunk enough to consider Mick's continued mooching for a head job.

Unable to sleep Corrie had progressed from the first-floor landing to the landing between floors, then as curiosity got the better of him he had kept moving down. He was sitting at the foot of the stairs, right outside the parlour door, when Mick emerged, heading for the back yard. 'What're you doing there, wee man?' Mick said. 'Shouldn't you be in your kip at this time of the night?'

'I can't sleep for the noise, Uncle Mick. And um, do you think it would be all right if I took a look?'

'Ohh, I don't know about that, Corrie. Remember what your ma said the last time.'

'Mum's not here. Is she? She told me she's the best worker at the Casino. That's why her boss makes her work every night. I know.'

'Aye, right enough, wee man. You've got me there.'

'Well, can I take a look then?'

Mick's eyes narrowed and his lips went thin. 'Ummm,' he croaked.

'Five minutes, Uncle Mick. Go on.'

'All right, but not a minute more. Do you hear me?'

Moments later, those nearest the door returned Corrie's smile as he entered the parlour. Anticipating that he would be successful in wangling his way into the party Corrie had dressed in joggers, jeans and a sweat shirt, and a baseball cap worn the right way round.

It wasn't long before Nigel Paterson noticed that the party goers, wishing to curry favour with Jimmy Macintyre, were gushing all over the boy. 'Who's that?' he said, sidling up to William.

'That's young Corrie. Jimmy's boy,' came the reply.

'Funny looking sort of a geek, ain't he? He's got no eyebrows or eye-lashes. Fuck all,' Nigel said, starting to bait, thinking it was time he made his move.

'That's the result of all that chem – medicine shite he has to take for his leukaemia. Poor kid.'

'Poor kid, my arse. I hate kids. All kids. Including that one. I can't work those paedophiles out. Imagine fucking the likes of that.'

'If I was you, mate,' William said, 'I wouldn't let his old man hear you saying that. That's a terrible thing to say.'

'Why don't you tell him what I said then?'

'I've a good mind to,' William snapped, thinking only of preserving the peace.

Unaware that Jimmy had slipped into the kitchenette, drawn by the aroma of the curry, Nigel Paterson approached Corrie and leaned in, shouting to be heard. 'Come in to the centre of the room a minute, son. I've got a nice surprise for you.'

Corrie beamed up at the stranger and allowed himself to be led into the middle of the improvised dance floor. He retained the smile, but shifted awkwardly when the stranger turned the music off, leaving him alone on the dance floor.

As soon as all eyes focused on Corrie, Nigel Paterson again eyed Shane's hair closely, having suspected that it was too neat to be anything other than a wig. Smirking, he snatched the wig from Shane's head and, knocking Corrie's baseball cap to the floor, planted it firmly on the startled boy's shiny bald head.

'There, that's better,' he laughed, his cackle the only sound to break the instant silence.

Jimmy returned to the parlour to see Corrie with his head down and crying, and Shane, immobilised by shock, with her hands clasped over the hairnet covering her hair. When he looked at Corrie, then at Shane minus the wig, flashpoint was instant. Transferring the whisky bottle to his left hand he moved quickly across the room.

Shane watched him approach and, seeing him as an avenger, forced a smile through her own tears of embarrassment. Corrie hung his head lower, allowing the wig to fall on the floor.

'It was that animal there, James,' William said, pointing, realising his brother thought Shane was to blame.

Jimmy stopped and glared at the stranger, his eyes raging and malevolent. Realising by his smirk and the way he positioned his feet that the man was ready for him he turned his attention to his son. 'What's the matter with you, Corrie?' he smiled, winking at the stranger. 'Can't you take a wee joke?'

Nigel Paterson was thinking that this was going to be easier than he'd anticipated, especially when Jimmy turned side onto him, placing his hands on Corrie's shoulder and nudging him towards William. He didn't see the look from Jimmy that had William usher Corrie away, keeping the boy's back to the action. Nor did he see, not before it was too late, the spinning kick that caught him flush on the testicles and dropped him to his knees in agony.

Jimmy moved quickly, seizing Paterson by the hair and tilting his head backwards, forcing his face, twisted in agony, to look up at him. After a glance around the room assured him that William had stolen Corrie away he shattered the half-empty bottle of Johnnie Walker across the man's face, breaking his cheekbones and the bridge of his nose and leaving his face in tatters. Then, like a weight-lifter, he hoisted the offender in stages until he held him at chest-height. With a heave he hurled him through the bay window, bringing a shower of broken glass and splintered timber down into the basement area on top of him.

The stunned gathering, making a scramble for the door, stopped dead when Jimmy shouted, 'Hoy. None of you saw fuck all. Remember that.'

Jimmy continued as soon as the room was clear. 'Mick, give William a hand to get that cunt out of the basement while I go and see if Corrie's OK.'

'What do you want us to do with him after we bung him out into the street, Jimbo?' William asked.

'I couldn't give a fuck. Leave the cunt there, for all I care. If anybody asks, tell them he fell down the fucken stairs.'

'I think he might be hurt pretty bad, Jimmy,' Mick said, traipsing after William. 'He was bad enough before you flung him out the window.'

'Serves the cunt right,' Jimmy called after him. 'I had my eye on him all night.'

'You take his arms,' William ordered Mick as they bent over.

'Did you happen to see where our Corrie went?' Jimmy popped his head through the tattered remnants of the window and peered down into the basement.

'I took him straight out the back,' William puffed to Jimmy, struggling under the dead weight and looking up.

'Mind his fucken napper you,' Mick protested when the unconscious man's head thudded into the cast-iron gate at the top of the basement stairs.

In the feeble glow of light escaping from the bare kitchen window Corrie stood in front of the converted tea-chest that housed his white rabbit. With one hand he offered the rabbit a piece of lettuce through the wire. With the other he wiped away the tears. When a shadow fell over the cage he turned around, startled. It was Jimmy holding a ten pound note in his hand. 'Here,' he said, getting down on his hunkers. 'Don't tell your ma.'

Corrie returned his smile and fell into his open arms. 'Why did that man do that to me, dad? Was he just trying to be mean?'

'Aye son, but don't you worry yourself about the likes of him. Bad things happen to people like that. I'm sure of it.' Jimmy swallowed hard and kissed the top of his son's bald head. 'It's a tough old world out there, Corrie, and you have to be a bit of a tough bastard to survive in it. But eh, you leave that to me for the time being. I'll make sure you survive, son, if it's the last thing I ever do.'

Corrie buried his face in his father's shoulder. 'Promise me,' he said, knowing that, try as his father might to pretend he was talking about life in general, he was actually alluding to the battle with leukaemia.

Jimmy again kissed him on top of the head. 'I promise,' he vowed.

'Will I ever get better, dad?'

Jimmy choked. 'Didn't I just promise you, eh?'

'I suppose.'

'What do you mean, you suppose? You're the eldest son of the eldest son. Do you know what that's going to make you?'

Corrie shook his head.

'The head of the Macintyre Clan, that's what.'

'Geez,' Corrie grinned.

FOUR

It was just before daybreak and the streets were beginning to stir when Donna alighted from the taxi in front of No. 38. She stepped over a pool of congealed blood on the bottom step and shook her head in disgust when she noticed that little remained of the bay window. All the signs were there that someone had gotten on the wrong side of her husband.

As soon as she opened the front door the smell of stale alcohol and overflowing ashtrays assaulted her, forcing her to pinch her nose and hurry past the open parlour door. It was a stench she could never get used to. On the way by she saw Old Davey sprawled unconscious and fully clothed at the foot of his chair. At the top of the landing she stepped out of her high heels and carried them into the flat, having no wish to waken her family at that hour of the morning. She needn't have bothered. Corrie was wide awake, and when she looked through the open bedroom door she saw her husband in a drunken coma, lying on top of the bed fully clothed with his feet dangling over the edge and his arms outstretched fully.

'Did you make plenty of tips at the casino tonight, mum?' Corrie asked.

'It was a good night, love. Friday nights are always good,' she replied, sitting on the edge of the bed-settee that cramped the already limited space in the living-room, tucking the blankets under his chin, and kissing him gently on the lips.

'When I get better you won't have to work so hard, will you, mum?'

'No darling, mummy won't have to work so hard. But you'd better get back to sleep. Do you know what time of the day it is?'

'Dad might get a job, then you can stay home.'

'Yes, I hope so,' she muttered under her breath.

'What did you say, mum?'

'I said, that would be nice.'

Donna ran her hand backwards over his shiny head and watched him twist away.

'I'm sorry. I forgot you don't like that,' she said, and began stroking him on the cheek instead.

If he didn't have such an important question to ask, he would have twisted away again. 'Do you think they've had any luck finding me a donor yet, mum?'

The combined noise from two double-decker buses, going in opposite directions, right outside the window gave her time to think about the relapse that had triggered the urgent search for a bone-marrow donor. She knew Corrie was aware that tests on family and friends had proven incompatible, but she didn't have the heart to tell him that the British Bone Marrow Donor Register and the World Donor Register had both failed to find him a matching donor. And she didn't want to tell him that, without a donor, his life expectancy could now very well be counted in months, or that she was pursuing what she considered her last possible hope. Barring a miracle.

'I don't think it'll be too long now love,' she answered, her forced smile belying the inner turmoil.

Corrie nodded solemnly in agreement. 'Geez, I hope so. Dad told me I was going to be the head of the Clan some day.'

'The what?'

'The Clan. You know. The Macintyre Clan,' Corrie answered, puzzled by his mother's ignorance.

'Ohh, that clan. Why didn't you say?' Donna kissed him on the forehead, rose and took the two steps to the sink where she began filling the electric kettle. In the bedroom, reacting to the cold rather than the noise of the new day, Jimmy raised his head. 'I'll have one of those,' he shouted, and let his head fall back on the bed.

With enough light sneaking around the curtains to spread a weak glow unevenly around the flat she carried the two coffees into the bedroom and shut the door with her heel. 'What bloody well happened downstairs last night, Jimmy?' she said, striving to keep her voice down.

'Ach, it was nothing. Some smartass decided to take

the pish out of one of the boys and I had to give him a wee bit of a slap.' Jimmy answered with exaggerated conviction, figuring that he was actually telling a form of the truth.

'I don't believe you. After all the promises you made, do you know that you never made it past your first day out without giving somebody a hammering? What if somebody had called the police?'

Jimmy sat up and laughed, cradling his aching head in his hands.

'What's so funny? I don't think it's a laughing matter. What if Corrie had seen it?'

Jimmy steadied his cup. 'Don't worry about the police, doll. There were no witnesses.'

'What about all the blood on the steps?'

'Ha ha. Oh, I don't think you should worry about that. My ma'll probably give it a good scrub when she gets up.'

Donna sat on the edge of the bed facing away from him, hitched up her skirt and began unfastening her stockings. She rolled them up and aimed them at the open clothes basket, watching them dangle over the edge. 'It didn't occur to you that I was thinking more of the person who bled all over the place, did it?'

'Why would you want to give two fucks about some useless prick? Anyway, it could've been avoided if you'd been here like you said you would.'

Too tired to argue Donna stood with her hands on her hips and leaned backwards, seeking some relief for her aching back. 'Do me a favour, love,' she sighed, climbing under the duvet. 'Give me a shove at nine o'clock, will yah? I've got a bit of running around to do.'

At nine twenty-five Donna entered the post office to check on the morning mail, looking and feeling like she hadn't made it home after a night on the tiles. She was at her wits' end and knew that if the mail didn't contain something positive, anything at all, she would struggle to find the strength to go on. Yet she knew that for Corrie's sake she had to find the will somewhere. The sight of the single envelope sitting in Box 1739 did little to instil confidence.

From the other side of South Lambeth Road Munro watched her hurry from the post office towards Stan's Cafe, still clutching the unopened envelope. Sharing her anxiety, knowing from the dwindling supply of mail to Box 1739 that the next step down from one reply was none, he made up his mind to confront her, find out what was going on.

Donna entered the cafe, ordered her customary cup of tea and looked around for a table, as usual managing to find one away from the window.

Munro, thankful that she was too engrossed to notice him, slipped past her to an empty table and watched her place the unopened envelope upright against a bottle of HP Sauce, obviously bracing herself for further disappointment. He saw her slit the envelope and begin to read, her stoic expression giving no hint as to the contents of the letter. When she crammed the envelope into her handbag and took a hurried drink of tea he suspected that she was preparing to leave. Thinking that he'd procrastinated long enough, he eased himself out of the chair, not wanting to bring attention to himself. He wasn't quick enough. Donna snatched her handbag from the table and hurried from the cafe, leaving some coins on the counter on the way out. By the time he'd fumbled for the price of his coffee and raced after her Donna had caught the lights, crossed the road and was already halfway up the steps of No. 38. Disappointed, he returned to the cafe to finish his coffee and contemplate his next move.

On her way up the stairs Donna winced at the sound of voices coming from her flat and hoped that Jimmy wasn't entertaining at this hour of the day. If he was, she decided, she was just in the mood to remind him of their long-standing agreement that she was entitled to a bit of peace and quiet during the day.

The sound of the key turning in the Yale lock, followed by the clatter of the ancient brass doorknob, brought Shane to her feet. She smiled tentatively in response to Donna's questioning stare and looked to Jimmy for an introduction.

'Oh aye,' Jimmy responded, taking the hint. 'This is Shane, Donna. She does a turn at the Wheatsheaf and ahh, she was at the party last night when I had to sort that guy out. She just popped in to see if anybody found an earring, and she was good enough to ask if everything's OK. I told her everything was hunky-dory, didn't I, Shane?'

'Hello, Donna,' Shane said softly.

'Hi,' Donna replied and casually angled for a closer look at the visitor. A move that didn't go unnoticed by Shane, contributing further to her discomfort.

Not bad, Donna thought, knowing that the stunning transvestite would have passed undetected in company less discerning or experienced in the ways of the world than herself.

'I was having a chat with your son Corrie before he toddled off to feed his pigeons. He seems a lovely kid. Nine, isn't he?' Shane said in a move designed to gain favour with Donna.

'Oh, he'll probably tell you he's nine and a half,' Donna smiled, warming to the visitor.

'Look, I know this is none of my business but your husband was telling me that you're searching for a bone marrow donor for Corrie and I was wondering, you know, if you don't mind someone, eh ... someone like me, I wouldn't mind, eh ... I mean I'd quite happy to do the blood test, or whatever it is they want me to do.'

'Would you really?' Donna enthused, responding kindly to the offer and making no mention of the slim chances for success. 'Look, that would be much appreciated. The more tests we do the better the chances of finding a compatible donor. That's right, isn't it Jimmy?'

'Aye, right enough. The more the merrier,' Jimmy replied, glad that the topic of conversation had been steered clear of the events of the night before.

In appreciation of the offer Donna put her hand on Shane's forearm and gave her a gentle squeeze. That was when she noticed the make-up covered bruising on Shane's right cheekbone.

'Are you all right?' Donna asked, glancing over Shane's shoulder at her husband.

'I'll be OK,' Shane said, gently feeling her cheek with the tips of her perfectly manicured nails and flinching despite the delicacy of her touch.

'Let me see that,' Donna demanded, all but touching the affected area. 'I'd hate to see that without the make-up, girl. You're lucky there's no swelling. Jimmy, have you seen this?'

'I was up half the night with an ice pack and a pound of steak,' Shane explained.

Jimmy wanted no part of it and said, 'Ach, sure you can hardly notice it. It was probably only a wee tap.'

'You had something to do with this, didn't you?' Donna accused.

'Giv'us a break, Donna doll. You know I wouldn't lift my hand to a woman.'

Shane interrupted. 'It's all right, Donna. I think I got caught with an elbow. It was my own fault, and it's not as if I hadn't been warned.'

The pressure on Donna's lips flattened them to

slits and endowed her with rarely seen dimples. 'They should've warned you not to be in the same room as him, Shane. And while we're on the subject, Jimmy Macintyre, you needn't think I'm paying for that window. No bloody fear.'

'The window's all taken care off, so you can just relax. Christsake.'

Donna winked at Shane and headed towards the bedroom, throwing her coat on the bed.

Shane winked back, the action distorting her face with pain.

'Be a love and put the kettle on, Jimmy. You haven't offered our guest a cup of tea yet,' Donna said, adding, 'Corrie should be back by now, shouldn't he?'

'He's probably playing with that stupid rabbit of his by now,' Jimmy answered. 'You should see it, Shane. As soon as you let it out for a bit of a run around it tries to fuck everything in sight, including our Mick. That's how stupid it is.'

With her leg cocked Shane put her hands on her hips and cooed, 'Ooh, where is it?'

Donna placed a tray next to a plate of sliced fruit cake on the coffee table and smiled at Shane. 'Just you mind your language in the presence of ladies, James Macintyre,' she chided, coaxing a grin from both.

After what Donna had been through lately, dealing with the horror of their son's relapse, Jimmy cherished her fleeting moment of cheer, knowing that a change of mood would cast a cloud over a room just as quickly as her smile had brightened it.

Shane drained her coffee and stood, smoothing the wrinkles in her tight grey skirt with the flat of her hand. 'When would you like me to do the test for that bone marrow stuff? I'm free most days.'

'Oh yes,' Donna said, rising also. 'Give me the details of where I can contact you and I'll get something organised ASAP.'

Using an eyeliner pencil Shane jotted down her particulars on a scrap of paper and handed it to Donna. 'Here's my address and phone number but I'm sure you'll be seeing me around. I'm at the Wheatsheaf three nights a week. Thursday, Friday and Saturday. Why don't you try and catch my act?'

'I'd love to, pet, but I work nights and those are my busiest. But I'm sure I'll get the chance.'

'Yeah. Whenever you get the chance,' Shane agreed.

Donna saw Shane to the door and noticed that she wasn't wearing a coat. 'Didn't you bring a coat, you silly girl? You'll catch your death of cold,' she scolded and moved towards the bedroom.

'It's all right, Donna. Honest. I'll be catching a cab.'

'You'll be catching a cold,' Donna quipped and went into the bedroom, returning with her black coat over her arm. 'Here, put this on before you do yourself a mischief.'

The sight of Donna's expensive black coat, and the thought of wearing it, reduced Shane's protests to a feeble smile. When she put on the coat she slung her handbag over her shoulder and dug her hands deep in the pockets, wallowing in the fragrance, the feel and the aura of Donna.

'I don't fancy going on stage with a face like this so I might drop the coat off at your work tonight, if you don't mind, Donna? Where did you say you worked again?'

Donna held the door open and exchanged glances with Jimmy, taking the shrug of his shoulders as the go-ahead to answer the question. 'Archer Street. 18 Archer Street. Just off Shaftesbury Avenue. But you needn't put yourself to any trouble. It's not my only coat, you know.'

'I wouldn't feel right,' Shane explained, stepping out onto the landing. 'Don't come down the stairs,' she added.

Donna stood at the kitchen sink under the window and watched Shane cross South Lambeth Road to the taxi rank opposite. 'That was nice of her to offer to do a tissue test, wasn't it, Jimmy?'

'Aye, that was me,' Jimmy said, taking the credit. 'I was telling her all about Corrie. Before you came home, like.'

'I could get to like her,' Donna said, resisting the urge to wave at the departing cab.

Outside, Shane looked up at the window. Not a bad effort, she thought, going over her progress. So far so good.

FIVE

Anton Winters slammed his fist down on the tubular metal framework at the foot of the hospital bed and glared at the unconscious Nigel Paterson. He was furious. Not because of the damage sustained by his emissary, but because someone, as if he didn't know who, had had the nerve to do it. 'He's fucken dead,' he muttered, drawing a look of reproach from the startled nurse reaching for the clipboard next to him.

'As soon as you get any sense out of him can you let me know? I want to bring him a bunch of grapes,' Anton sneered, shaking his head and walking away.

At six foot two inches tall Anton was broad-shouldered and powerfully built, a physique he'd sculptured in the gym. His dark hair, appearing black from the gel that kept it slicked back, was long enough to tie in a ponytail. He had brown eyes, hollow cheeks that emphasised the strength in his jaw, and olive skin. The classic Savile Row suits he favoured were intended to make him look like a legitimate businessman. They did nothing of the sort. He was a heavy, and nothing could disguise that.

'If you want something done properly, you have to do it yourself,' he muttered under his breath as he climbed behind the wheel of his black BMW 7 Series and headed towards Vauxhall Bridge, the quickest way from St Thomas's Hospital to South Lambeth Road.

Always in the shadow of Jimmy Macintyre, Anton had been moving slowly but surely through the ranks of Archie Kemp's burgeoning crime empire. From his position as an enforcer of some considerable reputation he had delighted in taking over much of Jimmy's patch the same day as Jimmy had gone down. It put him in the box seat to be assigned the caretaker role when, two months ago, Archie Kemp in turn went down.

Archie Kemp was London's reigning crime boss, a popular working-class villain who thrived on the attention of celebrities and the adulation of ordinary people from the same background as himself. Those he referred to as 'being in the trade' he ruled with an iron fist, meting out a deadly justice at the hands of enforcers such as Jimmy Macintyre and Anton, and lately Nigel Paterson.

Archie's firm was a crime empire with eight prestigious nightclubs in areas such as Soho, Knightsbridge and Islington, plus controlling interest, though no money had changed hands, in numerous pubs scattered throughout London; a drug distribution network linking the major cities in Britain; properties in Gran Canaria, Marbella and other parts of Europe, even Gstaad; front companies to launder the proceeds of fraud, racketeering and armed robbery. Money didn't change hands because, by intimidation, he took whatever he wanted.

Up until the time of his promotion Anton, as chief enforcer, was in charge of an impressive array of firearms, a job once filled by Jimmy Macintyre. Nigel Paterson, the man who in turn had filled Anton's shoes when he stepped up, a man more than adequately qualified, had volunteered for the task of teaching Jimmy Macintyre some respect – a labour of love Anton would've preferred to do himself if Archie hadn't counselled so strongly on the importance of being seen to delegate authority. Now it looked like he would have to do the job himself after all.

The Wheatsheaf was the obvious place to start. Nigel Paterson had phoned him from it the night before, confirming their suspicions that Macintyre would show up there, it being a pub he was known to frequent before he last went inside.

Anton, a total stranger at the Wheatsheaf, knew not to barge in and start asking questions about Jimmy Macintyre in his own patch. There was every likelihood that they would think he was the police, or someone equally as sinister, and just clam up. Old Davey Macintyre, seated with two others at a table with easy access to the bar, watched Anton stroll in and scan every corner of the room.

'Afternoon, lads,' Anton said with a smile.

'Afternoon,' they chorused, knowing a man who commanded respect when they saw one. Davey, for one, thought that if he was nice, there might be a drink in it for him.

'A Jack Daniel's with a splash of Coke,' Anton told the barman. 'And get the lads here whatever they want. I don't like drinking alone.'

'Fuck sake. I'm just the very man to keep you company,' Davey said, nodding his head. 'Sure as Christ.'

'You eh – you guys locals, are you?' Anton said.

'Not really,' Davey replied. 'I'm from Glasgow myself.'

Anton smiled. 'You know what I mean. Do you live around here?'

Davey grinned at his pals. 'Live around here? The wife thinks I actually live *here*. She's never done telling me.'

'Umm. If that's the case I think I might be talking to the right man,' Anton grinned.

'It depends what you mean by the right man. I don't think I've ever been called that before. Everything but.'

'Nah, it's just that I was supposed to meet a guy here and I don't see any sign of him.'

'You're out of luck, pal. Me and the boys are the only ones to set foot in here for the last hour or so. The three desperadoes. That's right, isn't it lads?'

'Umm, it's not like him.' Anton said, rubbing his chin.

'Who was you looking for, anyway? There's not too many folk around here me and the boys don't know.' Davey thought that if he could be of help, there was the chance of at least another drink in it for them.

Anton looked off to the side, his eyes narrowing in concentration. 'No, wait a minute. Now that I think of it, I'm pretty sure he said to meet him at the house. Jimmy's probably wondering where I am.'

'Jimmy who?' said Davey.

'Jimmy Macintyre. I'd be surprised if you didn't know him.'

Davey's companions, each in the process of taking a mouthful of ale, gulped quickly, intending to be the first to answer in the affirmative.

'Never heard of him,' Davey said emphatically, drawing puzzled looks from his friends. Looks that didn't go unnoticed by Anton.

'There's a quid in it for you, if that'll help your memory.'

Davey was resolute. 'Listen, mate,' he said, glancing sideways at his drinking companions and up at the barman summoned by the twenty pound note Anton was holding, 'when I say I never heard of Jimmy Macintyre, that means I never heard of him. OK?' Anton raised his eyebrows at the other two. 'What about you?'

Both shook their heads.

'Suit yourself,' Anton said and moved further along the bar, drawing the barman with him. 'What time does Jimmy Macintyre normally show a face?'

The barman shook his head and reached for a glass to wipe. 'The name doesn't ring a bell,' he said, avoiding eye contact.

'The old guy over there, what's his name?' Anton said suspiciously. 'The one with the Scottish accent.'

'Excuse me, sir,' called the barman, 'this gentleman was just asking what your name was.'

'Jock,' Davey shouted back, grinning. 'My friends just call me Jock.'

'All right, Jock,' Anton said, stopping at the table on his way out. 'When you see Jimmy Macintyre you tell him Anton Winters was looking for him.'

'Awh shit,' the barman said when the exit door slammed shut. 'Did he say Anton Winters? He's nothing but trouble.'

'I might've known,' Davey said. 'I didn't like the look of him as soon I clapped eyes on him. I thought he was a debt collector, or something. Cunning bastard. Let that be a lesson to you lads. You tell nobody nothing.'

Sitting in his car Anton took the mobile phone from his inside pocket and punched in the numbers. 'Donna Macintyre's still on the game, isn't she?' he said, adding, 'Good,' when the male voice on the other end answered, 'As far as I know. But you know she doesn't come under our banner. Her old man's Jimmy Mac –'

'I know who her old man is. That's why I'm looking for her,' Anton snapped. 'Find out where she operates from and give me a call back. Quick as you can.'

SIX

The well-worn path to the pigeon loft at the rear of the garden passed through overgrown and ill-defined beds that once boasted vegetables. Wraparound grey clouds hovered low, hiding the source of the thunderous roar that caused Corrie to look up. He saw a Concorde jet make a fleeting appearance in a break in the clouds. 'Look Dad, a Concorde,' he said, pointing up.

'Right enough,' Jimmy agreed, looking up to see the clouds devour the jet again.

Along the side wall there was a series of garden sheds defying the laws of gravity. To the left, dilapidated timber and wire fences in various stages of disrepair separated the back gardens of the neglected row of terraces. Shattered windows outnumbered unbroken ones, and four doors up a spiral of black smoke told Jimmy that the occupants of a squat were burning the plastic coating from copper wire, readying it for the scrap yard.

'Bastards,' he muttered under his breath.

Climbing over or squeezing through gaps in the dividing fences Jimmy strode up to the fire, and shielding his eyes from the flying sparks, began kicking it all over the place. 'This is the first and last time I'll be telling you cunts that your smoke chokes my pigeons. Now if I catch you again, I'll take a hold of you and stick your fucken heads in the fire. And the first one that opens their mouth will find out what I'm talking about.'

A ragtag collection of squatters and shabbily dressed dropouts, comprising as many males as females, was immobilised by fear.

Corrie retreated from the hole in the last fence his father had squeezed through as soon as he saw him returning. 'Did you make them put it out, Dad?'

'Aye, come on,' Jimmy said, leading the way back to the pigeon loft.

His mood mellowed noticeably as soon as he stepped inside the enclosure. 'Come here, my bonnie lass,' he whispered and cradled the elegant racing pigeon in the palm of his hand, allowing its legs to protrude through his fingers.

'Here,' he said, handing it to Corrie. 'Careful now.'

The streamlined racer at first looked bland and grey, but at the merest hint of light, the feathers shimmered like the rainbow.

Corrie held it the way he'd been taught and stroked it gently with his other hand. 'Who's a bonnie lass?' he said, mimicking his father.

Outside, the contrasting brightness forced Corrie to blink. 'Now?' he asked, holding the bird above his head.

'Go ahead,' Jimmy urged, simultaneously releasing another racer into the air. In a frantic flutter of wings both birds soared and converged to begin circling. On release, the rest of the racers caught up and completed the customary laps, swooping and turning and soaring, glad of the opportunity to spread their wings.

Craning his head upwards Corrie performed a shuffling circle on the spot, following the birds' progress. 'Dad, how do the pigeons know how to find their way home?'

Mick was making his way up the path when he heard the question. 'Everybody thinks pigeons are dead clever,' he began, 'but I bet you I could see the roof of my house if I could fly two miles up in the air.'

'Is that right, Dad?'

Jimmy shook his head and said, 'Don't keep him going Mick, yeh bam.' After a pause he added, 'Pay no attention to him, Corrie. It's got nothing to do with sight. Them birds have got a sixth sense.'

Mick winked at Corrie and Corrie grinned back. 'Come on, big man, are we going to get this window or what? I've got the lend of a van.'

Jimmy kept his eyes on the birds. 'You won't be needing a van,' he said, turning to face his brother after the last pigeon settled on the roof of No. 38.

'How no?' Mick said. 'There's no way I'm going

to hump a ruddy great window along the streets in broad daylight. No way.'

'You won't have to hump it far. I've got my eye on one three doors up.'

'Jimmy, there's folk living in there.'

'Squatters. I'm taking the window off them and if they open their yappers I'll take the roof as well.'

Donna was alone in the flat, filling the electric kettle when the rat-a-tat-tat of the heavy brass door knocker echoed up the stairs. Standing on her tiptoes she leaned over the sink, hoping to catch a glimpse of the caller should he or she step back from the door. She was horrified when she recognised the man as the same one who, last night, had paid her fifty pounds for a talk that never eventuated. The man with the American accent.

How dare he, she thought, skipping down the stairs and getting to the front door moments after Agnes. 'It's all right, Agnes, I think this gentleman's looking for me,' she said, waiting until her mother-in-law, giving her a look of reproof, returned to the parlour. In her line of work Donna had seen all kinds and she'd thought there was something odd about this guy when he'd paid her fifty quid and walked out the door. Him showing up at the house proved it.

'What the hell are you doing here?' Donna snapped. 'How did you get this address? If you've been following me I'll –'

Munro looked distraught. 'Look ma'am, I'm very sorry but I think it's time we had a talk. There's something very important I'd like to discuss with you.'

It still hadn't registered with Donna that the stranger was anything other than a troublesome John. 'Listen you, if you don't –'

'I believe you're looking for Tom Gilfeather,' Munro interrupted.

Donna, standing just outside the door, shot a look over her shoulder along the length of the hall then across at the bay window. 'Look,' she said in near panic, 'I can't talk to you here, but please, please meet me tonight at the same place as you saw me last night. You know, the place in Archer Street.'

'Fine. What time?' Munro said, looking into the darkened hallway behind Donna, sharing her anxiety.

'What about right now?' Donna said, coming to her senses.

'Suits me.' Munro began backing down the steps.

On her way back upstairs to get ready Donna hesitated momentarily and returned to the front door with the intention of telling Munro to meet her somewhere nearer. 'Blast,' she said when she saw no sign of him.

It was just after three o'clock when she stepped out of the cab in Archer Street and squeezed between two of the fruit barrows that lined the narrow street day and night. She exchanged pleasantries with the

Cockney stallholders and caught the apple one of them lobbed at her. 'What brings you up West in broad daylight, Donna? Doing a bit of overtime then?' one said.

Anton was driving towards Islington when the call came through on his mobile phone, relaying the message from the stallholder. 'It looks like Donna Macintyre just showed up, Anton. The geezer said you'd better get over there smartish. He said to tell you that she's not in the habit of hanging around if she makes an appearance during the day.'

'I'm on my way.'

Munro, standing in the shadows outside Donna's room, stepped forward when he saw her making her way upstairs towards him.

'I hope I haven't kept you waiting,' Donna said nervously. 'I got here as quick as I could.'

'No more than a couple of minutes,' Munro replied and followed her into the room. 'This isn't going to cost me fifty pounds, I hope,' he joked, attempting to break the ice.

Donna's weak, sarcastic smile warned him that she was hardly in the mood for jokes. 'What's this about Tom Gilfeather, Mr, eh . . .'

'Munro.'

'I don't suppose you happen to know where he is, Mr Munro?' Donna urged.

'If I knew that – Donna, isn't it? – I wouldn't be standing here.'

The penalty for allowing herself a glimmer of hope

was always the same. A plunge to a new depth of despair. 'I don't understand. I thought – I thought you must've known him. Known where he is. Known where the fuck he is.'

'You're half right,' Munro conceded. 'I do know Tom Gilfeather. Quite well.'

Stealing up to the ill-fitting, panelled door that the fruit stallholder had directed him to, Anton heard voices and put his ear closer to the wood, cautiously determining the lay of the land.

Donna lit a cigarette and paced the length of the room. 'Have you any idea where he is? Any idea at all?'

'Before I answer that, uh, I would need to know why you're looking for Tom. I mean, this seems all very sinister to me. And to be honest with you I'm, uh, I'm not sure what's going on here. Is he in some kind of trouble?'

'Look Mr Munro –'

'Call me Steve. Please.'

'OK, Steve, I was just going to say that it might not be a bad idea if you tell me what it's got to do with you.'

Munro squinted at her for several moments, deciding what to do next. 'Fair enough,' he began. 'I don't suppose it'll do any harm. I'm a reporter for the Chicago *Post* and –'

'A reporter?' Donna blasted. She was thinking that, at this stage, publicity of that nature was the last thing in the world she wanted. In her efforts to find Gilfeather she had been as discreet as humanly possible.

'Let me finish. Please. There's more to it than that. Believe me. You see, I'm looking for Tom Gilfeather myself. I saw your advertisement in my paper and decided to check you out. I thought, well I thought that between the two of us we might stand a better chance of finding him.'

Donna couldn't imagine any circumstances in which she would be willing to share Gilfeather once she found him. Not until she'd finished with him. On the other hand, if she didn't get some help to find him there would be nothing to share. 'How do I know you're not with the police or somebody like that? You could be anybody for all I know.'

Munro took his time to look around the room, implying by the expression on his face – a smiling sneer – that he was well within his rights to view her with equal suspicion. However, he'd had enough time to assess the situation and, believing she meant Gilfeather no harm, decided to take her into his confidence, trusting that she would reciprocate. 'Can I ask you something before I answer that?'

'Fire away,' Donna replied.

'Is the Tom Gilfeather you're looking for an American around about thirty?'

Donna thought for a moment, adding ten years to the Gilfeather she had first encountered. 'Close enough,' she said.

'If that's the case I think Tom Gilfeather might be my son,' Munro said.

'What do you mean, you *think* he might be your

son? Is he or isn't he?' Donna gasped.

'I found out that Tommy decided to go by the name of Gilfeather, my dead wife's maiden name. God knows why. So I hope, or should I say, that I'm sure we're talking about the same person here. All things considered.'

'How do I know you're telling the truth? How do I –'

'Hey, slow down there. All I know is that you've gone to a helluva lot of trouble to locate Tommy. Yes, and a helluva lot more trouble to keep it a secret. Your turn to do a bit of explaining.'

'If what you say is true, then I have a surprise for you. It seems that you and I are related by birth,' Donna told him. 'The birth of my son Corrie. You see, Tom Gilfeather is his biological father. It's a long story.' Donna took no heed of the surprised look on his face. She was too busy speculating on the increased chances of a compatible bone marrow donor.

'Well, I'll be a goddamned son of a bitch. How about that? A grand-daddy, eh? When can I see the boy?'

'You can't,' Donna snapped. 'You mustn't go near him. Do you hear me? Jesus, if my Jimmy ever finds out.'

'I have no problem with that. For the time being.' Munro's priority was to locate his son, without further complication.

'You don't understand. My Jimmy must *never* find out.'

'If that's the case, why have you gone to so much trouble to find Tommy? Surely not for child support payments? Not if you're so concerned about your husband finding out the truth. It doesn't make sense.'

'I think you'd better get something into your head, eh, Steve. My Jimmy is a violent man. Extremely violent. It's how he was brought up and until recently it was how he made a living. Eventually he solves everything with his fists. Or worse.' Donna stopped short of describing her love for her husband. Of how she placed sparing his feelings second only to the life of their son.

'Umm, I suppose that explains the secrecy all right,' Munro answered, squinting off to his right. 'But it doesn't explain why you're in such a god-damned hurry to find Tommy.'

'My son has leukaemia,' Donna answered softly. 'I need a compatible bone marrow donor, in, as you say, an awful big hurry. Gilfeather, your son I mean, might be my last hope. Unless you've got a swag of relatives stashed away somewhere?'

'I'm afraid there's only Tommy and me. But if this kid's family, and it doesn't take major surgery, I'll uh, I'll think about doing whatever the hell I can to help.'

Major surgery, Donna thought and laughed. 'We're only talking about a tissue test. It's a blood test.'

'From what you said, I gather that close relatives are the best prospect for a donor?'

'Correct. I'm looking for Tom Gilfeather, and they don't come any closer than that.'

'In that case I'll be glad to help. I consider myself family.'

'That's appreciated,' Donna smiled.

'And I'm sure that goes for Tommy,' said Munro, returning the smile.

'If only we could find him.'

'We'll find him.'

'That's all very well but where do we go from here? I've used police contacts, a bit of contra, to exhaust every avenue. Electoral rolls, motor registration. Even the deed polls, in case he changed his name again.' Donna's mouth shot open. 'Munro. I never thought to look under the name of Munro.' She was convinced she'd found the missing link.

'But I did,' Munro said, once again erasing a glimmer of hope. 'Since Tommy got out of prison here, I go through the same process year in, year out. Everywhere the Chicago *Post*'s tentacles reach. And a few more places besides. It's almost as if he's disappeared off the face of the earth.'

Or beneath the face of the earth, they thought simultaneously.

Anton backed away from the door, coming down off the tips of his toes when he reached the head of the stairs. Skipping down the stairs he squinted when he emerged in the comparative brightness of what was actually a dull winter's day. On his way to his car, which he'd parked half up on the pavement, he ignored the chain-reaction greetings from the line of stallholders, unlocked the car by remote control and plucked the mobile phone from the inside pocket of his suit jacket as he climbed behind the wheel.

Sitting in his open cell in Parkhurst Prison, surrounded by the privileges of his status, all the comforts of home, Archie Kemp tossed his head back and laughed at one of the characters in the television programme he was watching. With his distinguished silver hair, well groomed and lighter around the temples, he had a well-heeled look about him that even the dowdy prison fatigues failed to detract from. A gold sovereign, the centre piece of a chunky gold ring that he wore on his right pinkie, enhanced the image. He was still in his early fifties, fit and tanned from a pre-trial holiday jaunt, but the strain of waiting for his appeal was starting to tell on his nerves. That and having to rely on others to find Gilfeather, the key factor in the appeal.

A warder appeared suddenly in the open doorway, looked left and right along the corridor before he entered the cell. 'Anton was on the blower, Archie. He said you've to ring him straight back. Christ, make sure nobody finds out I'm taking messages for you, Archie.'

'Don't give me any of that crap. We're paying you as much again as you get for being a screw.' Archie eased himself out of his chair and ambled out of the cell towards the pay phone in the amenities block. It was halfway down an aisle formed by two-storey white painted walls, broken with lines of bars and a catwalk running its length. The warder who delivered the message escorted him all the way, delighted to be seen in his company.

Inserting a phone card, one of the prison system's many illicit currencies, Archie dialled the familiar number and said with suitable concern, 'Sorry to hear about your old mum, Anton. She was a good old stick. My condolences to you and your family.'

'Thanks. It was probably for the best. She was in a lot of pain. Anyway, she had a fair innings. Eighty-six she would've been.'

'Christ, I would never have thought. She looked like a woman half her age. She always looked so fit.'

'She went downhill fast.'

'When's the funeral?'

'We're burying her on Monday, but, eh, that's not what I'm ringing you about. I've been having a bit of trouble with Jimmy Macintyre since he got out and –'

'You didn't ring me just to tell me that I hope?' Archie interrupted, dispensing with the pleasantries and sounding more like his normal self. 'It's your job to handle things until I get out of this shithole. Not come running to me.'

'No, no, no. That's nothing. I was trying to find out where he lived. You know, so's I could pay him a visit. Anyway, without going into all the details I went round to see his old lady with the intention of –'

'And?'

With his eyes closed Anton gritted his teeth and counted to ten. 'I overheard her talking to some American geezer about that other American geezer you told me to keep an eye open for. You know. Gilfeather.'

'Good work, Anton. Good work.' Archie made a fist of his free hand and shook it triumphantly. 'What were they saying about him? Anything interesting?'

'For a start, the American guy said he was Gilfeather's father. I'm sure that's what he said. But from what I could gather they seem to be in the same boat as yourself. They seemed pretty keen to find him.' Anton paused. He hoped Archie would tell him why he was looking for Gilfeather. Without him having to ask.

'What else did they say? They must've said more than that, surely?'

'What did you say you were looking for this geezer for?' Anton chanced.

'It's a private matter,' Archie snarled. 'Hurry up and tell me what else they said.'

'I'll tell you what they did say. On a personal level like. It turns out this Gilfeather character is the father of Macintyre's son. I didn't even know he had a son. What am I saying? He hasn't got a son. He only thinks he has. Ha ha. I can't wait to see the look on his face when I tell him.'

'Anton. Listen to me. You'll do no such thing. Do you hear me?' The warning bells were ringing in

Archie's ears. He had known Jimmy Macintyre long enough to realise that there would be nothing left of Gilfeather if Jimmy ever got wind of what Anton had just told him. He needed Gilfeather in one piece. At least until his business with him was over and done with.

'I was looking forward to telling him,' Anton moaned. 'It would've been one of life's little pleasures.'

'There'll be plenty of time for that later. First things first.'

'I take it that it's OK to give him a slap?' Anton said sarcastically. 'He's been well out of order.'

'What's he done anyway?' Archie had a soft spot for Jimmy, never seeing the unambitious hardman as a threat to business. Not like Anton.

'He's been going the demand over in South London. Just walked in and took a fucken car off one of our customers. No beg your pardons. And him not out of Pentonville five fucken minutes either.'

'No respect,' Archie cut in.

'And if that wasn't bad enough he's put Nigel Paterson in the hospital. I made the mistake of thinking he could handle Macintyre by himself. Looks like I'll have to take care of him myself.'

'Umm, Nigel Paterson eh?' Archie pressed his lips together, forcing them down at the sides. 'Do what you have to do, Anton. But whatever you do, make sure Macintyre knows fuck all about Gilfeather. Not until I fucken say so. Are we on the same wavelength here?'

'I hear you.'

'Good. Here's what I want you to do. Flash over and see Macintyre's old lady. Tell her that you know the score. Tell her you'll tell her old man about the kid's real father if she doesn't weigh in with the goods on Mr Gilfeather. Make sure she gets the message. But I don't want her harmed. Know what I mean?'

'No problem. I'm as good as in Archer Street right now.'

'Good. Now as far as the American guy goes, just keep an eye on him for the time being. See where he goes. We don't want to scare him away, do we now?'

'That shouldn't be too hard.'

'Oh, and Anton. A word to the wise. If you're going to pay Macintyre a visit, make sure you go team-handed this time, eh? He can be a bit of a handful.'

Archie's words were like a red rag to a bull, insinuating, Anton thought, that he couldn't handle Jimmy Macintyre by himself. The well-intended advice only served to strengthen his resolve to prove that he was the better man.

Anton hung up, locked the car and hurried across the road, bowing his head when Munro emerged from the building where Donna conducted business. Briefly he considered following Munro, as per Archie's instructions, but deciding that his own needs came first he veered into the darkened hallway and took the stairs two at a time, striding into Donna's room without knocking.

Thinking that Munro had returned, Donna, though slightly peeved at the lack of courtesy, looked up unconcerned. When she saw that it was Anton, a man well known to her, she forced a smile and tried a bit of bluster to mask the sudden apprehension. 'It's polite to knock before you enter a lady's boudoir, Anton,' she said.

'If it had been a lady's boudoir I probably would've knocked.'

'Huh. I doubt if you'd know a lady if you saw one.' Donna knew that Anton had filled the vacancy left by her husband when he'd last been sentenced. She was also aware that he was running the show while Archie Kemp was waiting for his appeal to come up. She thought that if he was here with the intention of using her to entice Jimmy back into a life of crime, boy, did he have another think coming.

'Now, now, Donna. That's no way to treat an old friend. Not somebody who might be able to do you a good turn.'

Donna's eyes narrowed as she backed up to the bed and sat down, leaning back on her outstretched arms. 'The only good turn you can do me is piss off and shut the door behind you.'

'Tut tut. Don't you want to discuss the favour I was thinking of doing for you? Fair enough. I'll just show myself out.'

Prick, Donna thought and said nervously, 'What favour's this you're talking about? I didn't think you were capable.'

'I was thinking of telling that old man of yours that eh, that he – how can I put it? – that Tom Gilfeather is a very close relative of that son he idolises. Know what I mean? Nudge nudge, wink wink. I reckon I'd be doing you a real big favour if I kept that information to myself. That and the fact that you're hell-bent on finding him. What do you think?'

The smirk on Anton's face warned her that the denial she was contemplating would be a complete waste of time. 'What the hell do you want?' she said.

'Nothing too difficult. I want to know where your old man's living these days.'

'If you're thinking of trying to talk him into going back to work for Archie Kemp, then I'm afraid you're wasting your time. He's finished with all that crap.'

'Is he now? That's not what I heard. I heard he was up to his old tricks.'

'Well, I'm here to tell you that you're mistaken,' Donna told him.

'Whatever suits you. It's immaterial anyway. I just want to have a talk with him and if I have to go to any more trouble to find him I might as well tell him about Gilfeather while I'm at it. I'm sure he would be delighted to know. I know I would if it was me.'

'38 South Lambeth Road. But you have to swear that you won't mention Tom Gilfeather. Please, Anton,' Donna begged and got to her feet, 'my son has leukaemia and the only hope of –'

'I know all that,' Anton dismissed her. 'That's why you're going to tell me everything you know about this geezer Gilfeather. And Donna, don't think for one minute that I'm kidding. Archie Kemp's the one interested in finding Gilfeather, not me. Personally, I hope you decide to keep your mouth shut because nothing in this wide world would give me greater pleasure than to see the look on your Jimmy's face when I tell him who the father of his kid is. Nothing.'

As the implication of his words rammed home Donna slumped, seated on the edge of the bed. She didn't have to be told that Archie Kemp's involvement augured no good for Gilfeather, a turn of events likely to make him harder to find, if that was possible. But if Anton followed through with his threat she might as well pack up and put herself and Corrie on the missing list. With both Anton or Jimmy looking for him, Gilfeather, if he had any sense, would never surface again. And the consequences ... Even if Corrie survived it would mean the breakdown of the family and the loss of any hope for the normal life she craved. She wondered how much more she could take. 'How come you're looking for Gilfeather?' was all she could manage.

'That's got nothing to do with you.'

'It's got everything to do with me,' Donna began, then stopped. In her confusion she had failed to appreciate that Anton needed her help to find Gilfeather in one piece. Otherwise he would just turn

Jimmy loose. If she was careful she could string Anton along, keep him at bay until she found Gilfeather and satisfied her own needs. Dripfeed him information.

Anton clicked his fingers in front of her face. 'All you have to do is tell me when you find Gilfeather. That's not a high price to pay.'

How could she tell him what she didn't know? 'If I knew where Gilfeather was do you think I'd be standing here?'

'I realise that,' he said, pointing a finger. 'All I'm saying is that you've got a week to find him.'

'What's that supposed to mean?'

Anton moved towards the doors, stopping when he'd taken hold of the handle. 'After that I'm going to tell Jimmy the score and see if he can find Gilfeather any quicker.' He opened the door and let himself out, sure that he had maximised his position.

Donna fell back on the bed and buried her face in her hands. 'You bastard,' she wept.

Out in the street a tow truck had backed up to Anton's BMW. Anton strode up angrily and confronted the heavy-set man operating the winch at the rear of the vehicle. 'If you don't fuck right off I'll stuff you in this little toy of yours and burn you to the ground.' He gripped the man by the throat, ushered him to the cabin and slammed him into the door. 'No fucken respect,' he laughed as he watched the tow truck speed off, followed by a sustained tirade of abuse from stallholders and customers diving for cover.

'It's a diabolic liberty when you can't get a parking

spot in your own manor,' he muttered to himself and climbed behind the wheel. Drumming the top of the steering wheel with the fingers of both hands he waited for a car to pass and took off down Archer Street, turning left and right and heading for South London through Piccadilly Circus, Trafalgar Square and Whitehall.

SEVEN

Jimmy Macintyre stood on the footpath and watched William and Mick manhandle the bay window down the steps of No. 46, four doors up. 'Careful,' he ordered. 'Don't drop the fucker or we'll have to get another one.' He was rugged up against the cold, wearing a working man's reefer jacket and a head-hugging, black woollen cap pulled down around his ears.

Beads of sweat trickled down the side of Mick's nose. 'Mind you don't strain your fucken self there, big man,' he grunted.

From the other end of the window William agreed. 'I don't know how we would've managed without you, Jimmy.'

A lone delegate broke from the ranks of the squatters and warily approached Jimmy. 'Who gave you the right to take our window.' A quivering voice foiled her attempt at indignation.

'Who gave you the right to choke my fucken

pigeons? How many times do you have to be told?' Jimmy winked at Corrie and Corrie winked back.

'We think your actions are a bit heavy-handed and we demand you put the window back.'

'Oh do you now?' Jimmy's jaw jutted out and he spoke through clenched teeth. 'Go on, get to fuck the lot of you, before I knock youse all on your arse. Cunts, fucken ill-treating dumb animals. Go on, get.'

The squatter retreated to the ranks of those shaking their heads and filing back inside. From the gap where the window had been she watched Jimmy direct the progress of her window along the pavement to No. 38.

On the other side of the road, caught in a line of traffic, Anton watched the proceedings and thought, That's him, the man himself. 'Jimmy Macintyre,' he shouted, obscured by the tinted window he had wound down a fraction.

Jimmy turned around and smiled with his hand automatically raised ready to wave. A frown gradually replaced the smile when he failed to recognise a familiar face in the line of traffic moving off, or on the pavement beyond. Feeling slightly embarrassed he raised his other arm in a similar fashion and pretended he was stretching. 'I could've sworn somebody called my name there, Corrie,' he whispered.

Cursing the traffic Anton kept an eye on the rear-vision mirror while he waited for the break in the oncoming traffic that would permit a U turn.

The BMW swung sharply in a squeal of burning

rubber. Anton turned in his seat and fingered the driver of the car he had just cut off, annoyed at the persistent tooting. Seeing no sign of Jimmy, as he drove back up the street he turned left into Mawbey Street, parked next to the Macintyre house, and walked out into South Lambeth Road looking for him. William and Mick were sitting on the steps sharing a cigarette while they recuperated before the second stage of the operation. Installing the window.

'I'm looking for a guy called Jimmy Macintyre. They tell me he lives here,' Anton said.

In keeping with the normal family practice of being evasive to men dressed in suits who came calling at the door William answered, 'Never heard of him.'

Mick agreed. 'He doesn't come from around here, whoever he is. Who's looking for him anyway?'

'Me. Anton Winters. I'm fucken looking for him. What are you? Some kind of idiot?'

The brothers exchanged worried glances. 'Aye, right enough, Anton,' William began. 'Sorry, I didn't recognise you, big man. Jimmy's mentioned your name a time or two. But eh, I'm afraid you've just missed him. If you'd been here a wee minute ago you'd have seen him getting into a taxi. That's right, isn't it, Mick?'

'Aye, right enough. A wee minute ago. Offski. Away he went.'

Anton glared at them through narrowed eyes. Other than barge into the house and start kicking down doors he figured he would have to bide his time. 'You two wouldn't be at the fanny? Because –'

'I swear to god, mate. You just missed him,' William interrupted. 'I wouldn't bullshit you. No way.'

'You tell him Anton Winters was looking for him,' Anton said and walked away.

Mick peeked around the corner into Mawbey Street and withdrew his head the instant he saw the BMW perform a U turn and drive towards him. He waited until it had turned left into South Lambeth Road and disappeared from view before he raced up the steps ahead of William. As he made his way along the overgrown path to the pigeon loft Mick played with his breath in the encroaching darkness, seeing how far he could huff it in the crisp air. Inside the loft Jimmy and Corrie had made themselves comfortable, sitting next to each other on an old wooden crate, holding and caressing the pigeons they had each just removed from their roosts. Corrie's eyes were wide with delight as he listened intently to his dad, speaking softly, starting to tell of the plans he had to race the birds.

'Hey big man, and you too, wee man,' Mick said, ducking through the open door.

'You got that window in yet?' Jimmy cast an eye to the fading light.

'Giv'us a break. It took us long enough to get the bloody thing out.'

'I wouldn't leave it lying around, Mickey boy. You

know what people are like around here. They would steal the sugar out of your tea.'

'Hey listen, Jimbo, there was this punter out the front looking for you a minute ago. A big guy driving a flash car. I thought he might've been a mate of that guy you chucked out the window. He didn't seem too pleased.'

'What'd he look like, this guy?'

'I told you. A big guy wearing a suit. Hard-looking sort of guy. But I never let on you were here,' Mick was adamant. 'It was our William who let the cat out of the bag. You can ask him.'

Jimmy got to his feet, returned the pigeon to its roost and instructed Corrie to do likewise.

'Awh Dad,' Corrie whinged, 'can't you finish the story first?'

'Do as you're told, Corrie,' Jimmy snapped. Characteristically, he was apprehensive at the thought of a bit of aggravation. 'Off you go inside, mate, and I'll finish the wee story as soon as I come in. There's a good boy,' he added, annoyed at himself for raising his voice to the child.

Both men waited and watched Corrie dawdle towards the back door. To the accompanying drone of heavy traffic Mick listened to the pigeons cooing and watched them as they ruffled their feathers or intermittently poked their heads from their nesting boxes, seemingly unsettled at the continued presence of a comparative stranger in the loft.

'Right, Mick, on you go,' Jimmy urged.

Mick scratched his head. 'You ever tasted one of these fuckers?'

Jimmy's eyes narrowed, his tightened lips forcing his jaw to protrude. 'It would be more than your life was worth.'

'Ease up, big man, I'm only taking the pish. You'd probably have to cook the lot to get a decent feed.'

'I'm warning you, Mick. If you don't rap up and get on with it you'll feel the toe of my boot.'

'What?'

Jimmy looked off to the side and shook his head. 'Whadda you mean, what? I'm trying to get a picture of this guy to see if I can put a name to him.'

'Why didn't you say? The guy said his name was Anton Winters.'

Casting his mind back to the words of the car dealer, that Anton wouldn't be pleased, Jimmy concluded that the visit wasn't likely to be social. 'Did he say anything? Or did he just ask for me, like?'

'Let me see. What did he say now? Aye, he just said to tell you he was looking for you.'

His eyes blazing Jimmy said, 'Did he now, the cunt? You should have come and got me.'

'Sorry, Jimbo. We weren't sure who he was. Know what I mean?'

'Forget it,' Jimmy said, holding the door open for his brother to duck through.

Outside, the glow from the roadside street lights escaped over the rooftops, tingeing the cold night air amber. At the end of the path a light went on in the kitchen, flooding the yard with light.

'Come on Mick,' Jimmy said. 'We'd better get that window in or we'll never hear the end of it.'

Mick shook his head in disbelief. 'This'll be a world first. The big man doing a bit of graft.'

Disregarding the comment Jimmy paused at a chopping block outside the back door, eyeing the hatchet that was wedged in it. 'I think I'll sharpen this up,' he said, wrenching the small axe free. 'It might come in handy.'

'You'll have to. That thing's as blunt as fuck,' Mick said.

Two hours later Agnes stood back and proudly looked at the window. 'That's smashing,' she said. 'Pity you couldn't have got your hands on one with some decent curtains though. Anyway, not to worry. I might lash out and run us up some new ones.'

'Hurry up and get the grub on the table, ma. Our William's paying for the bevie again tonight,' Mick announced.

Slumped in a threadbare easy chair with his legs fully extended and the open paper draped across his chest William's head spun as if it was on a swivel. 'What's all this?' he demanded.

'That's what you said last night, my man. And there was plenty of witnesses and all,' Mick insisted. 'Yeh needn't think yer getting out of it.'

'Giv'us a break, for Christsake. Nothing I said last

night counts. I was legless, so I was. I wouldn't have a clue what I said.'

Old Davey, nursing the effects of his afternoon session at the pub, was swaying in front of the cracked mirror above the kitchen sink. The collar of his shirt was tucked under and the lower half of his face was covered in a lazy shaving foam he'd whipped up from the washing-up detergent. 'I'm a witness,' he lied, talking out of the side of his mouth.

Standing up, William folded the paper and stretched his arms out wide, feigning a yawn. 'Well, I'm sorry to disappoint you, but I happen to have made other plans for tonight. In fact, I'm feeling a bit knackered. I might even stay in.'

Old Davey rinsed his razor in the basin and swilled the cloudy water over his face with his cupped hands. 'I don't give two fucks where you go, our William, as long as yer wallet goes to the boozer. I haven't stood here and shaved for nothing, beh Christ. That's right, isn't it, Aggie?'

Agnes agreed wholeheartedly. 'Aye, and you needn't think I'm standing here with a head full of curlers just to sit in the house watching bloody TV.'

The landlord of the Wheatsheaf was sitting at Jimmy Macintyre's permanently reserved table, half listening to Shane and half nervously watching the door, hoping that the place didn't empty out when the punters got wind that the pub was to be without live entertainment tonight. 'I'm going to give Jimmy Macintyre a good piece of my mind as soon as he walks in that door,' he told Shane and butted out another cigarette in the overflowing glass ashtray.

Shane's eyes lit up and she stopped talking in mid-sentence when she saw Jimmy lead the Macintyres through the double doors. 'Have a look at who just walked in, Ronnie. You'll be able to tell him now.'

'Shit,' Ronnie muttered, springing to his feet. 'Me and Shane were just looking after your table for you, Jimmy. Here, sit yourself down.' He held the back of the chair for Jimmy and allowed Agnes and the others to seat themselves.

Shane took the ashtray to the bar and returned quickly to wipe the table. She flinched, but smiled, when Davey ran his hand up the back of her leg. If only it was Jimmy, she thought.

'Right, the first round's on me,' Ronnie rubbed his hands together at chest-height.

'Squeeze in beside my ma, if you like,' Jimmy told Shane and started scanning the room, wondering if Anton would show up.

As the evening wore on the haze of cigarette smoke thickened. At the bar and around the perimeter of the room the noisy patrons denied a seat jockeyed for position, anticipating that Shane would relent and take to the stage. Those near enough to Shane kept the pressure on. 'Come on, Shane. Give us a song,' they insisted time and time again.

Sick of the constant badgering and in the mood for

a bit of decent entertainment himself Jimmy shouted across the table. 'On you go Shane, or we're never gonna get a minute's bloody peace.' He made the order sound like a request.

Shane halfheartedly pointed to her face.

'You're carrying on for nothing. Sure you can hardly notice it. Dab a wee bit more of that powder stuff on it and I'm sure nobody'll give two fucks.'

A cacophony of whistling, shouting and applause accompanied Shane to the stage, alerting Ronnie the landlord, who was standing in his usual position at the end of the bar, that his star turn had relented. Ronnie's two-fingered whistle could be heard above the din.

Shane was halfway through her act when Anton Winters entered the lounge. Jimmy, sitting with as clear a view of the door as the crowded lounge permitted, locked on to him and monitored his progress all the way to the bar, wondering how long it would take Anton to spot him.

Anton recognised Jimmy immediately, but resisted the urge to acknowledge him with a nod. However, Jimmy's constant staring, coupled with the apparent lack of able-bodied assistance on his table, encouraged Anton to detour from the bar and get down to business. He had ample faith in his own ability to handle Macintyre, and anyway, he had a point to prove to Archie Kemp.

On reaching the Macintyre table he reversed the chair vacated by Shane and sat down uninvited, resting his elbows on the back of the chair. 'The great Jimmy Macintyre,' he scoffed.

Jimmy made no sign that he recognised Anton. He studied him in silence while the rest of the family leaned back in their seats. 'Did anybody invite this cunt to sit down?' he said.

'I hear you called in to see Bert Wright,' Anton persisted. 'Relieved him of a motor, I believe.'

'Only those I invite get to sit at this table. I don't remember inviting you.' Jimmy pointed a finger directly at Anton.

'The owner of that car yard pays good money to Archie Kemp to protect them from the likes of you. And well you know it.'

At the mention of Archie Kemp, one of the few men he had any respect for, Jimmy diverted from his intended course of action, that of upending the table on top of Anton and pouncing on him. 'Is that your way of asking for an invitation to sit down?' he sneered, giving Anton a rare chance to comply.

Instead Anton engaged Jimmy in a sullen stare. Eventually he said, 'I would've been happy enough to get the keys off you but I'm afraid things have gotten out of hand. You damaged one of my men last night. Put him in hospital so you did.'

'You sent that cunt into my house?' Jimmy said, getting to his feet and walking around behind Anton.

In a show of bravado Anton remained seated, craning his head left and right until Jimmy came into his peripheral vision. He was confident that, in response to Archie Kemp's edict that he tackle Macintyre team-handed, the couple of heavies he'd had the good sense to send ahead and blend with the crowd were already in position.

On stage, Shane tried to make eye contact with the two bouncers who were standing either side of the entrance doors. The security staff seemed intent on looking anywhere but in the direction of Jimmy Macintyre.

On cue Anton's men stepped forward menacingly, thinking that their presence was deterrent enough for Jimmy to behave himself. 'Why don't we step outside and discuss this?' Anton grinned.

Jimmy, having anticipated such an eventuality, reached for the hatchet concealed under his jacket and drove it into the table, splitting the timber under Anton's nose and forcing a surge of frantic bodies away from the table. 'Yes. Why don't we step outside and discuss this somewhere where there's no witnesses?' he replied, matching Anton's grin.

Before Anton had a chance to respond the reinforced bottom of a beer bottle struck one of his men on the side of the head, felling him like a tree. Jimmy instantly aimed the hatchet at Anton's head, assuring that the violence went unanswered.

Old Davey shrugged his shoulders in response to Jimmy's withering glare. 'You keep your bloody hands to yourself,' Jimmy told him. 'This has got nothing to do with you.'

'Did you see the way he was looking at you, the

cheeky article?' Old Davey protested and lined up the fallen man for a swift kick in the head.

'Don't you dare kick him, mister,' Agnes threatened.

'Hey, Aggie, if yeh get awarded a penalty kick, yeh take it.' In went the boot.

Anton, aware of the hatchet poised above his head, gazed at his associate lying unconscious on the floor, blood oozing from a deep wound at the side of his head and mingling with the cigarette burns on the carpet. 'There's no call for this, Jimmy. We only wanted to have a few words.'

'A few words eh?' Jimmy scoffed, holding the sharp end of the hatchet close to Anton's eyes. 'When somebody fronts up to me team-handed I've got no problem letting this handle my end of the discussion. Mind you, any time you feel like stepping outside, one to one, that's a different matter.'

Thinking about saving face Anton overtly cast an eye over the Wheatsheaf patrons, intimating that he regarded them as the hostile home crowd. 'This'll keep,' he said angrily and signalled to the second strongarm to help him manoeuvre his injured companion through the crowd to the door.

'You know where to find me,' Jimmy called after him. 'Fucken balloon,' he added.

Shane continued singing, watching the landlord and his bouncers belatedly arrive on the scene as soon as they deemed it safe. As usual, Ronnie the landlord apologised to Jimmy and paid for the spilled drinks.

'I meant to tell you, our Jimmy. That geezer, the one doing all the talking, was in here this afternoon looking for you.'

'Aye, well he fucken found me. Didn't he?'

By closing time most of the Wheatsheaf's inner sanctum were aware of the imminent party at the Macintyres'. The landlord breathed a sigh of relief and bolted the door behind the last carryout-laden customer joining the entourage for the two-steps-forward, one-step-back trek to No. 38.

Mick breasted the wall near the corner of Mawbey Street and South Lambeth Road, about to have a pee, when a passing police car forced him to abandon the idea in a hurry. On entering the house the toilet was overlooked as usual. Instead he went straight out the back and began peeing on the weeds, singling out an overgrown thistle for special attention. With the steam rising like a Turkish bath he marvelled at the durability of his country's floral emblem. It seemed to thrive on the urine he had rained on it over the last month or so.

A loud bang from the rear of the garden startled Mick. When he heard the sound again he peered into the darkness, wondering what was going on. He began backing up slowly until the sudden flood of light from the kitchen window extended far enough for him to make out the door of the pigeon loft banging in the breeze. He took a step forward then thought, Fuck it, I'm not going up there in the dark.

Jimmy was standing in a group admiring the new bay window. 'Hey Jimbo, you never did a very good job of shutting the pigeons' door,' Mick told him.

'What're you talking about, sure you were there when I shut the fucken thing? Not unless our Corrie went back up and left it open. I've warned him about that. I hope you shut the bastarding thing, did you?'

'Away and fuck yerself, Jimbo. There's no way I'm going up there in the dark. Them pigeons of yours don't like me, and for all I know they might be just waiting to attack.'

Jimmy left the gathering, walked up the garden path with a full tumbler of beer in his hand and checked the roof of the loft for any escaped pigeons. He contented himself with the knowledge that homing pigeons did just that. Always headed for home. On reaching into the darkness to feel for the light switch he was startled by a muffled sound coming from inside the loft. He found the switch quickly, flipped it down and stepped inside not knowing what to expect but ready for anything – except for what he found.

Corrie was sitting on a wooden crate sobbing bitterly, surrounded by the bodies of pigeons.

In a rising tide of shock, anger and despair Jimmy stared for long seconds at the mass of blood and feathers clogging the loft floor before he realised the pigeons' heads were missing. He slumped down beside Corrie and cradled the boy's head in his arms.

'Did you see who did this, son? Please tell me you got a look at them. Please Corrie. Tell your da.'

Corrie raised his reddened, tear-blotched face and nodded silently in time to his convulsive sobs. 'Half the pigeons are dead, dad.'

Jimmy heaved visibly and pressed his son's head harder against his chest, stroking the side of his face and staring unseeing at the top of his head. 'There, there, Corrie,' he consoled, guiding the boy out of the loft, down the garden path away from the carnage. 'Just you tell me who it was and I'll make sure he suffers. If it's the last thing I ever do.'

Corrie looked up again and shook his head.

The realisation of what his son was doing hit home. 'Don't do that, Corrie. Don't shake your head like that. I know you saw them. You as much as said. Was it those bastarding squatters? That's who it was, wasn't it?'

'No.'

'Christ Corrie, what do you mean, *no*? *No*, it wasn't the squatters, or *no*, you didn't see them?'

Before Corrie had a chance to answer Jimmy realised that they were abreast of the open parlour door. He shielded the distraught boy from the curious stares and whispers and escorted him up the stairs to the flat. A slurred query of concern followed them up the stairs, 'You all right there, Jimmy?'

'Give your face a wash, Corrie, and I'll be back up in a minute.' Jimmy said, ignoring the question and ushering Corrie into the flat.

Corrie nodded solemnly. 'The noise woke me up dad, but I was too scared to go up the back in the dark. I wish you had've been home.'

Guilt-ridden, Jimmy hurried downstairs, forced his way through the crowd to the radiogram on the other side of the room and lifted the record from the turntable, shouting, 'Right you lot, the party's over. Let's be having you. Everybody out.'

'Hey, what the fuck –' An elbow in the ribs silenced the lone protester.

'What did I tell you? Go on, get teh fuck the lot of you. On your bikes.' With his arms out wide Jimmy shepherded the concerned mob through one door, then the other, and made his way back upstairs.

'Now Corrie,' he said gently. 'I was asking you if it was the squatters. It was them, wasn't it?'

'It wasn't the squatters, dad. The man I saw was wearing a suit and tie. He was climbing over the wall, back in to Mawbey Street.' Corrie was shaking now, white-faced.

As if the slaughter of the pigeons wasn't bad enough, the effect it was having on his son exacerbated the problem à thousandfold. 'A suit, eh,' Jimmy said, an eerie look of delight mellowing his hardened features.

EIGHT

'Stop out the front of No. 38,' Shane said to the taxi driver as she pointed up ahead. 'It's the end house there.'

When the taxi performed a U turn and pulled into the kerb Shane alighted onto the pavement, wrestled the Christmas tree from the open luggage compartment and dragged it over to the railings next to the steps. Glancing up at the first-floor window she returned to the taxi, paid the driver and retrieved the rest of the packages, including Donna's coat.

The front door was opened to her before she reached the top of the steps. 'Can you manage with that?' Jimmy held out his hands to relieve her of the packages wrapped in Christmas paper.

'I'm OK with these but I could do with a hand with the tree,' Shane smiled.

'Nice tree.' Jimmy put his hand between the limbs and grasped the pine by its slender trunk. Holding it at arm's length he followed Shane up the stairs. 'Go on in,' he told her.

'You must've read my mind,' Donna smiled, looking up from the Sunday paper spread across her lap. 'I was going to take Corrie shopping for a tree today. He's been harping on. I normally would've done it ages ago but I wanted to wait until Jimmy got out. You know, so we could all decorate it together.'

Shane lowered her packages onto the coffee table and said, 'Oh, I hope I haven't spoiled things for you. It's just that I noticed you didn't have a tree when I was here yesterday and I thought I'd bring one when I returned your coat. Thanks a lot for lending it to me, by the way.'

'Don't worry, you've done me a favour,' Donna said. 'His lordship, Jimmy Macintyre there, hates shopping of any description. I wouldn't put up with him, if I didn't need him to carry the tree. This'll save me the bother. We can go shopping for presents without him. Do you fancy?'

Jimmy leaned the Christmas tree in the corner next to the sink and started picking at the sap stuck to his hand. The antiseptic fragrance of fresh pine needles dominated the stale morning air in the room.

'He's pretending he doesn't hear,' Donna grinned.

'I heard you all right,' Jimmy replied. 'I was too busy thinking, thank God for that.'

'Make yourself useful then, will you love, and give our Corrie a shove. We may as well get this tree up.'

Donna flashed a smile at Jimmy as he moved towards the bedroom.

'Up you get, wee man.' Jimmy gently prodded the sleeping boy on the shoulder and waited until he was awake before continuing. 'We've got a Christmas tree in the living room. Your ma wants a hand to put the decorations up.'

As if he'd heard the magic word Corrie sat bolt upright, blinked and bounded out of bed. Wide-eyed, with an earnest look on his face he hurried into the living room and zeroed in on the tree. 'Where are we going to put it?' he said.

'Aren't you going to say hello to Shane?' Donna said. 'She's the one who bought you the lovely tree.'

'Hi Shane. Thanks for the Christmas tree. It's a smasher.'

Shane exchanged smiles with Donna and went over and put her arm around the boy. Jimmy came out of the bedroom and put a ski-cap on Corrie's head, thinking that he must've forgotten about it. Corrie turned bright red and looked up at Shane.

'Come on, son.' Jimmy held open Corrie's dressing-gown, inviting him to put it on.

Corrie slipped his arms into the sleeves and managed to stand still long enough for Shane to get down on one knee and tie the cord. Brimming with compassion Shane locked eyes with Corrie and said, 'You call me Aunty Shane. Do you hear me?'

'Is Shane my aunty, mum?'

'Too right she's your aunty,' Donna confirmed,

winking at Shane. 'Who else but an aunty would buy you such a beautiful Christmas tree, eh?'

Jimmy grabbed hold of the tree and held it straight. 'What are we supposed to put it in? I'll have to go out the back and see if there's a bucket.'

'They come with a stand these days.' Shane reached for the green metal ring with the spiked upright in the middle.

'I thought that was a basketball ring, sure as Christ.' Jimmy got Corrie to hold the tree while he bent down and fastened the tree to the stand. As soon as he was satisfied that the tree was straight enough he stood back and allowed Shane to wrap the bottom in Christmas-paper.

Shane, grinning from ear to ear, placed the rest of her packages around the bottom of the tree and stood back. 'You can't open these until Christmas Day,' she warned.

'You didn't have to do that, Shane, but it was a lovely thing to do.' Donna smiled at Shane, seeing her as a lonely figure, much in need of a friend. Who else would buy Christmas presents for folk she hardly knew? 'Jimmy, that was a lovely thing to do, wasn't it?'

'Aye, doll. There's no two doubts about that. It's a cracker of a thing to do, right enough.' Jimmy couldn't see why Donna was making such a fuss. He was used to getting things given to him.

'I'll tell you what,' Donna said eagerly. 'What are you doing on Christmas Day, Shane?'

Shane shrugged her shoulders. 'The same as usual, I suppose. Dinner for one.'

'We won't hear of it.' Donna fixed Jimmy with a stern look, defying him to disagree with her. 'You can spend Christmas Day with us. We'll make a big family day of it. Plenty of presents and heaps of turkey and stuffing.'

'I like the bit about the stuffing,' Jimmy grinned.

Genuinely moved, Shane was momentarily stuck for words.

'Yippee,' Corrie boomed, his infectious cheer bringing big smiles all round. 'We're having a visitor for Christmas.'

'That settles that, I suppose,' Shane beamed.

'It does indeed. Now let's get this tree decorated so's we can go and do some serious Christmas shopping.' Donna edged towards the bedroom and paused when she saw Shane join Corrie in an impromptu dance around the front of the tree. She sensed a strange melancholy in their happiness. Like clowns crying behind their painted smiles.

Shaking herself, Donna went into the bedroom, returned with a bulging, green plastic bin-liner and began fishing out strands of silver tinsel, coloured balls and all sorts of other Christmas decorations. Each time she separated an item from the tangle Corrie, chuckling with delight, grabbed it and either handed it on to Shane or found a place for it on the tree. Jimmy stood back and offered unwanted advice, directing them to spots he thought in need of extra attention.

Like the spirit of Christmas, the more the tree took shape, the stronger the bond Donna felt with Shane.

NINE

'Hurry up Davey, for goodness sake. I think that's him coming now.' Agnes Macintyre parted the curtain separating the kitchenette from the parlour just enough to get a clear view of the door.

'Ach, away and fuck, sure I'm going as fast as I can.' Old Davey closed the lid on the cardboard box and began wrapping every inch of it with the wide sticky tape that William had brought home from work.

'Ah, there you are, Corrie.' Agnes's loud and cheerful greeting was intended as a warning for her husband to finish what he was doing. 'I see youse all went Christmas shopping, yesterday. I hope you remembered to get yer auld granny something nice?'

With a solemn look he thought appropriate under the circumstances Old Davey walked from behind the curtains, carrying the cardboard box at chest-height as if it was a coffin. 'I was going to give it a lick of black paint for you son, but ole misery-guts there said I'd make too much mess and that you'd end up with it all over you. Christ knows, she might have been right for once.'

Tears rolled down Corrie's cheeks and dripped onto the cardboard box he was now clutching to his chest. 'It doesn't feel very heavy, grandda. Are you sure they're all here?'

'Let me explain this to you, Corrie. You see, pigeons are made up mainly of feathers. You'd agree with that, wouldn't you?'

Corrie nodded twice.

'Good. Now you know how I've kept these pigeons out of the road for a couple of days so's we could give them a proper funeral, once things settled down a bit? I mean, we had to have a bit of a wake, not to mention the collection, didn't we?'

Corrie nodded again. But the look of complete bewilderment on his face prompted Old Davey to put his arm around him and persevere. 'Corrie, when things are dead they don't eat, and we all know what happens if you don't eat? You lose weight, don't you?'

Agnes raised her eyes to the ceiling and retreated to the ancient radiogram in the corner. 'On you go upstairs wee son and get your da,' she urged, and began sorting through a pile of old 45s.

Donna had on a long pink dressing gown when she walked into the parlour yawning and stretching and not looking her best. A barefoot Jimmy, looking no better, followed her into the room, dressed in a pair of faded blue jeans and an old white tee-shirt. 'What the hell time is it?' he croaked.

'I could do with a fag,' Donna yawned.

Jimmy leaned in and whispered, 'Whose stupid cunt of an idea was this?'

With his version of a subtle wink at Agnes Old Davey gave the order. 'Right, Corrie, grab the box, eh, I mean, grab the casket.' He held the door open to allow the procession, headed by the boy, to pass through. 'What's keeping you?' he narked, just as the needle settled on the record and Roy Orbison started belting out 'In Dreams'.

Jimmy shook his head when the kitchen window shot up and the mournful sounds from the radiogram accompanied them all the way to the hole dug at the back of the garden. He raised his eyes to the clouds when he spotted the makeshift cross Old Davey had nailed together.

'That reminds me,' Agnes whispered to Jimmy as she watched a tearful Corrie place the cardboard box in the hole. 'I see in the paper they're burying old Mrs Winters today. That was her son you had the trouble with the other night, wasn't it? The one you did time with? God, she must've been a right old age.'

'Shush,' Jimmy said, putting a finger to his lips and glancing sideways at Donna.

On returning to the house Agnes took half a step into the parlour and hesitated, holding on to the doorframe with one hand. 'Are you sure you don't want a cup of tea or something?' she shouted up the stairs.

'We're sure.' Donna retied the twisted sash of her

dressing gown and propped up her breasts with her folded arms.

Old Davey, looking like he was having a fit, frantically gestured for Agnes to shut the door. 'Christ, I nearly shit myself there, so I did. Come on, give me a hand to get rid of these feathers before somebody sees them. I'm knackered after all that plucking.'

'You'll be the death of me, Davey Macintyre, so you will,' Agnes told him.

'See you, you're nothing but an old moan, beh Christ. Aye, and I'll bet you, you won't be long putting your paw out if I get two quid a pair for these pigeons – er ... quail, down at the Brixton market, heh heh.'

'I hope you left me two for the soup?'

'Like fuck I did. If you want a pair you can get them down at the market the same as everybody else. Just bring the dosh.'

'You're nothing but a miserable old bastard, so you are, Davey Macintyre.'

Donna sat at the coffee table gripping the teacup by the rim and holding her cigarette at the end of two extended fingers, freeing her other hand to turn the pages of the morning paper. Over the past two days she had become increasingly aware of her husband's brooding mood. She knew that it had to do with the incident with the pigeons. If Anton had said more than he was supposed to, not that Jimmy had spoken of his visit, other than to play it down, all hell would have broken loose by now. She had been loath to broach the subject – the very thought of Anton terrified her.

Behind her, Jimmy hovered, impatient to check the death notices in the paper. 'You all right, love?' she said, flicking the page and glancing over her shoulder. 'You've been a bit on the quiet side lately. I thought you would've been raring to go.'

'Aye, I'm all right,' Jimmy said, coming around to face her. 'I've just been taking it easy.'

'They were only birds, you know.'

'Only birds, were they? Fuck sake, Donna, I thought you would've known better than that.'

'Well. You know what I mean. You can replace them.'

'That's not the point. Sure, you can replace them, but what about the effect it's had on our Corrie? Eh, what about that?'

'Jimmy, he'll get over it.'

'I'm fucken sure he will. But somebody's going to pay for it. No cunt's getting away with that. I've got to look at myself in the mirror.'

'So this isn't about Corrie. It's about you. *You've* got to be able to look at yourself in the mirror. What do you see anyway? Obviously not somebody who promised to put the needs of his family first.'

'That's brilliant, that is. I'm minding my own business and some cunt climbs over the wall and kills my pigeons, Corrie's pigeons, and I'm supposed to do fuck all about it? That'll be the day.'

'It could've been anybody,' Donna consoled herself, happy to remind Jimmy of the fact.

'Right enough,' Jimmy agreed. In Donna's present frame of mind he had no intention of telling her that he had his suspicions.

'I suppose you'll be sneaking off to the funeral, will you?' Donna said, raising an eyebrow. She could see he was agitated, waiting for the paper.

'I thought we'd just been to the funeral.'

'Not that funeral,' Donna said smirking. 'You know the one I'm talking about.'

'What one's this?'

'The one you can't wait to look up in the paper. The one your mother was talking about, out the back. Do you think I'm deaf or something?'

'Oh, that one. What makes you think I'd want to show a face there for? There's no love lost between me and Anton. There never has been.'

'That's what I was trying to work out. I thought ex-cons weren't ever allowed to consort with known criminals.'

'Give us a break, Donna. I would hardly call going to an old woman's funeral consorting.'

'So you are going?'

'Ach, I was only thinking of showing a face. The old lady never done me any harm. She was a good old stick.'

Exasperated, Donna slowly shook her head.

'I'll take Corrie with me and we'll do something afterwards. Go to the –'

'You needn't think you're taking our Corrie anywhere near a graveyard! No way.'

'Credit me with a bit of sense, will you? I was going to make him wait in the car. Christ, anybody would think we were talking about robbing a bank. Not going to some old lady's funeral.'

Corrie, whose ears had pricked up at the mention of his name, came out of the bedroom where he had gone to hide his tears. 'Please, mum. I promise I'll stay in the car. Honest.'

Looking from father to son, Donna said, 'You make sure you do.'

TEN

The cemetery was on a gentle hill overlooking a pond. Mallard ducks, some moorhens and an occasional Canadian goose drifted in and out of the reeds that spread unevenly from the manmade banks. At the whim of a biting northerly wind, fluffy grey and white clouds danced and rolled and occasionally parted long enough to grant a glimpse of a clear blue sky.

'Right, Corrie,' Jimmy said. 'Do the buttons of your coat up before you get out of the car. Me and you's going to take a closer look.'

'But dad, I promised mum I wouldn't get out of the car.'

'Listen Corrie, mate. I didn't want to mention this in front of your ma but I've got a funny feeling the guy who done the pigeons in might be here. You wouldn't want to let him get away with it, would you? Eh?'

Corrie sat bolt upright and craned out the window, his eyes narrowing as he scanned the mourners making their way to the graveside, many irreverently tramping on the surrounding plots.

'Put your hood up, son, and we'll go and take a closer look,' Jimmy said, seeing no sign of recognition in the boy's eyes.

Anton Winters stood back from the open grave, raised the collar of his long black coat and settled his dark glasses onto the bridge of his nose. He was surrounded by dozens of similarly attired associates all jockeying for position, trying to ensure that their presence was noted. Behind his dark glasses Anton took roll call, knowing that most of the mourners were there as a result of protocol.

As the wind caught the flowing cassock of the clergyman sprinkling a handful of dirt on the coffin and saying, 'Dust to dust, ashes to ashes,' Anton dipped his dark glasses and peered over the top. Jimmy Macintyre, accompanied by a boy, was standing off to the side, the two of them conspicuous by their casual attire. No sooner had Anton spotted them than a man came up on his right and whispered in his ear. With his head down and one hand rubbing the point of his chin Anton nodded as he listened attentively, all without taking his eyes off Jimmy for more than a second.

'I'm sorry for interrupting you at a time like this and I'm even more sorry for your loss, Anton, but Archie's been trying to get in touch with you. He says he wants to see you out at Parkhurst right away.'

Anton studied the ageing villain, guessing correctly

that he'd just been released from Parkhurst Prison that morning. He noted by the way the man's thinning grey hair was parted in the middle and his outdated, pencil-thin moustache that he'd stuck with the fashion of his youth.

'Christ Eddie, I can't even bury my mother,' Anton complained.

The messenger shrugged his shoulders apologetically and said, 'You know Archie. Business always comes first.'

'Tell Archie he doesn't have to worry. I never let trivia get in the way of business.' Anton nodded sarcastically towards the grave.

'I'm sure he'll be glad to hear that, but he wants to hear it from you. He says he wants to see you right away.'

Not for the first time did Anton dwell on the result of Archie Kemp losing his appeal. With Archie doing a long stretch he would move in to the top spot. Then he would be answerable to nobody.

As the service ended the two men held their coats shut and hurried to beat the deluge threatened by the first spits of rain blowing into their faces. In the shelter of the curved stone wall on one side of the heavy wrought-iron gates they stopped and backed against the brickwork. Anton knew that the mourners, including Jimmy Macintyre, would have to pass him to get out.

Eddie Simpson smiled warmly when he saw Jimmy and his son approaching.

'How are you doing, Eddie?' Jimmy said, ignoring Anton. 'Long time no see. When did you get out?'

Eddie shook Jimmy's hand and smiled awkwardly, shifting from one foot to the other. 'I, eh, I just got out this morning, Jimmy. How's yourself, anyway? I see you've managed to stay at large. You too, Anton. I hope I can say the same for myself.'

'Sorry to hear about your loss, Anton,' Jimmy said with more than a hint of sarcasm.

'We could've done without the likes of you here, Macintyre.'

'That's nice, that is. I came to pay my respects and all I get is ridicule.' Jimmy turned to Eddie and shook his head. 'I'm afraid times have changed for the worst, Eddie.'

Anton, looking at Corrie, suddenly changed his tune. 'This your boy, is it, Macintyre?' he said, grinning.

Corrie smiled awkwardly and stepped closer to his father. He failed to recognise the bitterness in Anton's voice. Not so Jimmy, who answered by putting his arm around the boy and drawing him close.

It took all Anton's willpower to stop himself from blurting out the details of the boy's parentage. He consoled himself with the knowledge that the day wasn't far off when he could do so. 'He looks nothing like you, Macintyre. Have you ever noticed that?'

Jimmy swept Corrie behind him, the action giving Eddie Simpson the chance to step between him and Anton. 'Neither the time or the place, gentlemen,'

Eddie said and steered Anton towards a waiting car.

'What did he mean by that, dad? I don't look like anybody except the other kids at the clinic.'

'Pay no attention to him, son. He's a fucken idiot. 'Scuse the French.'

Corrie sniggered.

'You didn't recognise anybody then?' Jimmy continued. 'What about that prick I was talking to?'

'Nah,' Corrie said, screwing up his face and shaking his head. 'Maybe if they'd taken off their sunglasses.'

Anton made good time on the drive from London, arriving in Southampton in time to board a ferry for the short crossing to the Isle of Wight.

Now looking up at the heavy blanket of sea-mist shrouding Parkhurst Maximum Security Prison he shuddered and wasted no time entering the side door next to the main gates. From there he was escorted to a visitor's room via a maze of drab, white-painted brick corridors. He wasn't surprised to see Archie sitting there like he owned the place.

'Nice of you to drop by, Anton,' Archie said, motioning to the chair on the other side of the table at which he was sitting. 'I hope you didn't mind me sending the message with poor old Eddie, but I promised him I would give him a few odd jobs to do, just to keep him out of trouble. You know the sort of thing I mean.' Archie was the epitome of charm and good manners. 'Oh, and once again, my condolences for the loss of your mother.'

'Thanks, Archie. It's been a hectic couple of days, what with one thing and another.'

Archie leaned forward in the chair, the sudden change of mood for which he was famous manifesting with the rage in his hazel eyes. 'Yes, be that as it may, but you make sure you keep the lines of communication open in future. Funeral or no funeral, you keep your phone switched on and take your calls. Here's me sending messages with Eddie fucken Simpson.' Archie leaned back in the chair like a man well used to getting his own way, and pushed his fingers through his thatch of silver hair and down the sides of a face kept lean by countless hours in the prison gym. His enforced healthy lifestyle had taken years off him, giving the impression that he was much younger than his fifty-five years.

'Archie, I just buried my mother. Come on.' Anton seethed inwardly, glad that there were no witnesses to his reprimand.

Archie mellowed almost as quickly as he'd flared up. 'I know. But eh, what's the word on Gilfeather? Any luck?'

'No. Nothing,' Anton spat out, his eyes blazing. Archie's total lack of respect was the last straw. No longer could Anton remain subordinate to the man who was ready to put him down. No. As far as he was concerned Archie Kemp could rot in jail.

Looking around the room, taking in the dainty

floral curtains covering the narrow barred window above head-height, and the array of framed prints breaking the tedium of the fresh coat of white gloss enamel on the much-painted brickwork, Archie took a long, deep breath and let it out slowly. It had just occurred to him that the ambitious Anton had more to gain by keeping him in prison. He could see it in his eyes. It was more than probable that Anton had worked out that it was in his best interests not to put much effort into finding Gilfeather. Alternatively, and more alarmingly, he might put every effort into finding him, then make sure he disappeared for good. Archie now regretted telling Anton that the success of his appeal hinged on Gilfeather being located.

'Listen, Anton,' he said, hitting on an idea, 'I've been thinking. God knows I've had plenty of time,' he laughed. 'As soon as I get out of here I'm handing the reins over to you. I'm getting too old for this caper. Time to get out.'

Anton laughed along with him. Not that he found his words funny. He thought it humorous that Archie Kemp expected him to believe a statement as far-fetched as that. A statement that simply told him that Archie was aware of his ambitions and trying, in his vulnerable situation, to fortify his position against them. The balance of power had shifted.

'Let's get you out of here first, Archie. Then we can sort things out.' Anton eased himself out of the chair, indicating that he was terminating the visit. 'You sit tight and try not to worry,' he added. 'If I can't find Gilfeather in London, nobody can.'

His words were of no comfort to Archie, who, with a weary look on his face, masked by the merest hint of a smile, stood and followed Anton as far as the door. 'Do your best,' he said, adding, 'Oh, how did you get on with Macintyre?'

'Unfinished business,' Anton answered curtly, without turning.

This obvious sign of disrespect added credence to Archie's suspicions. 'Listen, Anton, I don't want you, eh, I mean I'd appreciate it if you waited until you find Gilfeather before you finalise your dealings with Macintyre.'

Fuck it, Anton thought, Macintyre will have to wait. If I make a move on him now it'll send a clear signal of dissension in the ranks and give Archie time to react. 'You're the boss,' he smiled.

No sooner had the door closed behind Anton than Archie slumped back in the chair. Who's fooling who? he thought.

When he arrived in the West End, straight from Parkhurst Prison, Anton found Archer Street to be quite busy for a Monday night. The usual assortment of West End low lifes mingling with the wide-eyed tourists – not to mention the Christmas shoppers – and the raincoat brigade ducking their heads as they walked from garishly-lit sex shops with their plain brown packages under their arms.

Not surprised that Donna was absent from her pitch in the doorway he crossed the street, carefully side-stepping the numerous pieces of squashed fruit overlooked by the street cleaners. From the bottom of the dimly lit stairwell he looked up for a sign of light escaping from under her door. At the top of the landing he turned his head sideways to the door and listened, positive he could hear movement.

He was about to barge in when the menacing silhouette of the new in-house minder emerged from the shadows at the far end of the landing, gently tapping a pickaxe handle on the linoleum-covered floorboards as he approached. 'Looking for somebody are we, sir?' His tone, though pleasant enough, was brimming with menace.

Anton allowed him to come near without answering. Since he had recently installed the minder, instructing him to detain anybody answering Gilfeather's description, he was sure his employee would recognise him soon enough. Anton had figured that it wasn't beyond the realms of possibility that Gilfeather might show up here.

'Oh, it's you, Anton,' the minder whispered. 'Everything's under control.' He raised a finger in salute and retreated back to the shadows, inviting Anton to follow him.

'Nobody's been here who matches that description you gave us, guv. Otherwise I would've stiffened him with me pole here and got you on the blower.' The minder smiled shiftily and tapped the mobile phone concealed in the inside pocket of his leather jacket.

'That's magic, Freddie, but don't you hesitate to phone me the minute you see something. Day or night, it doesn't matter. You understand?'

The minder nodded his head eagerly. He couldn't wait to tell his mates down the pub that he was in the big league.

Alerted by the whispering, Donna, holding a short leather riding crop behind her back, opened the door a crack and peered out. Anton spotted her and shouted, 'Hoy, I want a word with you.'

'Not while I'm working,' Donna said and tried to shut the door. Anton's lunge prevented her.

'What are you doing? You can't come in here now. I'm with a punter.' Donna tried to block his view into the room.

A bound figure on the bed intrigued Anton, prompting him to crane over Donna's shoulder for a better look. 'Fair enough,' he threatened. 'Maybe you'd prefer me to call round and see you when you're at home.'

Donna stepped out into the hall, closing the door behind her. 'Make it quick,' she snapped, inadvertently tapping the side of her thigh-high boot with the riding crop.

Dressed the way she was, in black corset, sheer stockings and boots, Anton had trouble stopping his eyes from wandering. 'Go for a walk,' he said, addressing the minder and waiting until he was alone with Donna before he continued. 'I've decided to let your husband in on your little secret. He might be prepared to put a bit more effort than you into finding Gilfeather. His motivation might be stronger than yours.'

'That's impossible. There's a boy's life at st—'

'Oh, I don't know about that.'

'But, but – I thought we agreed Gilfeather would be no good to anybody if Jimmy ever got his hands on him. Think about it, Anton.' She was pleading now. 'It wouldn't do you, or me, any good.'

He wasn't about to tell her that the rules had changed. That he now wanted to make sure that Gilfeather was of no use to Archie Kemp. And he wasn't about to tell her that the only reason he hadn't gone directly to see her husband was because such an action would have alerted Kemp to his treachery, enabling him to instigate countermoves. No. Donna's motivation for finding Gilfeather was strong enough for him. All he was doing was giving her added impetus. He would tell Jimmy Macintyre all about Gilfeather when it best suited him. Probably before the week was out.

'Please, Anton. Think about what you're doing. You wouldn't want the life of a nine-year-old boy on your hands, would you?' It hadn't escaped Donna's attention that Anton had already figured out that, should she succeed in finding Gilfeather, it would be practically impossible for both their needs to be met. Did he expect her to hand Gilfeather over before she'd had a chance to convince him to do a blood test? Surely not. She could only presume that Anton considered her to be gullible. His mistake, she thought.

'I'll tell you what I'm prepared to do, Donna. You keep me posted. None of this 'out of sight, out of mind' crap. All right? You do that and I'll give you to the end of the week. After that, Bob's your uncle.' As he backed towards the stairs Anton grinned and ran his forefinger across his throat.

A bundle of nerves, Donna waited, making sure he was gone before she retreated into the room. With the door closed to the landing's feeble contribution of light she blinked and backed against the wall, steadying herself until her eyes adjusted to the subdued red glow cast by the bedside lamp. 'I'm sorry, I can't finish you,' she said approaching the bed and fumbling with the straps restraining her client. 'I've got to go.'

As she discarded her boots, stepped into a pair of shoes and donned her coat straight over her underwear she urged the disgruntled punter to get a move on, eventually ushering him out onto the landing to finish getting dressed.

On locking the door behind her she turned and spoke to the seemingly empty landing. 'I'm just popping out for a coffee, Freddie,' she told the minder, in case he decided to follow her. 'Can I bring you one back?'

'Ta very much, Donna. That would be lovely. Two sugars please.'

A steady rain brought the Holiday Inn's top-hatted doorman to the pavement's edge, where he stood to one side and held the umbrella directly over the taxi door, waiting for the passenger to pay the fare and exit. 'Umm,' he muttered, when Donna swung her legs onto the pavement, unaware for a moment that her coat had fallen open at mid-thigh level. The perks of the job, he thought as he escorted her quickly to the revolving doors.

Munro answered the phone on the third ring. 'Yes, that's fine. Just send her on up.' He debated whether or not to change out of his faded blue jeans and his white tee-shirt with the Chicago Bulls logo on the front. As a compromise he donned a pair of socks and his new Nike sneakers.

'The Chicago *Post* paying for this?' Donna tossed her handbag onto one of the beige armchairs and continued to look around the four-star room. She was frantic with worry but, in keeping with her resilient Northern nature, tried to present her host with a picture of complete composure. It was almost as if she was delaying the pain of raising the subject that brought her to his room.

'Can I fix you a drink?' Munro placed his glass on the walnut veneer cabinet that took up most of one wall. Stooping, he opened one of the doors to reveal a well-stocked fridge.

'I wouldn't say no to a nice cup of tea, if you can manage it?'

Munro walked to the wide floor-to-ceiling window

and took a last look before drawing the curtains. 'I like watching the rain. There's something peaceful about it,' he said and diverted to the tea-making facilities at the end of the long cabinet.

'Well, you've certainly come to the right place,' Donna said, forcing a laugh.

Munro took the tea-bag from the cup and handed Donna her tea, taking pains not to spill it. Fetching his glass he sat down opposite her on one of the two armchairs that filled the space between the queen-sized bed and the curtains. 'OK. What brings you here? Tell me what's happening,' he urged, using both hands to keep the long tumbler poised at chin level.

'Do you think you can make it for a tissue type test tomorrow? I'm taking Corrie to the clinic for his maintenance chemo.' On the way over to the Holiday Inn Donna had fantasised about Munro's bone marrow being compatible with her son's. The thought of the resulting end to the nightmare search for Gilfeather, and all that that entailed, comforted her. Until the reality of the situation sank in. Even though Munro was related to Corrie, the odds of success were still very remote.

'It'll be my pleasure,' Munro replied, smiling.

'There's something else.' Donna continued with the detailed news of Anton's visit and subsequent ultimatum.

Try as she did to disguise it, Munro could see that she was getting close to breaking point. Her voice was faltering and she seemed on the verge of tears.

'So there you have it,' she laughed pitifully. 'Not only is the heaviest team in London looking for Gilfeather, your son, but now it looks like they're definitely going to let my Jimmy in on the act.' She sucked in a deep breath at the mention of her husband's name and continued, barely raising her eyes above the level of the floor. 'In case you haven't already worked it out, my Jimmy ...' She paused again, shook her head and swallowed. 'Mr Munro, we've got to do something quick. I'm not kidding you.'

Munro returned his empty glass to the coffee table and, in search of a comforting answer, began rubbing his two-day growth. 'Tell you what,' he said, trying to sound optimistic, 'we can turn this to our advantage.'

'I'm not sure what you mean.' Donna's forehead furrowed, knitting the skin between her eyes.

Unable to look her in the eye he reached for her cup, took the untouched tea to the bathroom sink and emptied it. 'It's time I was getting my ass into gear. Up to now I've been sitting back waiting for Tommy to come marching out of the woodwork.' Consolatory as his words were designed to be, the truth of the matter was that, over the years, searching for his son, he had exhausted every avenue open to him, and some that weren't. Since his arrival in the UK he had, with the help of police contacts arranged by the *Post*'s London correspondent, covered the same old ground – deed polls, motor registration, etc. A check of his son's police record had failed to reveal anything new. At least he was staying out of trouble, Munro thought, looking on the bright side.

'What are we going to do?' Donna persisted.

'Plenty.'

Donna eyed him sceptically and said, 'I didn't think there'd be much you hadn't already done.'

'Obviously I've missed something. Haven't I?'

'I suppose. Obviously we've all missed something.' Donna rose, gathered up her things and walked to the door, pausing with her hand on the knob as if she'd forgotten something.

'What time tomorrow?' prompted Munro.

'I've been thinking about that. Could you come to the house about nine-thirty? It's about time you met Jimmy. It would save all the ducking and diving and explain any further contact I have to have with you. You could say you were doing research or something.'

'Sure. Leave it to me. I'll tell him I'm doing research for a story stateside. Maybe I could phone you in the morning? You know, introduce myself. Say I looked up your son's name in the, what was it you called it?'

'The International Bone Marrow Registry.'

'That's the one.'

Donna wrote the phone number on a scrap torn from the hotel stationery. 'Make it just after nine, will you?'

ELEVEN

Jimmy Macintyre watched his wife fluster about the room chain-smoking and eyeing the clock incessantly. He was familiar with that mood and took it for granted that it was motivated by their son's appointment at the clinic later in the morning. 'Come on, doll, stop stomping around the joint, will you? You're doing my fucken nut in, so you are.' He waited for the inevitable retaliation.

'Jimmy,' she answered playfully, 'how would you like a smack in the gob?'

'Huh,' he replied, fending off the playful assault. 'Cut it out.'

On hearing the muffled ring of the pay phone in the downstairs hall Donna stopped jabbing and bouncing around in front of him, waiting to see if the call was for her. 'It's for you, hen,' she heard Agnes shout up the stairs.

'I wonder who that is,' she said, raising her eyebrows.

On her return several minutes later from the wall-mounted phone, which was a relic from the days when No. 38 was a thriving boarding house, Donna said to Jimmy, 'That was some geezer, a Yank. He's doing some research into bone marrow transplants. For a story or something. He wants to know if it's all right to see Corrie. I told him it was OK by me.'

Jimmy nudged the coffee table when he got to his feet, forcing a lunge to save his cup from spilling, his frantic effort achieving the opposite effect. 'Now look what you made me do,' he accused, holding his hand at the edge of the table to stop the spill from flowing onto the rug. 'There'd better be a few bob in it.'

'I never thought to ask.'

'That's the first thing you should've done.'

'Away you go, Jimmy. You can't do that.'

'I suppose. Where'd they get our Corrie's name from anyway?'

'The International Registry apparently,' Donna said, bending over the coffee table to wipe it, her fitted skirt riding up and accentuating the contours of her backside.

'Stop messing about, Donna, you've got me all going here.' Jimmy put his arms around her from behind and pinned her arms to her side, nuzzling the side of her neck. Treasuring every moment of intimacy Donna responded like a purring cat.

Jimmy gently nibbled at her ear-ring, sucking it into his mouth and delicately twirling it with his tongue. 'We've got time before we go, haven't we?'

'Jimmy Macintyre, you're nothing but a prick, you know that, don't you?' Donna turned and sucked his tongue into her mouth. A second later the sound of the key turning in the lock forced her to step back and smile demurely at her son. 'I hope you haven't been running up those stairs?' she warned him.

'What time are we leaving?' Corrie asked, his lack of enthusiasm linked to the knowledge that he wouldn't be feeling so spritely after the morning's session of chemotherapy.

'Soon, but nip across the road to the Paki's and get me the paper and a packet of fags. Just tell him the ciggies are for your mum if he says anything.' Donna directed him to her purse knowing how important it was to treat him like a normal child. Provided he was feeling up to it.

'Aw mum, why didn't you ask me before I went out? Sure I've got to get ready for the clinic,' Corrie whinged.

'Do as your mother says, son. You've got heaps of time. And you be careful crossing the road. Make sure you use the lights.'

No sooner had the door closed behind Corrie when the mood in the room became serious again.

'That fucks that.' Jimmy sat on the couch with his legs wide apart and his elbows resting on his knees.

Donna reached for the cigarette packet on the coffee table and squashed it after finding it empty. 'That American geezer said he was on his way around anyway. We wouldn't have had time.'

'Ten seconds would've done me.' Jimmy shook his head and eased to the edge of the couch. 'This guy's on his way over now, is he?'

'So he says.'

A reverberating rat-a-tat-tat on the brass door knocker brought Donna to the window. She leaned over the sink and peeked down at Munro standing with his back to the door and nervously brushing the shoulders of his old blue Burberry with the flat of his hand.

Agnes, with Old Davey leaning over her shoulder, sneaked a look at Munro through a slit in the curtain. In her haste to answer the door she turned abruptly, nearly flattening her husband.

'Hey, for Christsake Aggie, watch what the fuck you're doing. For all you know it might be the police or one of them fucken debt collectors.' Old Davey moved into the position vacated by his wife.

Munro sprayed a quick blast of breath freshener and turned with a ready smile when he heard the door creak open behind him. Somehow it didn't surprise him that the person answering the door blended in with her surroundings.

'I'm here to see Donna Macintyre.' Munro rechecked the number on the door.

Agnes drew her head back in surprise then, in an effort to be discreet, leaned in and whispered. 'She doesn't work from home, son, I'm afraid.'

'I think you'll find she's expecting me. I'm from the press.' Munro was reaching for his press card when he saw Donna emerge from the stairs into the stream of light flooding through the open door.

'I see you've met my mother-in-law. Agnes, this is Steve Munro. He's here to see about Corrie.' Donna smiled and stood to one side, allowing him to pass.

'Pleasure to meet you, ma'am.'

Agnes flattened against the wall, making sure she got a good look at the visitor on the way by. She could smell money. 'Pleased teh meet yeh,' she gushed and followed them as far as the parlour door where she stopped and watched them until they rounded the stairs onto the first landing.

'Who the fuck was that?' Old Davey came out from behind the kitchen curtain where he'd gone to hide. 'It wasn't them fucken Morons again, was it?'

'Mormons, yeh edjit,' Agnes corrected him.

From the first-floor landing Munro stepped into Donna's flat, pleased that the pungent smell he'd encountered downstairs had confined itself there. Munro's first impression of Jimmy Macintyre was all he thought it would be, and more. He saw a handsome, well-dressed man about six feet tall with broad shoulders and a chilling look that did justice to his reputation. 'It's a pleasure to meet you, Mr Macintyre,' he said, nervously.

'Pleased to meet you.' Jimmy shook his hand and nodded. 'Donna says you're here to do some research into what's up with our Corrie? Speaking of who, where the hell is he? He should be back by now.'

'Yeah, that's right.' Munro flashed his press card,

hoping he wouldn't have to elaborate. 'Your wife said you were taking your son to the clinic today. Do you mind if I tag along?'

'It's all right by me.'

The sound of Corrie's footsteps carried up the stairs ahead of him bursting into the room. Munro was surprised to see that, other than the lack of facial hair – eyebrows and lashes – the boy seemed a picture of health. Not someone who was at death's door. The puzzled look on his face relayed his thoughts to Donna. 'He's in his second remission,' she explained. 'He has good days and bad days. So far this is a good day.'

Corrie was used to people talking about him and acted like any other child, relishing attention. He smiled confidently, allowing his mother to continue.

'This is Mr Munro, Corrie. He's from the paper and he wants to have a chat with you. Why don't you go and show him your pigeons?' Donna felt uneasy with her husband and Munro in the same room. 'I'm sure he would love to see them.' She smiled when she saw the unmistakable look of excitement in her son's eyes as he opened the door and invited Munro to follow him. She also saw the look of surprise on Agnes's face when she was caught floundering in the doorway, offering no explanation other than an embarrassed smile.

The instant Munro cleared the dingy downstairs hallway into the daylight the acidic stench of stale urine wafted up the concrete steps and attacked his nostrils like a dose of smelling salts. He pinched his nose with thumb and forefinger and cupped the rest of his hand over his mouth. Corrie turned eagerly, making sure he was keeping up. 'Uncle Mick's trying to poison that thistle,' he explained. Munro held his breath until he was upwind of the biggest thistle he had ever laid eyes on.

Hurrying the last few steps to beat a sudden downpour Corrie unlocked the door to the pigeon loft as fast as he could and held it open for Munro to duck in. The earthy smell of pigeon droppings, by comparison, was a more than welcome relief.

'We used to have a lot more pigeons than this but somebody broke into the loft and murdered half of them.' For a moment Corrie looked as if he might cry.

Munro reversed a piece of sacking lying on a wooden crate and sat down, inviting Corrie to sit on the crate opposite him. Corrie reached into a nesting box for a pigeon and delicately kissed the top of its head as he sat down. 'Me and my dad are the only ones allowed to touch the pigeons,' he apologised, holding the bird clear of Munro's attempt to stroke it. 'Aw, go on then,' he relented after first checking for approaching footsteps. 'One touch won't hurt. But make sure you don't tell my dad.'

At Munro's touch the normally placid bird bristled with fear and made frantic attempts to escape.

'Gee, I've never seen her do that before,' Corrie said and returned the terrified pigeon to its nesting box. 'It must be something to do with the other night.'

A sudden rapier-thin ray of sunlight streaked through the partly open door and dissected the loft at an angle between the two crates. Munro leaned over and shut the door, robbing of a stage the multitudes of previously unseen swirling and dancing particles. 'Sit yourself down Corrie and tell me how you're keeping. How has your life changed since you were first diagnosed?' Munro had decided to keep his emotions in check, distance himself from the boy and concentrate on finding his son. But that was impossible now that he'd met the child. Even if he wasn't his own flesh and blood.

Corrie's eyes lit up. 'It's great. You get heaps of days off school and when you're there the teacher doesn't give you a hard time any more.'

'Really?'

'Yeah, and you don't get picked on as much, and mum and dad hardly ever shout at me any more and Uncle Mick's forever taking me to McDonald's and the pictures.' Corrie leaned in and continued in a whisper. 'And sometimes he buys me stuff mum and dad say I'm not allowed to have.'

Munro nodded, urging Corrie to continue.

It was almost as if Corrie was boasting. Then suddenly and without warning his eyes misted over and he fell silent. He had been keeping the thoughts at bay of how he had shown his mother the lump he'd found under his arm. Of how he'd treated with excitement the ensuing trips to the doctor, and the subsequent attention it generated, as if the whole episode was a passing phase, like the time he'd had his appendix out. Of how the mood in the house changed the day the family doctor advised them of the worst. He remembered it well. The tears, the anger and the grief.

'You OK, son?' Munro prompted softly. 'Are you all right Corrie?' he repeated louder.

For a moment longer Corrie stared at the timber wall opposite, as if he could see straight through it to the future. 'I was just thinking that I might never have a girlfriend,' he said solemnly, adding a weak resolute smile.

Donna's approach was masked to the occupants of the loft by the amplified patter of rain on the tin roof, but she was in time to overhear her son's last remark. Over the last few days she had run the gamut of emotions, but now she was angry. 'Corrie,' she said, trying not to betray her mood, 'when are you going to get it through your head that we're going to find a donor? Geez, Corrie.'

The stern look on Donna's face warned Munro that the session was at an end, prompting him to proclaim it officially. 'That should do us for the time being,' he said awkwardly and slipped out of the loft, leaving Donna to cradle her tearful son's head to her bosom, the tears not those of a dying boy but the tears of a boy not used to being scolded.

'Come on Corrie,' she soothed. 'You don't want people to see you gurning, do you?'

Munro placed his hand over his nose once again and rushed past the overgrown thistle. At the top of the front steps he hesitated, thinking that it would be more prudent and less nerve-racking if he waited for Donna.

Jimmy, pacing beside the car now illegally parked outside the house, looked up and saw him. 'Listen mate,' he said. 'I'm having a wee bit of party for the kid on Thursday. For his birthday. You're welcome to come, as long you don't mention it to Donna. It's a surprise. Oh aye, and you don't have to worry about a present. Money'll do fine.'

'Sure thing,' Munro replied, turning when he heard Donna's footsteps in the hall behind him. 'I'll uh, I'll make my own way to the clinic,' he told her. 'I got a couple of calls to make.'

Though he wasn't too fond of London traffic – any traffic in fact – and at times like this wished that Donna didn't have an equal aversion to it, Jimmy was grateful that he'd had the sense to confiscate a car with automatic transmission.

'Who does that idiot think he's tooting at? If he keeps it up I'll get out and give him a right good clatter round the lugs.'

Donna half-turned in her seat and looked out the rear window, trying to see what the frantic hooting was all about. 'It's a taxi, Jimmy. I think he wants you to pull over.'

'Does he now?' Jimmy pulled into the side of the road, as usual viewing the situation in the light of impending violence. He leapt out of the car and was striding towards the taxi when Shane emerged from the kerbside passenger door. Waving and smiling broadly she said, 'Hi, Jimmy,' and walked straight past him.

'For the love of Christ,' Jimmy muttered and watched her climb into the back seat next to Corrie.

'Hi, everybody,' Shane announced, settling back and adjusting her coat over an expanse of sheer leg.

'Shane, what are you doing here?' Donna said, twisting in her seat.

'You haven't forgotten, have you?' Shane leaned forward. 'You have, haven't you? I wondered why you left without me.'

As it dawned on her Donna's chin dropped and her hand went up to her mouth. 'Ohh,' she said. 'This is the day I promised I'd take you to the clinic for your tissue type test. Shane, I'm sorry. I forgot all about it.'

'All's well that ends well. I'm here now, aren't I?' Shane smiled.

Jimmy double-parked near the Sidney Doolan Research Centre, enduring the wrath of a line of traffic forced to bank up behind him. 'Jump out everybody and I'll come back and get you in a couple of hours.'

'Awhh, dad, aren't you coming in?' Corrie whinged, voicing the opinion of the others.

'I've a wee bit of running around to do, son. Besides, you've got more than enough company with you today. Go on, get out of the car before somebody runs up the back of my arse.'

Dr Cullen, wearing his customary white coat, greeted Corrie and his entourage with a warm, lingering smile. 'How is everybody today? All in good spirits, I take it? I see you've brought a friend along today, Corrie?'

The doctor was in his early forties, but his billiard-ball head, while ingratiating him to his young patients, at first sight tended to make him look older. The redeeming factors were his ever-ready smile and the exuberance of his disposition.

All eyes focused on Corrie, who alternately looked from the doctor to his mother. Donna placed her hand on her son's shoulder and smiled sweetly at him in much the same fashion as the others were doing. 'Dr Cullen, I've got a favour to ask you. This is a friend of mine, Shane. Do you think you could fit her in for a tissue type test?'

'This is grand. I'm delighted to meet you, Shane.' Dr Cullen bowed and flamboyantly shook hands with Shane. 'Now,' he added, looking around and attracting the attention of a passing nurse, 'if you would care to go with Nurse Martin here, she'll be happy to put you through your paces.' Turning to the nurse he told her, 'Shane is here to do a tissue test.'

'Ah, here's Steve now,' Donna said, diverting Dr Cullen's attention away from Shane. 'He's the guy I was telling you about when I phoned you this morning.'

Munro sidled into the company. 'Made it,' he smiled.

Dr Cullen returned the smile and extended his hand. 'I'm Dr Cullen,' he said, waiting for the introduction.

'Eh, this is Steve Munro,' Donna began. 'He's – he's here to, ah, do a tissue test as well.'

'The more the merrier,' said the doctor. 'This is bloody marvellous, Mr Munro. We can use all the help we can get, and you make sure you tell all your friends.'

'Glad to be of assistance.'

'If you would like to follow me I'll get somebody to look after you.'

Crossing the reception area Munro observed Corrie enthusiastically greet other bug-eyed children. Some, like Corrie, had caps to conceal their baldness, and most were without a trace of facial hair. But all seemed so optimistic and completely filled with life that Munro vowed never to give up the search for his son. Not while there was still a breath in him.

After handing Munro over to a nurse Dr Cullen led Donna and Corrie down a passage leading off the reception area and into the room on the left at the far end. He instructed a nurse to start attaching the chemotherapy sachets and tubes to a chrome stand next to the bed. 'OK, Corrie, why don't you hop up on the bed and give me a good look at you?

'That reminds me,' the doctor continued, 'would you like me to tell you a joke?'

Corrie nodded, matching the doctor's grin.

'Right. This chap went to the psychiatrist. The psychiatrist said, "What seems to be the problem?" The man answered, "I think I'm a dog." "Oh," the psychiatrist said, "better hop up on the couch and give us a look at you." The man said, "I'm not allowed up on couches." Get it? I'm not allowed up on couches. Oh well. I suppose I'll have to stick to medicine.'

Further down the passage Shane waited nervously. She was dressed in a black, figure-hugging business suit and complementing patent leather stilettos, which combined to give the nurse the impression that she was a high-powered business executive. With her sheer black hose and austere black wig styled in a bob it was an image she readily fostered.

'If you would like to follow me, we'll process you as quickly as possible.' The nurse smiled and held the door open for Shane to follow.

'Shane,' Donna said as she came down the hallway, having left Corrie while the nurse busied about him. 'I was just looking for you.'

'Come and hold my hand, Donna. This is worse than the dentist.'

The nurse standing next to the bed laughed and patted Shane on the shoulder. 'I think you'll find that it's painless,' she said.

Donna laughed too. 'There's a guy in the room next door doing a tissue test for Corrie too. Well, for anyone lucky enough to be compatible with him, I suppose. Anyway, you'll probably meet him later.'

'You don't say,' Shane replied, looking sick. 'Hey, where do you thing you're going?'

'I can't stand still. I'm going back to see how Corrie is. I don't like watching when they're hooking him up.'

'Oh God. That's brilliant, that is.'

By the time they had finished with him Munro, in need of answers to a series of questions he had formulated while they were taking a sample of his blood, made his way back to the room in which Corrie was being attended to. 'Do you mind if I ask you a couple of questions, doctor? Just to satisfy my curiosity.'

Dr Cullen checked that all was in order with Corrie, then turned to face Munro, ready to answer.

Munro nibbled at the corner of his mouth and squinted up at the ceiling. 'In layman's terms what exactly are we dealing with here doctor?'

'We're dealing with chronic myeloid leukemia.' The doctor directed Munro to a group of chairs over near the window, where Corrie wouldn't be able to hear. 'I stress chronic because, after it gets to the acute stage, I'm afraid we've run our race. Bone marrow transplants are useless at that point.'

In the tradition of the professional journalist Munro, with notebook at the ready, kept his questions precise and to the point. 'What's the life expectancy of a child, or anyone for that matter, after diagnosis?'

'It varies, but the average is three years.'

The nurse popped her head around the door. 'Sorry to interrupt, doctor, but I wonder if you could spare a moment?'

'Certainly,' he told the nurse and added, smiling apologetically at Munro. 'I should only be a minute or two.'

Dr Cullen returned five minutes later and took Donna to one side, appearing as if he was pondering a subject that he found highly amusing. 'It appears your friend Shane – well, it appears that she is a he.'

'So?' Donna protested. 'Do you think Corrie, or anybody else for that matter, is going to give a toss whether Shane is anything other than a human being if her bone marrow is compatible?'

Dr Cullen placed both hands on Donna's shoulders and looked her straight in the eye. 'My sentiments exactly,' he beamed and leaned in to whisper. 'They wouldn't have known if he – if *she* hadn't put down on the form that she was male.'

Further down the hall Shane manipulated her toes through the black reinforced toes of her stockings and leaned back against the pillow, playing the sheen on her legs against the bright overhead lights. She enjoyed being the main attraction and relished the attention of every staff member who could be spared.

The doctor was still grinning when he returned to Munro and sat down again. It was as if any elusive moment of mirth in his often heartbreaking work-day was a moment to be savoured and cherished.

'Now Mr Munro, where the hell were we?'

'I was about to ask you about the success rate of bone marrow transplants.'

'I'm afraid it's only fifty per cent, Mr Munro, but maybe I should fill you in on the process prior to that. I'll keep it brief and do my best not to bore you.'

Munro nodded.

'The most suitable donor for a bone marrow transplant is a brother or sister if they are fully matched, that is to say, fully matched tissue type. Unfortunately only one patient in three has such a donor. But, I'm glad to say, over recent years medical advances have overcome many of the problems associated with the use of unrelated donors whose tissue type matches that of the patient.'

Munro could tell by the way the doctor's eyes were constantly darting towards his patient that his time was at a premium. 'I can see you're a busy man, doctor, but one more question please. How long has Corrie got?'

The doctor took a long, slow breath through his nose and released it hissing through his pursed lips. 'Corrie is in his second relapse. Unfortunately, once a relapse has occurred we are at the stage where a bone marrow transplant is vital to the patient's chances of survival. So far we have been unsuccessful in matching Corrie with a relative or anyone on the International Bone Marrow Registry. And unfortunately, once again, time is ticking away. I'm sure Donna won't mind me telling you this. It's not as if it's a secret, or anything like that.'

Getting to his feet Munro shook the doctor's hand appreciatively and stamped each foot in turn as he tried to restore lost circulation. 'Thanks a million, doctor, you've been a big help.'

'There's a comprehensive range of pamphlets in the waiting room. Why don't you help yourself?'

Munro, acknowledging the suggestion, waited until the doctor was busy tending to Corrie, before he clandestinely invited Donna to join him at the coffee machine in the waiting room. He went on ahead without waiting for an answer.

Donna was in two minds, but the sight of Corrie beaming with delight at all the extra attention, coupled with Munro's gentle persuasion, convinced her that it would be all right to leave her son for a few minutes.

Corrie looked up when the sound of high heels click-clacking along the corridor preceded Shane's grand entrance into the room. Standing in the doorway Shane held the back of her limp wrist to her forehead and, in typical Hollywood fashion, feigned a swoon. 'They all loved me,' she gushed. 'I'm a star.'

'There's no doubt about you,' Donna grinned at Shane and eased past her on her way to join Munro.

In the waiting room Munro placed the two polystyrene cups on the coffee table and fired several quick blasts from his breath freshener directly to the back of his throat. He was trying to mask the aroma of the neat bourbon he had swigged straight from his silver-plated hip flask, before Donna reached the room. His effort was futile. Donna had come to associate the breath freshener with the sweet smell of bourbon.

Well versed in the benefits of a reassuring touch Munro reached out and rested his hand gently on Donna's shoulder. He knew that Donna could not have been more vulnerable. 'I just want you to know that I'm prepared to do everything I can to help Corrie. Just you name it. Money. Anything.'

Donna was always emotional when she was at the clinic and nearly succumbed to her urge to cry, especially when she felt Munro's hand on her shoulder. To check the flow of tears she sucked her breath in through her teeth and bit her bottom lip to stop it quivering.

'Just help me find your son.' Donna paused to light a cigarette, inhaled deeply, blew the smoke out of the corner of her mouth and plucked a wayward piece of tobacco from the point of her tongue with the tips of her long red fingernails. Munro looked at her and tried to envisage what she must have looked like ten years earlier. He found it was hard to imagine an improvement on the stunner he was facing at the moment.

A young mother towing a grizzling child too healthy looking to be anything other than a visitor stopped briefly to inquire after Corrie. For the first time in his life Munro was glad to see a spoiled brat get his own way when he dragged his apologising mother away.

'I'd choke that little horror if he was mine,' Donna stated, matter of fact.

'It would be too quick for him,' Munro agreed.

Donna threw her head back and laughed, forcing Munro to see the humour and join in. He realised that it was the first time he had seen her laugh heartily.

As suddenly as it started the laughter stopped and the warmth vanished from Donna's eyes. In contrast it left them colder and harder than they were before, almost as if she was extracting a toll on herself for the stolen moment of happiness.

'Ah there you are. I thought I'd find you here.' Dr Cullen's infectious grin restored a semblance of a smile to Donna's troubled features.

'Sorry to interrupt you like this,' he continued, directing his apology to Munro, 'but I need to discuss a few things with you, Donna, and I'm afraid that due to other pressing matters now is the only chance I've got. I hope you understand?'

Donna smiled weakly at Munro and followed the doctor to his office next to the reception area. She doubted if there was anything else the doctor could tell her that would add to her despair. But from experience she knew that the knife in her heart could be twisted, and usually was.

The doctor sat behind his desk and rested his elbows on the bottle-green leather top. He tried to maintain a smile, but the sparkle was missing. Donna mirrored his expression almost exactly, in a subconscious effort to steel herself for the worst. Although she had become accustomed to hearing bad news she knew she would be devastated if the doctor told her anything other than that he had found a donor for Corrie.

'Firstly, Donna, I'm afraid there's no news on the donor front. No good news anyway.'

Before the doctor had finished the sentence, and despite how well she had prepared herself, and regardless of how often she had heard the words, Donna heart sank to a new depth. It was a physical shock.

As was his custom Dr Cullen got the bad news over with first. He worked on the premise that hope springs eternal and from there the only way was up. If only until Corrie's next six-weekly appointment.

'I hope this isn't an inopportune time to mention it, but – I take it you haven't told your husband exactly who Mr Munro is. I mean in relation to your son Corrie.'

'Under no circumstances,' Donna said, horrified.

'Good. You did convince me, at the time of Corrie's diagnosis, when your husband's tissue type test proved that he wasn't the boy's natural father, that it was in Corrie's best interests to keep this information to ourselves. You did rather stress the point.'

Donna gave him a pensive stare, neither agreeing or disagreeing. She wondered if he took her for an idiot.

'From what you've told me of your husband, I for one will sleep better at night if we keep it that way.'

'You and me both.'

'I take it that Mr Munro is sympathetic to your wishes?'

'As he said himself, "You bet".'

'Good. Because in the final analysis Corrie's welfare is of the utmost importance. I can't take the chance of him finding out about any of this. He loves his father dearly and might even give up the fight.'

'You're telling me.' Donna pointed back at herself.

Dr Cullen pressed on. 'Donna, in light of all the current activity, am I right in thinking that you still haven't had any luck tracing the boy's natural father?'

As she got to her feet Donna took a deep breath and looked off to her right. 'As soon as I get my hands on him doctor, you'll be the first to know. Make no mistake about that.'

Dr Cullen came round from behind his desk and hurried to open the door before Donna reached it. He knew that things didn't look good, but he wanted her to leave with something to cling to, something to give her the strength to carry on. 'We still have a little time. You to find his natural father and me to keep checking the new donors coming on to the registry.'

Donna appreciated his comforting words and rewarded him with the biggest smile she could muster under the circumstances. 'Thanks,' she croaked.

Leaning on the doorframe the doctor watched her walk off despondently. 'Donna,' he called after her, 'that fund raiser I mentioned the last time we spoke.

It's coming up, you know. Saturday the twenty-third, in Brighton.'

Donna took the two steps back and smiled apologetically. 'I don't think so, doctor. It's not the sort of thing –'

Dr Cullen interrupted, adding a confirming shake of his hand. 'No no no. There's no pressure on you to attend. I just meant that there'll be an immeasurable amount of publicity come out of this. A lot of big names have pledged their support. Not to mention the television coverage. We want our families to come if possible, that's all.'

'It sounds brilliant, but Saturday night's my busiest night.'

'No matter. As long as we've got bone marrow donors coming out of the woodwork.'

Donna gave him a wave without turning and continued along the corridor to the waiting room. Finding that Munro had left she retraced her steps past the doctor's office to the room in which Corrie was being treated. When she opened the door she was pleasantly surprised to see Jimmy standing beside Corrie's bed, relating a story that had the nurse cringing and Corrie wide-eyed with joy. She stopped to listen, marvelling at the way his presence always brightened up a room. On reflection she regretted not taking the opportunity to tell the doctor that Corrie wasn't the only one who dearly loved Jimmy Macintyre.

'Hey Donna,' said Shane, waving her friend to one

side. 'I was just telling Jimmy. One of the nurses was raving on about some big charity function they're having in Brighton. At the Sands Hotel, I believe. Why don't we doll ourselves up and make a big night of it? It sounds brilliant.'

'That's what I said. But nah. By the time you add the cost of everything to what I'd lose if I took the night off work, it's just not worth it. Besides, I've got nothing to wear.'

Winking at Jimmy, Shane enthused, 'We might get our heads on TV.'

TWELVE

On returning from the clinic Jimmy pulled into Mawbey Street, next to the house, and waited for his passengers to get out of the car, intending to move away from the double yellow lines. Mick, coming back from the deli across the street, spotted the car and diverted into the side street. 'Everything go all right?' he grinned, passing Donna and Corrie on the corner of South Lambeth Road. 'Hey Jimbo,' he called out, stopping his brother from driving off. 'Some geezer chapped the door looking for you. I told him you were out.'

Jimmy's eyes narrowed. 'Not another one. Did he give a name, this geezer?'

'Aye. He did as a matter of fact. Said his name was Eddie something or other. He seemed a pleasant sort of a cove. Not like that other cunt.'

'Eddie Simpson? Does that sound like the name?'

'The very man.'

The tension eased from Jimmy's face. 'I don't suppose he said what it was about?'

'No. But he said to tell you he'd be across the road in the cafe. Mind you, that was a good half-hour ago.'

'I'll see if he's still there. Here, jump in and move the motor off the double yellow lines.'

From his seat at the window Eddie watched Jimmy cross the road and stood to greet him as soon as he walked into the cafe, smiling and clasping him tightly by the hand.

Jimmy returned the smile and the firm handshake. 'I didn't think I'd be seeing you again so soon, Eddie. What brings you across the river?'

'I've been doing a few odd jobs for Archie and he asked me to nip over and see you.' Eddie sat down, nodding for Jimmy to join him, and held up a pointed finger to attract the attention of a passing waitress. 'I'll have a cup of tea and a paris bun this time, and whatever my mate here wants.'

'Nothing for me. Nah. Gimme a coffee. White.'

'Yeah. Archie said to ask you if you wouldn't mind popping down to Parkhurst to see him.' Eddie leaned across the table. 'As a matter of extreme urgency.'

Jimmy noted that what had started out as a casual request quickly turned into an order. His first reaction was to tell Eddie to tell Archie to go take a hike.

Aware of this Eddie took it upon himself to add, 'He said to say that you'd be doing him a favour for which he would be extremely grateful.'

'Oh, I don't know. I kind of promised Donna I was done with all that. It's the boy.'

'Sorry to hear about the boy. It must be murder.

But eh, Archie seemed to think you'd be doing yourself a favour.'

'What did he mean by that?'

Eddie shook his head. 'He never volunteered the information and I didn't think it was any of my business to ask. Why don't you find out for yourself? You're your own man. You can please yourself what you do, after you talk to Archie.'

Jimmy thought for a moment and said, 'Aye. Right enough, I suppose.'

'I think you're doing the right thing. Archie'll appreciate it.'

'Do me a favour, will you, Eddie? If you need to get in touch with me, leave a message at the Wheatsheaf over the road. If Donna thinks for one minute that I'm going back to my old ways, she'll fucken go apeshit.'

That's funny, Eddie thought. A guy who is frightened of nobody, shit scared of his old lady.

Jimmy took a seat at the table and waited for the screw to escort Archie Kemp into the visitors' room. Wishing to maintain a low profile, he was glad that Archie had enough clout to enable him to receive visitors away from the general public. A privilege, he thought, that was no doubt linked to the prospect of him winning his appeal and being at large.

'Glad you could make it, Jimmy,' Archie said, striding into the room. 'I knew you wouldn't let me down.'

Reaching across the table Jimmy shook hands, thinking how remarkably well Archie was looking. 'Prison life must be agreeing with you, Archie,' he joked.

'Like a boil on the end of my prick.'

'That much?'

'With any luck it might be a temporary situation.' Archie placed his elbows on the table and leaned in, resting his chin on his knitted fingers. 'With your help, that is.'

Jimmy wanted to put Archie in the picture. Tell him that he was under starter's orders from the wife. But common sense told him that, in this company, he would only be making a fool of himself. In any company except Donna's, he thought. 'I thought this might have had something to do with Anton,' he said.

'It has.'

'He's not too happy with me just now.' Keeping his voice down Jimmy eyed the screw over Archie's shoulder.

'I heard about that. All because of a motor, wasn't it?'

'Anton can go fuck himself. I was entitled to that motor.'

'You make sure you watch yourself there, Jimmy. Anton can be a right vicious bastard. But I'm sure I don't have to tell you that. You know him as well as I do.'

'He's a balloon.'

Archie smirked. 'I'm glad you think so because I

might be needing your help to sort him out. You'll be well looked after.'

'Oh aye. What's he done now?'

Pausing for a moment Archie picked at something caught between his teeth. 'Are you aware that Anton's got it in for you? And I don't mean a slap over the wrists like I'd have given you.'

'What? Over a Mickey Mouse car? He's not right in the head, the cunt.'

'You could be right. But eh, in answer to your question, he hasn't done anything to me. Not yet.'

'Not yet, eh?' Jimmy grinned. 'I always knew he'd end up causing you serious grief, Archie. Fucken power freak. I'm surprised you never worked that out for yourself.'

Archie had spent a sleepless night trying to figure out how to take Jimmy into his confidence without him finding out that Gilfeather was his son's natural father. He was well aware that Anton would tell him soon enough, turning him against Gilfeather. Part of the answer had come when Eddie Simpson relayed the message that Jimmy was on his way and that he might be reluctant to get involved, for reason that he'd received a serious ultimatum from his wife, of all people. That piece of information assured Archie that, provided he could command Jimmy's assistance, there was no likelihood of him betraying his position by discussing it with Donna, including the subject of Gilfeather. As far as the race to find Gilfeather was concerned Archie could only hope that Jimmy found him first. Gilfeather was sorely needed if he was to win his appeal, and there was no one quite like Jimmy for persuading people to do as they were told ... All this before Anton told Jimmy the truth about Gilfeather.

Another approach he had considered was to make no mention of Gilfeather and simply arrange for Jimmy to eliminate Anton from the picture altogether. But then who would find Gilfeather?

'I'm sure I don't have to tell you,' Archie began, then suddenly paused and looked off to the side. He had been about to tell Jimmy how the extortion conviction he was appealing against was the result of trumped-up evidence fabricated by Detective Chief Superintendent Ian Tate. A man well known to both of them. He stopped though, not because he realised that this was common knowledge, more for the reason that he was having second thoughts about taking Jimmy completely into his confidence. He'd given the subject some considerable thought, yet he took the time to mull it over again, squinting at Jimmy.

Should he tell Jimmy about the time, just before his bail had been revoked, when a geezer had contacted him by phone, offering to supply certain information that the caller firmly believed would convince that bastard Chief Superintendent Tate to change his tune? About how this information would be available only upon payment of a substantial amount of money? Considering his options, Archie decided that if he divulged this to Jimmy, then he would have to tell him that a request for more details had been met with a photostat copy of what was obviously an extract from a diary that was all very embarrassing, and incriminating, for the then detective sergeant Tate. Archie remembered with rancour that once he'd confirmed his interest, and that he was prepared to pay the asking price, provided he knew who he was dealing with, that the anonymous benefactor had – with surprising lack of concern – revealed himself, by way of correspondence, to be Tom Gilfeather. He cursed the impetuosity that forced him to make a rare mistake: that of thinking he would soon be in possession of all the damning evidence and approaching the chief superintendent with certain demands. The chief superintendent, he recalled, had expressed a willingness to comply, provided that all originals of the incriminating material were handed over. But lo and behold Mr Gilfeather, he remembered with increasing malice, as late as no more than a week ago, had decided to do a vanishing act. That had left Archie unable to complete the transaction, but worse, it meant that he had alerted Tate to the existence of the diary and unwittingly sent him in pursuit of it. The only redeeming factor was that Tate, as yet, had no idea who he was looking for.

On the strength of that, and the fact that Jimmy was too close to the action, he decided not to tell him anything about Gilfeather. He couldn't afford to make any more mistakes.

'Here's what the score is Jimmy,' Archie finally said, barely audible. 'I want Anton on the missing list.

But not until I get word to you. Fair enough.'

Jimmy nodded.

Good, Archie thought. Time to notify Eddie Simpson of his progress.

THIRTEEN

Detective Chief Superintendent Ian Tate reached for the diary on his desk, quickly turned to Wednesday 20th December and verified that his instructions to cancel all appointments had been carried out. Satisfied, he called for a car, saying that he would be driving himself. He was never in the mood for company when he made the tedious journey to Her Majesty's Parkhurst Prison.

Tate, tall, with a penchant for wearing suits that hid his abundant girth, waddled rather than walked to the car, setting his heavy jowls jiggling in time. What hair he had left was completely grey and swept from the left side of his head, just above the ear. His face was permanently flushed.

At his destination he was ushered quickly to a room painted in sky blue gloss enamel. The only furnishings there were a long Formica-topped table set between two backless benches. Archie Kemp was sitting lengthways on the far bench, his back resting against the wall and his legs stretched out along the seat. He was smoking a tailor-made cigarette and looked as if he had all the time in the world.

Tate was far from happy, a mood he intended using to his best advantage. Nodding at Archie he reached for the document in the inside pocket of his suit jacket and thrust it across the table. 'Take a look at this and tell me what you think.'

After several minutes of silence, other than the sound of Tate pacing the room and his own occasional sniffle, Archie placed the letter back on the table and said, 'You're in a spot of bother, old son.' His flippant attitude was at odds with the pain of reading the confirmation that he had been well and truly hung out to dry.

With Archie's frivolous comment adding to his foul mood Tate spat, 'Remember, Mr Kemp, if I go down on this, I'll make fucken sure that you'll never see the light of day again.'

'Tut tut, Chief Superintendent,' Archie interrupted. 'We can't have you losing sleep just because you're faced with the prospect of joining me in here. Better still, you'll probably end up in protective custody, locked up with all the deviates and child molesters.'

The chief superintendent's face drained of blood as the enormity of the convict's statement hit him. Though the ramifications of going to prison hadn't escaped him, having his worst fears verified by the most powerful villain in or out of the penal system was enough to scare him. As a distraction he reached into the side pocket of his jacket for the two unopened packets of Senior Service cigarettes and slid them across the table. His forced smile failed to fool Archie. Archie leaned off the wall and reached for the cigarettes, then slid them back to the policeman. 'Not my brand,' he told him.

Tate pushed the cigarettes back at him. 'Trade them for something,' he suggested.

'Fair enough. I'll trade them for a key out of here.' Archie slid the cigarettes back in front of the detective.

Pushing the cigarettes into the centre of the table Tate turned the document so that he could read it yet again. Archie leaned back on the wall, drawing his knees up to his chest.

'What are we going to do about this?' Tate asked, tapping the white paper.

Archie, deciding to treat the matter with the seriousness it warranted, flicked the piece of paper so that it faced him. The letter, cleverly written, took the form of an official invitation. It was headed, Dear Founding Member Of The Dirt Book Club and included a snippet of the information contained in the diary that gave the Dirt Book Club its name. The diary that contained the incriminating and embarrassing evidence against Tate.

The letter advised the price of membership and stated that the recipient of the invitation was in illustrious company, all of whom could keep the information contained in the diary from being made public simply by paying the annual fee. The penalty for non-compliance, it threatened, would be exposure to the highest-bidding gutter press. Further details would be furnished in due course and no correspondence would be entered into.

Archie's eyes narrowed. It was clear that Gilfeather, obviously seeing more profit in it for himself, had decided to bypass him and deal directly with Tate. A fact, he realised, that was not lost on the chief superintendent. 'What does he mean by annual fee? Christ, it looks like you'll be paying up for the rest of your life. Death by a thousand cuts, eh?'

The hint of humour in Archie's voice annoyed Tate to the extent that he only just managed to stop himself from pounding his fists down on the table either side of the paper. Lowering his head he looked up through his eyebrows and spoke softly. 'Let me put it like this. The quicker you help me, the quicker you'll be helping yourself. Does that make more sense to you?'

'How do I know I can trust you?' Archie said, grinning as he leaned across the table.

Tate was tiring of Archie's continuous game of cat and mouse. 'It's no longer a question of trust, Archie. There'll be no deal between you and me if I find our chum before you do. If you find him first, we deal. What could be simpler than that? Meanwhile, you can rot here knowing that I'll be out there looking for him.'

Archie's attempt to maintain a poker face was

betrayed by a succession of rapid swallows.

'What's the matter Archie? You're not stuck for words, are you?'

Archie placed a cigarette in the corner of his mouth and patted his pockets.

Tate reached across the table with his lighter. 'Face it, Archie. You've been left in the lurch, haven't you?'

'Yeah, but the advantage still lies with me. I know who the fuck I'm looking for. That's more than you can say.'

'I seldom know who I'm looking for,' Tate said, adding, 'At first.'

'You wouldn't know where to start looking.'

'Ha ha. At least I'm not banged up in here relying on others to do my legwork for me. I'd say that the advantage lies with me.' Tate took his weight on his knuckles and leaned forward on the table, looking Archie straight in the eye. 'I thought we could've worked together on this one, Archie, but I can see that it's every man for himself.'

Having said all he had to say Archie maintained a belligerent silence and held the policeman's gaze.

'So be it,' Tate said, walking out and slamming the door behind him.

'Amen,' Archie shouted after him.

Squeezing behind the wheel Tate looked in the rear-view mirror and headed for the ferry, glad to be putting Parkhurst Prison behind him. With a bad taste in his mouth, because he had gotten nowhere, he put in a call in to detective constables Curnow and Fallows. Curnow took the call while Fallows was at the bar getting another round of drinks and waved at his partner to hurry up. Fallows smiled at the bar manager and told him, 'Put it on the slate.' The manager forced a smile, as his boss had instructed him, and walked away wishing he had the nerve, just once, to ask them to pay for the drinks.

'What's the panic?' Fallows said, placing a Bacardi and coke and a beer chaser in front of his partner.

'That was Tate on the blower. He wants us to meet him back at the nick as soon as he gets back.'

'What've we done this time?'

'Nothing. He says he's got a job for us.'

John Curnow, at an inch over six feet, was half a head taller than his partner Peter Fallows. Unlike Fallows, who was stout and pot-bellied, Curnow had a wiry, athletic build. Fallows had a chubby face and fair hair which he wore flat to camouflage a receding hairline. The prematurely greying Curnow kept his thick crop of hair combed back, adding length to his already angular face. Both men were in their late twenties and kept postponing their sergeant's exam. They were on the take and, knowing that any promotion would entail a transfer and a stint back in uniform, resisted the move on the grounds that it would curtail their extra-curricular activities.

The detectives, handpicked by Tate, relished their role as revenue collectors. It made them feel important to be acting as middlemen in the widespread operation that provided a range of services to all manner of legal and illegal enterprises, including gaming, liquor licensing and drugs. As those they dealt with generally had reason to fear close scrutiny from the police, Curnow and Fallows enjoyed the power they had over them, even though Tate had taken pains to explain that, other than to line their pockets with money, the criteria were to allow business to be conducted profitably and without fear of prosecution.

Curnow was the first to acknowledge that he wasn't the most experienced detective in London. He did, however, realise that he had no business calling himself a detective if he hadn't worked out that, in the beginning, Tate had been at the mercy of Archie Kemp's generosity and that he had gradually asserted his authority, by way of demands for equal share of the proceeds, to the point where a serious conflict of interest occurred.

It was obvious to Curnow that Archie Kemp was in prison as a direct result of Tate's desire to rid himself of opposition and send a clear message to potential aspirants that the same fate awaited them. He could see that Tate was relaxed about the situation, knowing that Kemp couldn't incriminate him without further incriminating himself. Besides, if he knew Tate as well as he thought he did, the old man was bound to have enough buffers in place.

Chief Superintendent Tate ushered the two detectives into his office, switched the light on and shut the door behind them. 'Take a seat, lads,' he told them and produced a bottle of Beefeater gin and three glasses from the bottom drawer of his desk. 'Lads,' he continued, 'I need your help to find somebody, off-the-record like.'

'What have we got to go on?' Curnow said.

Tate sat back in his chair, planted his elbows on the vinyl armrests and nursed his drink in both hands. 'Ahh, that's the problem. Not much I'm afraid. Not even a name.'

'You don't want much,' offered Fallows.

'I want you to make this your number one priority. There's a lot at stake here, least of which is the nice little earners we all make on the side.' Tate knew that any hint of an interruption to the cash flow was bound to guarantee their undivided attention.

'No problem,' Curnow said, acknowledging his partner's silent nod of agreement. 'But, eh, if we're going to be doing this on the quiet, we'll need to know what we're up against. I take it that we can't rely on any back up? From the job I mean.'

'Correct. As far as the job is concerned, this conversation never took place.'

Tate glanced from one to the other, pondering to what extent he was prepared to take them into his confidence. Too much information could be dangerous.

'We'll need something to go on, sir,' Curnow said.

'Somebody's having a go at me,' Tate began. 'If we can't find him, it could end up being a costly exercise. It could even put us out of the game altogether. And I'm not just talking about money.'

Grim-faced, Curnow pushed his empty glass towards the bottle and helped himself. 'What have we got to go on?' he repeated, leaning back with a double ration of gin.

'I was getting to that. One of you can start by compiling a list of names of those who have done time with Archie Kemp over the years. The other, and it might as well be you, Curnow, check the computer and see what it spits out on prostitutes working the game in this or surrounding manors. I want you to concentrate on the ones who are still around after ten or eleven years. I know this doesn't give us much to go on, but at least it narrows the field. So get a move on.'

Fallows whistled and said, 'Archie Kemp.'

Nodding, Tate indicated that the meeting was at an end by replacing the top on the bottle and holding out his hand for the empty glasses.

Curnow got to his feet quickly and nodded for Fallows to follow him. With his coat over his arm and his free hand on the knob Curnow hesitated and turned to face Tate. 'Should we be concerned for our safety?'

'You should.'

FOURTEEN

Old Davey Macintyre was hanging around the curtain separating the parlour from the kitchen. He was trying to figure out how long it would be before the dinner was on the table. The last thing he wanted was to be roped in and given a job.

'Is that you mooching around out there, Davey Macintyre? If you're in such a big bloody hurry, why don't you do something useful like putting the knives and forks on the table, or you could butter a few slices of bread,' Agnes told him, knowing it was a sure way to get him out from under her feet.

Old Davey retreated to his fireside chair immediately and pretended to be asleep.

Agnes popped her head out into the parlour, holding the chip pan at arm's length behind her. 'Go on up and give our Jimmy and Donna a shout, will yah Davey? They're having their dinner with us tonight.'

Knowing that he would get no peace Old Davey

abandoned his sleeping act and trundled towards the door. 'Your tea's out,' he shouted up the stairwell and cocked his ear, waiting for the response that would save him the bother of going all the way up the stairs.

The light from the open parlour door filtered up the darkened stairwell and highlighted Mick and William bolting neck and neck down the stairs.

'I might have known it was you pair of gannets,' Old Davey growled. 'You could fucken smell grub a mile away, beh Christ.'

'I could smell you a mile away,' Mick replied. 'It must be time for your annual bath.'

Old Davey muttered something unintelligible and listened for several moments more. 'They must be fucken deaf,' he cursed and trudged up to the landing between floors. 'Your tea's on the table getting cold,' he shouted, pronouncing each word individually.

Donna bristled at the sound of her father-in-law's voice. 'You and Corrie go on, Jimmy, I'm not very hungry,' she said, hoping Jimmy would take the hint and go downstairs without her.

'Give us a break, doll. You know my ma's gone to a lot of trouble. You know she likes to do what she can to help.'

'Come on, mum,' Corrie pleaded.

Donna followed them to the door, her weak smile failing to disguise her discomfort. 'Come on then,' she said, suddenly realising that a lost opportunity to spend time with Corrie was one she might never recoup. 'But why do they have to eat so early? It's only just gone five o'clock.'

'Goody,' Corrie grinned.

'As long as it's not mince again,' Donna protested. 'They always have mince on a Wednesday. You can tell what bloody day it is by what they eat.'

Jimmy thought it best not to remind her that mince was likely to be on the menu on other days beside Wednesday.

'Hurry up and dish up, ma,' Mick said, reaching for another slice of buttered bread from the loaf-sized stack in the centre of the table.

Old Davey, with half a slice of bread in his mouth, spat crumbs all over the table in his haste to speak. 'That's the first sensible thing that edjit's said this year,' he mumbled, nodding towards Mick and laughing.

William wiped at the wet crumb that had lodged near the corner of his top lip. Unsure of what it was, he flicked out his tongue and dragged it into his mouth. 'Why do we have to wait for ma to dish up all of a sudden? We don't normally,' he said, adding, 'What do you think you're laughing at, our Mick?'

'I think that's them coming now,' Agnes said, ahead of Corrie bursting into the parlour, grinning from ear to ear.

Corrie was dressed in the height of juvenile fashion. Sneakers, baggy jeans and a knitted, woollen ski-cap. All the clothes were new and Corrie was clearly delighted.

'Are you off skiing, Corrie?' William grinned, winking at Jimmy and Donna who were acting strangely formal, as if they were real visitors.

'Don't be daft, Uncle William. East 17 started this fashion.'

'Pay no attention to him, son,' Mick advised. 'Sure he's only taking a lend of you.'

'That's a sin,' Agnes agreed, emerging from the kitchen wiping her hands down the front of her apron. 'The grub'll only be a minute,' she added.

'What's for tea anyway?' Jimmy inquired, helping himself to a piece of bread.

'It's your favourite,' his mother beamed. 'Mince, chips and peas, and I've made you some nice short-crust pastry to go with it.'

'Awh ma, you know I don't like chips,' William whinged.

'Shut your face. I've boiled you a couple of spuds, yah pest.' Agnes told him, unaware that Donna had rolled her eyes up to the ceiling. 'Sit down and I'll dish up.'

'About fucken time,' Old Davey mumbled and pushed his easy chair up to the table.

Jimmy and Donna took a seat next to each other, on the only two chairs that matched, and Corrie sat up on a rickety bar stool with an aqua vinyl back.

Agnes covered a chip in mince and forced it into her mouth sideways, speaking before she took the first bite. 'You're all dolled up, Corrie. Did Father Christmas come early this year?'

'Mum sent away to the catalogue for my new gear,' Corrie said, responding exactly as his mother had instructed.

Donna breathed a sigh of relief. The last thing she needed was the Macintyres thinking she had any spare money.

'Never you mind, son, it won't be long before Daddy Christmas comes to see you. Have you sent him a note up the chimney yet?' Agnes said, turning to adjust his ski-cap in exactly the way he didn't want it.

'Don't be like them pair of bams there, son.' Old Davey nodded at his sons. 'They stuck that many notes up the chimney they set the fucken thing on fire. The greedy pair of bastards.'

Amid the laughter William and Mick each pointed a finger, apportioning blame to the other. For Donna, in her present mood, the laughter and the fond memories of Christmas were the last straw, moving her to push her untouched meal away and run from the room to avoid bursting into tears.

Those gathered at the table exchanged glances, wondering what had been said to upset her. Agnes, thinking that it might have been her fault, looked sheepishly at Jimmy and pushed her chair back from the table, preparing to go after Donna.

'Go and see how your ma is, Corrie,' Jimmy said, raising a hand to bid his mother sit down.

As the door closed behind Corrie Jimmy shook his head slowly and nibbled at the side of his bottom lip.

'I can't make her out lately. She seems to be away with the fairies half the time.'

The others, with the exception of Agnes, continued eating in silence. 'God love her, she's got a lot on her plate, Jimmy son,' she said, raising her fork and threatening to stab Mick if he didn't leave Donna's chips alone.

'Hey listen, I've got the same weight on my shoulders and you don't see me carrying on like that, do you?'

'It's different for a mother,' Agnes reminded him.

'Meh arse. Are you trying to say that fathers don't have as much feeling? That's the stupidest thing I ever heard.'

Old Davey interrupted. 'I think what your ma's trying to tell you, Jimmy, is that women handle the situation a wee bit different than the men. Men bottle their feelings up and that's probably one of the reasons why we're never sober.'

'Listen to him,' Agnes said. 'The only reason he's never sober is because he's too fond of the bloody drink.'

'That's lovely, that is. If that's all the thanks I get I'll just sit here and keep my mouth shut, beh Christ.'

Jimmy paid no attention to the banter. 'Nah,' he said. 'Donna seems to be somewhere else half the time. Has anybody else noticed it, or is it just me?'

'Aye, she can be a bit funny at times, but I put that down to her being English,' Old Davey agreed, adding, 'Oucha,' and making no attempt to hide the fact that his wife had kicked him under the table.

After several seconds of silence, in which time Agnes shook her head and stared off to her right, Corrie bounced back into the room wearing a different ski-cap.

'Where's your ma? Is she coming back down?' Jimmy asked him.

'She told me to tell you she's having a lie down.'

'Hurry up and finish your dinner, Corrie, and I'll show you what we've got for pudding.' Agnes put her arm around the boy's shoulder and gave him two gentle squeezes. Corrie looked up at her and grinned.

'Tell your granny what's happening tomorrow, Corrie,' Jimmy said, leaning back in his chair and stretching.

'Dad's throwing me a birthday party and he's inviting heaps of people so that I get stacks of presents,' Corrie beamed.

Mick burst out laughing. 'Sure it's only been six months since the last birthday party we threw for him. Are you not worried folk'll think we're at it?'

It was Jimmy's turn to laugh. 'Who gives a fuck?'

All heads turned when the parlour door opened. Everyone expected to see that Donna had changed her mind and decided to join them, but with her head protruding around the door and her black leather glove gripping the edge of it Donna blew Corrie a kiss and indicated with a nod that she wanted to talk to Jimmy in private.

Jimmy responded to what he considered was her

earlier act of defiance by obstinately sitting where he was. Donna, with a fresh face of after-five make-up, wasn't in the mood for games either. 'If I'm going to be lying on my back I might as well get paid for it,' she shouted and slammed the door behind her.

'What does that mean, dad?' Corrie asked, holding the spoonful of ice cream short of his open mouth.

'Never mind her, son,' Jimmy told him.

Two minutes later Jimmy slowly got to his feet and ambled towards the door, trying unsuccessfully to give the impression that he was unconcerned.

'Oh oh,' Corrie said, as the door closed behind his father. 'Dad's getting pretty shitty.'

Jimmy stood on the top step, just outside the front door, and scanned left and right along South Lambeth Road. He checked the taxi rank opposite and the bus stop on his side of the road. Seeing no sign of Donna he went down the steps as far the pavement and repeated the exercise. She needs a good talking to, he thought.

Returning to the house he walked past the parlour door and on upstairs thinking that he'd like to see if Shane could shed any light on Donna's recent spate of mood swings. Tonight was Wednesday, so she wouldn't be at the Wheatsheaf. If he could get Shane's address off Ronnie he would call in and see her before she left for work. Approaching her in a more personal manner might guarantee a better result. At the top of the stairs he checked his watch and decided to phone the pub.

FIFTEEN

Wherever possible Jimmy stuck to the side streets, reaching Elephant and Castle less than fifteen minutes later and parking in a residents only spot right outside Shane's place. The hardest part had been sneaking out without Corrie asking where he was going.

Since his meeting with Archie Kemp Jimmy had been anxiously contemplating his position. It wasn't that he minded whacking Anton, that was self-defence, or the fact that he had to bide his time. It was the thought of Donna finding out and following up on her threat to leave. That was one thing he couldn't handle.

Shane responded immediately to the authoritative rap on the door. 'Hold on a minute,' she said looking through the peep-hole.

'It's me, Jimmy. Jimmy Macintyre.'

The door opened to the sound of a succession of sliding bolts and rattling chains, creating the impression that the door was being opened in a hurry.

'Goodness me,' Shane said wispily. 'What brings you here? I hope Donna's kicked you out.'

The subdued expression on Jimmy's face, despite his attempt to smile, convinced Shane that her joke had fallen flat. It was the first time she could remember him as being anything less than totally overbearing.

'Come in,' she said, stepping to one side.

'I need to have a word with you, Shane.' Jimmy followed her through the living room to the bedroom.

'Do you mind if we talk while I'm getting ready for work? I like to be ready in plenty of time.' Shane sat at a dressing table illuminated by a row of miniature bulbs around the outside edge of the mirror. The light from the bulbs concentrated on the immediate area, casting the rest of the room in shadow.

She wore a lilac satin dressing gown that fell open all the way to the top of her bare thigh the moment she sat down. And although her own dark hair was abundant and feminine, it was wavy, and not at all in keeping with the image she nurtured with the straight, jet-black wig she was reaching for.

Jimmy sat on the edge of the bed and studied Shane in the mirror, watching as her long red fingernails delicately flicked and teased at the hairpiece. 'I know you haven't known Donna for all that long, Shane, but I was wondering if she'd said anything to you? You know, woman talk.' He knew he had to be careful with what he said. If anything Shane's allegiance lay with Donna, and no doubt anything he said was likely to go straight back to her.

'As you say, I haven't known her for all that long, Jimmy, but I like to think of her as a friend.' Shane broke eye contact in the mirror as she turned to face him.

'I was wondering if you'd noticed anything funny about her lately? You know what I mean. Apart from worrying about Corrie.'

She locked eyes with him for several moments longer than she was comfortable with and then turned to face the mirror. Leaning in she lavishly applied lipstick between the lines she had previously pencilled in.

'I'm not sure what you mean by funny. Do you mean funny ha ha, or funny peculiar?'

Jimmy was about to ask her if she took him for a mug when he remembered that he had decided to beguile the information out of her. Instead he smiled and simply said, 'Funny peculiar.'

'It's hard to say. Maybe it's you who needs a change?' Shane laughed, pouting and looking up at him.

Jimmy silenced the laughter with a sullen glare. 'Shane, how would you like a good kick in the balls?'

Shane was mortified. Not at the threat of violence, to which she was no stranger, but at the reference to the genitalia which she considered to be the least significant aspect of her person.

'I was only joking,' she mumbled.

For no other reason than to glean some information from her Jimmy stood and began massaging the sides of her neck as tenderly and affectionately as he was capable of. Under the circumstances.

'Shane, if I tell you what's on my mind do you think we could keep this little conversation to ourselves? I'm a wee bit worried about Donna and I don't really want her to find out, in case I'm on the wrong track. I would feel stupid if I was imagining things.'

With her eyes closed and her mouth partly open Shane responded to his touch like a purring cat. She aided his manipulation by gently raising her chin and looking along each shoulder in turn.

Jimmy continued. 'I just get the impression that she's – I don't know – up to something.'

Shane opened her eyes momentarily. 'I'm not sure what you mean by "up to something". You don't think she's playing up, do you? Nah. Not Donna.'

'I'm not sure what to think. She's been sort of moody lately. One minute she's all right, the next minute she's away with the fairies.'

'She's under a lot of pressure Jimmy. You said so yourself.'

'I can understand that, but she eh – she's got something on her mind, and I'm not talking about our Corrie. I've known her far too long.'

'I doubt if I'd be acting any different if I was in her position.'

'I probably wouldn't have thought anything of it if she hadn't been ducking out at all sorts of funny hours. I thought to myself, uh uh, how long's this been going on? Christ, I remember when you couldn't get her out of the house unless she was going to work. She liked her peace and quiet.'

'Umm. Do you know what I'd do if I was you? You know, just to put my mind at rest. I'd mention it to her.' Shane paused and added, 'I'd be very surprised if it's what you're thinking.'

Jimmy's thumbs kneaded the muscles at the base of Shane's neck as his fingers manipulated their way over her shoulders, careful not to proceed beyond the natural barrier of her collarbone. 'Ahhh,' he sighed. 'That's the problem. She might tell me something I don't want to hear. Then again, I'd feel a right idiot if I was wrong. Know I mean?'

'Listen, Jimmy ... ' she sighed, intending to give the impression that she was willing to divulge as much as she knew, without making it obvious that her intentions were simply to keep the massage going for as long as possible.

'Go on,' he coaxed, and continued massaging, working his way up the side of her face, careful not to dislodge the wig.

'Jimmy, if I knew anything I would tell you, and that's straight up. But if I was you, and I was feeling a bit concerned about Donna, I'd go up West and keep a bit more of an eye on her.'

'What are you saying?'

'I'm not saying anything. It's just that there's all sorts of weirdos getting around up there and I was thinking that it wouldn't do you any harm to keep a bit more of an eye on her.'

His thumbs aching, Jimmy took a seat on the edge of the bed and watched Shane's face in the mirror. 'Umm. I suppose it wouldn't do any harm,' he said.

Shane, misinterpreting the reason for the sensual massage and acting on the urge initiated by it, opened the top drawer of the dresser and reached for the clear plastic bag containing the seamed black stockings she favoured for special occasions. Turning to the side, facing Jimmy, she crossed one leg over the other and stooped to roll a stocking up to the black suspender clip she produced from under the dressing gown. After she repeated the process she stood and provocatively let the dressing gown slip off her shoulders to the floor.

Jimmy had gone hard despite his wish to remain otherwise, but he managed to console himself with the knowledge that he had become aroused at a perfectly normal erotic image that, on this occasion, just happened to be an illusion.

'Do you know that you remind me of Donna in this light?' Jimmy told her.

Shane pressed what she saw as her advantage by stepping up to him and allowing her legs to rest against his knees. 'What about a head job?' she whispered and, trembling with excitement, forced his legs apart with her knees.

Jimmy studied the intricate frills on the black lace panties facing him at eye level, looking for the telltale bulge. 'Tell me something, Shane,' he began, looking up and trying not to laugh, 'what did you have in mind? Did you want to suck my prick or did you want me to suck yours?'

Standing with her hands on her hips Shane watched him back flip over the bed and take to the floor running, narrowly edging out of the door ahead of the cushion hurtling across the room after him.

'Hurry up and get dressed and I'll give you a lift to work before I shoot up West,' Jimmy said and opened the door without exposing himself to view. He was thinking that his offer of a lift was the least he could do to restore harmony. But mostly he wanted the opportunity to remind Shane of her promise to keep their meeting to herself. If she gives me any shit, he thought, I'll threaten her with telling Donna that she put the hard word on me.

Finding a parking spot in the West End at any time of the day was difficult enough, but finding one on the Wednesday night before Christmas in Soho was practically impossible. In Great Windmill Street, a few doors down and around the corner from where Donna plied her trade, Jimmy parked the car on the pavement and placed a previously prepared note under the windscreen. His actions drew a stinging tirade of threats and abuse from a Cockney chucker-inner spruiking in front of the garishly-lit strip club across the street.

Jimmy strode across the road thinking he would

just start laying into the doorman, no question.

'Sorry Jimmy,' the bouncer said, displaying his open palms and cocking his head to the side. 'I never knew it was you. On my life.'

Jimmy eyed him menacingly. The bouncer backed into the perceived safety of the doorway he was supposed to be minding and said, 'We don't see you up West much this weather, Jimbo.'

'Keep your eye on my motor, Kenny.' Jimmy relented and veered off into Archer Street, half-expecting to see Donna standing in the doorway of the three-storey building. As soon as he encountered the heavy foot traffic he realised that she was odds-on to be working.

The light creeping in from the street made it no further than the bottom of the steps two yards in from the front door. Beyond that the only form of illumination was the weak glow extending from the red light on the first-floor landing. Jimmy reached the first floor walking on the balls of his feet and put his ear to the door on his left at the head of the stairs.

'Looking for something, cock?'

At the sound of the voice, which was little more than a husky whisper, Jimmy turned abruptly and faced along the passage with his fists held low. The offence he took at the offhand remark was compounded by the sight of the intimidating silhouette of a man approaching from the other end of the passage, gently tapping the floor with what he took to be a baseball bat or a pickaxe handle.

'Hey you, are you fucken deaf or what? Didn't I just ask you if you were looking for something?' In the subdued lighting the minder stopped two paces back and held the pickaxe handle over his shoulder, looking like a Neanderthal man.

Jimmy was still primed from his brush with the bouncer around the corner. But mindful of the possibility that this could be a repeat performance he hesitated long enough to see if either of them recognised the other.

Donna raised her head off the pillow and peered at the door down the length of the grossly overweight man grinding away on top of her. She watched the cheeks of his backside pumping frantically below the level of his shirt tail and hoped he would get a move on. She had known by the strong stench of alcohol that she had her work cut out for her. As usual, when she was going through the motions with a client, she found herself dwelling on what little time there was left before Anton followed through with his threat. If nothing else, the raised voice outside her door gave her a moment's respite.

'What are you, some kind of creep hanging around in the dark listening at people's doors, eh?' the minder said, and manoeuvred to cut Jimmy's access to the stairs. He was thinking that if he hadn't been under specific instructions from Anton Winters to keep a hold of anyone acting suspicious he would have thrown the creep headfirst down the stairs by now.

'Do you know who I am?' Jimmy went against his

nature and better judgement in granting a short reprieve. It was only because he knew exactly where the confrontation was heading. He had gathered by the minder's lack of protocol and respect that he was either new to the game, or the area, or both. Either way he was due a slap.

'No, and I don't give a fuck. All I know is you're creeping around here in the dark and it's my job to keep creeps out.' The minder transferred the thick end of the pickaxe handle to the floor and leaned on it with both hands. He jutted out his head in an obvious act of defiance.

Jimmy stood square to his target and threw the punch from his hip. He could tell by the dull thud and the sweet familiar jarring all the way to his feet that the minder was unconscious before he hit the ground.

Donna, fearing the worst, thrust with her hips in a well-practised movement that dumped the startled punter onto the bed beside her. 'Hey. I haven't finished yet,' he shouted, rolling onto his back and watching her dart towards the door.

She paid him no regard and opened the door a fraction, fully expecting to see the minder doing what he had openly boasted he would do if he caught anybody getting up to any hanky panky with his girls. Instead she saw her husband kneeling over the minder, systematically beating his face to a pulp.

'Christ, Jimmy,' she screamed, trying to drag him off. She was heedless of the skimpy way she was dressed or of the other similarly clad girls chancing a look from behind chained doors. 'You're killing him,' she screamed louder. 'Help me, Lavender,' she pleaded, her cry for help falling on a door slamming shut. A second later, when she'd unchained the door, Lavender pounced from the room.

In desperation the two women locked their arms around Jimmy's head and neck and threw themselves backwards onto the floor, toppling him on his side. In an instant Donna was aware of him looming over her with one hand clutching her throat and the other poised ready to smash into her face. Her eyes pleaded, 'It's me, Jimmy,' but the words failed her. Out of the corner of her eye she saw Lavender slink back into her room and slam the door shut behind her.

'Donna,' he said suddenly, as if she was the last person in the world he expected to see there. 'When are you ever going to learn? Never get in my road, woman. Not when I'm giving some cunt a slap. You should know well enough by now. It's the worst thing you could do.'

'A slap, is that what you call it? For Christsake, Jimmy, take a look – you've nearly killed the poor bugger. And he was probably only doing his job.'

Jimmy dragged Donna to her feet and fought to quell the revived surge of anger. He had perceived her remark as adding insult to injury. 'Only doing his job? I'll tell you what he is. He's a cheeky fucker and he's lucky that's all he got. And eh, while we're on the subject, what do you mean, only doing his job? Is this something else I know fuck all about? I'll tell you one thing Donna, you've got some fucken explaining to do.'

The biting cold on the landing reminded Donna of her near nakedness and she returned to the room with Jimmy close at her heels. 'I've got a punter in here, Jimmy,' she reminded him, and tried to block his access with her body, intending to put on her dressing gown and, if nothing else, tend to the needs of the stricken minder before she answered any questions.

Jimmy had different ideas and pushed past her into the room, breaking one of his cardinal rules. 'You. On your bike,' he shouted, pointing directly at the hapless punter.

The punter, not waiting to be told twice, pulled on his trousers straight over the condom shrivelled up on the end of his flaccid penis.

'Come back another time and I'll make it up to you, Harry,' Donna promised him and escorted him to the door, steering him as far away from Jimmy as possible.

'I thought we agreed you wouldn't come in the room when I was with a punter, Jimmy? I thought that we agreed it would be bad for business.' Donna looked at him coldly and realised by the look in his eyes that now wasn't a good time to debate the issue.

'Fuck the punters. Fuck every cunt. I came all the way up West to see my wife and I get accosted right outside her door by some fucken smartass waving a pickaxe handle right under my nose. What was I supposed to do? Call for help?' Jimmy threw his head back and sniggered. 'Heh heh, it's me you're talking to.'

Donna pushed her open fingers through her hair and reached for the dressing gown hanging behind the door. With a relaxed grip on the doorknob she held the door partly open and waited for the usual kick that would slam the door shut. 'Did you try telling him who you were? No, that would have been too easy, wouldn't it?' When the expected kick failed to materialise she chanced opening the door the rest of the way.

Seeing that she was determined to assist the still unconscious minder Jimmy followed her out onto the landing and watched her painstakingly dab the blood from the man's swollen and broken face. He breathed a sigh of relief when the gurgling stopped and the minder opened his eyes and dislodged a saucer-sized mixture of blood and phlegm onto the floor beside him.

'He'll be all right. Just let him sit there for a minute,' Jimmy ordered, and steered Donna back to the privacy of the room. 'Now,' he continued, 'are you going to tell me what the fuck that minder's doing here or do I have to go out there and ask him myself?' Jimmy strode towards the door without waiting for an answer.

'Who's looking after Corrie?' Donna said, making it sound like an accusation.

'Who's watching him?' Jimmy answered, stopping

before he reached the door. 'Who do you think's watching him? It's the same people who normally watch him when you decide to take yourself off to work. Don't forget you were supposed to be staying home tonight.'

'I thought I left him with his father.'

'You did. Until I decided to come up here and find out why you've been so touchy lately. Why you stormed out of the house for nothing.'

Donna, knowing she was at the stage where she would have to tell him something, answered sarcastically, 'What? Apart from all the worry with our Corrie?'

'Yes, Donna. Apart from all the worry with our Corrie. And you can start by telling me why you've got a minder guarding your door.'

'Anton Winters installed him here.'

'Anton fucken Winters. Not him again? What the fuck's he up to now?'

Since Anton's last visit Donna had become increasingly aware that it was inconceivable to believe that Jimmy could, or would, be kept totally in the dark. Her dilemma was how to tell him enough, selective, facts without revealing vital information. She began nervously. 'I don't suppose you remember about ten or so years ago you sent me a message with a guy called Tom Gilfeather? You were doing time together and he got out the day before you.'

'That twisted cunt? He could crawl up a pipe backwards,' Jimmy said, fascinated. 'Did you know that he was Archie Kemp's bum boy? Not that he had any say in the matter, mind you. Poor cunt.' Jimmy shook his head and continued. 'It was supposed to be on-the-quiet, but eh, after they stuck Gilfeather in with me – me of all people – I made sure Kemp left him alone. I wouldn't put up with that kind of malarky. No fucken way.'

A look of complete surprise came over Donna's face.

'Don't look so surprised. These things happen in the best of jails,' Jimmy told her.

The fact that Gilfeather was a bum boy is what Donna found so incredible. It didn't tally with her perception of the young man who, having turned up on her doorstep with a message from her husband, stayed and spent nearly every penny he possessed on an all-night session. She remembered it well because his striking good looks had caused her to break a golden rule: that of servicing acquaintances of her husband. But above all, the memory was etched in stone, not just because of his insatiable sexual appetite and the vigour that caused the condom to burst, but because of her ensuing pregnancy. If only she hadn't gone off the pill, in anticipation of Jimmy's release.

'Anyway, what's all this got to do with Anton? Don't tell me he was humping him and all.'

Donna gulped, preparing herself to relate the story she had gone over countless times in her head. The story she dreaded telling because it would focus her husband's attention on Gilfeather. 'Anyway, while you were in prison I started writing a diary. I think I might have mentioned it in a letter, did I? Then the diary was stolen.'

'Donna, stop fucking around and get to the point, will you?'

'After your mate Gilfeather handed me the envelope from you, because I wanted to read it in private, I placed it on the mantelpiece and went to put the kettle on. When I was in the kitchen I thought I could hear a noise in the bedroom on the other side of the partition and when I went into the living room, sure enough, there was Gilfeather coming out of the bedroom. I wouldn't have been out of the room for more than a minute.'

'Are you sure that it was Tommy Gilfeather who took the diary? Let's face it. He probably wasn't the only one to go into the bedroom that day.'

Donna propped up her bosom with one arm and rested her elbow on the back of her hand, keeping her cigarette poised at her lips. Before she answered she continued studying her husband for a moment longer, trying to gauge his reaction so far. 'Are you kidding? As soon as I got rid of him I checked to see if anything was missing. I couldn't find the diary.'

Jimmy shook his head again. 'It must've been some fucken diary. What was in it anyway?'

Donna paced further into the shadows, away from the rich velvet glow cast by the red light above the bed. 'Anton came up here to see me. Last week some time,' she confirmed, trying to hold the tremor in her voice. 'And he was asking about Gilfeather. Apparently he –'

'Why would he be asking you about Gilfeather?' Jimmy interrupted. 'What's that cunt got to do with you?'

'That's the first question I asked myself. I couldn't work it out. Then I remembered the diary and put two and two together. Gilfeather must be up to something with the diary, I thought. It couldn't be anything else.'

'Did Anton mention the diary?' Jimmy said, intrigued. He was thinking about the meeting with Archie Kemp, knowing that there had to be a connection.

'No. Not really.'

'Well what makes you think this had anything to do with the diary then?'

'It wasn't that hard to figure out really. Providing I'm on the right track. That was the only contact I ever had with Gilfeather and I haven't set eyes on him from that day to this.'

'What's in the diary? Details about all the no-hopers who can't get a fuck without paying for it? Some big names in it, I suppose?'

'Some of them are big names now, all right.'

'What? They weren't at the time?'

'Not really.'

'Umm. It looks like Gilfeather's decided to get into them,' Jimmy said, thinking aloud. Even in that inadequate light he could see how reticent Donna was.

Christsake, he thought, surely she would have mentioned it, even if it was only in conversation, especially after I told her about Anton's visit to the Wheatsheaf. Maybe Anton Winters could provide the answer without all the fucking around.

'If I go and see Anton Winters is he going to tell me something I don't want to hear? Because, if he is, it might be better coming from you, Donna. I mean, why didn't you mention this a lot sooner? Why did you wait until I brought the subject up?'

'You're joking, aren't you?' Donna snapped indignantly. 'I thought I made it clear that we, me and Corrie, don't want you having any more to do with the likes of him.'

'Fair enough,' Jimmy retorted. 'But, eh, you haven't mentioned how Anton managed to trace the diary to you.'

'That's because I don't think he has. I think he would've mentioned it otherwise.'

His eyes narrowing, Jimmy thought for a moment and said, 'OK then. Tell me something else. How did Anton come to associate you with Gilfeather? And don't tell me he popped in on the off chance.'

After a prolonged silence in which time she fussed about looking in her coat pocket for a cigarette, Donna answered, 'He's probably doing the rounds asking everyone the same question.'

'It's an answer, I suppose,' Jimmy said, smiling and thinking that there was only one way to verify it. Go see Anton.

'Did Anton give you a hard time?' he added, stopping with his hand on the doorknob.

'No,' Donna assured him, over-enthusiastically. 'He was quite polite, actually.'

'Aye, OK. But you better get yourself on home. I've got a bit of running around to do.'

Out on the landing Jimmy had no trouble convincing the minder to give Anton's current phone numbers to him.

'You never got those numbers from me,' the minder said, whispering down the stairs after Jimmy.

'What numbers?' Jimmy whispered in return and hurried out into Archer Street in search of a working phone box. Turning into Great Windmill Street he spotted the mobile phone in the hands of the young bouncer standing wide-stanced in the doorway of the strip club across from where his car was parked. 'Hey, Kenny,' he said, nodding the doorman closer.

The doorman abandoned the belligerent expression as soon as he realised who it was. 'How yah doing, Jimmy,' he asked, offering his hand in a thumbs-up grip. 'I done a good job looking after your motor, Jimbo. Only had to tell a couple of likely lads to get on their bikes.'

'That's magic, Kenny. Much appreciated. But eh, is that a phone I see you've got there?'

Kenny looked alert, eager to impress. 'Yeah,' he said, holding it up. 'It's one of them ones you can cart around with you. You can even talk to people while you're having a shit.'

A wry smile came over Jimmy's face. 'I could be doing with one of these,' he said.

The young doorman was no fool. 'It's yours,' he told Jimmy, saving face, knowing that the mobile phone had just been taken off him. 'Anything to oblige,' he added, backing into the doorway.

Crossing the street Jimmy stood beside the car and dialled Anton's number. After he'd heard the engaged signal for the fourth time he muttered, 'Fuck it,' and got behind the wheel.

Anton Winters had no sooner hung up when the phone rang again. 'Is there no peace?' he moaned, hesitating with his hand poised above the phone. 'Yes, what is it,' he answered gruffly.

'Hooray fucken at last. Is that you, Anton? Jimmy Macintyre here.'

'What do you want?' Anton said, dispensing with formalities.

'I think it's time me and you had a wee bit of a talk.'

'Where are you?'

'I'm in Great Windmill Street.'

'I'm in Islington. Feel free to take a run over? Or you can say what's on your mind right now.'

'Nah. I can't talk about it over the phone. Why don't you meet me at the Marquis of Granby in Shaftesbury Avenue?'

'That's just around the corner from where you are now.'

'Neutral territory,' Jimmy said.

Anton held the phone away from his face and focused on his whitening knuckles. 'Give me half an hour,' he snapped.

'Keep your eye on my motor again, will you Kenny?' Jimmy shouted, and walked out into the Piccadilly Circus end of Shaftesbury Avenue.

The Marquis of Granby, like most West End pubs, was old and comfortable, a succession of owners having stuck with the original decor of heavy timber beams and walnut panelling. Even the frosted glass in the top half of the door behind the bar, bearing the name of the pub, was original. Jimmy took a stool at the end of the solid oak bar and positioned himself for an uninterrupted view of the doors.

'What'll it be sir?' he was asked, in a broad Belfast accent.

'A pint of heavy, and you better bung us a packet of nuts,' he answered.

'Right yeh be Jock,' the barman replied, and casually tossed a handled pint glass from one hand to the other, doing his poor man's version of a cocktail waiter.

'Hey dynamite,' Jimmy said, leaning over the bar and beckoning the barman closer. 'Don't call me Jock and I won't call you Paddy. Fair enough?'

'Fair enough, sir.'

Jimmy settled back on his stool. 'What's your name anyway?' he asked, deciding that the young, black-haired barman was all right after all.

'Meh name's Paul, but my friends call me Woody.'

'OK then, Woody, give us a nip of one of your best single malts. Let me see, aye, you better make it Laphroig.'

'A good drop of stuff, this,' Woody winked and added an extra measure.

Rather than throw the whisky straight back like he'd normally do Jimmy sniffed it and then swilled it around his gills, savouring every last drop. 'Same again,' he said, settling down to wait for Anton.

Fifteen minutes later Anton strode in, peeled off his black leather gloves and said, 'This had better be good.'

Or what? Jimmy was on the verge of saying, but decided on a more tactful approach. 'Aye, well it all depends what you mean by good, doesn't it?' he retorted.

'A gin and tonic,' Anton told the barman.

'Donna tells me you paid her a visit? Something 'bout looking for Tommy Gilfeather. Is that right?' Jimmy said, trying to gauge the look on Anton's face.

Anton took a long sip of his drink and studied Jimmy from over the top of his glass. He was immediately concerned that this turn of events would rob him of the leverage he had over Donna. How could he continue to threaten her with telling Jimmy about Gilfeather, if Jimmy already knew?

'That's correct,' he said, hoping to ascertain by Jimmy's reply if he was in possession of all the facts.

'How did you come to associate my Donna with Tommy Gilfeather? What made you think she'd have any idea where to find him?' While he was patient enough to await Archie Kemp's sanction to get rid of Anton Jimmy was concerned that a show of belligerence on Anton's part might force him to act ahead of schedule.

That was the question Anton wanted to hear. It confirmed that Jimmy was fishing, and that Donna could still be manipulated. He was pleased that the opportunity wasn't lost for him to give Jimmy the bad news about Gilfeather. A delightful task he would be undertaking soon enough. 'Not that it's any of your business but I was acting for Archie Kemp,' he said, distancing himself from accountability. 'To tell you the truth I went up to see her so that I could find out where you lived. You know, regarding that little bit of unfinished business with the car. I thought I might as well ask her about Gilfeather while I was there.'

'So you didn't go there just to ask her about Gilfeather?' Jimmy said, now more concerned with finding out what Archie Kemp's role was in all this.

'That's what I said. I've lost count of the folk I've asked about Gilfeather. In fact, if you take the trouble you'll probably find the word's out on the street that I'm looking for him. I don't suppose you've come across him yourself by any chance, have you?' Anton, still convinced that his best chances of finding Gilfeather lay with Donna, smiled at Jimmy, trying not to annoy him.

'What's Archie Kemp looking for him for? D'you know?'

Anton couldn't resist it. 'I'll give you the same answer I got when I asked. It's none of your business.'

'It will be, if I make it my business.'

'Why bother? It's no big deal.'

No big deal, Jimmy thought. Here was Archie Kemp, on the one hand, issuing Anton instructions to find Gilfeather, and on the other hand, lining me up to whack Anton. But not until Anton found Gilfeather, by the look of it. There seemed to be a lot hinging on Tommy Gilfeather turning up. With the diary, if I'm not mistaken. He wondered if Anton knew anything about the diary. Not that he was prepared to discuss it with him, in case he alerted him to its existence.

'It depends whether or not you've got any more business with Donna,' Jimmy said.

'No. Not really. But if she comes across Gilfeather, tell her to give me a call.'

'What about me? You got any more business with me?' Jimmy spoke as if he was issuing a challenge.

'That business with the car. Forget it. Archie said we can live with it.'

If Anton hadn't been so eager to oblige, Jimmy might have taken him on face value. Under the circumstances he was left thinking that certain self-serving individuals – Archie, Donna and Anton – were taking pains not to acquaint him with all the facts.

SIXTEEN

As soon as Detective Constables Curnow and Fallows returned to the police station early Thursday evening Curnow resumed studying the names on the computer screen, stopping occasionally to bring himself up to date with the current form of some of the girls he was familiar with. As instructed he paid particular attention to those whose charges went back ten years or more. Not that there were many who lasted that long. 'Christ,' he said, wheeling round to see his partner peering over his shoulder at the screen. 'Have you been eating garlic again? Buy yourself some chewing gum, for goodness sake, man.'

'What're you talking about?' Fallows huffed his breath into his cupped hand and tried to sniff it. 'You know what your problem is, Curnow? Your head's too close to your backside.'

'You've been at Vine Street longer than me. Have a swatch at the screen and tell me what you see,'

Curnow said, making sure that Fallows was standing in front of him.

'Pussy. Shitloads of pussy.'

'You're getting predictable, Fallows. That's exactly what you said this afternoon.'

'Don't tell me it's still Thursday. I feel as if I've been on my feet for days.'

'Why don't you do what the old man said and concentrate on H District? He was right when he said that there wasn't too many slags who could last ten years on the game. I reckon they either make their money and get out, or shoot it into their arms and stuff themselves right up.' Curnow poked his head at the screen a last time and began walking away.

'Hey, where do you think you're going?' Fallows called after him.

'I'm going to get a gas mask before you choke me to death.' Fallows laughed. 'Black, two sugars.'

'Forget the coffee. Tate wants to see me. So hurry up and print us out a copy of those names on the screen there and I'll meet you at the car.'

'Yes sir. You wanted to see me,' Curnow said, knocking the door and walking on in.

'Come in, come in.' Tate rose and walked around to the front of his desk. 'How're you going with that list?'

'Not much luck yet, sir, but Fallows is doing another printout now. We're down to the last few names though sir, and it's like you said. Not many go the distance in that game.'

'Take this and see if anybody on the list can match the handwriting.' Tate handed Curnow a slip of paper. It was a photostat copy of an incomplete sentence, taken from the sample sent to him by Archie Kemp when he'd asked Archie to prove that he was in possession of material incriminating him.

'What's it supposed to be, sir?' Curnow said, trying to make sense of the wording. 'Care if you've got somebody,' he read aloud. 'That doesn't make sense.'

Tate wasn't about to tell him that he'd lopped the sentence at both ends for that very reason. 'That's immaterial,' he said, adding, 'Just get the ones on your list to write the same words and leave the rest to me. All I'm looking for's a match for the handwriting. It's all I've got to go on. If necessary, you might have to go over a bit of the ground you covered earlier.'

'We'd better go and make a start then, sir. Fallows should be waiting for me in the car.' Curnow was none too pleased at the thought of having wasted most of the day.

'Before you go,' Tate followed Curnow to the door, 'make sure nobody actually sees that sample. I don't want anyone to recognise their own handwriting and start playing funny buggers. You know, trying to disguise their writing or use the wrong hand. Watch out for all that.'

'No problem.' Curnow left the chief superintendent's office and made his way to the car park.

'What kept you?' Fallows said. 'I thought we were in a hurry?'

Ignoring the question Curnow said, 'Right. Who's first up for the honour of our company tonight?'

'Ahhh, let me see,' Fallows said, checking the list. 'The privilege belongs to that old cow Rochelle.'

'Rochelle it is then.'

With Fallows at the wheel the two detectives did the rounds, checking quickly down the list. A short time later the unmarked police car pulled into Greek Street in Soho and guttercrawled to the other end, enticing bizarrely dressed streetwalkers from the shadows to the pavement's edge. On the return lap Fallows pulled up opposite the building they were looking for, parking half up on the pavement.

'They can smell us a mile away.' Curnow looked in either direction down the newly deserted street.

Alighting from the car they clutched their coats in the middle and darted across the road to the comparative shelter of the dowdy, three-storey terraced building opposite. The tenant registry was a makeshift affair, stuck either side of the main door. Without exception, they advertised the services of a stunning young model or a fully qualified masseuse, all of whom preferred to use a single, colourful name. Starr was the next on the list.

The hall smelled of cheap perfume contesting the mustiness of rising damp, accentuated by poor housekeeping. Hearing the echo of several pairs of high-heeled shoes click-clacking hastily up the stairwell,

Curnow and Fallows took to the stairs running.

'I see you finally made it to the top, Starr,' Fallows joked breathlessly and stuck his foot in the door before she could slam it shut in his face. 'Now now, that's no way to treat somebody who only wants a friendly chat,' he scolded, pushing past her. Once inside he looked with disgust at the peeling, mildew-affected walls and the clothes scattered around a floor badly in need of a clean. One look at the only item of furniture in the attic room, a single bed covered by a filthy, faded red duvet, and he wondered why anybody would want to set foot in here, never mind pay for sex.

'What do you want, Fallows? You're not due anything.' Starr was referring to her weekly contribution to the police coffers. Once a beautiful, high-class call girl she was now an empty shell, battling years of heroin addiction and struggling to keep body and soul together the only way she knew how. She looked at least twenty years older than her thirty-one years.

Curnow opened his clipboard and looked at the slip of paper given to him by Tate. 'Here, write the words, "care if you've got somebody", on this piece of paper. There's a good girl,' he said, handing her a fresh sheet of A4. 'If you can still remember how to write, that is?'

Starr backed up under the lone attic window and looked at them incredulously. As the distant, bright lights of Regent Street and Piccadilly Circus flitted over the rooftops and filtered into the attic, basking one half of her wasted face in shadow, she sat on the edge of the bed and wondered what the catch was.

'Just do as he fucken well told you,' Fallows snapped and stepped forward menacingly.

'Here, lean on this,' Curnow took his closed clipboard from under his arm and offered it to her. Fallows looked at him as if he was mad. 'Ugh. I wouldn't let her touch anything of mine.'

After Starr, resembling someone learning to write, painstakingly wrote the words 'care if you've got somebody', Curnow compared it with Tate's sample. Under no circumstances, he thought. And that was allowing for the ravages of her addiction.

'Well?' Fallows asked and moved round to see for himself. He knew there couldn't be many more names on the list.

Almost word for word and in the same tone of voice Curnow asked Starr the sequence of questions he had asked the other girls. 'You, eh, you've been around a long time, Starr,' he began, looking left and right around the room, determined not to come in contact with anything that remotely resembled a needle. 'Take a look at the names on this list and tell me if you can think of anybody who's been around for ten or more years and managed to stay off it. Do you know what I mean? Somebody with no convictions. No police record.'

Her confidence building Starr regarded the question as a likely source of revenue. She would trade her answer. 'What's it worth?' she demanded, speaking with her lips barely apart, unsuccessfully trying to hide her ragged and rotten teeth.

'Where have we heard that before, partner?' Curnow mocked.

'It's got a very familiar ring to it. You'd think that those who operate outside the law would be only too happy to help the police with their inquiries, wouldn't you?' Fallows gripped her by the hair and forced her head back.

A look and a shake of the head from Curnow forced him to let go of her hair, after which he inadvertently wiped his hand down the side of his trousers.

Continuing with the good guy, bad guy routine Curnow lit a cigarette and exhaled slowly. After another long draw he offered it to Starr. She accepted it gladly and took two deep draws in quick succession, forcing the smoke out through her nose. 'I think Starr might have something to tell us, detective. That's right isn't it, Starr?'

'Ta,' she said, and offered to return the cigarette.

'It's all right, you keep it,' he told her, matching the anguished look on his partner's face.

'You get nothing for nothing these days,' Starr reminded them, thinking she was in a position to trade.

Fallows responded to a surreptitious wink from Curnow. 'Maybe you'd like to continue this little chat back at the station? I'm sure we could come up with something to keep you occupied until the morning.'

Starr reacted, as anticipated, to what the detectives

knew was the junkie's equivalent of dying and going to hell. 'No, no. You can't do that,' she screamed and scurried across the bed to the far corner of the room. 'Please, I haven't done anything.' She needed a hit now, and the prospect of climbing the walls down at Vine Street police station was more than she could bear.

Making sure his gloves were on tight, Fallows approached the whimpering Starr, gripped her tightly above the elbow and hurled her clear across the room. Curnow cringed at the force with which her emaciated body hit the wall. 'Careful,' he whispered. 'We don't want to have any explaining to do.'

Fallows followed Starr across the room, his face distorted in a scowl and his fists clenched tightly by his side. 'Get up, you cow,' he ranted, and kicked her full force on her bony hip.

Curnow realised at once that Fallows had stepped outside the parameters of their normal routine. Stepping forward he gripped his partner's left fist just as he was drawing it back. 'She won't be much use to us if you keep this up,' he said.

Still dazed from the kick and the force with which her head had met the wall Starr watched the blurred outline of the two detectives take shape.

In his most compassionate voice Curnow told her, 'I don't think I can stop him locking you up, Starr. Not unless you stop messing us about.'

'There's a girl from up North,' Starr spat out, careful to avoid looking at her tormentors. She had no intention of mentioning Donna by name for fear of her husband. She was more intimidated by the thought of Jimmy Macintyre than she was by the threats of the police.

'We'll need more than that. A name at least.' Fallows said.

'I don't know her name,' Starr lied. 'All I know is that she comes and goes.'

'That's a good one. I thought it was supposed to be the punter who comes and goes.' Fallows laughed, well pleased with himself. 'Do you get it? Comes and goes?' he explained.

Curnow was running out of patience. 'You wouldn't be making this up, because if you are, I'm fucken warning you?'

Starr remained silent, regretting having said anything.

'You tell me where we can find her and we'll owe you one,' Curnow said, recognising the need for further inducement. 'That's the same as a get-out-of-jail-free card.'

Starr chose her words carefully. 'According to the word on the street there was a bit of trouble yesterday, over in one of the houses in Archer Street. If I was you I would start looking for her there. Oh, and you didn't hear it from me.'

'Is that the best you can do?' said Curnow.

'You're lucky I remembered that much.'

'If this doesn't check out we'll be back.' Fallows responded to his partner's nod to follow him downstairs.

'May as well head for Archer Street. It's only around the corner.' Curnow said climbing into the car.

'Archie Kemp controls that area,' Fallows noted as he turned the key in the ignition. 'That's probably why none of the cats have got charge sheets. We should've looked there first.'

'I hate to admit it, but I think you're right.'

In Archer Street there were several premises providing a range of sexual services. All were at the opposite end of the scale to Greek Street and all the girls, with the exception of Donna, paid protection to Archie Kemp. Donna didn't pay because of her husband's long-standing association with the crime boss. Archie, in turn, paid a percentage of the take to the police, buying the girls a cordial working relationship with the law. Until recently the agreement with the police had been amicable.

After meeting with no success at their first two ports of call Curnow and Fallows looked up at the building where Donna worked. 'I don't know about you but I'm going to go and scrounge something to eat. Do you fancy a kebab or something?' Fallows saw a break in the traffic and darted across the narrow street. 'What do you fancy?' he called.

Answering 'No,' Curnow opted to continue alone. He was feeling his way up to the first floor when a minder loomed at the top of the stairs, leaning on a pickaxe handle and looking, with his face and cheekbones in a mask of plaster, like some demented

Viking. The minder stood his ground, blocking Curnow's advance.

'Police here.' Curnow whipped out his badge, approaching from behind the presumed safety of it. 'I was wondering if you would mind answering a few questions?' he added, stopping abruptly when the minder suddenly transferred the thick end of the timber to his right shoulder.

'They're selling those fucken Mickey Mouse badges in Woolworths,' the minder sneered at him.

Annoyed at his own impetuosity Curnow chanced a look over his shoulder to see if there was any sign of his partner. 'Take it easy there,' he told the minder. 'I just want to ask you a couple of questions. We can do it here or we can do it down at the station. Please yourself.'

'Let me see that badge again.'

'What happened to your face?' Curnow held up the badge and squeezed past him onto the landing.

'I fell down the stairs.'

'You must've fallen all the way to the bottom, by the looks of you.'

The minder answered with a sullen glare.

'I'm looking for a girl from up North. Does that sound like anybody who works here? There might be a bung in it for you if you can point us in the right direction.'

The minder looked around as if the walls had ears. 'Never heard of her,' he said aloud.

Both men looked down the stairs when Fallows made an appearance, munching on a hot dog.

'What happened to you?' Fallows said to the minder and wiped his mouth with the empty hot dog bag. 'Whatever it was, it looks like you came off second best.'

'He fell,' Curnow answered and beckoned his partner to follow him up the stairs. When they reached the top floor he said, 'If we don't get a result we'll talk to that idiot on the way out. The less I see of him the better.'

The detectives wound their way back downstairs with a sample of each girl's handwriting and nothing else. Thinking that Donna might be the one the police were inquiring after the girls were reluctant to divulge information that might carry repercussions. The treatment of the new in-house minder at the hands of Jimmy Macintyre was uppermost in their minds.

With one room left to check Curnow rapped on the door several times in the unmistakable calling card of the policeman. Greeted by silence he tried again and shouted, 'Police here.'

'Who normally occupies this room?' Fallows turned to the minder emerging from the shadows at the other end of the passage. His question met with obstinate silence.

'He asked you a question,' Curnow shouted, his pretended anger alerting Fallows to commence the old routine.

'Why don't we just take him back to Vine Street and see how a night in the cells affects his memory?'

The minder's only allegiance was to the one who directly paid his wages. He had responded to Donna's natural kindness and would have gone into bat for her in most circumstances, but it didn't extend to being locked up for her. Especially after the beating her husband had given him. 'There's nobody in that room.' The minder was stating a fact, rather than making a conscious attempt to defend Donna.

'That's not what he asked you. I can see there's nobody in the room. I asked you who normally occupies the room.' Fallows exchanged glances with Curnow and overtly nodded towards the stairs in a gesture designed to intimidate.

Looking down the length of the uncarpeted stairs the minder had no trouble in getting the message. 'Donna Macintyre, Jimmy Macintyre's old lady, uses that room but she's fucked off. Don't ask where to, cause I haven't got a clue.'

The detectives exchanged nervous glances. Although they'd never had any dealings with Jimmy Macintyre personally, older heads had spoken of him with awe, often referring to him in the past tense, usually to prove how easy the new breed of detectives were getting it. It was common for them to be reminded how lucky they were that the Glasgow hard man was in the habit of spending as much time in prison as he was out.

'Where does Donna Macintyre come from? She's not Scottish, is she?' Curnow was thinking about Starr's claim that, possibly, the girl they were looking for was from the North of England. In a way he was hoping that this was a lead he wouldn't have to follow up on.

'No way,' the minder stressed. 'She's not a Jock. She's one of us, mate. She's English.'

Thinking that the minder had a cheek mentioning himself in the same breath as them Fallows was about to put him right when Curnow recognised the look and held up his hand to restrain him. 'What part of England are we talking about here?' he persisted.

'I'm fucked if I know. Up north somewhere. Try Yorkshire.'

The detectives, disregarding the minder, started down the stairs. 'Hey,' the minder shouted after them, 'what about me bung?'

'Think yourself lucky we didn't bung you down the stairs,' Fallows shouted back.

'What do you make of that?' Fallows added as soon as they'd cleared the building.

'It's not what I make of it. We're going to report this to Tate and see what he makes of it. We've done our job.'

'Not until we get a sample of her writing, we haven't.' Fallows threw his partner the keys of the car and added, 'Your turn to drive.'

'Anyway,' he continued as soon as Curnow reached over and unlocked the passenger side door, 'it's getting late. I doubt if he'll be at the station. Why not call ahead?'

'Because I'm not doing anything until I see what we're up against. That's why we're going back to the nick to check Jimmy Macintyre's form.'

The two remained silent until they were in the Vine Street car park. Separately and without discussion they were contemplating the ramifications of a run-in with the infamous Jimmy Macintyre. Fallows, for one, welcomed any confrontation, viewing it as a chance to make a name for himself. 'What do you reckon about this Jimmy Macintyre character?' he began. 'From the stories going around he either started young or he must be well past it. He's probably dead by now, anyway.'

Curnow wasn't so sure. 'That's not what I heard. I think you'll find that he's not much older than us. Anyway, we'd better have a word with Tate before we go rushing in. Don't forget we're on our own on this one, mate. There's definitely no back up. No cavalry to come to the rescue. I've got a feeling we're playing with the heavy team here, and I don't like it. Not when we're playing by their rules.'

Despite the butterflies in his stomach Fallows wouldn't be deterred. 'Fuck him. Macintyre's only one man. Besides, we just want a sample of his wife's handwriting to help us with our enquiries. It's hardly a declaration of war.'

'Ohh, I'm not too sure about that. I heard it doesn't take much to annoy him at the best of times. I'm doing nothing until I check his form.'

'All right then, look at it this way. If we don't get a sample of his old lady's handwriting by tonight she might get wind of what we're up to and, eh, make adjustments. That's if she got anything to hide. No, I reckon we should move now.'

Curnow drummed his fingers on top of the steering wheel, well aware of his partner's persistent stare. 'I'll tell you what I'm prepared to do,' he relented. 'If Tate's in his office we'll tell him what's going on, and if he's not, we'll look up the form on the Macintyres and eh, and see what the next move is.'

The balding desk sergeant looked up from the paperwork he was sorting through. 'Nice to see we're burning the midnight oil, lads,' he teased.

'Is Chief Superintendent Tate on the premises?' Fallows asked, choosing to ignore the quip.

'Nah, you've just missed him.'

Without responding Curnow went on ahead to his office and logged into the computer. Fallows arrived several minutes later balancing two coffees. 'Do you know what's got me baffled, John? I can't understand why Donna Macintyre's name never surfaced when we did the run-through earlier. You'd think that somebody who's been around for as long as her would have a bit of form, wouldn't you?'

'You would think so.' Curnow agreed without taking his eyes off the screen. 'She's either squeaky clean or she's got friends in high places.'

'Or her husband has had some influence on her career. From what I can gather around here, the gutless bastards are all shit scared of him. And I'll tell you what John, it fucken wouldn't be me. I'd just shoot the bastard and be done with it.'

'I think you'd have to. Take a look at this.'

Fallows stepped up to the computer, remaining silent as he focused on the screen.

'It seems our Scottish chum always resorts to violence when it comes to sorting out disputes. Serious violence,' Curnow said.

'It's a wonder somebody hasn't shot him by now.' Fallows turned away from the screen. 'One of our lads.'

'You still keen to go and see his old lady?' Curnow asked with a wry smile, noting the look of hesitation on his partner's face.

Indignantly Fallows copied down the last-known address of Jimmy Macintyre's next of kin and stormed out of the office. 'You can stay here if you want,' he spat.

Shaking his head Curnow shut the computer down and followed Fallows out to the car park.

SEVENTEEN

With Fallows at the wheel of the unmarked car the detectives crossed Vauxhall Bridge and cruised along South Lambeth Road, slowing down when they neared No. 38. Following normal police procedure, they pulled into the kerb outside the Pakistani's shop and sat in the car while they watched the Macintyre house. Fallows checked his watch. 'Not much happening,' he said, noting that the house was in darkness save for a light burning on the first floor. A room he presumed was a bedroom. 'They must be out,' he added. 'Probably down the boozer – where we should be.'

Across the road Corrie checked his image in the full-length mirror next to the door. Well pleased with all his new gear he adjusted the ski-cap, wishing he at least had some eyebrows. He wasn't feeling the best, a side-effect of the chemotherapy earlier in the week. But, on the pretext of trying on the rest of the new clothes his mother had bought him, he got ready for the party his dad had promised him.

'I can't understand why you want to get all dressed up at this time of the night. It's nearly ten o'clock. You should be in your bed.' Donna looked over his shoulder and smiled at him in the mirror. 'Your daddy should be home soon.'

'Can I stay up until he comes home, mum?' Corrie was concerned that his mother, knowing nothing about the party, would put a stop to it on the spot. He thought it was silly of his dad to organise a party so close to the day he got his chemo.

'As long as he's not too late,' Donna said, still annoyed at herself for going to work when she should've been at home. At least the chemo hasn't knocked him around as much this time, she thought.

The sound of people laughing outside the front door drew Donna to the window. She saw that a procession of others equally as loud were making their way around the corner from the direction of the Wheatsheaf. 'He would not,' she said and stormed downstairs, standing aside as Agnes and Old Davey led the drink-laden caravan into the parlour. Hands on hips she accosted Jimmy as soon as he set foot inside the door. 'Not tonight, Jimmy. Please.'

Jimmy took her to the relative quietness of the hall beyond the parlour door. 'I'm having a bit of a birthday party for our Corrie. You're normally at your work.'

'A birthday party?' Donna couldn't believe her ears. 'Jimmy, it's not his birthday. Why on earth would you be throwing him a party?'

'Because I'm making up for the ones I've missed,' Jimmy said, adding solemnly. 'Besides, he might not be around for the next proper one.'

'You're a big softy,' Donna said, putting her arm around his waist. 'But do you not think that a few of his friends at McDonald's would've done?'

'Get away. I don't mind taking presents off this lot, but I wouldn't do it to his wee friends. They'd be too clever anyway.'

'You're something else, Jimmy Macintyre,' Donna responded, allowing herself to be steered into the parlour.

'Mick,' Jimmy said, spotting his brother leading a conga line up the steps, 'nip up the stairs and get Corrie. But don't let him into the parlour until I've got the you-know-what ready.'

'Come on, wee man, they're all downstairs waiting for you,' Mick said, bursting into the room and pulling the ski-cap down over Corrie's eyes.

'Goody,' Corrie laughed.

'Put your hands over your eyes, Corrie, and don't take them away until I tell yeh.' Mick told the boy to stop outside the parlour door and made sure his instructions were carried out. 'No peeking,' he warned, and began leading Corrie into the room. For good measure he covered Corrie's eyes with the flat of his hand and popped his head around the door. 'Ready,' he said, guiding Corrie into the darkened, deadly quiet room.

On the kitchen side of the dividing curtain Agnes

was having trouble getting the candles to light. Somebody in the crowd thought they saw the curtain move and erupted into 'Happy Birthday to you', then stopped abruptly when no one joined in.

'See these bloody candles,' Agnes muttered, causing Corrie to snigger.

Mick went behind the curtain to see what was causing the hold up and said, 'That'll do, ma, sure he's only going to blow the bloody things out.'

'Watch you don't set fire to my good curtains, our Mick.' Agnes rushed to hold the curtains to one side.

'Happy birthday to you,' Mick sang at the top of his voice, his confidence encouraging the others to join in.

'For fuck sake,' he shouted, when a gust of wind blew out all the candles before Corrie had a chance to get near them. 'Who left that bastarding door open?'

Corrie tried not to laugh. 'Is it all right if I open my eyes now, Uncle Mick?'

'Aye, on you go, mate. It was far too big a job for one wee fella anyway. Blowing out all them candles.' Mick grinned and placed the cake on the table.

Old Davey wasn't having it. Closing one eye in order to focus he stumbled his way across to the table. 'Giv'us a look at them fucken candles,' he spluttered. 'Christsake, this might be the last chance the boy gets to blow the candles out on a birthday cake.'

No sooner had he uttered the words when, even in his advanced state of inebriation, he realised what he had said. A silence accompanied the stolen stares and whispers. Bewildered, Corrie slowly scanned the faces in the crowd, looking as if he didn't know whether to laugh or cry. He needed his parents to reassure him that it was all a joke. Despite every effort having been made to convince him to the contrary, Corrie was well aware that he was living on borrowed time, but this was the first time it had been confirmed in his presence. After the exhilaration of having his dad home, and the promises his mum had made, of the things the family would do once he was better, this was devastating.

Stunned by what they had heard Donna and Jimmy were slow to react. Old Davey, sobered by the reaction and motivated by the need for self-preservation, let out a laugh. 'Aye son,' he said, putting his arm around Corrie's shoulders. 'If we don't hurry up these gannets will eat all the cake before we get a chance to light the candles again.'

Donna placed her hands on Corrie's shoulders from behind and kissed him on the cheek. Jimmy took one look at his son's beaming face and decided against what he had been about to do. Everyone in the room breathed a sigh of relief, none more so than Old Davey.

'Right, get the bevie up,' Mick shouted and began relighting the candles.

The crowd stood around the cake singing at the tops of their voices and Jimmy stooped and took a photo of the soft light from the candles playing on

Corrie's smiling face. With Corrie still blinking from the effect of the flash he squeezed his way to the door and let himself quietly out of the room. He took the stairs three at a time and let himself into the room next to his flat. On the bed was a hamper-sized package wrapped in Christmas paper and tied with a big red bow. He carefully picked up the package with both hands and even more carefully made his way back down stairs. All heads turned to face him as soon as he walked into the room.

Corrie looked up from unwrapping the small parcel his granny had given him, his face beaming with glee. Jimmy placed the package on the table next to the cake and stood back matching the look on his son's face. Donna put her arm around Jimmy's waist and leaned her head on his shoulder. She blinked and sent tears running down her face.

Standing on a chair Corrie yanked feverishly at the red bow. As soon as he saw the wicker basket he stopped and looked at his dad with his eyes wide open and his mouth agape. It was exactly what he wanted, a new basket to transport the pigeons.

'Go on, Corrie, open it up,' Jimmy urged, and pulled the Christmas paper away from the sides of the hamper.

Corrie's jaw dropped even further when he raised the lid of the wicker basket and peered in. 'Awh,' he gasped. 'Thanks dad,' offering his dad a kiss on the lips and reaching into the basket.

Donna leaned forward. 'While you're dishing out

the kisses don't forget about your mum.'

Corrie responded by drawing his parents close and nuzzling his face in between theirs. Jimmy swallowed hard and Donna gripped the two of them for grim death. She was fighting a wave of panic and thinking that she would never let them go.

'Come on, Corrie, we'd better put the pigeons out the back before everybody scares the shite out of them.' Jimmy eased himself out of Donna's grip and pecked her softly on the cheek. In response to her tacit anguished plea he sucked in his breath through his teeth and winked at her solemnly.

Thinking it unlikely that Shane had finished work for the night Donna, nevertheless, turned and slowly scanned the room looking for her. She was surprised when she saw Munro standing in the bay window, looking decidedly out of place and nursing a long can of McEwens Export that Old Davey had thrust into his hand. 'What on earth are you doing here?' she asked him, trying to imagine what he must be thinking of the Macintyres and their antics. She didn't have to imagine what the Macintyres thought of him. They had smelled money and treated him accordingly.

'I got an invitation from your husband the day we went to the clinic. He said it was a surprise party and that I wasn't to mention it to anybody. Especially you.'

'It was a surprise all right,' Donna smiled. 'But I don't know what you must be thinking about this lot.'

'Well, it's always nice to see the locals in their native environment.'

Donna laughed and said, 'I think you mean, natives in their local habitat, don't you?'

Munro agreed, not that he was prepared to admit it. 'Interesting people,' he said, noticing Old Davey hovering to his right. Donna noticed him too and, recognising the look in his eyes, steered Munro away from him.

'If that toothless old bastard asks you for any money, tell him to piss off,' she warned him.

'Thanks for the advice,' Munro replied, more amused by her colourful turn of phrase than the description of her father-in-law.

'I wouldn't exactly call it advice. If I was you I would take it more as a warning.'

'Listen, Donna, I hope you don't mind me dropping by like this.'

Before she could answer her attention was caught by the two men sitting in the car on the other side of South Lambeth Road. 'No. Not at all. As long as you don't mind,' she answered vaguely, and moved closer to the window.

'I think you're wanted in the kitchen, doll.' It was Old Davey tugging on Donna's sleeve. 'Agnes wants a hand with the grub.'

Realising that it would be quicker to see for herself if her father-in-law was telling the truth or trying to prise her away from an intended victim Donna said, 'Remember what I told you, Steve,' and began squeezing around the dancers congested in the middle of the room.

'How's yer can going there, mate?' Old Davey

wasted no time making a move, his intention being to sell the beer at exorbitant prices.

'I'm glad you asked,' said Munro. 'I was just wondering where the can was.'

'You don't have to worry where it is mate. I've got plenty.'

'Oh, if you could just point me in the right direction I'm sure one will do me for the time being.'

'It'll cost you.'

'To go to the toilet?'

'Whaddaya mean, to go to the toilet? I thought you said you want a can?'

Munro laughed. 'Back home the can is the toilet.'

Old Davey shook his head. 'It's upstairs on the first landing,' he said walking away.

When she came out of the kitchen Donna could see that Munro was no longer by the window. Wanting to take another look at the occupants of the car illegally parked across the road she pushed past Old Davey prancing about at the edge of the dance floor, mimicking the dancers as best he could and performing his version of the twist. 'You didn't happen to see where the American geezer went to, did you Davey?' She decided it would be a waste of time to rebuke him for sending her into the kitchen for nothing.

'He must've went for a shite, cause he asked me in a roundabout kinda way where the lavvy was and I –.'

'Spare me the details.'

In the hallway Munro looked through the open

back door, attracted by light from the pigeon loft at the rear of the garden. He could see Jimmy and Corrie moving about in the loft before they shut the door. At the bottom of the stairs he almost bumped into Agnes. 'I beg your pardon, ma'am. I didn't see you in the dark.'

'Don't mention it.' Agnes smiled and followed him with her eyes as he stepped around her and made his way hesitantly up the dimly lit stairs. 'Second door on the left,' she called after him.

Curnow and Fallows sat in the car watching the parlour window. 'It must be some knees-up,' Curnow said, alighting from the car and stretching. He was viewing the timing of their visit with even greater misgivings.

Fallows thought differently. 'If they're having a piss-up our luck might be in. A gathering of the clan, eh?'

'That's all we need. A clan of them,' Curnow muttered under his breath and hurried across the road after his partner.

They found the front door open when they reached the top of the steps. After a moment's deliberation they entered the darkened hallway uninvited and paused outside the parlour door, listening to the wails of someone singing along with an old rock and roll record. As they looked at each other and cringed, the door opened suddenly and one of the Wheatsheaf regulars lurched out ahead of a blast of cigarette smoke, bouncing off the doorframe like a human bagatelle. 'On you go lads,' he said, and continued on out the back, pulling his trouser zip down before he reached the back door.

The detectives took one step into the room and craned over the heads of the crowd at a couple jiving and holding centre stage. Fallows turned to Curnow and nodded. 'Not bad, are they?' he whispered.

As the record ground to a halt the middle-aged man swung his partner around his neck and onto the floor where she performed her version of the splits. Those nearest the detectives turned to look at them and started a wave that quickly spread around the parlour until everyone, including the dancers, was looking at them in silence. Those farthest from the detectives held their noses and began complaining about the smell.

Fallows held up his badge. 'We're looking for Donna Macintyre,' he said, his confidence growing after a fleeting scan of the room convinced him that there was no one in attendance that he couldn't handle.

The gathering breathed a collective sigh of relief. All, for numerous and various reasons, had no wish to come under police scrutiny.

Donna stepped forward, having watched them cross the road. She hoped she could find out what they wanted and get rid of them before Jimmy and Corrie returned from the back yard. 'I'm Donna

Macintyre,' she told the detectives and pushed past them into the hallway, drawing them with her.

'Is there somewhere private we can have a quiet word, Donna?' Fallows spoke in the pleasant manner he reserved for dealing with goodlooking women, the same suave approach that he often referred to as his bedside manner.

'This is as private as it gets around here,' Donna replied, focusing on the back door.

Curnow followed her eyes to the back door, feeling more ill at ease by the second. 'Listen Donna, I'll tell you what it is. We need a sample of your handwriting. So if you'd oblige me by writing the words "care if you got somebody," on this piece of paper we'll let you get back to the party. Somebody's birthday, is it? I saw a cake.'

The back door swung open violently, crashing the handle into the wall behind it and sending chips of plaster flying. As if the noise hadn't startled them enough the sight of Jimmy Macintyre framed in the doorway was nothing less than terrifying.

Jimmy glared at them and said, 'Aye, it is somebody's birthday and I don't remember inviting the pair of you.'

Neither detective bothered to ask who he was.

'Take it easy, Jimmy,' Curnow said, offering his hand. 'We just want to have a quiet word with your missus. Don't worry, she's not in any trouble. We just want a sample of her handwriting so that we can eliminate her from our inquiries. It'll only take a moment.'

Ignoring the proffered hand Jimmy stared at the detective, forcing him to look away. 'She'll be giving you fuck all,' he stated.

The detectives, knowing that they had been baited, looked at each other nervously. Curnow's eyes counselled caution.

Fallows played his ace first up. 'We can always finish this little chat down at the station, if you like? Or you can let your missus give us a sample of her handwriting and we'll let you get back to the party.'

'You'll let me go back to the party, will you?' Jimmy sneered, and positioned himself between the detectives and the front door. 'And who the fuck do you think would stop me? Not you.'

The message was received loud and clear. Curnow wanted to withdraw immediately. Fallows saw strength in numbers and stepped forward boldly, but only level with his partner. Jimmy continued his cold stare and turned side on to them. With a flick of his head he ordered Donna to get behind him.

Donna recognised the look in her husband's eyes and moved quickly, knowing that once he started it would be impossible to stop him. 'It's all right Jimmy,' she whispered. 'I don't mind doing it. Honestly. It'll get it over and done with.'

'Fuck them,' Jimmy snapped. 'They're getting nothing.'

'Listen, Jimmy.' Curnow spoke in a conciliatory and condescending manner. 'There's no need for this.

We only want to eliminate Donna from our inquiries. That's all.'

Fallows added. 'I'm sure you'd like to continue with the current goodwill the lads up West extend to your wife.'

'Ha.' Jimmy pointed directly into the detective's face and spoke with his teeth clenched, 'Every time you open your mouth you come out with a threat. Now the next time you do that, I'm going to take a hold of you and kick your cunt in.'

Donna tugged at Jimmy's sleeve and pointed at Corrie standing in the doorway at the top of the back steps. No amount of tugging or pointing would have distracted him if Corrie had not been standing in his direct line of vision. 'Go and sort the new pigeons out, Corrie, and I'll be there in a minute. There's a good boy.' Jimmy waved him away.

'Nice boy you've got there.' Curnow smiled awkwardly, hoping to defuse the situation.

'Come here quick, dad,' Corrie urged, beckoning with his hand.

The detectives were forced to stand aside when Jimmy pushed past them and put his arm around Corrie. 'What's the matter son? Are you OK? Are the pigeons all right?'

'Come and take a look.' Corrie ran off towards the loft.

Jimmy hesitated momentarily. 'Give them pair of bastards nothing,' he said, jabbing a finger directly at Donna. 'I'll only be a minute.'

Donna followed them as far as the back door and watched them all the way to the pigeon loft. 'Quickly, give me the pencil,' she asked Curnow, impatiently shaking her hand, looking urgent.

The detective handed her the pencil and turned his clipboard to face her. 'Just write "care if you've got somebody",' he said, following her eyes to the back door.

To waste time Donna purposely dropped the pencil. While the detectives fumbled for a replacement she bent down and scanned the darkened floor, stealing glances at the back door, expecting Jimmy to return immediately.

Jimmy looked at the tiny eggs that Corrie was pointing at and grinned, just like his son. He drew Corrie close and kissed him on top of the head. Corrie put his arms around his waist and buried his face in his chest. 'You stay here and keep an eye on them, son, and I'll be back in a wee minute.' Jimmy waited until he was clear of the loft before he quickened his stride.

Donna saw him coming and said, 'Found it. Quick, what do you want me to write?'

In near-panic Curnow replied, 'Care if you've got somebody.'

Judging Jimmy's progress along the garden path, stalling, Donna said, 'What's that supposed to mean?'

'It's not meant to mean anything. Just write the bloody words, will you?' The pressure was proving too much for Fallows.

Gripping the clipboard Donna wrote as directed. 'There,' she said, handing back the clipboard. 'If I was you I'd take this and get the hell out of here.'

As he reached the back door Jimmy was in time to see a sudden draught catch the front door and slam it shut behind the departing detectives. Both policemen thought that Donna was responsible.

With his teeth clenched and his jaw set square Jimmy backed Donna against the wall. 'Where'd them fucken pair of snakes go?' He was in two minds whether or not to go after them or wait until he'd heard what Donna had to say.

Donna replied with equal venom. 'Who do you think you're talking to? This isn't one of your lackeys, you know.' She had reasonable grounds to be brave. If he'd lifted his hand to her, it would have been for the first time.

Jimmy looked at the front door, fighting the urge to put his fist through it. 'Did you, or did you not, write anything down for those two cunts? That's all I want to know.'

Her moment of hesitation was answer enough to send Jimmy running towards the door.

Munro, listening from the landing above, took the opportunity and sneaked down the stairs. Encountering Donna in the hall he raised his eyebrows and nodded towards the front door. 'What was all that about?'

'I've got no idea.' Donna took him by the arm and pushed him into the parlour. She was thinking that the less he knew on that score the better.

Across the road the detectives were congratulating themselves on a job well done when their attention was drawn, by way of an angry driver continually sounding his car horn, to Jimmy Macintyre stuck in the middle of the road between the opposing lanes of traffic. 'By the look of him I don't think he's on his way to the Paki's for a packet of ciggies, do you?' Curnow undid his seat belt to gain access to the car keys wedged at the bottom of his trouser pocket.

'I doubt it, but I'm not in the least bit interested in finding out. Hurry up, will you?' Fallows said, dispensing with the bluster.

The same rush of traffic that was preventing Jimmy from moving away from the centre of the road was also stopping the detectives from driving off. Jimmy could see that the car had its indicator lights on and its front wheels angled towards the traffic. He made a lunge for the other side of the road, enduring another fusillade of pumping horns.

'Up yours too,' he shouted, and presented himself squarely in front of the unmarked police car.

'Drive over him,' Fallows urged.

'Too many witnesses.' Curnow pointed at the Pakistani shopkeeper and his family lined up on the footpath to see what all the noise was about.

Fallows wound down his window and called out to Jimmy, 'Would you mind getting away from the front of the car? You're interfering with police business.'

Turning to his partner he added, 'Now you can run over the bastard.'

'Nah, we better see what he wants. There would be too much paperwork.' Curnow switched off the engine and watched Jimmy move onto the pavement and approach the open passenger window. He was glad that it was his turn to drive.

Jimmy looked through the window and for several moments silently focused on the passenger's nervous grin. Turning suddenly he ordered the shopkeeper and his family back inside. When his original request met with some resistance he shouted, 'Go on, Ali. Get to fuck when I tell you.'

Curnow didn't like the look of it. 'Watch yourself, Fallows,' he whispered.

Focusing on the clipboard resting on the detective's lap Jimmy considered grabbing for it, or at least the top page, where a sample of his wife's handwriting could be clearly seen. He saw Fallows tighten his grip on the clipboard and knew that if he lunged for it he was in danger of being dragged along by the car. Instead, he reached in, gripped Fallows by the lapels of his suit jacket and yanked him headfirst through the open window. With the flat of his foot firmly pressed against the car door he hauled him the rest of the way out and dumped him on the pavement, still clutching the clipboard.

Fallows scurried on his hands and knees over to the tiles at the bottom of the shop window. Curnow leapt from behind the wheel and ran around the front of the car, in his haste, struggling for traction. At the pavement's edge he stopped abruptly and held up his open hands. 'Easy now, Jimmy,' he pleaded. 'We don't want this to get out of hand, now do we?'

Jimmy, knowing by the look in their eyes that neither man was prepared to make the first move, casually bent down and tore the top page from the clipboard. 'The next time either one of you pair of cunts comes around here and touches something that doesn't belong to you it'll be the last thing you ever touch. Get the message.'

Both detectives remained silent until Jimmy was halfway up the steps to No. 38. 'No respect for the law, that's his problem,' Fallows said and stooped to retrieve the clipboard. 'Who does he think he is, anyway?'

'Get in the car,' Curnow barked, annoyed that he had gone against his better judgement in confronting Jimmy Macintyre in the first place. The fact that they were not on official police business, with no prospect of assistance from the uniformed branch, only exacerbated the problem.

Now that the danger had passed Fallows became decidedly braver. 'I'm for just going straight back in there and placing him under arrest,' he said, knowing full well the impracticality of such a move.

'So what are you going to charge him with?' Curnow answered sarcastically. 'Stealing a page from an inquiry that doesn't exist, or assaulting a police officer in the course of investigating a non-existent case? Have a bit of sense, will you?'

Fallows shrugged his shoulders. 'Well, if you're so clever, what have you got in mind? At least my way we found out that Jimmy Macintyre was desperate not to give us a sample of his wife's handwriting. That must tell us something, surely?'

'Not really. No matter what we were after he wasn't going to give us it. Besides, his old lady didn't seem to have any problem obliging.'

'Where does that leave us then?'

'Did you check her handwriting against the sample when I handed you the clipboard?'

'What are you talking about?' Fallows scoffed. 'That lunatic showed up before I had a chance. Did you?'

'How could I? You snatched it off me as soon as we got in the car. Remember?'

'What now?' Fallows asked.

'Simple. We'll just tell the guvner everything we found out and let him work it out. I think we've done enough for one night. Talk about over and above the call of duty.'

'I'll drink to that.'

'And I'll join you.'

As the unmarked car cleared Westminster Bridge and turned towards Whitehall the mobile phone in Curnow's coat pocket began to ring. 'Blast,' Curnow said and handed the phone to Fallows. Fallows took the call, intermittently saying, 'Yes sir.' On hanging up he told Curnow. 'The drink will have to wait. Tate wants to see us right away. Go back towards Westminster Abbey.'

Donna was sitting at the bottom of the stairs when Jimmy stormed back through the front door and waved the sheet of paper in front of her. 'You know what this is all about, don't you?' he ranted. 'That fucken diary of yours, that's what. Have you no sense? Couldn't you see what the pair of bastards were up to? I'm surprised at you, Donna. I really am.'

'I'm surprised at you being surprised at me,' she answered glibly.

The hardened look on Jimmy's face softened gradually and gave way to the hint of a smile. 'You make me laugh sometimes, Donna, you really do.' He sat beside her on the stairs, placed an arm around her shoulders and drew her close. 'Shit,' he said suddenly and sat straight up, 'I forgot all about our Corrie. He'll be wondering where the hell I got to.'

'Stay where you are.' Donna placed a restraining hand on his knee. 'He came looking for you again and I took him up to bed. He's been staying up far too late since you got out, Jimmy. We're going to have to settle him back into his normal routine.'

'Christsake, Donna. He's been getting plenty of rest during the day. You can only sleep so much, you know.' Jimmy began tapping the sheet of paper with the back of his fingers. 'Anyway, why were you so keen to give the police a sample of your handwriting when you knew it had to be connected to that bloody diary? You should know by now that you never give those bastards anything.' His tone was both gentle and probing.

'Ha ha. With you around I knew they wouldn't be leaving with anything. You don't think I'm that stupid, do you?'

Jimmy's eyes narrowed. 'Very clever. I think I might have underestimated you. That was well done.'

'It was either that or incriminate myself by refusing to give them a sample. Sort of like refusing a breath test.'

'Anyway, no harm done.' Jimmy got to his feet and looked down at her. 'Those two are obviously involved in a little extra-curricular activity, otherwise this place would've been crawling with uniforms by now. And without this piece of paper the pair of bastards are none the wiser.'

'Yeah. As long they've got enough sense between them to work out that by giving them a sample of my writing I was proving that I had nothing to hide. Anyway, we'll just have to wait and see.'

'I'm convinced they're doing their own thing, you know. The cavalry's well overdue.'

'You're saying that if they don't come back straight away, it means they're at the fanny? They're too young to be mentioned in the diary. Obviously they're acting for someone else.'

'Exactly. It looks as if that idiot Gilfeather, or

whoever's got your diary, is farting around with a senior member of our illustrious police force. If you think back far enough a name might spring to mind. Any clues?'

'Hardly,' she said. 'It's not a high priority remembering johns.'

'Give it some thought and let me know. I'm just going up to see Corrie before he goes to sleep.'

'Wouldn't you be better off getting that lot out so that he can get to sleep?' Donna called after him, directing his attention to the noise coming from the parlour.

In the flat, bathed in the murky glow from the street lights and the beams of passing cars fleetingly playing on the walls, Jimmy saw that the made-up bed-settee was undisturbed and he crept into the bedroom, listening to the muffled sounds of the sing-a-long reverberating from the floor below. Standing beside the double bed he looked down at the sleeping boy, smiled and stooped to kiss him on the forehead. 'Lucky boy,' he whispered and pulled up a chair beside the bed. 'You're looking more like your mum every day. Night night, son.'

Curnow and Fallows pulled into the kerb along from the busy hamburger stall opposite Westminster Abbey. They witnessed a ragtag collection of the homeless and other people of the night mingling with the more affluent slumming it after a night on the town. Occasionally one of the down and outs could be seen asking for the price of a cup of coffee.

'I don't suppose this waste of space has got a liquor licence?' Fallows joked and followed his partner onto the pavement, doubling his step to fall in line.

'You'd have more chance of getting a snort of coke,' Curnow replied and stepped up to the chest-high counter. 'Two teas please.' When the aroma of frying onions got too much for him he added, 'You'd better giv'us a couple of your hamburgers,' and flashed his badge for payment. Fallows nodded in agreement and stepped to one side, allowing the woman standing behind him access to the counter. When she was in front of him and Curnow had turned to face him, Fallows grinned and simulated entering her from behind. Curnow shook his head and walked to the edge of the pavement.

'That little trick of yours is going to backfire on you one of these days,' Curnow told him, and nodded towards the car sitting behind a black Sierra.

Chief Superintendent Tate strode towards the detectives with an unmistakable air of authority. Fallows and Curnow approached him holding their hamburgers and teas out to the side. 'Evening, guv,' they said in unison.

The chief superintendent took one look at the burgers brimming with onions and steered the detectives away from his car. 'What have you got for me?' he asked.

Fallows took an oversized bite of his burger and

half-turned to face the other way. He needn't have bothered. Curnow knew that the question had been directed at him and began relating their night's activities as quickly and efficiently as he could. But not fast enough to finish before his untouched tea and hamburger had gone cold.

The anguish first showed on Tate's face at the onset of Jimmy Macintyre's inclusion in the story. It steadily increased until he looked as if he was in pain. 'It was a mistake to approach Macintyre's wife while he was around. You should've waited for the opportunity to get her alone.'

'With respect, sir,' Fallows cut in, 'we felt we had to act before she got wind of what we were doing. Word travels fast up West.'

Tate shook his head. 'You said she was quite willing to give you a sample of her handwriting. She didn't use her left hand or anything like that?'

'I was watching her like a hawk, sir,' said Fallows.

'OK then,' Tate continued, 'what can we deduce from that? Either this has got nothing to do with her or she's trying to divert attention away from herself by appearing to be willing to give us a sample. Eh? Them's questions we have to ask ourselves. Maybe she was confident that that nutter of a husband of hers would react exactly as he did and retrieve the sample before we had a chance to look at it. She's cunning enough.'

'You know her quite well, do you sir?' Fallows grinned.

Tate moved quickly towards his car. 'When you've been around as long as I have, chummy, you get to know a lot of folk.'

'What do you want us to do now, sir?' Curnow followed him to the car, waiting while his boss reached across and wound down the passenger side window.

The chief superintendent's eyes narrowed; he stared at Curnow as if he wasn't there. Then, focusing, he answered, 'I don't want you to do anything other than forget everything you've just told me. I'll take it from here. Understand?'

EIGHTEEN

'Ah there you are, Donna,' Munro said, shouting to be heard above the continuing din. 'I think I'll make myself scarce,' he added, grimacing and nodding at the crowd.

Donna, her pained smile indicating that she understood, put her hand on his shoulder and walked him as far as the door. 'Catch you later,' she said.

Returning to the party she checked her watch, thinking that it was about time for Shane to show a face. She'd half-expected to see her ages ago, seeing that most of the Wheatsheaf regulars had emptied out into Agnes Macintyre's parlour long before closing time.

In a way she was glad that Shane had failed to show. She was uncomfortable with the drunken partygoers and figured – only because Corrie had gone to sleep for the night and Jimmy was home to look after him – that she would be better off going to work. The thought of not reaching her minimum nightly budget was slowly niggling away at her. The quicker she reached her targeted level of savings the quicker she could get off the game and lead her family to a normal life. A night missed at this end was a night tacked on the other end.

If only I didn't have to share Jimmy with half the drunks from the Wheatsheaf I might stick around, she told herself, and checked her watch again. 'That's it,' she said aloud, to no one in particular, and began forcing her way through the crowd, intent on going upstairs to change into her working clothes.

When she walked into the bedroom she wasn't surprised to see Jimmy still sitting in the chair, looking down at the sleeping boy. Draping her arms around him from behind she said, 'I don't know how he can sleep with all that noise. He must be exhausted.'

Jimmy responded by clutching her arms to his chest and smiling up at her.

'I'm just going to get ready and take myself off to work. The quicker I get the stash up the quicker we can get the hell out of here.' Donna said, her mind wandering. Jimmy's gentle touch had kindled a desire.

'You'll be all right, will you?'

Caressing his chest she sighed and whispered, 'Do you think the crowd downstairs could spare you for a while longer?'

'Spare me? What're you talking about?'

She answered by delicately undoing the buttons of his shirt and gently massaging down over his stomach, finding him hard by the time her fingers crept under the waistband of his trousers.

Jimmy reached behind him and held her by the back of the neck. 'Stay home,' he said softly.

'No, no. I can't.' She had already decided to call in on Shane on the way to work.

'Please yourself.' Jimmy faked indignation.

'Are you going to stay here with Corrie?'

'I've no intentions of budging.'

'In that case you can drag yourself away for a couple of minutes?' Donna rested her chin on his shoulder and nibbled on his ear.

'Umm, I think I can manage that.' Jimmy stood and drew Donna to him, delicately exploring with his tongue the area just inside her mouth.

'Ohh,' she responded, thrusting her pelvis against his as she felt him reach behind her and grip her by the buttocks. She took her weight on her arms and wrapped her legs around his waist, sucking his tongue into her mouth as he walked her towards the bed-settee in the other room. As one they tumbled onto the bed, tearing at the lower parts of each other's clothing. When he felt her take him in her hand he resisted the urge to enter her immediately, instead succumbing to her probing, sensuous kiss. After the daily, mindless drudgery of unsatisfying sex she had a need to make love. No quirks or pandering to deviate tastes here. Just unequivocal love. She needed to be loved. Real love.

Breaking from the kiss she directed Jimmy to her

breasts, feeling him cup them in his hands and nuzzle and kiss and suck each of them in turn. A push on top of his head and she felt his tongue trace a path over her navel and pubic hair, lingering when it parted the lips of her vagina, probing for her button-hard clitoris. Arching her back she gasped, her jaw shuddering as the wave of orgasms began. After the climax, becoming soft and limp, she whispered breathlessly, 'I want you inside me.'

Later, when she became aware again of the noise carrying through the floor and the streak of light from the partly-open bedroom door falling on her face Donna turned to Jimmy and gave him a gentle nudge with her elbow. 'You awake?' she asked.

'Aye. I was just lying here thinking,' he answered and hoisted himself up onto the pillow.

Donna rested her head on his bare chest and began absentmindedly running her fingers through the dark hairs extending down from his chest and thinning out on the way to his navel. 'Oh yeah. And what are you thinking about?'

'I was just lying here thinking that you're dead right. We've got to put everything behind us and start again.'

'I thought we'd already agreed on that?'

'We did. But it's only just dawned on me that you're right.' Without mentioning that he intended to finish the business with Archie Kemp first he diverted his eyes from high on the wall facing him and looked down at the top of her head. He tensed his muscles and waited for the inevitable reaction.

Donna slapped him on the stomach. 'You better believe it,' she said, kicking the sheet off her legs and springing out of bed.

'Come here,' Jimmy cajoled, holding his arms out wide.

Donna stopped rummaging in the chest of drawers and looked at him sideways.

Jimmy added a wry smile and held his arms out wider. 'Come on,' he coaxed.

She relented and sat on the edge of the bed, looking at him dewy-eyed then falling into his open arms.

'It would probably be the death of Corrie if anything happened to you, Jimmy. You know that, don't you? You realise it would take the fight out of him.' Her head rose with his deep sigh and she felt him kiss the top of her head.

'I'll be doing nothing to jeopardise our Corrie. You can rest assured of that.'

Donna pecked him on the lips. 'Promise me again,' she demanded, easing out of his arms and returning to the drawers.

'What did I just tell you?' he replied, raising his voice and pretending to be insulted. 'How many times do you want me to tell you?'

Plucking her working underwear from the open top drawer she sat at the foot of the bed facing away from him and continued dressing in silence, feeling his eyes on her. Wearing her black coat she pulled on the skintight black leather gloves and watched him get out of bed and approach, gripping his rockhard penis at the base. She took it in her hand and watched his eyes glaze over as he reacted to the softness of the leather. Without letting go she led him back to the bed. 'Not when I'm dressed for work,' she smiled.

It worried her that when his libido increased it always corresponded with the prospect of violence. Backing from the room she blew him a kiss and said, 'Be good.'

In South Lambeth Road she hailed a taxi about to pull into the empty rank in the side street opposite. 'Drop me around at the Wheatsheaf for a minute, then you can take me to Archer Street, up West,' she told the driver, and prepared to rebuff the customary attempt at small talk.

Donna, together with a much smaller than normal crowd, watched Shane finish the last number of her last set like she was only going through the motions. As soon as she stepped off stage and out from under the rose-tinted spotlights Shane spotted Donna standing by the bar and her face lit up. 'Old grizzly guts there is raging because half his customers left to go to the party at No. 38. They tell me he hates it if a party starts before closing time.' Shane nodded over her shoulder at the landlord standing in his usual spot at the end of the bar and looking up whenever the door opened, smiling if someone came in, glowering if customers left.

'He's a sleekit git, my Jimmy. You know he never

breathed a word about the party to me. He knows I wouldn't have put up with it. Two birthday parties in the one year. Have you ever heard the like of it?' Donna shook her head and cast her eyes to the ceiling.

'I'm sure he had good intentions,' Shane replied.

'I might have stayed if you'd been there.'

'Wild horses won't stop me going now that I'm finished for the night. Why don't you stick around until I get ready and I'll come back with you.'

'Actually, I've already decided to go to work. But eh, I was wondering if we could have a bit of a natter. I might need a favour.'

'Sure. If I can. Is everything all right?'

Donna traced the pattern in the carpet with the heel of her shoe and answered, 'I'm not sure but I don't want to take any chances.'

'Anything you'd care to discuss?' Shane was careful not to pry.

'Maybe one day, but eh, I was wondering if you could put me and Corrie up for a while? Not now. Only if I need somewhere in a hurry.'

'You're not leaving Jimmy, are you?' Shane was astounded.

'No, no,' Donna laughed. 'Nothing like that. He'd probably be coming with us.'

'Ohh,' Shane winked. 'A man about the house. Stay as long as you want.'

'Thanks pet.' Donna leaned in and pecked her on the cheek. 'Some day I'll explain it all to you.'

'Don't go away, I haven't had a chance to go to the loo since I came off stage.' Squeezing her legs together and performing an impromptu jig Shane made a face and darted towards her allocated toilet in the private quarters upstairs.

'Wipe the lipstick off your cheek,' Donna called after her, paused and headed to the public phone in the entrance. She smiled at the bouncer standing near the door and began flicking through her address book, stopping at the spot where she'd concealed Anton Winters' phone number. Dialling, the phone rang once before it was answered. 'Is that you, Anton?' she responded to his curt greeting. 'It's Donna Macintyre. I told you I would get in touch if there were any developments.'

There was no mistaking the frosty edge to Anton's voice. 'Then why didn't you tell me that Jimmy was on his way to see me yesterday?'

'Christ. Has he been to see you already? That's one of the reasons why I was calling. I kept trying your number but your line was engaged. I thought your phone was off the hook.' Donna didn't bother asking him if he'd betrayed her to her husband. She knew she would have been the first to know as soon as Jimmy had walked in the door.

'Yes, already. But don't worry, our little arrangement still stands. I didn't tell him anything he didn't already know.'

'What did he say?' Donna was wondering if Jimmy had mentioned the diary.

'What do you think he said? He wanted to know why I paid you a visit.'

'Is that all?'

'He knows I'm looking for Gilfeather. But enough of that. I called around to see you tonight. I was told that a couple of detectives, Curnow and Fallows from Vine Street, had been doing the rounds of Soho asking all sorts of questions and making a nuisance of themselves. Apparently they were trying to match the handwriting of selected working girls with a sample they were carting around with them. I hear they were very interested in you. I hear they even made a house call.'

Donna, realising that he must be having her watched, approached the subject cautiously. 'That's the other thing I was calling about, Anton,' she lied. 'But seeing that you already know, maybe you can tell me what the police were up to?' It was Donna's way of pleading ignorance.

Anton laughed. 'Spare me the bullshit, Donna. I'm not in the mood.'

'The police asked me nicely for a sample of my handwriting and I gave them one. Anyway, according to you I wasn't the only one they asked.'

'What about the carry-on with Jimmy dragging the copper out the window of the car? I'd say that that was the actions of somebody with something to hide.'

Continuing with the fabrication Donna laughed and said, 'That's news to me, but I'm not surprised. You know as well as I do that Jimmy wouldn't give them breath.'

'Where are you now?' Anton said at length.

'I'm in a pub.'

'Right. Unless you want me to call around there, just you get yourself on up to Archer Street right away. I want to discuss this further.'

As the phone went dead in Donna's hand the taxi driver came through the outer door convinced that his fare had done a runner. On seeing Donna he smiled and pointed to the taxi, indicating that he would be waiting outside.

Donna stepped onto the pavement and turned to address the doorman standing back out of the wind. 'Can you please tell Shane that I'll catch up with her later.'

At close to midnight Donna alighted from the taxi in Archer Street wondering if she was making the right decision. It didn't help matters when she saw a well-dressed man, drunk and fat and ugly, being seen off the premises by the minder. At the top of the stairs the girl who occupied the room next to hers was hurling dog's abuse and instructing the minder to, 'Giv'im one for me, Freddie.'

'One of those nights, is it?' Donna stated, squeezing past her and turning the key in the lock.

Lavender, as she preferred to be called, was a bottle blonde with greenish blue eyes, full lips and a reasonable set of cheekbones. She was good-looking, but a big nose, accentuated by her platinum hair, detracted from the overall package and dropped her down a division. 'You're telling me,' she said. 'That's the second punter I've had to fling out tonight. Is it a full moon or something?'

Donna opened the door and as usual looked behind it and under the bed before she hung up her coat on the wire hanger dangling from the frieze. Lavender followed her into the room uninvited and was looking around as if she was seeing it for the first time. It dawned on Donna that she *was* seeing it for the first time and it surprised her that Lavender had set foot in the room at all. The girls in the building were in the habit of keeping themselves to themselves.

'Anton was around earlier looking for you. He didn't seem too pleased to find out you weren't here. He seemed even less pleased when he found out that the place had been crawling with cops.' Lavender sat on the edge of the bed and bounced up and down a couple of times, testing the mattress. 'I was thinking that if you had to give up the room, I wouldn't mind putting my name down for it. If it's all right with you, that is?'

'I don't work for Anton so why on earth would I want to give up the room?' Donna strode over to her and looked down accusingly.

'It was something I heard them say.' Lavender replied, looking like a schoolgirl anxious to pass on a secret. 'I could hardly miss it. Anton was talking to the minder right outside my door.'

'No doubt you had your ear to the door.'

'No doubt,' Lavender agreed.

Desperately trying not to show her concern, Donna swallowed hard and nonchalantly went to fetch her cigarettes, checking her handbag first, then her coat. She was determined to find them before she listened to another word. 'You haven't got a cigarette by any chance, have you?' she said at length.

'Sorry, don't use them. Not ordinary ones anyway.'

'Wait here and I'll bring us back a coffee,' Donna told her and hurried from the room clutching her bag.

Outside there was no sign of the minder or the man he had been dragging down the stairs. Following a trail of fresh blood to the adjoining lane Donna found the man lying unconscious along the bottom of the wall. 'Bastard,' she muttered angrily, making a mental note to apologise to Jimmy for condemning his assessment and handling of the minder. Walking on, she entered the cafe three doors down on the other side of the street, anxious to get served and get back to find out what Lavender was on about. 'Two coffees and a packet of –'

The muffled explosion that stopped her in mid-sentence sounded close. Startled, she, the shopkeeper and several other customers gaped at each other in disbelief and began edging towards the door. Without exception they all thought that the IRA had been active in nearby Piccadilly or Shaftesbury Avenue.

At the door of the cafe, peeking around one another, the customers were surprised to see a thick cloud of smoke billowing from the stairwell of a building opposite. The shock registered on Donna's face as she began to run, the sound of her heels breaking the deathly stillness that had settled over the street. She stopped close to the door of the building where she worked and stepped back, repelled by the thickening smoke. Frantically she looked around for help.

Slowly, a large black dog emerged from the smoke, completely disorientated and bordering on collapse. With the smoke stinging her eyes Donna approached it warily, thinking, in her confused state of mind that she would shoo the hapless animal away. When it failed to respond she stamped her feet and clapped her hands, prompting the big black head painfully and mechanically to look up at her. At the sight of the distinctive greenish blue eyes pleading with her, her hand shot up to her gaping mouth and she jumped back in absolute horror. She was looking at a woman, almost completely charred and naked, crawling on her hands and knees.

In her panic Donna ignorantly placed her hands on the woman's blackened shoulders and guided her towards the red-brick wall, leaving her sitting up with her legs apart and her arms dangling by her side, like a discarded marionette. As the burned skin began to peel in sheets from the woman's face and body and the deep facial wounds refused to bleed Donna fell to her knees and looked into the shocked and disbelieving eyes. She was aware of the emergency vehicles' sirens and the presence of others, seemingly reluctant to get too close to the abhorrent sight.

'Listen, Lavender, the ambulance is on its way. You can hear the sirens getting closer.' Donna spoke soothingly through her tears, but stopped short of touching her again. There was no sign of recognition in Lavender's eyes.

'What happened, Lavender? How did this happen?' she urged.

'I'm all right. Honest, I'll be OK in a minute.' Lavender answered all too quickly and coherently. To Donna and the others standing around in shock her words exemplified the hopelessness of her condition. It was like watching a corpse speak.

'I'll take over, miss.' Donna became aware of two ambulance officers, one kneeling either side of her. It was a calming influence amid the controlled frenzy of the fire brigade dragging hoses and shouting orders.

The phone in Jimmy's inside pocket started ringing, startling him. He doubted if the call was for him. He had only commandeered the thing yesterday and was yet to tell anyone that he had it.

'Is that you, Jimmy?' the voice said.

'Aye. Who's that?' Jimmy walked to the bedroom door and checked to see that Corrie was still asleep.'

'It's Kenny the bouncer. I gave you the mobile phone.'

'Aye, right enough, Kenny. I didn't recognise the voice. There's a bit of a party going on downstairs.

Hey listen, pal, while I've got you, what number is this contraption?'

The bouncer recited the number, continuing when Jimmy repeated it after writing it down on a scrap of paper, 'Listen, mate, you better get your arse up here right away! That building where your missus works has just gone up. The whole place is crawling with the Old Bill and the fire brigade. And the ambulance has just carted a body away.'

Jimmy felt his knees go weak. 'Did you see who it was, Kenny?'

'I'm sorry, Jimbo. They had a sheet over the head. But they said it was a woman.'

Switching off the phone Jimmy hurried downstairs, uttering a prayer for the second time in his life. 'Please God in heaven, don't let it be Donna.'

'You all right Jimmy?' Mick said, responding to the wave that beckoned him into the hall. 'You look like shite.'

'I want you to nip up the stairs and look after Corrie for me.'

'What's up?'

'Nothing's up. I've just got to go a wee message.'

'You're no driving I hope, big man? You've had a few bevies, don't forget.'

Without responding Jimmy turned on his heel and headed for the car.

The drive up West was an ordeal, full of dreadful, morbid thoughts. Jimmy could visualise Corrie's face when he told him his mum was dead. He found himself rehearsing the words in his head. This gave way to thoughts of the funeral and the vision of the distraught family surrounding the lowering coffin. At that moment he realised just how empty his world would be without Donna.

Unable to drive any closer because of a road block, he parked the car in Rupert Street, just off Shaftesbury Avenue, and ran the short distance to the crowd blocking the narrow entrance to Archer Street. His first reaction was to find out if the dead body had been identified. Fear stopped him. The sight of the burned-out building where Donna worked, with its obvious concentration of damage on the first floor, did nothing to dispel his fears.

He waited until the policeman controlling the crowd at the top end of the street turned his back before he darted down the side of one of the fire engines and mingled with those the police had segregated for questioning. Donna wasn't one of them.

'Hey Sammy,' Jimmy said, recognising the owner of one of the all-night cafes, 'did you see where my Donna went?'

Sammy's 'No' sent a wave of panic surging through Jimmy's body. 'But she was here a few minutes ago,' Sammy added. 'I think she said something about going back to my shop to make a phone call. Hey Jimmy, did you know she was standing talking to me when this shit went up? Lucky girl.'

Jimmy picked him up and kissed him dead centre of his bald head.

'I think he likes me,' Sammy grinned.

Donna was second in line waiting to use the phone and making no contribution to the strange carnival atmosphere that prevailed in the shop. Doing his best not to startle her Jimmy tapped his wife on the arm. As she jumped back and sucked in her breath he doubted if he could have frightened her more if he'd tried.

'Jesus, Jimmy!' she said, closing her eyes and touching her forehead with the fingertips of her right hand. 'You frightened the –'

'Shite out of you,' Jimmy grinned, finishing the sentence for her. The relief of finding her unharmed, written all over his face, masked temporarily the realisation that she was in danger – a reality he had come to terms with on the way up West. He had already settled on an irrevocable course of action to deal with this. But right now all he wanted to do was get Donna away from here. To somewhere safe, while he worked out what to do – and to whom.

He wondered if her tear-stained face was a result of emotion or the consequences of standing too close to the smoke. 'You look like shite,' he told her, taking her by the hand and steering her through the shop and on out to the narrow lane at the rear.

'I hope you're not over the limit?' Donna said as soon as she set eyes on the car.

'Don't worry,' he told her. 'I've never been more sober in my life.'

To be on the safe side Jimmy kept his eyes

frequently on the rear-vision mirror and silently concentrated on his driving until they were well clear of Soho and heading over the Thames via Waterloo Bridge. Expecting not to get a word in edgewise while Donna furnished him with all the details of what had happened he found her persistent silence puzzling. He had made no allowance for shock.

'Well,' he said, when he was convinced that they weren't being followed, 'are you going to tell me what happened or do I have to do what Saddam Hussein did after he launched one of his Scud missiles?'

The absurdity of the question managed to penetrate the haunting thoughts of Lavender's charred body. 'What's it got to do with Saddam Hussein's missiles?'

'He had to run into the house and switch on the telly to see where they landed, that's what he did. And it looks like I'm going to have to do the same thing if you don't tell me what the fuck happened.'

'You're not saying it was a missile, are you?'

'Donna, are you winding me up? That was supposed to be a joke. You know, one of those things that are supposed to make you laugh.'

'I don't see anything to laugh about,' Donna said, sniffing back a tear. 'You didn't see the state poor Lavender was in.'

Jimmy looked suitably chastised. 'Umm. Lavender, eh. Bad, was she?'

Donna shook her head and sucked her breath in through her teeth. 'You should've seen her, Jimmy.

Burnt black. I thought she was a big dog the way she came crawling out. I'll never forget it as long as I live. I swear to God.'

'The fire must've been in her room then?' Jimmy had been convinced that the explosion was meant for Donna.

'She was in my room at the time, Jimmy. I'd only set foot out the door a couple of minutes earlier.'

'Bastards.' Instead of turning left towards Lambeth Palace Road and following the river in the direction of home Jimmy drove straight ahead along Waterloo Road into Newington. He intended circling Kennington and the local suburbs before heading home. Donna suddenly gasped and put her fingertips up to her lips, startling him and forcing him to check the rear-vision mirror again.

'What about Corrie?' Donna blurted out.

'Mick's looking after him. You don't think I'd –'

'Jimmy, go straight home and get him out of the house. For Godsake, hurry.'

Braking hard Jimmy took the next turn to his right, running an amber light.

'They're capable of anything,' Donna muttered.

'*They*? Is this Anton fucken Winters we're talking about here?'

Donna was lost for words. She could hardly explain to her husband that Anton had nothing to gain by killing her, and everything to gain by making sure she stayed alive. Unless the bomb, intended to intimidate, had been tossed into her room after she was seen to leave?

Jimmy continued. 'OK then. If it's not Anton fucken Winters then who is it? Is it your mate Gilfeather? Was it the prick who sent those two coppers to the house? Eh? It's got to be one of the three. Talk to me about this, Donna.'

'What's there to say? As far as I'm concerned you can take your pick.'

'I'll take my pick all right,' Jimmy said. 'I'll pick the three of them. I'll do them all in, just to make sure I get the right one.'

Horrified, Donna screamed, 'You'll do no such bloody thing. You'll just hide us somewhere until this blows over. Do you bloody well hear me?' After a pause she added. 'For Godsake, Jimmy, use a bit of sense. Nobody can harm us if they don't know where the hell we are.'

She's missing the point, Jimmy thought. I can't let these cunts get away with this. I've got to look at myself in the mirror.

'Well?' Donna urged.

'Where do you want to go then? Jimmy said, ignoring the main thrust of her argument. 'Scotland?'

Calmer now, she said, 'For Corrie's sake we have to be near the clinic. That means we have to stay in London. Just in case they find a donor.'

'A hotel'll cost money.'

'I was thinking about staying at Shane's.' Donna made no mention of the fact that she'd already cleared it with Shane. 'She might be at the party by now.'

'Fair enough, but what about this fire? You said

something about that poor girl being in your room. What was that all about?' Thanks to some jail time spent in the company of a suspected paramilitary bomber, one whose touch was similar, if not identical, to that evident in the Archer Street blast, Jimmy had someone to go to for advice. 'Tell me what happened before the blast.'

A solemn, almost tortured look replaced the trepidation on Donna's face. 'I was just standing there talking to Lavender. She was saying that Anton Winters had paid a visit. She said that he wasn't too pleased that the police had been around asking questions. She told me she overheard him talking to the minder right outside her door. Then she said a funny thing. Oh, by the way, you were right about the minder. What a nasty piece of stuff he turned out to be.' Donna stopped deliberately, wondering if it was prudent to continue. She rationalised that it was, thinking that any small diversion away from Gilfeather was justification enough.

'What do you mean funny?' Jimmy urged, ignoring the reference to the minder.

'It wasn't what she said as much as the way she said it. She asked me if I minded her putting her name down for my room, as if I wouldn't be needing it.'

'Is that right,' Jimmy stated, rather than asked. 'And this Lavender, or whatever it was you called her, was she in the habit of going into your room?'

'It was the first time she'd ever set foot in it.'

'Umm,' said Jimmy, reaching into his pocket for

the mobile phone. He was thinking about dropping Donna off and pursuing the matter alone. 'What's Shane's number?' he added, his thumb poised ready to press in the numbers.

Thinking that his driving was bad enough Donna relieved him of the phone. 'I could've managed,' Jimmy said.

'Yeah, but I'm ringing the Wheatsheaf to see if she's still there. Where'd you get this thing anyway?'

'I confiscated it,' he said, matter of factly.

'Oh. She's already left,' Donna said, talking into the phone. 'OK, thanks.' Turning to Jimmy she added, 'Did you hear that? Go straight home.'

'Where do you think I'm going?'

Jimmy pulled up at the kerb outside No. 38 and ran around to open the car door for Donna. He checked the streets again and ushered her up the steps, keeping his hands on her shoulders. As soon as the front door closed behind them he took her by the hand and led her into the parlour, smiling as if nothing had happened. The music was blaring and the party was still in full swing, a fair indication that all was in order at the house. Near the bay window Shane, cornered by William, responded gladly to Jimmy's delicate nod in the direction of the door.

Jimmy steered Donna back to the door, explaining to those shouting greetings from all around the room that he would be back in a minute. Shane had guessed by the strained smile on Donna's face that all wasn't well. The nod from Jimmy confirmed it.

'Giv'us a song, Jamesy,' William bellowed from across the room and began singing at the top of his voice, 'Oh flower of Scotland, when will we see yir likes again, that fought and died for yir wee bit hill and glen ...'

As soon as she cleared the parlour door Shane, suitably serious-faced, asked, 'Is everything all right?'

Jimmy waited until they were on the landing before he acknowledged the question. 'I want you to do me a wee favour, Shane,' he told her, putting his arm around her shoulder. 'I want you to put Donna and Corrie up for a couple of days, or whatever, while I get a few things sorted out.'

Shane grinned at Donna and nodded her head in agreement. Donna led the way into the flat. Mick, having heard their voices outside the door, was on his feet, eager to join the party. 'The wee man never opened his cheeper,' he said, making his way to the door.

'What's going on?' Shane said, turning to Jimmy when Donna hastened on into the bedroom.

'Ask Donna, she knows more about it than me.' Jimmy followed Donna into the bedroom, intending to tell her to get a move on. His heart skipped a beat when he saw her sitting on the edge of the bed, her chin quivering and silent, convulsive sobs shuddering her head and shoulders. He could see that Corrie, lying deathly white with his eyes closed, was failing to respond to her touch.

In panic, he shouted at the top of his voice, 'Corrie.'

As she spun around to face him Donna's chin

dropped and her eyes bulged in fright. Shane burst into the room minus one high heel and clutched the door for support. Through the haze of an exhaustion-induced sleep Corrie rubbed his eyes and wondered what all the fuss was about.

'Next time you want to waken somebody, Donna, don't bloody well pussyfoot around. You could give a man a heart attack doing that.'

'Don't talk to me about a heart attack.' Donna sighed with utter relief. 'I thought he was gone. Honest to God,' she added, turning away from Corrie and mouthing the words.

'What's happening, mum? Have they found a donor for me?' Corrie could think of no other reason why he would be plucked from his bed in the middle of the night.

'Not yet, son, but I'm sure it won't be long.' A look of utter disappointment was etched on Donna's face.

'Oh,' said Corrie.

Angrier now, at the thought that someone out there was trying to add to his family's misery, Jimmy waited impatiently for Donna to fill an overnight bag and herded everyone towards the car. He promised to return later for the rest of the gear. Once he satisfied himself that the coast was clear he drove towards Brixton, cutting through lanes and side streets that only a local could know. In Brixton, he lapped the dormant market and headed back towards Elephant and Castle, sticking to back streets once again. He exercised the same caution until the door of Shane's mews flat was securely locked behind them.

Corrie, fully awake now and invigorated by the sense of adventure, looked wide-eyed around the living room of the modernised apartment. Although nobody had explained what was going on he sensed the charge in the air. 'That's a smashing Christmas tree. It's exactly the same as the one you gave us,' he said, drawn by the flashing fairy lights in the corner.

'Would anyone like a drink?' Shane assumed the role of host, sharing Corrie's interpretation of the situation. 'What about you, Corrie? I've got some Milo.'

'Yes please,' he answered, grinning from ear to ear.

Jimmy shook his head. 'Not for me.' He was already eyeing the door and inching his way towards it.

'Where do you think you're going?' Donna fired at him. 'You're not thinking of leaving us on our own, are you?'

'Don't start,' he snapped. 'Nobody knows you're here. Why do you think I took us down all the back lanes? Giv'us a wee bit of credit.'

Not wanting to discuss the matter in front of Corrie Donna followed Jimmy over to the door.

Jimmy opened the door and turned. 'You be a good boy for your ma and I'll see you in the morning. And keep this door locked, Shane.'

Donna practically pushed him out into the hall. 'Just where the hell do you think you're going, Jimmy? And what am I supposed to tell those two, eh?'

'I'm sure you'll think of something.'

'Jimmy Macintyre, come back here this minute.'

As he passed Hyde Park on the way to Kilburn, two suburbs on, Jimmy remembered the mobile phone. He knew that the Harp had a late licence and wanted to find out how late, in case he was making the trip for nothing. He wasn't.

The Harp had seen better days. It seemed in harmony with its predominantly working-class customers, many of whom had yet to make it home from their jobs on the building sites. In the corner, through the customary haze of cigarette smoke, Jimmy saw a three-piece Irish band and steered towards the end of the bar that was as far away from them as he could get. He was over-dressed for this place, but the crowd singing along to 'Red Rose Cafe', paid him no attention. Unless he came into their direct line of vision.

A waist-high timber dado matching the front of the bar ran the extent of the lower walls. Above it, distributed about the room on the nicotine-stained paintwork, was a collection of Irish memorabilia consisting mainly of several old Guinness signs, a set of crossed hurley sticks and a few faded Irish tri-colours. There were cleaner patches on the walls, all within reach, where the souvenir hunters had been active. Some mirrors had been broken, presumably in fights. On a wall just in from the front door posters advertised the nightly entertainment.

Knowing that some of the people in attendance

liked nothing more than a good fight Jimmy moved carefully through the crowd, anxious not to bump anyone or antagonise them by looking at them for too long. He was as courteous as possible, but knew that the first one to take a liberty would get his head to play with. Nothing surer.

Dermot Mulholland, a regular customer when he wasn't doing time, saw him coming and moved to the end of the bar, seeking a wall at his back. Jimmy registered the move.

'Well if it isn't yer man Jimmy Macintyre.' Dermot smiled and held out his hand, reaching as far as he could, like a wary boxer touching gloves before a fight. Jimmy shook the hand and answered him in his own vernacular, 'What about yee?' he said, intently studying the man's eyes.

'What brings you all the way over to Kilburn, Jimmy? I thought you would've been tucked up in yer bed by now. The word is you've settled down. They say yer old lady's got you by the balls. How is Donna anyway?'

'She's all right, what about yourself?' Jimmy wondered if he was being paranoid, or if it was just a coincidence that Dermot had asked after Donna. Knowing Dermot as well as he did he had trouble convincing himself that it was the normal thing for him to do.

'Where's that fucken barman? Sure a man could die of thirst around here and nobody would take a blind bit of notice. Eugene, get your fucken arse up here and get me another pint of the good stuff. And you'd better fix me mate up with whatever he wants. Fuck him, give him a pint of Guinness. It'll do him the world of good.'

A resigned smile formed on Jimmy's face as he shrugged his shoulders and studied the mousy-haired Antrim man waving a ten pound note as bait to lure the barman away from his friends at the other end of the bar.

Somewhere in his mid-forties, with a full head of hair tied back in a ponytail, Dermot had a slim physique at odds with the amount of Guinness he put away. He had grey eyes and a thin upper lip camouflaged by an unfashionable Zapata moustache. His nose had been broken more times than he cared to remember.

'Christ of almighty, Dermot, we haven't seen hide nor hair of you all night long and now you want to drink us dry. And it nearly on closing time.' The young barman conspicuously winked at Jimmy, making sure that Dermot noticed and understood that he was only joking. 'Sure you've got a terrible thirst on you tonight, Dermot, so you have.'

The thick white froth from the Guinness lodged in Dermot's moustache when he drained half the pint glass with one effortless gulp. Most of the froth vanished with a practised flick of his tongue, the rest with a deft wipe with the back of his hand.

'What can I do for you Jimmy? I've a notion you never came all the way over to Kilburn to sip

Guinness like an Englishman. Get it into you man, before you give me a bad name.'

Tiring of the Irishman's annoying but good-natured banter, Jimmy laboured with a bigger mouthful. 'I need a favour, big man,' he whispered, glad of the relative quiet now that the band had left the stage for the night.

'What kind of a favour would we be talking about here, Jimmy? Would there be a small profit involved?' Dermot held up his hand, pressing his thumb and forefinger together.

'There's a monkey in it for you. But things must be bad if you can't do a wee favour for a friend without charging for it?' Jimmy knew he was stretching the truth by using the term 'friend'.

'Aye, right enough, you are a bit of a mate, I suppose. But what are mates for if we can't scratch each other's back. Eh?'

'You haven't changed much Dermot. I see you're still as mercenary as ever.'

Leaning in close enough for Jimmy to smell the Guinness on his breath Dermot said, 'A man has to make a quid somehow.'

Jimmy's eyes narrowed. 'That wouldn't extend to a bit of freelancing by any chance?'

Dermot's eyes darted left and right. 'We'd better talk about this elsewhere. They don't hold with that kind of talk around here. Very dangerous. Very dangerous indeed.' Dermot eased himself off the stool and drained the rest of his Guinness. Jimmy took another sip of his and abandoned it to the counter as soon as Dermot turned his back.

Instead of heading towards the exit door, as Jimmy expected, Dermot led them to a newly vacated alcove at the other end of the bar. 'Now what's this yer yabbering about?' he said.

'Did you hear about that blast up West tonight?' Jimmy kept his voice to little above a whisper.

'There was mention of it. Why?' Dermot suddenly seemed as suspicious as Jimmy.

'Because it was my Donna they tried to blow the shite out of.'

Dermot rested his elbows on the table and leaned in. 'Your missus isn't involved with any radicals, is she?'

'Donna? No chance.'

'No. I didn't think so.' The look on Dermot's face implied that Jimmy's reply posed more questions than it answered.

'Why?' Jimmy urged.

'Well, to tell you the truth Jimmy, certain people are wondering about that blast themselves. They're worried about the reference on the news that it had all the hallmarks of the Provisional IRA. They're not pleased about that.'

'They would be less pleased if they were me. I noticed a distinctive stamp as well.'

'The Provos claim their handiwork, Jimmy. Everybody knows that. Otherwise there'd be no point.'

'So I believe. But it doesn't stop me wondering if somebody's doing a bit on the side.'

'If one of the Provos was doing a bit on the side there's not a whole lot you could do about it, Jimmy. Even the SAS are no match for some of those guys.'

'Yes. But you are.'

Dermot laughed. 'I know we've done time together, Jimmy. And I know that you probably know more about me than what's good for you, but surely you don't expect me to pass on information the likes of that? We take care of that kind of business ourselves.'

'No. But you could tell me who put them up to it. That wouldn't be interfering with your business. Would it?'

Preening his moustache with thumb and forefinger Dermot turned and squinted towards the bar. 'You could be right. People like that need to be discouraged.'

'Don't forget there's a monkey in it for you.'

'Forget the monkey. This one's on the house.'

Jimmy went to the bar for a pen, jotted down the number of his mobile phone on a coaster and slipped it to Dermot. 'As quick as you can, eh?'

NINETEEN

Ignoring the residential parking restrictions Jimmy pulled up outside Shane's place and again scanned the length of the narrow mews. On alighting from the car he eyed the three milk bottles sitting outside a neighbour's front door. He swooped on a bottle and opened it on the spot, drinking half the contents in one go. Outside Shane's flat he leaned beside the door and knocked gently, guessing that either Corrie or Donna would be asleep on the settee. He took another swig from the milk bottle and knocked again, slightly harder than before.

Corrie appeared at the door in his pyjamas and stood rubbing his eyes. 'Shush,' he said, holding a finger to his lips. 'Mummy and Shane are still asleep.'

Jimmy winked and kissed him on top of the head. 'Go back to sleep,' he told him, and guided him back towards the settee, negotiating his way with the aid of the street light filtering through the curtains.

He sat on the edge of the settee and stroked

Corrie's forehead until he drifted back to sleep. Occasionally he leaned forward and kissed the sleeping boy softly on the cheek, pecking several times at the same spot. He tucked the blanket up under Corrie's chin and settled down in the armchair opposite. Reclining with legs straight out and the milk bottle balanced on his chest he drifted off to sleep.

Shane had thought she'd heard a noise and lay perfectly still, listening to the beat of her heart, ready to shake Donna awake if she heard it again. A minute that seemed like ten passed without her hearing anything other than the softly, rhythmic sound of Donna breathing. Donna groaned softly, smacked her lips several times and rolled over.

In the morning, freezing, Jimmy awakened with the empty milk bottle toppled on his chest and squinted at the square of light framing the curtain to his left. He prised the shoes from his swollen feet and tiptoed over to the bedroom, glancing down at Corrie on the way past. At the bedroom door he listened, trying to establish if anyone was awake. He heard nothing and opened the door just enough to pop his head into the room. There was sufficient light for him to see his wife and Shane laying as close as possible to the edges of their respective sides of the bed. 'Wakey, wakey,' he said, switching on the light.

Donna was nearest the door and looked up at him in surprise. She then peered over her shoulder and down at Shane. Shane responded with a fleeting grin. 'Morning,' she croaked.

'Aye, aye, what have we here?' Jimmy joked, switching on the light and advancing into the room. 'All the girlies in bed together, eh?'

Donna continued to stare at Shane for several moments longer, forcing her to partially obscure her face with the sheet and look away.

Jimmy seemed amused. 'If I can't trust you, who can I trust, eh Shane?'

Shane rolled over and buried her head under the blankets.

'I thought you would've brought us in a nice cup of tea, Jimmy. I hope you put the kettle on, at least?' Donna swung her feet onto the carpeted floor and reached for the pink dressing gown draped over the end of the bed. On her way to open the curtains she stopped to check on Corrie, ran her hand over his cheek and stooped to kiss him on the forehead. She pulled on the curtain drawstring and looked out of the window at the smattering of up-market cars parked in the mews below, then sat up on a stool at the breakfast bar separating the lounge from the kitchen. Jimmy reached for the electric jug and held the spout under the hot water tap.

'You're supposed to use cold water, you know,' Donna said, and smiled at Shane yawning in the bedroom doorway, wearing a dressing gown not much different to her own. She saw that Shane had put her face on before she put in an appearance.

Corrie stumbled over and switched on the television, switching channels at the sound of a newsreader's voice.

'Switch it back, Corrie. I want to watch the news.' Donna smiled.

'Awh mum,' Corrie gurned.

'Do as your ma says,' Jimmy snapped, crabbit from lack of sleep. 'There's a good boy,' he added when he saw Corrie pout his bottom lip as he ambled back to the television.

'An overnight explosion has rocked London ...' the female newsreader began.

'You don't say,' Donna said, looking at Jimmy and Shane. 'Shush,' they said in unison.

'... Last night police cordoned off an area surrounding Archer Street, W1, after an explosion claimed the life of a young woman. The explosion, believed to have caused extensive damage to a building in the narrow Soho street, disrupted traffic late into the evening. A spokesperson for the Provisional IRA was quick to distance that organisation from the explosion. More on that when news comes to hand.'

Shane, her mouth agape, sucked in her breath and shot a look at Donna. After she glanced at Corrie, she said, 'The poor soul.'

'You can switch it over now, Corrie,' Jimmy said, shaking his head and adding, 'They're getting a bit nonchalant, the authorities, when it comes to this type of thing.'

Congregated at the breakfast bar, Shane and Jimmy on the lounge room side and Donna in the kitchen, the three looked over at Corrie, wondering if they should discuss it.

Donna finished making the coffee and pushed the cups within reach of the others. 'What do we do now?' she said.

'Did you mention anything to Shane?' Jimmy nodded in Shane's direction.

'Of course I did,' Donna said defensively. 'I told her exactly what I told you. What else was I supposed to do?'

Shane stood back from the breakfast bar, holding up her hands in surrender. 'Keep me out of this,' she said and went to join Corrie on the settee.

'She's got a right to know something. Christ, Jimmy.'

'I never said she didn't.'

'Well then, why are you looking at me as if I've gone daft?'

'You went daft a long time ago,' Jimmy quipped, trying to lighten things up.

'For goodness sake, Jimmy, can't you take anything seriously?'

'I'm not taking this serious, huh? Is that what you think? You just stick around and I'll show you what serious means.'

'You promised me you wouldn't pull one of your stunts.' Donna looked scared.

'Do you see that wee boy over there? That boy's my whole life. And so are you.' Jimmy paused and lowered his voice to a whisper. 'Christ, Donna I can't sit back and watch this crap. You know me too well for that.'

Horrified, Donna turned to see if Corrie had overheard the conversation. Jimmy, following her gaze, felt much the same way. They were both relieved to see the boy chuckling away, his eyes glued to the cartoon characters on the screen.

Donna steered Jimmy over to the window. 'If that boy's life means anywhere near as much as you claim it does, Jimmy, for the love of God will you please back off.'

Exasperated, Jimmy headed for the door, detouring to grab his jacket from the back of one of the dining-table chairs.

'Where do you think you're going?' Donna sprang for the door, failing to reach it first.

'I'm going around to South Lambeth Road to get the rest of the gear. So you needn't worry.'

Corrie looked up in time to see his mother catch the door before it slammed shut. 'Mum, can I have the day off school? I'm not feeling too well. Honest.'

'As long as you stay inside.' Donna wrapped her arms around him, turning her face to hide the tears.

TWENTY

Chief Superintendent Tate walked into his Vine Street office, shook the melting pellets of sleet from his coat and looked over his shoulder at the plain white envelope lying on his desk. The envelope was heavily banded with transparent tape and clearly marked 'Private and Confidential'. He guessed that it had arrived by courier or by the hand of the correspondent. More than likely the former, he thought, sniffing the article and holding it up to the light.

He hung his coat on a hook in a row of three on a narrow varnished board in the middle of the cream-painted wall and left his office to go and speak to the desk sergeant in person. 'Phil,' he said, holding up the envelope, 'did you happen to see who delivered this?'

'It's funny you should mention that, sir. It was just sitting there on the front counter. It couldn't have been delivered by a courier because they would've got me to sign for it.'

Tate's eyes narrowed in exasperation. 'Haven't you

got any idea who left it there? Surely you know who comes in and out of the nick?' The sergeant shook his head. 'Not if they don't want me to. I do have other things to attend to. Sir.'

On the way back to his office Tate stopped at the desk of a young female constable. She had seen him coming and was over-zealously flipping through the paperwork of a routine accident report.

It was Tate's custom never to open mysterious correspondence himself. 'Use your paperknife to open this,' he said and gingerly placed the envelope on her desk. 'Bring it straight to my office when you've finished.' Tate hurried to his office, along the passage leading off at right angles from where the constable was sitting.

The young policewoman swept her wavy fair hair behind her ear and reached for the paperknife. She had the point of the slender, silver dagger poised at the top right-hand corner of the envelope, ready to begin slitting, when she stopped to answer her phone. As soon as she hung up the phone rang again.

'Sorry sir,' she told Tate. 'I had to take a call. Yes sir, I'll bring it to you right away.' Replacing the receiver she slit the envelope and headed for the chief superintendent's office.

Tate quickly got to his feet and approached her before she reached his desk. 'Take the correspondence out of the envelope and leave it open and upside down on my desk,' he told her and hurried into the passage, standing well clear of the door.

Probationary Constable Angela Murray pulled the document from the envelope and laid it on the desk. Leaving the office she smiled apologetically at Tate. Tate forced a perfunctory smile and returned to his office. Back at his desk he selected one of several paperknives protruding, along with an assortment of pens and pencils, from a brightly polished Jaguar V12 piston. Standing back as far as he could he flicked the contents of the envelope right side up. Only then did he reach for the spectacles in his shirt pocket and settle down to read.

Dear Chief Superintendent Tate,

Against my explicit instructions it appears that members of your personal staff are showing a keen interest in my affairs. If you don't back off I will be left with no alternative other than to furnish the press with enough incriminating and embarrassing evidence to assure an immediate investigation into your current illegal activities.

Be warned. Complying with this demand doesn't release you from the monetary conditions imposed in my previous correspondence. In that regard I expect to see you on Saturday night, 7.30 sharp, at the Sands Hotel, The Esplanade in Brighton. You will, of course, bring the £10,000 first instalment with you.

Incidentally, I have enclosed another extract from the dirt book. Sorry I haven't enclosed a photo. Yet.

Without turning the page the chief superintendent placed the document on the desk in front of him. Pounding it as hard as he could with the edge of his clenched fist he sent objects on the desk bouncing into the air. Raging, he began to read.

That big fat prick sergeant Ian Tate called in tonight. Drunk again. He hasn't been around here long, but he must be stupid if he doesn't realise that I know who he is. And he doesn't care if you've got somebody with you or not. He just comes marching in and expects you to drop everything just for him. Geez, he makes me sick and I wish something really horrible would happen to him. Like getting caught and being demoted to Wales or somewhere. Anyway, he'll get his when I write my memoirs. If he hasn't gotten himself fucked to death by then that is, the dirty old bastard. Somebody should tell his wife.

He brought all this clothes-line with him and made me tie him up. You should've seen his face when I strapped on the dildo he brought with him. Geez, I felt stupid when I looked at myself in the mirror. But the look on his face was more than worth it, and it'll probably come up great in the photo. As long as he doesn't remember me taking it and come back to get it. I don't think he will, cause he took a sniff of that Amyl whatever it is you call it stuff he carts around with him in that little bottle and his eyes went all glassy. If it hadn't been so sick, it would've been funny, and to think he was getting it for nothing. At first I thought he just wanted me to pull him off and I rolled him over onto his side, me with this great big thing strapped between my legs. What does he do? He shakes his head and makes me take the gag out of his mouth for a minute. 'I want you stick it up me,' he says. I said, 'What am I supposed to do with your legs?' 'Spread them and tie them to the corners of the bed,' he says. I thought he was coming while he was speaking. No such luck. And to think this is somebody's son. God, I was sure I was going to burst out laughing.

When I finally got on top of him and managed to get the thing in, he screamed that much that I thought I'd killed him, but as soon as I stopped, the abuse was something chronic. Right, you dirty perverted, kinky old bastard, I thought, and rammed it up him as hard and as fast as I could. I thought, if you can stand the pain pal I can stand the shit. And I felt like telling him, If you come back for more after this, you're a better man than me Gunga Din. I'll probably never see the end of him now. Anyway, he blew all over the place and then had the cheek to ask for more. You'd have thought he'd at least have offered to pay for my ruined stockings, but no.

Tate looked up furtively, double-checked that he'd no waiting visitors and read the extract from the dirt book again. On finishing he rested his elbows on the desk and buried his face in his hands. Deep in thought he shifted his hands to the side of his head and stared down at the document, wishing he could turn back the clock. He was one of the youngest chief superintendents in the Met and he wasn't prepared to let anything jeopardise his position.

Leaning back in the chair with his hands behind his head he focused on the expanse of blank ceiling and began considering his options. In his mind's eye the ceiling was a whiteboard on which he would put the pieces together. If only the encroaching thoughts of his humiliation, as described in the letter, would stop playing over and over in his head.

It became clear that he would have to approach the problem of the dirt book from another angle. One that would deflect attention away from himself. He suspected that the avaricious Anton Winters harboured aspirations to take over from Archie Kemp. Tate thought that if he could get Kemp removed to a place where he would be unable to contact or influence Anton, he could harness Anton's ambition and turn it against Kemp. When he was done with Anton, he would rid himself of him.

Straightening up he put in a call to Eric Matheson, an ex-colleague, now the ambitious second-in-charge of Parkhurst Prison. Before he went to work on Anton he had to take steps to ensure that Archie Kemp was unavailable for consultation. 'Listen Eric, I need a favour,' he said.

At the other end of the line Matheson, with his slicked-down grey hair and his black, pencil-thin moustache, practically stood to attention as he listened, nodded intermittently, and occasionally muttered, 'Uh huh.'

'It's as good as done,' he said, when given a chance to speak.

'Call me on this number as soon as you get a result. And Eric, I'll be sitting here waiting.'

Half an hour later, Tate glanced at the clock, thinking for the umpteenth time that he would give Matheson another five minutes before he called to check on his progress. One minute into the latest extension the phone rang in his hand. 'Tate here,' he answered.

'This is Matheson. The job's right.'

'And?' Tate wanted some details.

'And Kemp's banged up for ten days. Total loss of privileges. No contact, nothing. It's an impossibility for him to get anything in or out.'

'Are you sure?'

'As sure as shit.'

'That's one I owe you, Eric.'

'Don't mention it, Ian, just remember who your friends are.' Matheson was speaking into a line that had already gone dead.

On his way to the car park Tate hesitated, wondering if he should just roll up, or phone ahead to make sure that Anton was on the premises. Rationalising that there was no point telegraphing his punches he continued to the car. On the way across town to Islington he pondered his line of attack: whether to go in with both guns blazing or try the subtle approach. The latter was against his nature, but not beyond the realms of possibility if he thought it would get a quicker result.

Anton Winters worked from a luxurious suite of offices above the Temptation, one of Archie Kemp's many acquired nightclubs. Tate, on being ushered in by a young, female employee he thought striking enough to be a model, was much more than impressed. He was envious. The touch of one who could afford the best was very much in evidence. Imported furniture and carpets that looked too good to walk on.

'You're lucky to catch me,' Anton said, making no attempt at a welcome.

Even without the lavish surroundings Tate could tell that Anton was ambitious. It was written all over his face. He knew that men like Anton regarded subordination merely as a stepping stone and would, if he was any judge, do whatever had to be done to reach the top. Very similar to himself, he thought.

'Somebody's been up to a bit of hanky-panky in my manor,' Tate said, also dispensing with a greeting.

'Don't you mean that somebody's been taking liberties in Archie's bought-and-paid-for manor? *My* manor.' Beneath his calm exterior Anton hid the uneasiness he always felt when he was in the company of a high-ranking policeman. Especially one such as Tate who had thought nothing of asserting his authority by stitching up Archie Kemp.

'*Our* manor then, if you like,' Tate said, exhibiting a rare degree of diplomacy. 'And that's what I want to talk to you about.'

While pouring drinks Anton watched Tate in the mirror at the back of the black, marble-topped cocktail bar. 'Chivas Regal all right?' He placed the scotch on the matching black marble coffee table and eased himself into one of the beige leather easy chairs set either side of it.

Tate settled into the other chair and reached for his drink. 'I thought it was time we had a friendly chat,' he said, pausing to gauge Anton's reaction so far. He wanted to see if he was being taken seriously.

'This little chat. It wouldn't involve money, by any chance?'

'I would like to think it did. And plenty of it. But that's not what I came here to talk to you about. I want to put a proposition to you.'

'Oh yeah,' Anton scoffed. 'What makes you think I'd trust the likes of you? After the way you fitted Archie up.'

'That's the point of my proposition. In the words of Bob Dylan, Archie didn't want to play ball with the law. Maybe you've got more sense?'

Much as he would've liked to show Tate the door Anton knew that if he didn't compromise he ran a real risk of falling foul of the policeman in much the same way as Archie had. He was ready to listen. 'OK. You've got the chair.'

'Archie Kemp's finished. He'll be an old man by the time he gets out. Agreed?'

'Agreed,' Anton smiled.

'Then why should he have any further say in matters that he has no real control over? No. I propose a different arrangement. Up to now I've been getting the crumbs from your – shall we say – business activities. The proceeds from protection, gambling, prostitution, et cetera, will now be subject to a fifty–fifty split. And remember, without me you'll have nothing to split. You control things at your end and I'll do the same at mine. You collect the money and I'll make sure you don't get hassled. A marriage of convenience, if you like.'

'Provided you can keep Archie locked up,' Anton said, knowing that, even with a fifty–fifty split, he would come out of the alliance well ahead. Not counting the added prestige.

'That's where you come into it.' Tate, having dangled the carrot, wanted to remind the villain that the service he provided was essential to his being able to continue operating with impunity. 'Anton, you do realise that our on-going success depends upon me being able to take care of things at my end?'

'That's what you'd be getting paid for.'

'So you'd agree that if somebody took steps to remove me from the picture things could get difficult?'

'I can't see it making things any easier,' Anton conceded.

Tate leaned across the table. 'Then what would you

say if I told you that Archie Kemp was trying to do just that?'

'I'd say that we should put a stop to that.'

Tate raised his glass in a salute and leaned back in his chair. 'Archie's trying to blackmail me. But he's firing blanks. The trouble is, the live ammunition is still out there somewhere.'

'I should've guessed it was something like that,' Anton said.

By the way he'd answered, Tate realised that Anton, like himself, was in possession of certain facts, but lacked the necessary pieces to finish the puzzle.

'I think it's time to pool our resources,' Tate continued.

Reclining in the chair Anton crossed his legs, pulled a cigarette from the packet with his teeth and slid the packet towards the policeman. This was the break he'd been waiting for.

Tate caught the packet before it slid over the edge of the coffee table's smooth black top and helped himself to a cigarette. Leaning across the table he accepted Anton's offer of a light. He allowed himself a flicker of a smile now that he had Anton's undivided attention. 'I need your help to find out who's behind this. Before Kemp does.'

'Then what?'

Tate ran his finger across his throat.

'I thought somebody had already made a start. It wasn't you, was it?' Anton grinned.

'If you're referring to that business in Archer

Street, it was brought to my attention that you were showing a lot of interest up there. That's another reason why I thought we should talk. I was going to ask you the same question.'

In silence each man studied the other.

Anton maintained the grin and slowly and deliberately shook his head. 'It wasn't me.'

'Well then, it looks as if we're dealing with a third party.'

'You're telling the story.'

Looking off to the side and squinting Tate mumbled, 'Who else has got an interest in this?' Anton shrugged his shoulders. 'When I mentioned that Archie Kemp was firing blanks, in relation to the blackmail, you said something like, "I should've guessed it was something like that." What did you mean?'

'Not much. Archie's too cunning to give much away. But he's had me looking for somebody by the name of Gilfeather. He said it was very important to his appeal. He wouldn't tell me why.'

'Gilfeather?' Tate sat forward, excited. He didn't recognise the name but he presumed it had to be the author of the dirt book. 'This Gilfeather character – I take it you haven't had any luck finding her?'

'Her?' Anton pressed his lips together and shook his head. 'I think you'll find that Gilfeather is a he.'

'So you did manage to find him?' Tate got to his feet and glared down at Anton.

'Take it easy. You're as bad as Archie. Christ, I'd

love to know what this geezer's got on you. It must be good stuff.'

'Sorry. It's very important that we find him.' Tate was glad that Anton was in the dark. He realised that if Anton had knowledge of the dirt book he could well decide to use it against him. Exactly as Archie Kemp was doing. 'Are you sure Gilfeather's a man?' he added.

'Sure I'm sure. His first name's Tom.'

'That could be a red herring.'

'Not from what I hear. Or should I say, overheard.' Anton smiled, enjoying the look of anguish on the policeman's face. He might be forced to work with Tate but he didn't have to like him. 'This is the part I like,' he continued. 'Apparently about ten years ago this geezer Gilfeather did the dirty on Jimmy Macintyre. You'd know that name. Fucked his wife, he did. Anyway, there was a kid came out of it. Macintyre thinks the little bastard's his. He'll learn the truth soon enough when I te—'

'Wait a minute. Slow down.' Tate paced towards the window, trying to hide his excitement. 'Where did you come by this information? Who was talking about him?'

'She was telling some American geezer.'

'She?'

'Who do you think? Donna Macintyre. Who else?'

Looking out the window Tate clenched his fists by his side and inhaled deeply, sucking the air in through his teeth. The pieces were coming together. 'Right,' he said. 'It's time we had a serious word with Donna Macintyre. You organise to –'

'Before you go any further,' Anton interrupted, 'I've been through all that. I've even told her I'd tell Jimmy who the real father of his kid is, if she doesn't tell me where to find Gilfeather. She's desperate to find him too, you know. Probably more than you.'

'What? Do you mean to say that, after all this, she doesn't know where he is?'

'She'd love to know where he is. Her kid's got leukaemia and she's thinks that Gilfeather might be a chance of a marrow donor, or some fucken thing like that. That's why she doesn't want Jimmy to find out. She knows what he'd do to Gilfeather. And so do I.'

'What about the American geezer? Where does he fit in? Can we put our hands on him?'

Anton looked pleased with himself. 'I can tell you every move he makes. We've kept an eye on him. He's staying at the Mayfair Holiday Inn, if you want to talk to him.'

Tate clasped his hands together at chest-height. 'Right,' he said. 'At least we've got somewhere to start. You get a hold of the American geezer and find out everything he knows. Then get rid of him.'

'Oh yeah. And what are you going to do?'

'This business with the marrow transplant, or whatever it was you called it. Supposing Donna Macintyre did manage to find this Gilfeather character. She would have to put him in touch with doctors somewhere, wouldn't she? I mean, it stands to reason. We're dealing with a highly specialised field here.'

'I was just wondering about that myself,' Anton said, thinking back to when he'd overheard Donna telling Munro about Gilfeather.

'You follow up on the American geezer and I'll look into this.' Tate finished his drink and handed Anton the glass, suggesting a refill. 'I'm supposed to be handing over a substantial sum of money tomorrow night. I would like to short-circuit that process.'

'Tomorrow night? You don't want much, do you?'

'I'm due at the Sands Hotel in Brighton by 7.30. The shifty bastard has picked a very public arena to complete this year's transaction.'

Anton, with a hint of facetiousness, said, 'This year's transaction? What is this? A perpetual trophy?'

'I'd call it an annual drain on company funds.'

The smirk faded from Anton's face. 'Why don't we just go down to Brighton and do the damage? Sort this out, once and for all?'

'I don't want it to come to that, but you'd better allow for that eventuality. Presume that we'll be in Brighton tomorrow evening.' Tate sauntered towards the door, turning as he gripped the handle. 'If Gilfeather and Macintyre were in the same room, what do you think Macintyre would do if you told him that Gilfeather was the father of his son?'

'Coming from me, the way I'd put it, I think that that would be the end of Gilfeather.'

Tate thought for a moment and said, 'Excellent.

Make that Brighton thing a definite. Organise yourself to be down there well before 7.30 and book in. I'll be in touch later with the details.'

Anton looked troubled. 'Seeing as we're going to be working together, I may as well tell you: I've got a score to settle with Jimmy Macintyre and he knows it.'

'I worked that out for myself.' Tate was preoccupied, thinking about the forthcoming trip to Brighton.

Annoyed, Anton retorted, 'Did you work out that Archie Kemp summoned him out to Parkhurst on the QT. Eh? Because if you did, then you'll know that Archie's put a contract on me.'

Interrupting, Tate said, 'Who told you this?'

'A wee birdie told me. But that's not the point. Macintyre's out of the game tonight. I'm not waiting for him to make the first move. Nobody's ever survived that.'

'You can't do that.' Tate was emphatic. 'We need Macintyre in Brighton tomorrow night.'

Anton shook his head. 'Nah. I back off and I might not be around to see tomorrow night.'

'Listen to me, Anton. I intend to get Jimmy Macintyre down to Brighton for the express purpose of having you tell him the truth about Gilfeather. Can't you see it?. You impart that little gem of information to Macintyre and we kill two birds with one stone. So to speak. Gilfeather will be off our backs and Macintyre will be up for murder.' Tate paused and added, 'Plus, this way you'll get the satisfaction of knowing that he's living with the torment of finding out that he's not the boy's father. Think about it.'

With narrowed eyes and lips pressed tight Anton reached for another cigarette and ambled over to the window.

'Well?' urged Tate.

'I suppose I could always make myself scarce until tomorrow night.' Anton held up a warning finger and continued, 'Not that Macintyre scares me, mind you. Just to be on the safe side.'

The receptionist at the Sidney Doolan Centre looked at the senior policeman's identification and forced a nervous smile. 'Dr Cullen's handling that case. If you like, I'll page him for you, chief superintendent?'

'That would be appreciated.' Tate responded with a flick of a smile and turned to cast a curious eye around the foyer. Browsing quickly through a revolving rack of brochures next to the Christmas tree he moved on to reading the various notices dotted about the walls. A full-sized poster, coloured and glossy, caught his eye. The only item on the wall of a non-medical nature, it beckoned all to that establishment's forthcoming gala benefit. Tate was particularly drawn to the time and place of the function. The Sands Hotel in Brighton, on Saturday 23rd December.

'We wanted to hold the benefit close to Christmas and that was the only date available. We figured the guests would be in a more giving mood. You know, the spirit of goodwill and all that.'

Startled, Tate turned abruptly.

'Sorry. I didn't mean to make you jump. I'm Dr Cullen. You wanted to see me.' The doctor waited to hear what the visit was about. He hoped it was nothing personal.

Offering his hand Tate said, 'Yes. But not on official business. Is there somewhere private we could go for a quiet word?'

Considerably relieved, Dr Cullen glanced at the policeman's identification and led the way into his office. 'Sorry about the mess,' he said, waving his hand over his desk. 'I never seem to have a minute.'

'That poster in the foyer,' Tate said, completely digressing from his intended line of questioning, that of beguiling the doctor into revealing the identity of any prospective donors introduced to the clinic by Donna Macintyre. 'The one advertising the benefit in Brighton on Saturday night. What can you tell me about it?'

'Ahh, the benefit.' Dr Cullen perked up considerably. 'An endeavour close to my heart. What would you like to know?' Before Tate had time to answer the doctor added, 'It's a registered charity. All perfectly legal.'

Tate managed a laugh. 'I'm sure it is, Dr Cullen. I was inquiring more from a personal point of view. I was actually thinking of attending.'

'You'd be more than welcome. There are still some

tickets left. I could bet on it. Not that I would, mind you. Ha ha. That would be illegal.'

'This, eh, benefit. Are there many people going?'

'Oh yes. Certainly. You would've noticed who the guest artists are. How could we go wrong?'

'What's the set up? I didn't get time to finish reading the poster. Is it an all-seated affair?'

'Very much so,' said the doctor proudly. 'Apart from the entertainment, there's a four-course dinner with all the trimmings. We'd prefer you to fill a table for ten but if that's not feasible we'd be perfectly willing to make up a table. Provided you don't mind sharing.'

'I think the latter,' Tate said, squinting and rubbing the end of his chin. 'It's a bit late to be making up a table.'

'I understand perfectly.'

'Out of curiosity, I don't suppose I could see a copy of the floor plan? The seating arrangements, or whatever it is they call it these days.' Tate reached for his wallet and begrudgingly handed over one hundred pounds, the price of two tickets. 'Pay you, do I?'

'By all means.' Dr Cullen grinned and reached for the money. 'There's a small prize for the one who sells the most tickets. It could be me by the looks of things.'

'You were going to show me the floor plan, doctor.'

'Now that's the one thing I haven't got. I imagine you'd have to check with the Sands for that kind of information. But I can put your mind at rest. They're all good seats.'

Far from pleased Tate forced a smile. 'You eh, you said you were the top ticket seller. I don't suppose you sold a ticket to this chap, did you?' The detective reached into the inside pocket of his suit jacket and produced a photograph of a young Gilfeather. One he had acquired from the files.

The doctor held the photograph at arm's length and squinted down his nose at it. Shaking his head he responded, 'No. He didn't get a ticket from me.' After a pause he added, 'Why? Is he in some kind of trouble? Not something we should be worried about, I hope?'

'Oh no,' said Tate. 'Nothing like that. But you could get in touch with me if you ever come across him, I'd very much appreciate it.'

With a hint of suspicion Dr Cullen handed the photograph back to Tate and said, 'Why not?'

Scribbling a number where he could be contacted on his note pad Tate tore out the page and handed it to the doctor. 'Any time, day or night,' he smiled, turning and reaching the door by the time the doctor reacted.

'Just a moment,' said the doctor. Tate turned in anticipation. 'You can pick up your tickets at Reception on the way out.'

TWENTY-ONE

Placing two cups of coffee on the breakfast bar, Donna glanced at her husband sitting in front of the television, smiling when she saw that he was peeking at Corrie over the top of the newspaper he was supposed to be reading. She was worried about the effect her not working would have on their finances. Their nest egg. But the look in Jimmy's eyes told her that now wasn't a good time to discuss it. She knew that haunted look well. It was one born of heartache and despair.

'Here's your coffee, love.' She smiled and placed an encouraging hand on his shoulder. 'It'll be all right,' she whispered, gently squeezing.

Jimmy returned the smile, avoiding eye contact. 'Ta,' he croaked.

'What about you, Corrie, would you like some Milo?' she added, upbeat and cheerful. It was as much her intention to lift Jimmy's spirits as to stop herself sinking to his level. God forbid the day when they reached the lowest ebb together.

'Can I have a cup of coffee like you and dad?' Corrie beamed.

'That coffee's no bloody good for you. It's full of caffeine and it makes you fidgety.'

Jimmy winked at Corrie and watched Donna place a mug of milk in the microwave oven. 'Here,' he whispered, handing Corrie his cup. 'Watch you don't burn yourself.'

Donna, her back to them, smiled as she monitored their reflection in the microwave's opaque black door. 'You must think I'm a right edjit,' she said softly, glad to hear Corrie's muffled giggles as the sight of Jimmy creeping up behind her.

Jimmy reached around her waist, winked at Corrie again and began nuzzling her neck. Donna rested her head on his left shoulder and clutched his hands to her midriff. 'It's a pity we couldn't send Corrie out to play,' she sighed.

The timely intervention of the microwave's buzzer, as well as breaking the spell, brought Shane out of the bedroom where she'd been resting before getting ready for her night's work at the Wheatsheaf. 'Oh, was that the kettle I heard whistling?' she asked, making her way to the breakfast bar.

It must cost Shane a small fortune in make-up, Donna thought, noticing again that her friend never made an appearance without close to a full face on. 'The microwave didn't waken you, I hope? I forgot all about the racket they make.'

'No no,' Shane replied. 'I was lying there awake

wondering what the time was. I haven't missed the seven o'clock news, have I?'

'Corrie, switch that TV over for Aunty Shane, there's a good boy,' Jimmy said, and grabbed his jacket from the back of the chair.

'Where are you going dad? Can I come with you?' Corrie stood, eyes brimming with hope. 'Go on, dad.'

'Not just now, son.' Jimmy's heart sank when the look of expectation in Corrie's eyes turned to disappointment. 'But I'll tell you what I'm prepared to do with you,' he added quickly. 'I'll get your Uncle Mick and your Uncle William to come over with a video and a big bag of sweeties. What do you think of that?'

'Less of the sweets,' Donna scolded, before Corrie had a chance to answer.

'Sure one or two sweeties'll do the boy no harm.' Jimmy pulled his son's woollen cap down over his eyes and kissed him on the lips.

Corrie ran the back of his hand over his mouth and said, 'Yuk.'

'Right. That means no sweeties for you, mister.' Jimmy pretended that his feelings had been hurt.

Corrie smiled awkwardly, not knowing whether his father was up to one of his tricks. 'Sure I was only kidding, dad,' he said.

'Nah, that's it, you had your chance so you did. Sure you'll give your ma a big kiss but not your poor auld da. If that's the way you want it?' Jimmy tilted his head to the side and looked up, pressing his lips together.

Over at the breakfast bar Donna and Shane exchanged smiles as they watched the expression on Corrie's face fluctuate between a half-hearted grin and a look of bewilderment. 'Your poor daddy,' Donna said, going along.

Relenting, Corrie approached Jimmy with his arms out wide. 'OK. You can have a kiss on the cheek.'

Jimmy stooped and offered his cheek, indicating with the tip of his index finger the exact spot where he wanted the kiss. As Corrie's pursed lips were about to connect with his cheek Jimmy turned abruptly and took his son's kiss flush on the lips. 'Ha ha,' he laughed, taking the startled boy in his arms and lifting him clear of the ground. 'Your auld man's too fly for you.'

'Careful, Jimmy,' Donna protested. 'You'll bang his head on the ceiling if you're not careful.'

'I'm for the off,' Jimmy announced, as soon as Corrie's feet touched the ground.

Donna adjusted the collar of his jacket where it was sticking up at the back. 'How long do you think you'll be?' she said. 'I don't like you leaving us here on our own.'

Jimmy leaned in and whispered. 'For Christsake, Donna, don't let our Corrie hear you say that. He's already wondering what the hell's going on here.' Standing back he continued in a normal voice. 'Why do you think I'm sending William and Mick over?'

'You couldn't bring us back a couple of fish suppers, could you?' Donna turned to see if her suggestion had met with Shane's approval.

A pained look came over Jimmy's face. 'Christsake, I'm trying to get out the fu – bloody door. Why don't you just cook something?'

'Don't bother your arse then,' Donna snapped.

'OK, but you can just hit your satchel. I'm skint. I haven't got a bean.' Jimmy said and as proof pulled his trousers pockets inside out. 'Do you want to see my impersonation of an elephant?' he added with a mischievous grin, and started to undo his fly.

'Don't you bloody well dare, mister. There's women and a child present,' Donna said.

Pouting, Shane rolled her tongue around the inside of her cheek and looked at Donna sideways. 'Don't let me stop you,' she grinned.

Donna smiled and went to the bedroom, returning with a twenty pound note. 'I want my change,' she demanded.

'Some chance.' Jimmy placed the money in his back pocket along with the rest of his stash and let himself out.

'Never mind the sweets,' Donna called after him. Turning to Corrie she added, 'Your father spoils you, so he does.'

Jimmy parked behind the taxi rank in the street opposite No. 38. Alighting, he raised the collar of his suit jacket against the biting wind and hurried past the taxis and the corner shop. He was hoping to catch his brothers before they went out.

'Look at that sleekit auld git,' Agnes was saying. 'He won't do a hands bloody turn so he'll no. Sitting there in front of the fire like a big dumpling. But see as soon as I sit down and open a bottle, up he jumps. Go on get, it's no good mooching around me, mister, you had your rations this afternoon, so you did.'

'Nice to see everything's normal,' Jimmy said.

Old Davey, wobbling next to the table where the rest of the family was seated, squinted and craned over towards the door. Not sure of who was there he pursed his lips like a duck and tried leaning back.

'Watch yourself, man.' Jimmy's lunge caught him just before he toppled over backwards.

'Fuck me, if it's not the bold Jimmy.' Old Davey licked his lips and lurched forward as far as his eldest son's grip would permit.

A grim-faced Agnes, sitting with her arms folded across her chest and her glass of sweet sherry poised handy to her lips, raised her foot level with her teetering husband's backside and pretended to kick. 'You should've let the auld skitter fall, our Jimmy. He might've killed himself and put us all out of our misery.'

Old Davey matched his wife's expression. 'See you,' he pointed a waving finger. 'See me. This is the kinda thing I've got to put up with in my own fucken house. Yis have me demented, the fucken lot o yeh. See if I wisnay here yis'id all know the score, beh Christ. Aye yeh widnay last five minutes without me. None of yeh.'

'Ach away and giv'us a minute's peace, yeh stupit auld edjit yeh,' Agnes laughed.

William shook his head and grinned at Jimmy. 'Their patter never changes, does it, big man?'

Jimmy went around behind Mick and began reading the paper over his shoulder, flicking through the back pages.

'There's no boxing in it, if that's what you're looking for,' Mick told him.

Jimmy ignored him, took the paper and kept flicking through it all the way to the front. 'The police haven't been round here, have they?' he said, directing the question to his mother.

In the process of scanning the table for the bottle of sweet sherry that Agnes had placed on the floor beside her feet Old Davey shut one eye and tried to focus on the direction from which he thought he'd heard the voice.

'Over here, da,' Jimmy said, shaking his head. 'Christsake, it's enough to put you off the bevie.'

'There was these two guys chapped the door this afternoon. Wearing suits so they were,' Old Davey spluttered.

Jimmy looked at his mother for verification. She replied with a silent shake of her head and relayed the look around the table. William and Mick shrugged their shoulders.

'Was it the police, da?' Jimmy urged.

'How teh fuck would I know? I never opened the door to the pair of bastards.'

'Did they look like the police?'

A sly look came over Old Davey's face. 'Aye, well now that you mention it, they must've been. I could tell by what they shouted up at the window at me when I asked them what teh fuck it was they wanted.'

'Are yeh going to tell us or are you going to –'

Suddenly Old Davey seemed alert. 'Ohh,' he said licking his lips, 'I've got a shocking case of the heebee-jeebees. Maybe if yer mingy auld ma could see her way clear to giv'us a scoof out of that bottle she's got planked, it might jog the auld memory, know what I mean?'

'Give him a mouthful, ma, before I go over there and –' Jimmy stopped and shook his head.

'Yer nothing but a pest,' Agnes said, gripping the end of the bottle so that her husband couldn't tilt it as far as back he intended to.

'Christsake,' he moaned. 'I never even got meh gob wet. You couldn't expect me to remember fuck all with that.'

Agnes put the bottle on the floor and gripped it between her feet. 'You'll remember all right if somebody hits you over the nut with the bloody thing. Go on, tell our Jimmy what yer on about and I might give you another swig.'

'Aye, well eh, let me see,' Old Davey began, his intention being to embellish the story enough to earn another drink. 'They ah, these two punters, they just asked if Donna or you was in. I telt them yis didnay stay here any more. I telt them yis'd moved out, the pair of you.'

'What did they say to that?'

'How the fuck would I know? They just kinda looked at one another for a wee minute and fucked off. Just as well for them. If they'd tried to come through that door they'da had me to deal with.'

'Nay danger, da,' Mick smirked. 'You'da showed them, wouldn't yeh?'

'Hey, less o' the taking the pish. See in my day, they used to call me –'

'What time did all this happen, da?' Jimmy interrupted.

Agnes butted in. 'It must've been about the back of three o'clock when I was over at the wee shop. It had to of been, because other than that, I never set foot out of the house. Unless yer da's away with the fairies again?'

Jimmy placed one hand on the edge of the table to support himself and leaned under the table to reach for the bottle secured between his mother's feet. He had no wish to include his father in the conversation and used the sweet sherry to lure him over to his seat in front of the fire.

'That bottle's got to last me all weekend, our Jimmy,' Agnes whispered when he got back to the table.

Old Davey turned and leered at the table with righteous indignation. 'Oh by the way, if this is you getting yersel in trouble again, our Jimmy, don't forget what yer Uncle Hughie told yeh.'

'What's he on about?' Jimmy said.

'Remember the first time yeh got yersel huckled by the police, the time they gave yeh the three years GBH? Aye, well if yeh cast yer mind back, the brand-new suit yeh borrowed aff yer uncle Hughie got three years along with yeh. He wasnay too pleased, I can tell yeh. The fucken thing was out of style before he clapped eyes on it again.'

'It was a crap suit anyway,' Mick laughed. 'I'm sure that's what got our Jimmy the three years in the first place. Best place for a suit like that, the jail. Anyway it should've been well used to them conditions, the fucken thing was never out of the pawn.'

'Never mind the suit, I didn't come here to talk about shite like that,' Jimmy said.

Old Davey squinted over his shoulder. 'Oh aye, and what shite did yeh come here to talk about?'

Jimmy reached into his back pocket and pulled a ten pound note from the centre of the wad. 'Here,' he said, handing the money to his father. 'Go and get yourself blootered.'

I'm no as daft as I look, Old Davey congratulated himself as he grabbed his jacket from the hook behind the door.

Jimmy went to the bay window and waited until his father turned into Mawbey Street before he rejoined the others at the table. 'Do you think he was at the wind up?' he asked nobody in particular.

They all shrugged and shook their heads.

'Anyway, the less he knows the better. For that matter, the less youse all know the better.'

Mick reached into the centre of the table and helped himself to the last piece of bread, cramming it into his mouth. 'What's the score anyway, big man? Are yeh gonna tell us what teh fuck's going on?'

Agnes and William, both stern-faced, nodded in agreement.

Jimmy remained silent, waiting for the windows to stop rattling after the double-decker bus had passed. 'It would deafen you that,' he said, adding, 'I want you two to come with me. I need you to look after Donna and Corrie for me while I take care of a wee bit of business. You wouldn't begrudge me that, I hope?'

While William appeared nonplussed the look of intrigue on Mick's face gradually gave way to that of pain. 'Giv'us a break, Jimbo,' he moaned, adopting the role of spokesman. 'Sure me and our William were going up the thingwy to get bevied. Weren't we, William?'

'It's bevie night, Jimmy. Sure we're entitled,' William said.

Jimmy shook his head and looked at his mother for support.

Agnes leaned back in her chair and raised one hand in the air. 'Keep me out of this,' she told him.

Jimmy sighed and slowly got to his feet. He went around the table and stood between his brothers, placing a hand on the back of their necks. 'See that fucken window over there?' he said.

'For Christsake,' shrieked Agnes. 'Them's meh brand new curtains.'

The thought of the guy with the Manchester accent flying through the window and lying wrecked in the basement below was far too fresh in his memory for Mick to continue with the token resistance. 'Ach sure we're only winding you up Jimbo, kidding yeh on. Sure me and the bold William widnay let yeh down. That's right, isn't it William?

'Christ aye,' Mick continued. 'You get the carryout and I'm yer man. It's all the same to me where I get blootered. Where we going anyway?'

'We're going over to Shane's, but not a word to anybody.'

'Fuck, that'll do me. I've always fancied a good rake around in Shane's drawers, so I have.'

'You keep yer hands to yersel, Mick, or I'll cut the fuckers off.' Jimmy grinned, brushed the curtain aside and went into the kitchenette.

'Christ, can yeh no take a joke?' Mick mumbled.

On a bare wooden shelf next to the window above the kitchen sink sat a handleless mug containing Old Davey's shaving gear. Standing out among the discarded assortment of blue disposable razors was a fine bone-handled, cut-throat razor. Plucking it from the mug Jimmy opened it and delicately checked the cutting edge by running his thumb across the blade. Not satisfied, he reached for the usually redundant razor strop hanging from the cupboard door beneath the sink. When he returned to the parlour he said,

'See you later ma,' and nodded his brothers towards the door.

'You're no away already? Sure I was just about to get up off meh arse and get you a bite to eat. I could do you a nice pair of Aberdeen kippers.'

'Nah, it's OK, I'm in too big a hurry ma. Come on you two. Get a move on. We haven't got all night.'

'Here, you can take the kippers with you.' Agnes said, getting to her feet.

'Ma, I'm OK, honest.'

'Ah well, please yersel. Auld garbage guts'll probably have them for his supper. If he's in any fit state when he gets in.'

Holding his worn suit jacket closed in the middle Mick turned his head sideways to the driving rain and sprinted across the road ahead of his brothers. 'Fuck me,' he said, diving under the awning of the Pakistani's shop and wiping the rain from his face. 'Don't forget the carryout,' he added, grinning and nodding towards the shop window.

'Half a dozen big tins between you,' Jimmy said, handing him the money. 'I don't want the two of you getting blootered. I want you semi-sensible.'

Going by the look on Jimmy's face Mick knew there was no point in arguing. 'I could drink these meh fucken self in twenty minutes,' he muttered, as soon as he was out of earshot.

'Where's William?' Mick said, climbing into the front seat of the car a minute later, nursing the six cans of McEwan's Export and thinking that he'd had a stroke of luck.

'Away to get the fish suppers. We've to pick him up out the front of the chipper.'

'I hope you told him to get plenty?'

'You're nothing but a pig, Mick.'

Jimmy eased the car into the junction and waited for the traffic on his left to pass. He was forced to back up when the traffic on his right arrived before he had a chance to complete the turn. 'I see yer driving's no improved any, Jimbo,' Mick teased.

'You shut your gob.'

'There's the bold William now.' Mick pointed at his brother standing at the pavement's edge.

On the way to St Oswald's Mews the demister was struggling to keep up with the steam escaping from the small hole William had torn in the parcel of fish and chips.

'Christ, don't tell me Shane lives in this gaff?' William said, genuinely astonished. 'This place must be worth a right few bob. You wouldn't think a few gigs at the boozer would be enough to pay for a joint like this, would you?'

Mick was equally impressed. 'Fuck me you wouldn't credit that, would you?'

'She doesn't just sing at the Wheatsheaf, you know,' Jimmy explained. 'She's got other gigs.' Corrie eased himself up off the couch as soon as he heard the key turning in the lock. 'Uncle Mick,' he shouted, and as best he could, bounded across the room and latched his arms around his uncle's neck.

'Take it easy, wee man, or yeh might coup the bevie.' Mick walked to the table with Corrie swinging from his neck.

'Giv'us a burl, Uncle Mick.'

'Come on then, before yer Uncle Mick gets on the bevie.'

Shane appeared from the bedroom dressed in a blue satin evening gown. As she walked, a shimmering leg protruded from the thigh-high split running down the left-hand side of the dress. With the exception of her lips, which were outlined in red pencil, her face was made up ready for work.

Mick checked her up and down and whistled. 'Do you always get this dressed up for a feed of fish and chips, Shane?' he grinned.

'No. Just for you, sweetie,' Shane placed her hand on her hip and cocked her leg.

Donna opened the parcel of fish and chips and helped herself to a few crispy bits. 'Better hurry up and eat this before the chips go mushie,' she suggested.

While Donna busied herself buttering bread and making tea Jimmy diverted his eyes away from the split in Shane's dress long enough to coax Corrie over to the steaming parcel of food. Shane, enjoying the continuing attention of Mick and William, immodestly took bigger steps and performed a lap of the room that wasn't altogether necessary. Back at the breakfast bar she daintily selected a chip with her long red fingertips and equally as delectably bit it in half without touching it with her lips.

As soon as everyone had rejected Donna's offer of a plate, preferring to eat from the paper, Jimmy directed her over to the settee and sat her down. 'I'm going out for a wee while and I don't want to be worrying about you and Corrie. I've worded the boys up, but I don't want you complicating things by setting foot outside that door. Not unless I'm with you.'

A smile formed on Donna's face before Jimmy finished speaking.

'What's funny?' he asked her.

'I can't see those two doing much good. God, I think our Corrie would be capable of doing more damage than the two of them put together.'

Jimmy's lips narrowed in exasperation. 'Donna, I know they're a pair of doo-lallies, but I'm not expecting them to go into battle for you, or anything like that. Nobody knows you're here, for Christsake. If I thought for one minute that your safety depended on those pair of bampots, I wouldn't budge outside the door. What sort of mug do you take me for anyway?' He was loath to tell her that he had simply told his brothers to keep an eye on her and make sure she never left the house.

Donna merely smiled and said, 'Where are you going anyway?'

'For a kick off I'm going to the Wheatsheaf to see who shows a face. After that, I'll have to wait and see.'

'I don't understand why you have to go out, Jimmy. It's almost as if you're inviting trouble.'

'Ach away and shite, Donna. Sure trouble and me are perfect strangers these days.' Jimmy didn't want to remind her that his attitude was no different now than it was when he was growing up in Glasgow. You didn't hide from anybody. 'Come on, Shane. Get your coat on and I'll give you a lift up the road.'

Shane popped the rest of a half-bitten chip into her mouth and swallowed her index finger all the way to the hilt. Looking at Jimmy she sucked in and slowly extracted the finger. 'Won't be a tick,' she grinned and stepped into her high heels.

TWENTY-TWO

Donna moved to the window as soon as the door closed behind Jimmy and Shane and watched through a slit in the curtains until the car's headlights moved off down the mews. Fetching her handbag, she went into the privacy of the bedroom where she started thumbing through her address book.

In the living room William sat on the couch next to Corrie and joined him watching Mick kneeling in front of a set of cabinets and shelves, which, apart from two rows of books, housed a television, some state of the art stereo equipment, and whatever was behind the lower doors.

'Hey Mick.' William whispered and glanced towards the bedroom door. 'What do yeh think yer hokeying about in there for? You'll get us shot, so yeh will.'

Mick held his finger over his lips and drilled his brother with his eyes. 'Shush up a minute. I'm trying to find us a few more supplies before we run out. Ahh what's this?' he added, gripping the neck of a bottle of red wine in each hand.

'Fucken firewater,' William told him. 'One sniff of the cork and yer blootered, man. Remember the last time yeh got us bevied on the jungle juice we woke up in fucken Wales. Mertnyrfuckentydfil of all places. How in the name of fuck we managed that I'll never know.'

'Hey Willy, mind the fucken languange. The wee boy's sitting there.' Mick indicated to Corrie tugging at William's sleeve.

'Oh sorry, wee man. Yer auld Uncle William got a bit carried away with himself there for a minute. What was yeh going to say?'

Corrie's nose wrinkled in anticipation. 'Nah, it doesn't matter,' he said, after a short pause.

'Yeh sure? There's not much yer Uncle Willy doesn't know, yeh know.'

'Nah, it's just that I was wondering if Aunty Shane was my real aunty. If she was, then there would be a better chance of her bone marrow being compatible with mine, wouldn't there?'

'Not even a prick relation,' Mick said emphatically, before he had a chance to think. 'Mind you, I'd be just the very man to do something about that.'

Corrie was none the wiser.

'Hey wee man, pay no attention to that bam,' William said, angling his face so that his look of rebuttal went unseen by the boy. 'Of course yer Aunty Shane's yer real aunty. She's yer Aunty Shane, isn't she?'

'Right enough,' Mick said, winking at William after he'd got the message. 'What I was trying to say wee man was, if yer aunty was a man she'd be yer uncle, know what I'm getting at? But because yer aunty's no a man then she must be yer aunty. Know what I'm saying? Ach for Christsake, yeh know what I mean. If yer uncle was a woman he'd be yer aunty, just like Aunty Shane.'

In the bedroom, while she waited for the phone to answer Donna crossed her legs and inadvertently ran her free hand up and down her stockinged leg, massaging, and enjoying the softness of her touch. She had been on hold since the reception desk at the Holiday Inn had informed her that Mr Munro wasn't answering in his room, and if she liked, they would page him at the bar.

'Donna,' Munro answered, the slur in his voice impossible to mistake. 'To what do I owe the unexpected pleasure?'

'Steve, are you all right? You sound a bit –'

'Socially confused,' Munro interrupted, adding a laugh. 'Yes, I guess you could say that. I'm afraid it's been one of those days, but I doubt if you've called to hear that.'

Donna adjusted the pillows and took her weight on the wall behind her. 'There's a few things I think you should know, but I'm not sure if I can tell you over the phone. Do you think I could meet you somewhere, you know, so we can have a bit of a natter?

The only thing is, I'm not sure if it can wait until the morning, and by the sound of you, you're ready to call it a day.'

Munro laughed. 'My dear Donna I can assure you that I'm well practised at operating under these conditions. It'll be no trouble at all. The night's a pup.'

Donna stared into the mouthpiece and shook her head. 'It might be a better idea if you stay where you are, Steve. Give me a chance to get ready and I'll see you in an hour or so.'

'That's a great idea. Have you eaten yet?'

She was about to tell him that Jimmy had brought home a big feed of fish and chips, but thought better of it when she realised that her chances of getting some sense out of him would increase if he wasn't drinking on an empty stomach. 'That sounds like the shot,' she told him.

'Grand, I'll book us a table and meet you at the bar. Unless you would prefer to go to Langan's around the corner? I hear it's pretty good, but it'd mean we'd have to put the glad rags on.'

'Langan's sounds fine,' Donna agreed, hoping that the time he took to shower and get ready would help to sober him up.

Munro hung up and looked himself up and down. Seeing no room for improvement he brushed a hand over the front of his suit trousers and the shoulders of his jacket and headed straight back to the bar.

In the Wheatsheaf Jimmy sat alone at his usual table and kept an eye on the front door of the fast-filling lounge bar. Uncomfortable, he responded to the greetings of only a few. By presenting himself in public he was declaring not only that he wasn't shying away from confrontation, but that he was inviting it. He knew that if anyone was looking for him the Wheatsheaf would be the first place they'd look.

When a measure of scotch was placed on the table beside three other untouched drinks he didn't bother looking up to see who had sent it.

'Like a fly around a shite,' Jimmy smirked, looking at Old Davey gripping the back of a chair and wobbling precariously at the other end of the table.

'Like a fly man around a table full of bevie, yeh mean,' Old Davey laughed.

'Sit down before you fall flat on your coupon.'

'Yeh look like yeh could be doing with a wee hand with that, son,' Old Davey said, turning on the charm and casting a concerned eye over the drinks. 'Yeh don't want folk thinking the Macintyres cannay handle their bevie, son, now do yeh?'

'Away you go. By the looks of you you've had more than your fair share. How the fuck do they serve you in a state like that, da? I'll be having a word with the management.'

With one eye shut and the other threatening to join it Old Davey's tongue poked out and painstakingly lapped his lips, along the dark line of residue built up by his day-long session. 'Ach well, if yer going to be like that there's nay much chance of yer auld da remembering what that geezer was on about this afternoon when he rang yeh. Christ, I've already forgotten once and there's fuck all stopping me forgetting again?'

'Do you not get tired of your stupid little games, da?' Jimmy pushed two of the drinks to within reach of his father, keeping the palms of his hands clamped firmly over the top of them.

Old Davey licked his lips again and tried prising the drinks loose, muttering under his breath. 'As soon as you stop your fucking about and give me the message you can have the bevie. Fair enough?'

'Yer nothing but a sleekit git, so yeh are.'

'Aye, well on you go then.'

'The doctor rang up looking for Donna. I told him I hadnay a clue where the fuck she was. He said to tell her to ring him as soon as possible.'

Jimmy shook his head in disgust. 'How could you forget a message like that? It could've been about a donor.'

'Wise up. Do yeh no think the doctor would have said? Christsake, something as important as that.'

The three-piece band had just walked onto the stage ahead of the lights being dimmed when Jimmy stood and gently manhandled his father towards the door. Across the standing-room-only lounge bar the constant chatter subsided to a controlled whisper of anticipation. At the same time Old Davey protested and looked longingly over his shoulder at the drink he considered was going to waste. 'Yer a fair scunner,' he moaned, his feet barely touching the ground.

At the door the bouncer standing with legs wide apart and rigid, his hands cupped over his groin, sprang into action when he saw Jimmy coming and pushed the door open for him. The bouncer on the outside completed the double act by reaching for the ornate brass handle, preventing the door from swinging back.

'Do me a wee favour, Roland. Walk my old man around to the house, will you? He's doing my nut in.' Jimmy's tone suggested no hint of a request. 'Don't worry about the door. I'll look after it for you till you get back.'

'It'll give me something to do,' the bouncer agreed, winking at Jimmy and guiding Old Davey away. 'Come on, Davey, and we'll get you home.'

Old Davey tried to reef his elbow away and would have fallen backwards onto the road if Roland hadn't caught him. 'Ach, yeh couldnay knock the dust of a bap, the pair o yeh. And yeh can get fuckt and all, I'll be taking my business elsewhere from now on. A man cannay get a minute's peace to have a quiet bevie, for Christsake.'

'Carry him if you have to,' Jimmy called after them.

A relentless wind howling down the side street quickly consumed the continuing tirade of abuse and forced Jimmy back into the comparative shelter of the doorway. 'Fuck this for a mug's game,' he mumbled, and blew into his cupped hands. It reminded him of the days when he'd done a bit of bouncing. Before he realised he could make more money by simply going the demand.

He had the collar of his suit jacket clutched about his neck and was alternately hopping from one foot to the other or jogging on the spot when he peeked out of the doorway and noticed the headlights turning into the street. The vehicle crawled towards him and reversed into a newly vacated parking spot on the other side of the road.

Distracted by the grating sound of high-heeled shoes approaching from his left he looked away from the lone occupant of the car long enough to swing the heavy door open. 'Good evening, ladies,' he smiled, warming to his role.

'God, don't tell me you're working as a bouncer, Jimmy? Things must be bad.'

'No way, Norma,' Jimmy said, addressing the older of the two women. 'I'm just holding the fort till Roland gets back from doing a wee message for me. Christ, if I'd known I was going to freeze to death I'd have been as well doing the fucken thing myself. Pardon the French.'

'Well, you always know where to come if you want to warm yourself up,' Norma told him, grinning.

'Get in there and behave yourself,' he replied, returning the grin.

When the door closed behind the two women he went over to the pavement's edge and held his middle finger to the side of his nose. After checking to see that nobody was watching he snorted the effects of the cold weather onto the road. When he turned his head to repeat the process he realised that there was no one behind the wheel of the car, or any sign of the driver on the street. Unconcerned, he cleared the other nostril and checked the dimly lit street as far as his watering eyes could see, guessing that the driver had disappeared into one of the terraced houses opposite. A quick scan halfway to the corner revealed a figure watching him from a doorway shaded in the darkest point between two street lights. He was about to stroll up and see what was going on when a car approached from the other end of the street, slowed down and double parked right in front of the pub.

Cheeky fucker, Jimmy thought, watching the driver get out of the car and lock it.

'Hey dynamite, where the fuck do you think you're parking? You're blocking these cars in.'

'You be a good little boy and keep your eye on it for me,' Tate scowled, not bothering to produce his ID. In his usual self-opinionated manner he thought that there wasn't a doorman in London, worth his salt, that could fail to pick him for a policeman.

Jimmy returned to the doorway and leaned against the side wall with his foot firmly planted on the wall opposite. He had recognised the policeman as soon as he'd stepped within the range of the dull glow emanating from the coloured lights fringing the arched canopy over the door. It made him all the more determined. 'You've only been here less than a minute and you've made two mistakes already. Make it three and I'll take your warrant card out of your pocket and jam it up your clacker for you.'

Tate angrily eyed the leg barring his access to the pub. He was contemplating all manner of retribution when, after a closer look, it dawned on him who the doorman was. It mellowed him considerably. 'Jimmy Macintyre,' he said, grinning nervously. 'You're just the very man I'm looking for. Have you got time for a quiet word? We can sit in the car if you like.'

'Me and you have got sweet fuck all to talk about.'

'Sorry to disturb you while you're working, Jimmy, but there's something I think you should know.'

After the policeman's sudden backdown Jimmy thought it more important to preserve his image. 'I don't work here, by the way. I'm only holding the fort till the guy gets back.'

'We could jump in the car and drive around the corner, if that's what's bothering you?' Tate persisted. 'I'm sure you'll find what I've got to say interesting.'

Before he could answer Jimmy became aware of Roland running up the middle of the street towards him.

'Everything all right?' Roland asked breathlessly.

'Aye, but did you deliver that message OK?'

'Message? Oh yes. Mission accomplished.' Roland completed the transaction in his usual thumb-grip handshake.

Walking towards the car Jimmy turned and said,

'I'll be back in a minute. If I'm not, break out the militia.'

'Thanks for your time, Jimmy,' Tate said.

As the car proceeded slowly along the street Tate glanced sideways at his passenger, noting, by the way he looked out the window to his left, then over his shoulder, that something had caught his eye.

'As long as you're not wasting my time.' Jimmy said, his eyes now flicking from one side of the street to the other.

In search of somewhere to park Tate deliberately headed for the brighter lights of South Lambeth Road. The reality of being alone with Jimmy Macintyre had turned out to be more daunting than he'd anticipated.

'I want to discuss a guy by the name of Tom Gilfeather.' Tate pulled into the side of the road and twisted around in his seat, trying to gauge Jimmy's reaction.

'You said you wanted to tell me something? Not discuss something.' Jimmy opened the door, hesitated, and turned to face the detective.

Tate put a hand on Jimmy's shoulder, retracting it the instant Jimmy looked down the length of his nose at it. 'I'm getting to that. But first I have to clarify a few things.'

Jimmy eased the door shut.

'According to my records, you and Gilfeather did time together. In fact, if you cast your mind back, you might remember that you shared a cell at one stage.'

'So?' Jimmy continued staring straight ahead.

Despite the ex-convict's well-documented ability to remain calm in times of extreme duress Tate detected an edginess that would have escaped the attention of all but the most diligent of investigators. It raised a question regarding Jimmy's involvement in all this. For all he knew the Glasgow hard man could be pulling everybody's strings. Without risking Macintyre going off half-cocked he intended to have him in the right place at the right time and in the right frame of mind.

'I was talking to Anton Winters this morning. I don't think he likes you.' Tate lit a cigarette, blew the smoke out of the side of his mouth and half turned to grin at Jimmy.

'The feeling's mutual,' Jimmy said.

'He had some interesting things to say about our friend Gilfeather. Things I doubt you're aware of.'

'What makes you think that I'd be interested in anything he had to say, period?'

'If you're not interested in what he has to say about Gilfeather you might be more interested in what he had to do with the fire bomb up in Archer Street.'

'Is that what this is all about? I was wondering when I was going to get a visit.' Jimmy had registered everything the detective said but wished to convey indifference.

Tate continued. 'I've put myself in charge of that case, and you can consider this the visit, but that's not what I came here to talk about.'

'Hold on a minute, pal. You sit there and, casually as fuck, mention an attempt on my Donna's life. Then you say that you're not here to talk about it. Why the fuck not?'

'I was leading up to that. If I could find out who did it, would you be interested in knowing?' Tate paused, lit one cigarette off the butt of the other and raised an eyebrow at Jimmy.

Jimmy didn't have to ask why the chief superintendent was confiding in him. As soon as he'd set eyes on Tate he'd wondered if he was featured in the diary. Now totally convinced that Tate was the star attraction in it, Jimmy suspected that the policeman was manipulating everyone in a desperate attempt to save his own neck. 'Any cunt capable of harming a woman would be no loss,' he said.

'I couldn't agree more.'

'So how close are you to finding out who did it?'

'I've got to be in Brighton at 7.30 tomorrow night. The Sands Hotel to be exact. If you happened to be in the area, you might consider dropping in. I'm sure I'll have the answer by then.'

'Ach, I suppose I could grab my bucket and spade and head down there. It's been a while since I've been in for a paddle.' Jimmy's frivolous reply masked a far more serious mood. He was thinking that the big Irishman, Dermot Mulholland, had better come up with something quick. Failing that, the finger had been pointed at Anton. Not that he needed an excuse to sort him out. That was a done deal. His only concern was to make sure he had the right person. He didn't like the idea of somebody getting away with it.

Aiming his smoke at the slit of the partly open window Tate turned the key in the ignition and checked both rear-view mirrors, looking for a break in the busy Friday-night traffic. 'Can I offer you a lift somewhere, or would you prefer to go back to the pub?'

'No offence, but I think I'll walk it from here.' Jimmy alighted from the car and leaned in. 'See you in Brighton then.'

'Before you go, that business I mentioned about Anton having something interesting to tell you about Gilfeather. Anton insists on telling you himself. He said to tell you that he looks forward to seeing you in Brighton tomorrow night.'

With his hands in his pockets and his shoulders hunched against the chill Jimmy hurried towards the Wheatsheaf thinking that Archie Kemp was due a call. No offence, he would tell him, but if Anton fucken Winters is behind the bombing in Archer Street, then all bets are off.

As he turned the corner into Mawbey Street his thoughts drifted to the Sands Hotel, wondering why the name suddenly sounded so familiar to him. He had the Wheatsheaf in sight before it dawned on him. It was the venue for the big charity gala for the clinic Donna and Shane had been discussing after the last time they were at the clinic.

TWENTY-THREE

Donna dried herself off and wrapped the towel around her upper body, fastening it high on her chest. She sat on the edge of the bed facing the floor-length mirror, wondering what she was going to wear and what excuse she could use to get out. First things first, she thought, rising and going to the chest of drawers beside the mirror. 'Tart,' she smiled, when a quick rummage through Shane's underwear drawer revealed nothing in the way of tights. It was stockings and suspenders or nothing, unless she stopped along the way and bought a pair of tights. Thinking that it would be a waste of time, by the time she bought the tights and found somewhere to change into them, she selected a black barque similar to the ones she wore to work and put it on, glad that at least it seemed that she and Shane took the same size. She sat on the edge of the bed and put on the stockings, having checked them by running each of them over the back of her hand, all the way to the black reinforced toe.

She slid open the wardrobe door thinking that Jimmy could've saved her a lot of trouble if he'd brought the rest of her gear, like he'd promised. After several minutes spent browsing and holding various outfits up to her neck for appraisal she opted for a waisted, black suit with a fitted, knee-length skirt and put it on, thinking that it was a safe enough choice. She had seen Shane in the outfit and remembered at the time thinking how smart it looked.

When she'd put the finishing touches to her makeup and stepped into her own high-heeled shoes she reached for the phone and dialled the memorised number of Combined Cabs. 'Just toot the horn and I'll be right out,' she told the dispatcher.

As soon as she heard the distinctive sound of the black cab pulling up outside she grabbed her coat and handbag and popped her head around the bedroom door. 'Mummy's got to go out for an hour,' she said, turning to blow Corrie a kiss as she made a hasty beeline for the front door.

Mick had a half-pint tumbler of cabernet sauvignon raised to his lips when it dawned on him that Donna was leaving. 'Hey Donna doll, where do yeh think yer going? Me and our William are supposed to be keeping an eye on yeh.'

'What's all the racket?' William said, hurrying out of the toilet to see the front door lying open and his brother, his top lip ringed in red, standing on the footpath with a nearly empty glass in his hand.

'It's Donna, she's fuckt off. Done a runner,' Mick told him.

'You were supposed to be watching her, Mick. Christ, I can't even have a shite in peace!'

'Aye, that's right, blame me. If you hadnay been in there having a wank for twenty minutes yeh would've been out here to give me a hand. Don't forget you're the fucken oldest, so yeh are.'

'Oh, so that's yer game is it? All of a sudden I'm the fucken oldest, am I?'

'Don't be so fucken stupit, William, sure you've always been the oldest.' Mick chuckled and lurched back inside.

On the way to get Jimmy's mobile phone number from his jacket pocket William stopped at the coffee table and picked up the empty bottle of cabernet sauvignon. 'Did you drink this whole bottle yesel while I was having a shite?'

Mick drained the last of the red wine and peered into the empty tumbler, holding the rim to his eye. 'I only had the two glasses,' he laughed.

'You'll be laughing on the other side of yer face, my man, as soon as our Jimmy gets a grip of yeh. Yeh won't think it's so funny then, mister.'

'Hold yer horses, Willy,' Mick said, the gravity of the situation at last starting to penetrate the alcohol fog. 'Donna might only be five minutes. As long as she comes home before our Jamesie he'll be none the wiser.'

Shane's phone began to ring before William had a

chance to answer his brother. Mick darted for the phone as if the call was for him. 'Sorry pal,' he said, 'you've just missed her. She's just away to her work. You'll catch her at the Wheatsheaf in South Lambeth. No, Donna's not here either.'

'Who was that?' William said, worried.

'Don't worry. It was only the doctor. At least that's who he said it was.'

William shook his head and began dialling. 'There's no doubt about yeh, Mickey boy, yer a right fucken comedian, so yeh are.'

In the Wheatsheaf, as the clapping, whistling and cheering peaked Shane took her final bow and left the stage, promising she'd be back after a short break.

'Can I get you a drink?' she asked Jimmy, hovering over his table.

Jimmy nodded at the growing collection of untouched drinks on the table in front of him. 'No, but grab yourself one and sit down. There's something I need to talk to you about.'

Intrigued, Shane decided to make do with the half-full bottle of Perrier water she'd taken with her from the stage.

'You remember what we were talking about the other night?' Jimmy paused to acknowledge Shane's nod of agreement. 'As it turned out you, eh, you were pretty well spot on. Donna could've done with a bit of looking after. But, eh, I've been wondering what she said to you to make you think that? It was obviously something you discussed.'

Shane's face darkened. 'It's weird that, you know. I just had a funny feeling. Call it woman's intuition.'

'Call it *what*?'

'You know what I mean.'

'Did she ever mention anything about a – Fuck it, this phone's turning out to be a nuisance.' Jimmy reached for the mobile in his inside pocket. 'Hold on a second, William, I can hardly hear you.'

'Go through to the back.' Shane suggested, and stood with the intention of escorting him behind the bar.

'It's all right. I know where it is. But don't go away, I haven't finished talking to you yet.'

No sooner had Jimmy cleared the hatch at the end of the bar when one of the barmen waved Shane over. 'That was good timing,' he told her. 'There's some geezer on the blower for you.'

'For me? I'll take it out the back, if you don't mind, love?' Shane went behind the bar and through the door leading to the passage. Although she was curious as to who would be phoning her at work she still managed a smile for Jimmy on the way past.

Thinking that she'd followed him in order to eavesdrop Jimmy told William to hold on.

Shane made sure the door was closed before she picked up the receiver. 'Ahh, Dr Cullen. Yes, I'm fine. And you? That's good.'

As soon as the doctor began speaking Shane's eyes

narrowed and she glanced towards the door, aware that Jimmy had gone quiet. Resisting the urge to comment she simply whispered, 'If I can't coax Donna into going down to Brighton, I don't think anyone can. Yes. Leave it to me. You're welcome.'

Jimmy winked at Shane when she came out of the office and waited until she'd returned to the bar before he continued speaking. 'OK William, go ahead,' he urged.

'It's your Donna,' William blurted out. 'She's done a runner. There was fuck all I could do about it. I sat down with the paper to have a shite and the next thing I knew she was out the door and gone. Mick said he saw her jumping into a taxi, all done up.'

'What do you mean, all done up? Sure she never had any good gear with her?'

'That's what he said Jimmy. All done up. She wasnay going to work, was she?'

'Pair of fucken clowns, that's all youse are. A pair of balloons,' Jimmy ranted.

It was clear why Donna hadn't protested too much when he'd told her he was going to send his brothers over. He had played into her hands, providing her with babysitters for Corrie.

'Ask Mick if he saw what kind of taxi it was. Better still, put him on, go on, hurry up.'

'How's it going, Jimbo?' Mick slurred.

'Don't fucken tell me you're bevied already? Didn't I tell you I wanted you semi-sensible for a change?'

Mick winked at William and made a face at the

phone. 'It must've been the two glasses of red wine I had with meh fish and chips that blootered me, big man. I'm no used to plonk.'

'See, if you're taking the pish, Mick?' Jimmy warned, recognising his brother's smarmy tone.

'Jamesie, it's me yer talking to.'

'Aye, well listen. William was saying you saw Donna getting into a taxi. Did you happen to see what kind it was?'

'Too right I did. It was one of those big black fuckers.'

'Mick, for the love of fuck, don't be such an edjit. I'm talking about the name of the taxi company. Did you get a swatch at that?

'To tell yeh the truth, Jimbo, I didnay. The thought never crossed meh mind. But doesn't Donna always use the same outfit.'

Without answering Jimmy hung up and returned the mobile phone to his inside pocket. Shane would have to wait, he thought, leaving the pub and running the short distance to the car. As he drove out of Mawbey Street and crossed South Lambeth Road he pulled up beside the only taxi in the rank and woke the snoozing driver with a short, sharp toot on the car's horn.

'Cheers, Jimmy. What's happening?' The driver said, winding down his window.

'Alfie, just the very man I want to see.' Jimmy got out of the car and went around to the cab, climbing into the back seat out of the cold. 'Listen, mate, do me a wee favour and ask your dispatcher if one of your cabs picked up a woman in St Oswald's Mews in the last fifteen or twenty minutes. It's very important, so don't use the open channel.'

'Say no more,' the driver winked, and began relaying the message.

'Ask him what her destination was,' Jimmy urged, as soon as he heard the dispatcher confirm that a female fare had indeed been picked up in the mews.

'Can you confirm the passenger's destination please?'

'Still on route to the Holiday Inn Mayfair,' the dispatcher complied.

'Thanks, Alfie. That's one I owe you.' Jimmy reached through the open sliding window and patted the driver on the back.

The top-hatted doorman at the Holiday Inn moved quickly to the pavement's edge as the taxi pulled up at the kerb. 'Welcome to the Holiday Inn,' he smiled, and escorted Donna to the revolving doors, using his angled umbrella to protect her from the wind.

Donna returned the doorman's smile and stepped into the foyer, pleased that she blended easily with the luxury hotel's well-heeled clientele. On her way to the cocktail bar to meet Munro she ducked into the Ladies to assess and repair damage inflicted by the wind and rain. A dab of powder here and there and a fresh application of lipstick, followed by a two-handed tizz of her hair and she was ready to make an entrance.

From the hallway leading past the lifts to the restaurants and bars she glanced to her right and saw Munro, flanked by two-well dressed men, leaving by the wide, hinged door next to the revolving doors. As she got close to the full-length, tinted windows she could clearly see the relaxed, drunken look on Munro's face. A bid to attract his attention by lightly tapping on the window succeeded only in alerting his escorts to the need for more haste. She made it out into the street in time to see Munro being driven off in a light blue Sierra.

She rushed outside and tried with no success to commandeer a taxi waiting for the doorman to accompany three Japanese businessmen from the foyer.

'Sorry princess,' the driver said, locking eyes with her in the rear-vision mirror. 'Those three Japanese geezers have booked me for the night. Sorry.'

Frantic now, and fearing that Munro was in danger, she scrambled from the taxi looking left and right for any sign of another taxi entering the street. When a car pulled into the street she automatically raised her hand to flag it down. Not until the car swerved over to her side of the road did she realise who it was.

'Shit,' she muttered, knowing that she'd been spotted and that it was too late to do anything about it.

'Get in,' Jimmy demanded, winding down his window.

Donna's mind was racing. While she welcomed Jimmy's help she was terrified that it would lead him a step closer to finding out the truth about Gilfeather.

'Hurry Jimmy,' she said, trying to buy time to think. 'Two heavy-looking geezers in suits have just driven off with Steve. They're in a light-coloured Sierra. Jimmy, I didn't like the looks of them.'

'Steve? Who the fuck's Steve?'

'You know. Steve Munro. That American jounalist geezer.'

'This better be good.' Jimmy accelerated flat out along Berkeley Street to the corner. 'Are you going to tell me which way?' he added.

'Left. They turned left into Piccadilly. Hurry.'

'The Christmas traffic's pandemonium and she says hurry.'

'Just drive, will you?'

In silence Jimmy dodged and weaved through the heavy traffic looking for the Sierra. He was entering Piccadilly Circus when he thought he spotted the car. It was turning right at Haymarket and heading downhill towards Pall Mall East and Trafalgar Square.

'Does that look like the motor there, Donna?'

Donna reacted with a start. Apart from desperately searching for the Sierra she was trying to think of a reason to justify her presence at the Holiday Inn. 'Where? Yes. That's them. Quick, don't lose them.'

'Don't bother yourself about that, Donna. The old radar's locked on.'

'Down there, Jimmy. Look.' Donna pointed past the sparkling Christmas tree in Trafalgar Square to the Sierra crossing Duncannon Street and entering the Strand. 'Don't lose them, for goodness sake.'

'By the way, Donna. Are you going to tell me what you were doing at the Holiday Inn?'

Half-telling the truth she said, 'It was doing my head in, being cooped up in the flat.' As soon as the words cleared her mouth she realised how inadequate her answer was. 'I was worried about missing out on work so I got in touch with a client. You know, while William and Mick were there to look after Corrie.'

'So you thought you'd take a wee run up to the Holiday Inn to see a client, eh? And while you were there you just happened to see the American guy getting captured by a couple of heavies? You must take me for a right mug.' Jimmy took advantage of a sudden stop in the traffic to turn and smile at his wife.

Thinking quickly she said, 'I was worried that something like this would happen so I decided to kill two birds with one stone. Don't forget that Steve could've been seen in our company. I thought we owed it to him to warn him.' After a pause she added, 'Doesn't look like I was quick enough, does it?'

'Well, if that's the case me and you will have to sit down and compare notes as soon as I hear what your mate Steve has to say about things.'

Donna was angry at the stationary car in front indicating and trying to merge with the traffic flowing freely on her left. 'Why is this the only lane to have stopped Jimmy?' she asked anxiously. 'Can you see what the hell's going on? I think there's a car stopped at a green light. Give the stupid bastard a toot, for goodness sake, before we lose the Sierra.'

'Take it easy, doll. I'm not that stupid. It's the Sierra that's causing all the problems.'

'Can you see what they're doing?'

'They're just sitting there at a green light. Doing fuck all by the looks of them. I hope they've broken down.'

As soon as the green light changed to amber the Sierra sped through the intersection, leaving the traffic lined up behind it to face a red light.

'Bastard!' shouted Jimmy furiously, and thumped the top of the steering wheel with the heels of both hands.

Donna seemed unconcerned, almost relieved. It had just dawned on her that, one way or the other, she would be better off if she could keep Jimmy away from Munro. At least until she had time to alert him to the fact that Jimmy would be asking questions. If something were to happen to Munro in the meantime, it might be a blessing in disguise. One less worry.

'Well that's that,' she said, hoping with her tone to influence Jimmy into abandoning the chase.

'Maybe not. There's a place down by the river

where – Nah, you don't want to know about that. But it looks like that's where they're heading.'

'Don't tell me.'

'They must be from the old school.' Jimmy turned right behind the Savoy then left along the Victoria Embankment on the north side of the river and continued driving in silence until they had cleared the Blackfriars Bridge underpass and were heading along Upper Thames Street in the direction of Queenhithe Docks.

'According to my old man, the doctor phoned you this afternoon,' Jimmy told her, sounding as if it was an afterthought. 'Were you expecting to hear from him?'

'Excuse the language Jimmy, but what sort of a stupid fucken question is that? Of course I was expecting to hear from him. Aren't we always expecting to hear from him, or had it slipped your mind? Christ Jimmy, why didn't you tell me? Did he say what he wanted? I mean, I can't remember him ever phoning the house. It's always been me phoning him to hear the bad news. He was always saying he'd get in touch as soon as he had anything important to tell me. Jimmy, take me home. Now.'

Jimmy turned into High Timber Street and pulled over to the side of the road. He reached for the mobile phone in his inside pocket and handed it to Donna. 'Here you go,' he said, 'There's nothing you can do at home that you can't do from here. And before you go getting yourself all worked up, I think the doctor would have done a lot more than just leave a message to ring him back if he'd anything exciting to tell you. Besides, if it was that important why didn't he just ask for me, eh?'

As he got out of the car and gently shut the door behind him Jimmy watched Donna punching in the numbers and knew she hadn't heard a single word he'd said. No problem, he thought, and began making his way towards the river, walking on the balls of his feet and hugging the shadows along the building line. When he was close enough to the Thames to hear the sound of water lapping at its banks he stopped dead, cocked an ear and peered off into the darkness. Hearing nothing other than anonymous, waterfront murmurings, he moved slowly along the cobbles between the ancient sandstone buildings on his right and the low parapet wall running parallel with the river. He continued walking for over five minutes and was seriously starting to doubt his earlier conviction when the sight of a lone car parked up ahead enticed him to go on. Back in the days when he'd done a bit of freelancing for Archie Kemp this general area was known to be the drop-off point for soiled or unwanted goods. With the knowledge that only a few had made the return journey from here, and other places like it, he quickened his pace until the darkness up ahead surrendered the garbled sounds of someone running out of patience.

By the time he'd inched close enough to decipher fragments of what was being said he could make out the darkened form of two men, both of whom he judged to be the aggressors. Donna's presence at the Holiday Inn, coupled with Munro's abduction, had aroused his suspicions. Now all he wanted was to hear what Munro had to say. It didn't bother him if the information had to be knocked out of him. It's probably the quickest way and it saves me the bother, he thought.

Steve Munro, drunk as he was, had known as soon as he felt the shudder of the cobbles and saw the solitude of the area they were driving into that his companions were not the police, as they had purported to be. He had been too concerned to speak in the car, seeking solace in ignorance and the hope that they would re-enter a lit-up area. Having no previous experience in these matters, and with the alcohol partly acting as an anaesthetic, he had resisted the first firm but cordial request for information. It would have helped if they hadn't been seeking answers to the very same questions that he himself wanted answers to.

The two men exchanged knowing looks and forced Munro backwards to the parapet wall, keeping hold of him to stop him from going all the way over.

After claiming yet again that he had no idea of the whereabouts of Tom Gilfeather Munro found himself being hoisted over the wall and dangled. From his upside-down position the vast array of lights on the other side of the river now formed a ceiling, appearing as if the crescent of light was shining down. And the mud, that putrid, contaminated sludge revealed by the retreating tide, produced an immediate return of his senses. He primed himself for an impact as he saw the exposed cobbles of an abandoned slipway glistening thirty feet below.

'Hurry up. I can hardly hold him.'

Jimmy was near enough to hear this and to attribute it to the taller of the two figures bent over the waist-high wall.

'Do you hear what he said?' the other shouted. 'This is your last chance. You either tell us what connection you have with Tom Gilfeather, right now, or we drop you on your head. If the fall doesn't kill you, you'll lie there crippled until the tide picks you up and drowns you.'

You're between the devil and the deep blue sea, mate, Jimmy thought, knowing full well that they would drop him anyway, as soon as he told them what they wanted to hear. 'Tell them,' he muttered under his breath, thinking that it would be nice to hear what Munro had to say before they dropped him.

With the strain telling in his voice the taller of the two said, 'Tell us what you know about that slut Donna Macintyre and we'll lift you up.' He knew this was impossible. It was draining all his strength just to hold on to Munro.

Enraged, Jimmy stepped out of the shadows behind the two men. He was intent on grievous bodily harm, but stopped suddenly when Munro began to answer. Nobody called Donna a slut and got away with it, but this was what he wanted to hear.

The deep burble of a passing river cruiser festooned in strings of brightly coloured lights, apart from muffling Munro's reply, sent its stern wave lapping over the cobbles in its wake. Munro could feel the grip on his legs weaken and slip along his shins to his feet. With his head and face completely gorged with blood his frantic reply quickly turned to an impassioned scream for help. In the ensuing struggle, in which his intentions were to at least turn around so that he would fall with his arms out in front of him, he managed only to drain his captors of their last drop of strength and move them further along the wall.

'I can't hold him,' a voice screamed in panic. The taller man fell backwards onto the seat of his pants with Munro's right shoe in his hand. He was joined by his companion holding the other shoe lost in the leg of Munro's trousers.

As soon as he heard the scream Jimmy knew that Munro had fallen. It was obvious to him that there was nothing he could have done. Not that he'd intended to do anything that would have jeopardised his chances of hearing what he had to say. One move from him and it would have been over quicker. He knew that.

'That was a naughty thing to do,' Jimmy said with a wicked smile.

In fright, the two men rolled onto their hands and knees and scurried over towards the parapet wall where they got to their feet simultaneously and turned to face the unseen protagonist. Both relaxed when they saw that there was only one man to contend with.

'You, eh, you got something to say, pal?' the taller one said and moved off to his left, nodding at his partner to begin circling to the right.

Before they had taken two steps Jimmy stepped forward and presented himself. His action stopped the two men dead in their tracks and forced an exchange of worried looks. 'Jimmy Macintyre,' the one who had been doing all the talking said and held up his hands, cocking his head to the side. 'There's nothing personal here, Jimmy. This is strictly business. Me and Terry were only doing our job. That's right ain't it, Tel, we were only doing our job?'

Terry's tacit nod of agreement masked an ulterior motive. He was a new face from the North of England, hired by Anton to replace the inept Nigel Paterson. But now he saw the chance to make a name for himself at the expense of Jimmy Macintyre.

Without moving into striking distance Jimmy took another step forward. Apart from the need to sum up the opposition he wanted to get close enough to read the look in their eyes. He immediately recognised Eddie Simpson, not from their pleasant discussion at the funeral of Anton's mother, but for the two-faced bastard that he was.

'Does Archie know what company you're keeping?' Jimmy leered, at the thought of Archie telling him that, in effect, Eddie was his eyes on the outside.

'It's a question of showing your loyalty to the right

person, Jimmy. You could take a leaf out of my book yourself. You could do yourself a lot of good. Business is business.'

Spitting at the ground in front of Eddie Simpson's feet Jimmy turned his attention to the other man. He could tell by the look of contempt on the man's face that he was harbouring evil intentions and that he wasn't in the slightest bit intimidated by the Macintyre reputation.

'That's right, is it, Tel?' Jimmy goaded, standing with his arms folded across his chest.

Terry shrugged his shoulder and forced a sullen smile. 'Yeah, you know the game. Business is business.'

Laughing, Jimmy shook his head and let out his breath in a protracted sigh of derision. 'A right fucken pair of wankers. Two balloons. You two cunts have been watching too many gangster movies for your own good. Who the fuck do you think you are, Don Corleone or somebody?'

Eddie Simpson laughed nervously. He was more aware than his partner of just exactly what they were up against and didn't have to guess that they were being baited. Jimmy Macintyre was well known for his fun and games before the kill. Just like a cat. Except this time he had bitten off more than he could chew. Terry Smith, looking like he was as wide as he was tall, was fast making a name for himself and had been brought in specifically to handle Macintyre. And provided they went at Macintyre together there was every reason to be confident that he would soon be feeding the fish along with the drunken American. The thought of the consequences of returning to Anton empty-handed was daunting, but Eddie imagined Jimmy Macintyre's scalp in tow would be compensation enough.

'Don't be like that, Jimmy.' Eddie held his hands out to the sides, palms up. 'Why don't we go up the boozer and have a bit of a natter over a pint? 'Ere Tel, fancy a pint?'

Having now heard both men speak Jimmy knew the answer to his next question before he asked it. 'I'll tell you what I'm prepared to do with you, Eddie. You tell me exactly which one of you pair of cunts called my Donna a slut and I'll happily go and have a bevie with the other one. That's fair enough, isn't it?'

Terry Smith fixed his dark, malevolent eyes on Jimmy. He had recuperated long enough after his struggle with the American and just wanted to get on with the business. 'I called the slut a slut,' he lied with a sneer and took one step forward, offering himself as a target.

'Well then, it looks like you won't be joining us for drink, will you?' Jimmy mocked, and contrary to what Terry expected him of him, remained exactly where he was, with his arms still folded across his chest.

'Watch him, Tel,' Eddie said, abandoning the pretence as his eyes flitted rapidly from one man to the other.

Terry circled to his right with the intention of

forcing Jimmy to turn his back on Eddie. When he was side on to Jimmy and saw that he hadn't budged an inch he looked beyond him to his partner and held up a hand. 'He's mine,' he said, confident that he was in a no-lose situation.

Jimmy stared straight ahead and remained standing with his arms folded tightly across his chest. He kept Terry in his peripheral vision knowing by the way he had admitted to calling Donna a slut that he was ego-driven, and would make the first move. Eddie Simpson, the jackal that he was, was well-known for moving in for the pickings after the danger had passed.

On cue, Terry sprang forward in a crouch, intending to floor Jimmy with a waist-high rugby tackle and nullify him with his superior strength. This was a tactic that he had never known to fail. It invalidated his opponent's ability and technique and reduced the conflict to a test of strength.

In one fluent motion Jimmy side-stepped like a matador and deftly brought the cut-throat razor he'd kept concealed in his folded arms across the face of the rampaging Smith. The glistening blade sliced horizontally across the man's left eye, bisecting it like a grape. It travelled over the bridge of his nose, diverted over his cheekbone and off the side of his face, cutting his right ear in two. A torrent of blood quickly masked the fleeting glimpse of bone and gore and gristle.

Terry Smith covered his face with his hands and rolled on the ground in shock. A bone-chilling scream gurgled out with the blood oozing between the fingers that uselessly tried to hold his tattered face together.

Eddie Simpson was backing away when Jimmy spun to face him. He held up his hands, signifying surrender. The razor arced through the air and sliced his fingers to the bone. Eddie tucked the hand under his arm and fell to his knees and cried.

'Hey Eddie, if you'd owned up about calling my Donna a slut I might have accepted an apology.' Jimmy calmly raked the razor across the kneeling man's face in a back-handed action. The blade entered his left cheek just below his ear and travelled across his mouth, breaking contact on the other side of his face. His jaw unhinged, exposing a gaping red hole the width of his face.

'Try calling Donna a slut now, yah cunt.'

Out of curiosity Jimmy went over to the wall and peered down into the river. He didn't have much of a head for heights and gripped the stones as hard as he could, fighting the sensation that he was going to float up and over the wall. Fuck this for a game of soldiers, he thought, and backed away from the parapet.

He toyed with the idea of tipping the two men over into the river, but after he checked that he'd been nimble enough to dodge the blood he abandoned the idea, thinking he'd like to keep it that way. For the same reason he declined to put the boot in on the way past. Instead he wiped the blade clean on the seat of

Terry Smith's pants, telling him, 'You should put a sticking plaster on that.' To Eddie he said, 'Come on, I thought we were going for a bevie?'

Jimmy was halfway to the car when he saw a shaded figure hurrying towards him. Judging by the absence of footsteps, especially the click-clack of high-heels, he was convinced that it wasn't Donna and stepped into the first darkened doorway. As Donna passed, clutching her shoes in one hand and hiking up her skirt with the other, he cheekily whistled after her. It had the desired effect. She froze in her tracks.

'You're going the wrong way,' he told her.

'Christ, Jimmy, you didn't half give me a fright.'

'Put your shoes on, pet, before you catch your death of cold.' Jimmy put his arm around her waist and steered her back in the direction from which she had just come.

'What the hell was all that noise? Is Steve all right?' Donna urged.

'I had to give those pair of cunts a right good slap. That's probably what all the noise was about.'

That was one thing Donna didn't have to be told. In the space of seconds she had detected by way of his amorous affection and his barely contained excitement that he'd been up to his old tricks again. In a big way. 'Jesus Jimmy, who were they anyway?' she sighed.

'A couple of Anton's clowns, but who gives a fuck? Doll, they were calling you names. Fucken well out of order the cunts.' Jimmy stopped and turned his wife to face him. Reaching around behind her he gripped her buttocks and drew her in. 'They should've got worse.'

Donna could feel his erection pressing up against her and knew that what they had got was bound to have been bad enough.

'Did, eh, did Steve have anything to say, did you hear?' She stood on her tiptoes and looked over his shoulder, off into the darkness. 'Where is he anyway?' she added.

'Ah well, let me see now. Yep, I reckon he could be floating somewhere between the Tower Bridge and the Isle of Dogs.'

'Christ,' Donna sighed.

'Aye,' Jimmy agreed, acting compassionately. 'The dirty pair of bastards flung him over the wall. There was nothing I could do. Ach, at least I gave them a sore face.'

Taking the mobile phone from her coat pocket Donna stopped under a street light and began dialling.

'What do you think you're doing, Donna?'

'What do you think I'm doing? Somebody's got to ring the police. We're talking murder here, aren't we?'

Jimmy eased the phone out of her hand and pressed the off button. 'We'll be talking blue murder if you ring the police,' he replied. 'Am I not just after telling you that I gave those guys a right sore face? Would you like me to spell it out?'

Donna held his gaze for several moments. Sickened, she shook her head and walked away.

'Come on Donna. I wasn't going to let anybody call you names. Fuck that for a joke.' Jimmy shrugged his shoulders and trundled off after her.

One consolation, Donna thought: judging by Jimmy's reaction he obviously hadn't overheard anything that troubled him; otherwise she would have known all about it by now.

'Did you manage to get a hold of the doctor?' Jimmy doubled his step and fell in line with her. Walking fast was never what he considered one of his strong points. Something to do with his build. He'd always thought that if you had to get somewhere in a hurry, you'd be as well running, or catching the bus.

'Hey, am I talking to my fucken self here, or what?' he said, breaking into a slow jog.

Donna climbed behind the wheel and greeted him with an outstretched hand. 'Keys please,' she said and added after a pause, 'I've had enough of your driving.'

Jimmy plopped the keys into her hand and said, 'I'm waiting.'

'The doctor never said anything.'

'What do you mean he never said anything? He must've wanted you for something. Fuck sake. Nobody phones you up for nothing.'

'If you would just let me finish,' Donna snapped. 'He's gone away for the weekend and he won't be back until after Christmas.'

Not that he thought he had any real reason to doubt her, not when it came to the subject of Corrie's health, but there was something in her nonchalant response that didn't sit easy with him. 'I see. He phoned you to tell you he was going away for the weekend. That was helluva nice of him. I hope you told him to send us a postcard?'

'I hate it when you try to be clever, Jimmy,' Donna told him, completing the three-point turn as fast as she could. 'I didn't speak to the man. All I got was an answering machine. But I phoned the clinic to see if he left a message at reception. They said, no he hadn't.'

'There. What did I tell you? I told you you were panicking for nothing, didn't I? Didn't I say the doctor would've kept trying if it had been anything important? Christ, I tried to tell you. I mean to say, it stands to reason, doesn't it? Something as important as all that.'

Donna, in defiance of Jimmy's instructions to stay on the Victoria Embankment, headed for home by way of the brighter lights of Ludgate Circus and Fleet Street. She was barely aware of his incessant chattering but just to keep him happy she occasionally said, 'huh huh,' hoping that her timing was right. As she cleared The Strand and turned left into Whitehall she said, 'I wonder if the poor bastard's got any family, Jimmy?'

Jimmy said, 'What poor bastard?'

'Munro. I'm talking about Steve Munro. Who do you think I'm talking about?'

'How was I supposed to know? What do you think I am? A mind reader?'

'It's no use talking to you when you're like this. Jimmy. You're away with the fairies.'

'I'm talking a load of shite about football and you ask me if the poor bastard's got any family, and you accuse me of being away with the fairies. I know who's away with the fairies, doll, and it's not me.'

Donna laughed. 'You haven't got a leg to stand on, mate. As soon as you opened your mouth and started talking about football, you proved it. You're lucky there's no witnesses.'

The banter continued in one form or another until they were over the Vauxhall Bridge. Donna wanted to go straight ahead to St Oswald's Mews where she considered they would be safe, at least for the time being. But Jimmy had different ideas. 'Take me up to my ma and da's a minute, will you doll? There's something I want to see my old man about.'

Although she suspected that it was only an excuse for a drink, and probably the first stop on an all-night celebration of his earlier exploits Donna knew it would be a waste of breath protesting. She could see he was so hyped up that it was likely to be the best thing for him. At least he hadn't headed up West to gloat, or wanted to party on with his brothers back at Shane's place.

'Do you mind if I just drop you there, Jimmy? I want to get back to Corrie.'

'Ach away and – Listen Donna, when was the last

time me and you had a decent bevie together, eh, answer me that? I'm talking about a good night out with plenty of bevie and a bite to eat. Straw hats and trumpets material. And don't give me any of that shite about our Corrie because he'll be in his element looking after those two dopey uncles of his.'

Donna agreed for no reason other than wanting to keep an eye on him and keep him well away from his usual haunts. 'As long as we're not too late,' she smiled, thinking she would start by steering him well clear of the Wheatsheaf. 'But we're not setting foot in the Wheatsheaf.'

'Magic,' Jimmy said, rubbing his hands together.

TWENTY-FOUR

Old Davey was sprawled in his chair asleep. He was snoring softly with his chin resting on his chest and a continuous slobber sopping his pouted bottom lip. An almost empty can of McEwan's Export had escaped his feeble grip, spilling the dregs over his crotch. He eventually awoke to his son's increasingly vigorous shakes.

'Look at the state of you, da,' Jimmy laughed. 'You've pished yourself, you dirty old bastard.'

Agnes looked up from her knitting. 'Christ, Jimmy, don't start him. I was hoping that was him asleep for the night.'

'That's a shame,' Donna said.

Old Davey ran the back of his hand over his mouth and stared down at his crotch until it and the empty beer can came in to focus. He shook the empty can and raised it to his lips, tilting his head straight back. 'Bastard,' he wheezed, and shook the can again. 'Have you been at this?' he accused his wife.

'Not after you've been slobbering all over it. What do you take me for anyway?'

'I must've pished mehsel right enough,' Old Davey said, peering down at the wet patch circling his crotch. 'I'm always doing that this weather.' He preferred to believe he'd peed himself rather than the alternative of having wasted good drink.

Jimmy brushed the curtain aside and went into the tiny kitchenette. He quickly took the cut-throat razor from his inside pocket and washed it thoroughly under the tap. That done he restored it to the handleless mug on the shelf above the sink. When he returned to the parlour Old Davey was trying to persuade Agnes to tell him where she'd hidden the rest of his cans. With a wry smile giving her away she was trying in vain to convince him that he'd polished them off. Donna, who was sitting at the table sorting the mail into two piles, junk mail and bills, maintained a grin as she monitored her in-laws' antics.

'Anything interesting?' Jimmy said and sidled up beside her to see for himself.

'Just the usual. Junk and a couple of bills.'

A loud, prolonged rap on the front door startled all of them, none more so than Donna.

'Who the fuck's that chapping the bloody door at this time of the night?' Old Davey scowled. 'Whoever it is better have a carryout or they can get to fuck.'

Jimmy made a lunge for the parlour door and got there in time to steer his father away. Agnes put her knitting down and darted for the bay window, getting there ahead of her husband and son and leaving Donna slack-jawed at the table.

'Christ of almighty.' Jimmy hurried from the room without explanation. The look of wonder on his face left them all considering if he was going to answer the door or bolt it.

Donna's anxiety eased when she heard the front door opening ahead of the sound of Jimmy's laughter. 'You'll never guess who the cat dragged in?' Jimmy kept everyone in suspense by making an appearance in the doorway by himself. 'Bung me a tenner, will you Donna? It seems our guest has lost his wallet and he hasn't got the price of the taxi.' Jimmy turned and spoke into the darkened hallway. 'Come here and give us a look at you, mate. Come on, don't be shy. It's nothing they haven't seen before.'

'You can bung me a tenner while you're at it, pet,' Old Davey said, showing more interest in Donna's handbag than he was in whoever was standing in the hall.

Steve Munro stepped into the doorway as soon as Jimmy vacated it. With his bare legs blue with cold, his hands held clear of his body and his wringing wet underpants sagging well below his crotch he stood and shivered out of control. Never more sober in his life he stood motionless, his persistent chattering failing to produce a single word of sense.

'Come in and give yersel a heat in front of the fire while I get you a wee drop of something to warm you up.' Agnes guided Munro closer to the fire.

'You've done well for yersel, mate,' Old Davey grinned mischievously. 'Getting a drink off that auld bag. It's more than I could say for mehsel. What did you do? Throw yersel off a bridge into a river, or something? Christ, it's an extreme measure, but I might give it a try meh fucken self, before I die of thirst.'

Agnes returned from where she'd hidden the bottle of sweet sherry and helped herself to a drink from the glass she'd filled for Munro, convinced there was a danger he would have spilled it otherwise. 'If you're going to jump off a bridge,' she said, turning to glare at her husband, 'make sure it's over the M1.'

Munro took the glass in both hands and backed up to the fire. With no way of knowing why, he could tell by Donna's long face that his less than auspicious appearance had been met with mixed emotions. 'I g-g-got m-mugged and left out in the rain,' he explained quickly.

Jimmy exchanged a worried glance with his wife. On his return from paying the taxi he had intended waiting patiently for Munro to settle down and stop shivering so much before he asked him how he'd survived the fall. But Munro's unexpected explanation had left him with a bad taste in his mouth; one, by the look on Donna's face, that was obviously shared by her.

'Can ehh, can I have a word with you in private, mate?' Jimmy said, nodding towards the door.

'You'll do no such thing,' Donna butted in. 'Not

until after he's had a nice hot bath. Why don't you make yourself useful and dig him up some clothes?'

Jimmy was far from pleased. 'Why don't you dig him up some clothes if you're so keen? And you'd better make sure they're our William's because my trousers will be too tight around the waist for him. You've only got to take one look.'

'Well, do you think you could run him a bath then, if that's not too much trouble?' Donna retorted.

'Don't bother yer arses,' Old Davey said, hoping to curry some favour. 'I'll run the poor bastard a bath before he founders. Come on mate, get that down yer neck and follow me.'

'Oh no you don't.' Agnes elected to run the bath herself, having hid the bottle of sherry and the rest of the beer in the bathroom on the landing, a room that her husband seldom used. 'You have a rake in our William's wardrobe and see what you can come up with,' she ordered her husband.

As Munro and Agnes left the parlour Old Davey leaned into the hall and called after them. 'Yeh must've got mugged in a sewer, mate. Yeh smell worse than one of her farts, so yeh do. Fucken minging.'

Grinning, Jimmy said to his father, 'You stay where you are, blootery. I'll go get the guy some gear.'

Donna was carrying the junk mail to the plastic supermarket bag Agnes used as a kitchen tidy when Old Davey's eyes suddenly lit up. 'Fuck me, I nearly forgot,' he said, going to the mantelpiece and fetching an envelope lying on top of a pile of old paperback books. 'This was lying in the hall for you.'

'For me?' Donna replied, her nose wrinkling with surprise as she noticed that there was no stamp on the envelope. 'When did this arrive?'

'Some time this evening. I came across it after that useless article of a husband of yours papped me out of the boozer. If I hadn't tripped over the step on the way in, it'd probably be still lying there.'

Donna stared at the envelope for a moment as if it might yield the contents without having to be opened. She opened the envelope and sat down, reading the opening lines then referring to the front of the envelope to make sure there was no mistake with the name and address. Satisfied, she continued reading, wondering who on earth had sent her two tickets for the benefit at the Sands Hotel in Brighton. Especially at such short notice. By the time she'd read to the bottom of the page the blood had drained from her face. 'Here's a wee something for you,' she said, slipping Old Davey a ten pound note. 'If you don't mention this I'll give you another tenner tomorrow. OK?' She knew that, come tomorrow, he would remember nothing.

Hearing Jimmy's footsteps padding down the stairs she just managed to return the note to the envelope and place it under the bills before he walked into the room. Jimmy went straight to the small bundle of mail and began sorting through it, transferring the top envelope to the bottom when he found it to be of no interest.

'They're only bills, Jimmy,' Donna told him, trying to control the panic in her voice. 'Nothing of interest to you.'

Jimmy returned the mail to the table and went over and popped his head through the curtain into the kitchenette. 'Ah, there you are, you old bastard.'

'What's up?' Donna said, springing to Old Davey's defence.

'Somebody's been upstairs.'

'What do you mean, somebody's been upstairs?'

'It's all right. The only thing that seems to be missing is a half-bottle of Johnnie Walker. What does that tell you?'

'It wasnay me,' said old Davey, poker-faced.

Fearing that her father-in-law was likely to sell out Donna thought it best to get Jimmy out of the house until the old bugger's memory gave out. 'Listen Jimmy,' Donna said, slipping the mail into her handbag. 'Do you think you could take me around to the Wheatsheaf? I wouldn't mind seeing if I can catch Shane's last set. Steve'll be all right here.'

Jimmy checked his watch. 'I don't know about that. It's one thing me being seen there but I don't know if I fancy the idea of you jumping around the place.'

'You'll be there, won't you?'

'Make up your mind, Donna then. One minute you don't want to go to the Wheatsheaf, the next minute you do.' Donna wasted no time gathering her coat and heading for the door.

Intending to tell Munro to sit tight Jimmy hurried

upstairs to the bathroom. In the half-light of the landing he encountered Agnes drying her hands down the sides of her dress.

'If you're looking for the Yank, he's in the bath,' Agnes told him.

'Do me a favour, ma. Tell him to wait here till I get back, eh? I'm just nipping around to the boozer for half an hour. Don't let on to that old pest.'

'You couldn't bring us back a nice wee bottle of something, could you son? I'm down to my last drop.'

The doorman at the Wheatsheaf opened the inner door and stood to one side, allowing a blast of amplified music to greet Jimmy and Donna on their way in. Jimmy immediately glanced at his permanently reserved table, half-expecting to see Anton Winters sitting there waiting for him. Donna gazed beyond the thick haze of cigarette smoke trapped in the lone spotlight hoping Shane could see her waving. Both were mildly disappointed, Jimmy because his table was empty and Donna because Shane was oblivious to all except the cheering and the smiling sea of appreciative faces closest to the stage. As soon as they sat down Shane spotted them though and, without missing a beat, gave them a dainty, feminine wave.

Three numbers and two encores later Shane, leaving the stage to a round of tumultuous applause, joined Jimmy and Donna at the table. 'Phew, that's it for another night, thank God,' she said, poking out her tongue and panting just once.

Donna offered her a drink of her Diet Coke and checked that Jimmy was otherwise engrossed before she nodded towards the Ladies. Shane took the hint on the second nod and said, 'Got to go spend a penny and touch myself up. Want to come?'

'I think she means her make-up.' Donna grinned and fell in behind Shane as she started squeezing through the tightly packed crowd. Instead of going directly to the public toilet Shane steered towards the hatch at the end of the bar and ducked under it, hitching up her skirt. Shouting above the din she said, 'I figured by the look on your face that you'd prefer somewhere a bit quieter.'

Donna nodded in agreement and followed her through a door to the right of the hatch and down a cardboard-box strewn passage to a room with a homemade silver star pinned to the door. Shane sat on a padded, pink stool in front of a mirror fringed with lights and dabbed at her make-up as she studied her friend's reflection.

'Take a look at this,' Donna said, moving to the side of the mirror and looking down on Shane.

With a swish of nylon Shane crossed her legs and plucked the letter from the envelope, barely breaking eye contact with Donna. When she finished reading she said, 'OK. So you've got two tickets for the benefit in Brighton tomorrow night. What's the big deal?'

'What's the big deal?' Donna said incredulously.

'Here's me been looking half-way around the world for Tom Gilfeather, the signature on the letter in case you didn't notice, and all of a sudden he sends me an invitation to come to Brighton tomorrow night. Shane, I can't think straight. You're going to have to help me. I'm a gibbering wreck.'

'Well, the first thing we're going to do is get you settled down. Wait here a minute.'

Shane returned with a double scotch and thrust it into Donna's hand. Donna at first tried to drink it straight down as instructed, but as soon as the full malt whisky hit the back of her throat she faltered and screwed up her face. 'Ugh,' she shuddered. 'The cure's worse than the cause.'

'Now. This guy Gilfeather. Has he got something to do with all this shit that's going on? Obviously he has.'

'That's an understatement.'

'Are you going to tell me why?'

'You don't want to know. Not yet.'

'Suit yourself.' With a long face Shane, swivelling on her stool, kept track of Donna as she paced the room.

Donna stopped, placed a hand on Shane's knee and said, 'Sorry, love. It's for your own good. I don't want to get you caught up in this any more than you already are.'

Thinking that it was a bit late for that Shane forced a smile and said, 'All right. Let me see if I'm reading this right. The invitation to go to Brighton, I'm taking it that you're not in a position to mention a word of it to Jimmy?'

'Christ, you'd have to be bloody joking, wouldn't you? He's the last person I want to find out about this. Shane, this is the answer to my prayers, but it could be the start of an even worse nightmare. You have to promise me you won't say anything.'

'That's OK as long as I know.' Standing, Shane placed her hands on Donna's shoulders and manoeuvred her to the seat she had just vacated. 'Sit down, for goodness' sake, will you. It's like watching the bloody tennis.'

'I'm sorry. I've gone all nervous.'

Shane continued, 'You'll want to get down to Brighton without Jimmy then. Correct?'

'Correct. But I'm not going anywhere without Corrie.'

'Do you think that's a good idea?'

Donna already had some serious misgivings. Speaking of her fears she said, 'It might be somebody trying to get me away from Jimmy. It might be the one responsible for the fire bomb up West.'

'It's something you have to consider.' Shane placed a comforting hand on Donna's shoulder. 'But if I know you, it not going to stop you. Is it?'

'No. And presuming that this is genuine, I'm hoping that one look at Corrie and Gilfeather will consent to do a tissue test. What kind of person could refuse?'

Shane's silence, coupled with the intense look in

her eyes, suggested to Donna that her friend suspected that there was every probability of a refusal.

'Well, what am I supposed to do? I can't very well ignore it. I could never forgive myself if this turned out to be legitimate and I hadn't done anything about it. No. There's only one way to find out.'

'Well I'm bloody coming with you then. I'm not letting you go down there, just the two of you.'

'Would you?' Donna was overwhelmed.

'Somebody's got to be there. I mean, from what you tell me, you won't see hide nor hair of Gilfeather if he thinks Jimmy's floating about. That's for sure.'

'You're a doll.' Donna rose and put her arms around Shane.

Shane rested her chin on Donna's shoulder and said, 'This'll keep Dr Cullen happy. He phoned me to see if I could get you to change your mind about going to Brighton.'

'I thought that must've been all he wanted.' Donna pulled her head back and held Shane at arm's length. 'You won't breathe a word of this to anyone? Not now.'

'Scout's honour.' Shane gave the three-fingered salute and continued, 'We'll tell Jimmy we're going to take the Chunnel to Paris for an extra day's Christmas shopping. We'll tell him we'll spend the night there and come back on Sunday. He shouldn't have any problem with that. In fact, he might be glad to get you out of the road for a couple of days.'

Donna's eyes lit up. 'Do you think you could make

it look like it was your idea? It would sound better coming from you. I'm sure of it.'

'Leave it to me.' Shane winked.

Donna headed back to the bar, stopping suddenly halfway along the passage. 'Shane, is there a phone handy I could use? Somewhere away from the noise.'

'In the office. First door on the left.' Shane showed Donna to the door and added, 'I suppose I'd better think up a good excuse why I won't be able to work tomorrow night.'

Smiling and easing the door shut Donna went to the cluttered desk and reached for the phone.

At No. 38 the phone answered on the first ring. 'Hello,' Agnes said softly.

'Uhh, hello Agnes, It's me Donna. I was wondering if the American geezer is out of the bath yet?'

'Hold on a minute pet and I'll see. You've caught me as I was about to order some takeaway for old garbage guts in there. You know what he's like.'

'Yer wanted on the phone, Mr Munro.' Donna heard Agnes bellow up the stairwell, followed by, 'He says he'll no be a minute, hen. Och, here he is now. Hold on and I'll put him on.'

'Is that you, Steve?'

'Donna? Where the goddamn hell are you? I need to –'

'Listen to me, Steve, I haven't got much time. Jimmy saw you being thrown into the Thames. I'll explain later, but for Godsake when he tackles you about why you made up the story about being mugged you had better have something ready. Why did you say that anyway?'

'I'll tell him exactly what I'm going to tell you. What else was I supposed to say in front of your in-laws?'

'That's good, that's good. Stick to that, Steve. But listen, I've got something else to tell you. I think Gilfeather has – eh, I mean Tom – I think Tom's been in touch,' Donna paused, waiting for her words to impact. 'Hello, hello, are you still there?' she added after a long-enough silence.

Munro held the phone flat against his chest. He could hear Donna's tiny voice asking if he was all right. Leaning off the wall he cleared his throat and said, 'This isn't some kind of joke is it, Donna? I mean to say.'

At that moment Shane put her head around the door and said, 'I wouldn't be too long if I was you. Your old man will be wondering where on earth we've gotten to.'

Holding up two fingers Donna gripped the mouthpiece with her other hand and whispered, 'Two seconds.' She kept her hand over the mouthpiece until she heard the noisy burst of chatter that escaped when Shane entered the bar. 'You still there, Steve?'

'Where the hell do you think I am? Of course I'm still here.'

'Listen, Steve. I've got to go. If you make an excuse to hang around No. 38 there, if you can stand it that is, I'll get back to you some time tomorrow. I promise. Sorry I can't be more specific. Bye.'

'Donna, for god in heaven's sake listen.' Munro realised that the line had gone dead and rested his head against the wall, allowing the phone to drop from his grip. His eyes were shut tight and a faltering breath accompanied his gentle butting action.

'You all right there, Mr Munro?' Agnes said, sneaking a look around the corner.

When Donna ducked under the hatch at the end of the bar last drinks were being called, making it even harder for her to reach the table against the flow of patrons rushing the bar.

'You took your time,' Jimmy said accusingly. 'I thought you must've fallen down the chanty.'

'You can't look this good without a bit of effort. That's right, isn't it Shane?' Donna cocked her leg and placed a hand on her waist, adding an exaggerated feminine shimmy.

Jimmy was unimpressed and said, 'Shane tells me you're thinking of shooting off to Paris for a bit of shopping. What's the script?'

'Only for the day, love. It's one of those cheap specials.' Donna's smile turned to a grimace when she felt Shane kick her under the table, 'But it could be late before we get back.'

'It's all right for some,' Jimmy said, trying to hide the fact that he was secretly delighted.

Shane smiled at Donna. 'I'll look after her for you Jimmy, if that's what's worrying you.'

'You weren't thinking of going without Corrie? It'll do him the world of good to get a wee hurl on a train.' Jimmy allowed himself the faintest of smiles, thinking he'd offered enough token resistance.

'We'll bring you back something nice.' Donna leaned across the table and planted a kiss smack on his lips. Jimmy wiped his mouth with the back of his hand and checked for traces of lipstick. 'Fucken ease up, will you? You'll get me a bad name.'

A frown too easily replaced the smile on Donna's face. She knew that, come what may, she was going to have a lot of explaining to do if her trip to Brighton was successful. With time fast running out for Corrie it was a matter of the end justifying the means.

For the second time that evening Jimmy left a row of untouched drinks on the table. Unlike others of his ilk he had never been inclined to drink when things were playing heavily on his mind. On the way to the bar to get the bottle he promised Agnes he ran the gauntlet of backslappers asking if there was a party on the go. 'Not tonight lads,' he told them, and scooped the bottle off the bar.

Once outside he stayed close to Donna until they reached the car. 'Take me around to No. 38, will you pet?' he told her. 'I want to drop this bottle off for my ma.'

'You weren't thinking of hanging around, were you love? It's just that me and Shane were talking about getting an early start in the morning.'

'It might be a better idea if you drop me off at the

corner and piss off back to Shane's by the back roads.'

Donna pulled up at the kerb in Mawbey Street. 'Be as quick as you can. I'll wait here for you.'

'Nah. On you go. I want to make sure the pigeons get a bite to eat.'

'You and your bloody pigeons. Can't you get somebody else to feed them?'

'Don't start, Donna.' Jimmy alighted from the car, shut the door gently and waved the car away. He watched it turn right at South Lambeth Road, the opposite direction to St Oswald's Mews, and satisfied himself that it wasn't being followed before he clutched his suit jacket closed at the waist and hurried across the side street to the house.

As soon as he walked in the door Old Davey flashed a toothless grin at him. 'Did you bring a wee message for your auld da, like a good boy? Sure I've pulled the house asunder looking for that bottle of hers. I think the greedy pig's gobbled the lot. Look at the fucken state of her, would yeh? And me standing here drier than a witch's tit.'

'Ach away and give us peace, will yeh? You've had more than your fair share of bevie for one day, pal. Do you never get sick of being pished twenty-four hours a day?'

'Huh, listen to Lord Muck, would yeh?'

A poker-faced Agnes took the hint and walked towards the door, plucking the bottle Jimmy was holding behind his back. 'Oh,' she said, leaning on the doorframe and holding the bottle at arm's length out along the passage wall. 'If you're looking for the Yank, I've put him up the stairs in your flat.'

'Thanks ma.' Watching the darkness at the end of the passage consume his mother as she went off in search of a new hiding place for the bottle Jimmy closed the door behind him and headed up the stairs.

At the sound of footsteps on the landing Munro bristled and looked around for something to use as a club. By the time the footsteps reached the door he was holding a poker and standing with one hand on the mantelpiece. As soon as he heard the key turning in the lock he put the poker down and, rushing to unhook the security chain, peeked through the slit in the door. 'Sorry,' he said. 'Can't be too goddamn careful.'

Pushing into the room Jimmy said, 'Listen pal. It's about time you and me had a wee bit of a talk. There's one or two things I'd like to discuss with you. Know what I mean?'

'If you're talking about the mugging, I can explain that.'

Jimmy smiled. 'Aye well, why don't you grab that jacket my ma found for you and come for a wee walk out the back with me.'

Following Jimmy downstairs and out the back to the pigeon loft Munro detected in his hardened features a hint of the underlying malice that Donna had repeatedly warned him against provoking. The temperature in the pigeon loft, though a welcome change from the freezing conditions outside, was no compensation for the coldness in Jimmy's eyes.

'Sit yourself down.' Jimmy leaned against the wall and pointed at one of the upturned nesting boxes.

After what he had already been through Munro was wondering how much more of this he could stand.

'You can start with that bullshit about being mugged.' Jimmy said.

'That's easy, Jimmy. I didn't want to say anything in front of your family.' Munro's voice, like his eyes, implored grace and understanding.

'I'm listening.'

'The truth of the matter is, two men claiming to be policemen, their IDs looked genuine enough to me, said they wanted to have a word with me down at the station. To be honest with you, I wasn't exactly sober.' Munro knew he had to be careful about what he told Jimmy. 'Anyway, to get to the point, they took me down beside the river somewhere and dangled me over a wall. In short, they wanted to know why I was so interested in Tommy Gilfeather. Sons of bitches.'

'Sounds to me that around about there you should've told them.'

'That's just it, I did. But the noise from a passing boat drowned me out. Next thing I knew I could feel my pants slipping and I realised they couldn't hold me. I was staring at the cobbles thirty or forty feet below and I knew if I didn't do something I was a goner.'

'What did you do?' Jimmy asked, genuinely interested.

'All I could think about was turning around so that I would fall face first, with my hands out in front of me. As if that would save me.'

'Obviously it did, or you wouldn't be here to talk about it.'

'Lucky for me the bank was quite steep there and the cobbles were covered in mud. It was like doing a belly flopper on the slippery slide. All I did was skin my elbows. Look.' Munro pushed up his sleeves and offered his elbows as proof, finishing with a short, apologetic laugh, as if he was trying to dismiss the whole episode to the ranks of insignificance.

Jimmy casually leaned off the wall and delicately reached into one of the nesting boxes. Tenderly clutching one of the birds to his chest he kissed it on the top of the head. He slowly moved to the door which he bumped shut with the seat of his trousers and rested his back against it. 'A situation you couldn't expect to get out of twice in the one night, surely?'

With the strangely soothing cooing of well-contented pigeons for company and the sweet, inoffensive smell of their droppings lingering in the air Munro sat bathed in the tinge of street light filtering through the head-high wire mesh and realised the subtlety of the uncompromising threat. There was no way he was going to let the situation deteriorate to a life-threatening level again.

'What *is* your interest in Tom Gilfeather?' Jimmy held the pigeon up to the meagre light and looked it in the eye.

Munro, unnerved by the chill of Jimmy's apparent indifference, surprised them both with the speed and brevity of his reply. 'He's my son,' he said.

For the first time since taking the pigeon from its roost Jimmy diverted his eyes to Munro. 'Your son?' he answered, incredulously. 'I thought your name was –'

'Gilfeather is my wife's maiden name. I can only presume that Tommy started using it not long after she died. Don't ask me why.' Shrugging his shoulders Munro sighed and continued. 'My wife was a woman of independent means. She left him all her money.'

'My next question was going to be, what's all that got to do with my Donna?' Jimmy said, and resumed looking at the pigeon. 'But what I want to know now is, how did you come to associate him with Donna? How did you connect him to Donna?'

Munro thought that after all he'd been through he would give it one last shot. If that didn't work, he'd tell Jimmy the whole truth. 'Jimmy, you have to realise that I'm a newspaper man. It's my job to keep my ear to the ground. A guy in Classifieds, I wouldn't exactly call him a friend but he knows a bit about the family history. Anyway, he brought to the editor's attention a copy of an advertisement that had been running in the paper.' Munro stopped talking and reached into the inside pocket of his jacket before he realised the garment was borrowed. 'Somebody was looking for a Thomas Edgely Gilfeather and they gave a PO Box in London as the address for all correspondence. That advertisement was placed by Donna.'

Watching for Jimmy's reaction Munro became aware that he was holding his breath and tried unsuccessfully to exhale noiselessly. Jimmy returned the pigeon to its roost, kissed it softly on the back of the head again and turned to stand directly over Munro. 'You were looking for your son. What was Donna looking for?'

Munro feigned surprise and said, 'I thought you would've known?'

'Oh fucken did you now?' Jimmy snarled in the first overt show of aggression. 'I'll tell you what I'll do with you, pal. Seeing as you seem to be the one with all the answers I'll let you explain it to me.'

Munro grimaced and rubbed his aching neck, using it as an excuse to avert his eyes. 'To tell you the truth,' he began sheepishly, terrified that Jimmy could see through the fabrication, 'I was hoping you could tell me. All I know is that some pretty heavy guys seem to have an interest in your wife and my son. Donna won't say and I can't find my son to ask him.' Munro inadvertently held his breath again as he awaited Jimmy's response. In the ensuing silence he realised that he would somehow have to get to Donna first, to warn her of what he had been forced to tell her husband. If only he knew where to find her.

Jimmy stormed from the loft, breaking into a run when he was halfway to the house. Taking the back steps two at a time he continued down the passage and straight out the front door, cursing when he saw that there were no taxis in the rank across the street.

Munro reached the front door in time to see him hurry off down South Lambeth Road, towards the Elephant and Castle. His immediate reaction was to follow, but commonsense told him that would only result in him reaching Donna after Jimmy. Backing into the hall he opened the parlour door a fraction and beckoned Agnes over. 'Psst.'

With a concerned look on her face Agnes checked that her husband was still asleep in the chair and crept towards the door. 'What is it, son?' she whispered, stepping into the hall.

'I've got to get in touch with Donna. It's very important. Do you know where I can find her?'

Agnes eased the door shut behind her. 'Oh, I don't know about this?' she said, confirming her reply with a single sideways shake of her head.

Once again Munro forgot that he was wearing borrowed trousers and reached for his hip pocket – a move Agnes quickly zeroed in on. Realising his mistake Munro kept his hand behind him and continued. 'There's twenty pounds in it for you.'

'It would be more than my life's worth.'

'Fifty pounds?'

Looking left and right Agnes leaned in and whispered. 'Ach. I suppose I can trust you. But make sure you keep this to yourself. I think they must be staying over at Shane's.'

'You think?'

'That's the best I can do,' said Agnes, holding out her hand.

'Is there any way I can verify this? A phone number or something?'

Agnes grinned and pointed directly at a recently scratched number in the square of varnished timber surrounding the wall phone. 'Try that one,' she said and again held out her hand.

'You'll have to take a raincheck.' Munro took off upstairs in search of some small change.

Agnes called after him, 'No bloody fear, mister. I don't accept cheques.'

Returning to the phone, after first confirming that Agnes had returned to the parlour, Munro inserted the coins he'd found on the cabinet beside the bed and dialled the number.

'Hello,' said Shane.

'Uhh. It's Steve Munro here. Put Donna on please.'

Shane went on the defensive. 'I think you've got the wrong number. There's no one here by that name. Who did you say was calling?'

'Shane, this is Steve Munro. I'm a friend of Donna's. If she's there, put her on please?'

Reacting to the plea in Munro's voice Shane put her hand over the phone and mouthed at Donna, 'Steve Munro.'

Donna reached for the phone and said, 'Steve. What is it? How did you get this number?'

'I haven't got time to go into it, but I had to tell Jimmy about the advertisement in the Chicago *Post*. I'm sorry. I never had a choice. He –'

'Oh no. You never. Don't tell me.' Donna's face drained of blood. 'Where is he now?'

'I think he's on his way to see you. But listen,' Munro continued, desperate to atone. 'As soon as I get off the phone I'm going to ring the Holiday Inn and tell them I want a bigger room. I'll tell them my family's coming to stay for a couple of days. I'll tell them –'

'Steve. Steve. Settle down. I'm hanging up now, and I agree with what you just said, but forget about the Holiday Inn. I want you to book us in to the Wilsmere Hotel in Cranley Gardens, Fulham. Have you got that? The Wilsmere in Cranley Gardens, Fulham. Ask the operator for the number. I'm not setting foot near the Holiday Inn.' Hanging up Donna looked at Shane and said, 'We're out of here, girl. Grab a few things and let's go.' Smiling at Corrie she said, 'Come on, mate. We're going to stay in a hotel tonight.'

In answer to Shane's look of bewilderment Donna whispered, 'I'll have to explain later.' She followed with a glance in Corrie's direction.

'You've still got a surprise for me, haven't you mum?' Corrie said, catching Donna's furtive look.

'You better believe it.' Donna draped his coat over his shoulders and planted his ski-cap on his head. Patting him gently on the bottom she added, 'Now let's go.'

With her hand on the side of the door, ready to close it behind her, Donna hesitated for a moment and hurried over to the notepad sitting beside the phone. She wrote, Decided to go tonight. Hope you don't mind. Love you. Donna.

At the door she bumped into Shane returning from the car. Grinning apologetically Shane hurried into the bedroom and returned with two gowns, still on coat hangers and covered with plastic wrapping. 'Mustn't forget these,' she said, nursing the garments on her lap as Donna sped out of the Mews.

The flat was in darkness when Jimmy's taxi pulled into the Mews. He let himself in and switched on the light, at first thinking that he'd beaten Donna and the others home. As he approached the breakfast bar the note was conspicuous in the middle of the polished timber top. After he read it he screwed it up in a ball and squeezed it until his knuckles turned white. In the absence of any evidence to the contrary he presumed that Munro had phoned Donna with a warning. Cursing himself for letting Munro out of his sight and vowing not to make the same mistake again Jimmy left the flat, leaving the lights on, and headed to find another taxi back to South Lambeth Road.

Munro had been in a quandary from the minute Jimmy ran out the door. After making the booking at the Wilsmere Hotel, a long drawn-out process where a bit of fast talking took the place of a credit card number, he had to decide whether to drop out of sight, and save himself a lot of cross-examination at the hands of Jimmy, or stay close to the action, with the prospect of finding his son. As he went to the sink for yet another nervous drink of water he looked down on South Lambeth Road and saw Jimmy pay off a taxi and hurry up the steps. Ashen-faced, he was still standing next to the sink when Jimmy exploded into the room.

'Did you phone Donna and tell her I was on my way, yeh cunt?' Jimmy spoke with teeth barely apart and a nose wrinkled in a vicious snarl.

Munro took another sip of water and shook his head. 'How could I? I've got no idea where she is.'

'That makes two of us.' Jimmy held a pointed finger a few inches from Munro's nose and continued. 'Why all the bullshit? Why didn't you just come out at the start and tell us who the fuck you were?'

Ever the coward, Munro answered, 'That's something you're going to have to ask Donna. For some reason she didn't want me to divulge who I was.'

'What's this? More bullshit?'

'No. No way. Your wife seemed to think that Tommy was in some kind of danger and that I would only complicate matters if anybody knew who I was. After what happened to me tonight I think she was right.'

'Since when did this include me? Eh?'

Munro diverted his eyes. 'As I said, that's something you're going to have to ask Donna.'

Leaning in, close enough to get a whiff of the lingering smell of stale alcohol on Munro's breath,

Jimmy told him, 'That's exactly what I intend to do. And you're going to be there when I ask her.'

'I thought you said you didn't know where she was?'

'I don't know where she is right now but I've a good idea where she's going to be.' Jimmy was thinking about the arrangement he had with Tate, to meet him in Brighton tomorrow night. With things the way they were with Corrie he should've realised that it would take something exceptionally important to entice Donna away from the immediate vicinity of the Sidney Doolan Centre. Not some piss-farting trip to the Continent.

TWENTY-FIVE

Corrie leaned forward in the back seat he had to himself and eagerly watched the outskirts of Brighton come into view. He was thinking how exciting it was. Maybe not as exciting as it was last Christmas, but certainly as exciting as it had been on his real birthday. 'It's Brighton,' he shouted with glee, supplying the answer to what his mother had promised was to be a surprise destination.

Donna and Shane turned to face each other and smiled.

When the car pulled up outside the Sands Hotel Corrie beamed and said, 'Crikey, is *this* where we're staying? Gee! I thought the place where we stayed last night was pretty big but have a look at this: it's huge.'

Shane craned up at the grandeur of the ornate, white-painted building and said, 'Better check that address, girl.'

'I don't have to,' Donna began. 'If I read it once I must've read it a thousand times. But that's not what's worrying me. I'm more concerned with what they expect us to pay for a room in one of these joints. I mean, you could probably spend a month in any one of the bed and breakfasts for the price of one night in a place like this. We don't want to give ourselves a showing up if it's too bloody dear. God, I'd be mortified.'

'Too late,' Shane whispered, linking arms with Donna and falling in behind the maroon-suited porter who had just swooped on their luggage.

'Can we go for an ice-cream, mum?' Corrie pleaded, latching on to his mother's free hand.

At the top of the steps Donna spun them all around to face the Esplanade and the windswept breakers relentlessly pounding the pebble-strewn beach beyond. 'You must be mad, son,' she said, touched by his contagious excitement.

'Let me do the talking,' Shane said, winking and squeezing up to the reception desk in front of her friend. 'I want to see if he notices.'

'Notices what, Mum?'

'Nothing, love,' Donna replied, but was inwardly amused. She looked around the high-ceilinged foyer, taking in the sheer opulence of the place, with white-painted walls, rich burgundy carpets and matching floor-length curtains.

A bony nudge from Shane got her attention. 'That's a bit of all right,' Shane said, leaning in to whisper. 'This geezer's only after telling me that our suite has been taken care of. Did you hear what I said? He said our *suite* has been taken care of.'

Corrie was delighted. He thought Shane had said sweets. All the way up in the lift and along the passage he envisaged a room full of chocolate and the like.

The two women, drawn by the panoramic view of the sea, walked out onto the fifth-floor balcony just as a hint of sun, already low in the crisp winter sky, managed to penetrate the cloud cover and set the windows and water glistening.

'Come and have a look, Corrie,' Donna called out.

'Yeah, come and see what you're missing, Corrie,' Shane agreed.

Corrie had installed himself in front of the television, clutching the Mars bar he'd found sharing a tray with an assortment of other confectionery, nuts and crisps. The tray was on his lap and he had no intention of moving. Unless it was for an ice-cream.

'I hope you don't intend sitting in front of that television for the duration, our Corrie. You could've stayed home and done that. Come on, get your coat and scarf on, me and Aunty Shane want to go for a walk before it gets too dark.' Donna removed the tray from Corrie's lap and added, 'Make that Mars bar last you because that's the only chocolate you'll be having. And hurry up, son, we don't want to take all day.'

'As long as you buy me an ice-cream, Mum.'

'We'll have to see about that.'

Anton Winters, as instructed by Chief Superintendent Tate, for all outward appearances had come to the Sands Hotel alone. The thought hadn't occurred to him to book a room in advance. It never did.

'Sorry Mr Winters,' the check-in clerk said pleasantly. 'We don't seem to have any rooms available. There's a big function in the ballroom tonight and all the guests have reservations.'

'Not good enough.'

The clerk, a first-year trainee barely clear of pimples, knew an awkward customer when he saw one. 'Perhaps the manager could be of more assistance, sir,' he advised Anton, and evacuated his post for the safety of the adjoining office.

There was nothing like a fully-booked hotel to boost the confidence and alter the approach of a manager normally desperate for custom at this time of the year. 'What seems to be the problem, sir?' the manager said, straightfaced and aloof.

'I don't have a problem, mate. You do. My name is Anton Winters and all I want is a room. Why don't you make a phone call, or do what you have to do, so that you can show me to my room.'

The manager was visibly taken aback, even though he was aware of Anton by reputation only. 'Mr Winters,' he said, cocking his head to the side and extending his arms in welcome. 'How remiss of me not to recognise you. Allow me to register you personally.' At the click of a finger he summoned a porter and directed him to the overnight bag at Anton's feet.

As the lift door opened, much to Corrie's annoyance, his mother was still fussing with his scarf, making sure there was no bare skin showing under his baseball cap. He managed to adjust his expression and return Anton's sympathetic smile just before he and Shane noticed the shock registering on his mother's face.

'Fancy meeting you here,' Anton smiled, and stepped into the lift.

Clutching at Corrie, Donna shielded him with her body and steered him out of the lift without saying a word.

'Who was that man, mum?' Corrie craned over his shoulder at the grinning stranger, trying to figure out where he'd seen him before.

When the lift door closed behind Anton, Donna thrust Corrie at Shane and went over to the reception desk. 'I don't suppose you've got a guest registered under the name of Gilfeather, by any chance?'

The clerk scanned the computer screen and slowly shook his head. 'I'm afraid not, madam.'

'Nah,' Donna agreed, 'it was daft of me to think you would.'

With Corrie in the middle, firmly clutched by the hands, the two women swung him down the steps and turned left along the Esplanade. Enjoying the strong tang of salty air delivered by a playful wind gusting over the incoming tide they hurried past an assortment of souvenir shops and empty amusement arcades. Donna was looking for a cafe, intending to install her son in a corner while she had a quiet word with Shane.

Corrie had other ideas. 'Oh, mum, let's go for a walk along the pier. It looks super.'

One look at the grey outline of the pier, with the rolling sea crashing through its stout, wooden piles and the spray lashing it like giant handfuls of grit, and Donna succumbed to her son's sustained harping for an ice-cream. Steering him into the nearest cafe she said, 'Hurry up and tell the girl what you want, Corrie.'

'I want two banana splits please,' Corrie told the sweetly smiling lass behind the counter.

'After you make him *one* banana split could you get us two caffe lattes as well, please,' Shane added.

'It's caffe lattes now, is it?' Donna teased. 'What the hell's a caffe latte?'

'You don't get out enough.' Shane led Corrie to a table overlooking the street and sat him down. 'While you're waiting for the girl to bring you your ice-cream why don't you –'

'Give you a bit of peace,' Corrie interrupted.

'Yeah. Close enough.' Shane pulled the cap down over his eyes.

Joining Donna at a table nearer the back of the cafe Shane placed a consoling hand on her shoulder and said, 'You're going to have to settle down, Donna. You've come too far to let this get to you.'

Donna was almost in tears. 'Did you see who that was in the lift?'

'He's one of the guys I saw talking to your Jimmy in the Wheatsheaf last week, isn't he?' Shane said.

'Anton fucken Winters, as Jimmy calls him. That's who it was. Shane, we're just going to have to get the hell out of here.' After a pause she added, 'Shit, I wish my Jimmy was here. I wish it was possible for him to be here.'

Shane tried to sound sympathetic. 'Why don't you just phone him and ask him to come down then? It might be better. You could tell him we changed our minds and decided to come to Brighton instead.'

Donna looked at her as if she was mad. 'It was only a wish.'

'It was only a suggestion,' Shane countered.

'I'd rather put up with two Anton Winters than one of my Jimmy. At least with Anton we'd have a chance.'

'I think you're exaggerating.'

'You think so, do you?' Donna retorted.

With Corrie arriving at the table and whingeing for another ice-cream they finished their coffee and emerged on the footpath to the welcome of a seemingly infinite string of winking and windblown, coloured lights extending either direction along the foreshore and out along the pier.

'Last one back to the hotel is a dirty rascal,' Corrie announced and took off in a plodding run before the words were out of his mouth.

'Look at him,' Donna said, her eyes moistening over. 'He thinks he's got all the time in the world.'

Shane forced an awkward smile and tried desperately to think of something appropriate to say. Words failed her.

In the inappropriately named Bayview Hotel, an inconspicuous establishment tucked away in one of the back streets running parallel with the Esplanade, Chief Superintendent Tate was propping up the bar, a roaring log fire and a bored barman for company. When he saw Anton passing a series of much-painted windows a click of his fingers summoned the bow-tied barman away from the glasses he was polishing at the other end of the bar.

'Same again for me.' Tate turned to see Anton backing up to the open fire. 'And whatever my assoc – whatever this gentleman wants.'

That's fair enough with me, Anton thought, I'd rather be a called a gentleman than an associate of yours. Better a compliment than an insult.

'You managed to get a room in the Sands all right then?' Tate deliberately placed Anton's scotch and water on the mantelpiece rather than into his outstretched hand.

'Absolutely.'

'Good. That's important. I was worried you'd left it a bit late. You'd have noticed that there's a bit of a function on there tonight. Some charity do or other.'

'Yeah. What's the story there? I saw Donna Macintyre there with that kid of hers and some other piece of stuff. She never let on she knew me so I didn't say much. I thought I'd wait and see what the score was.'

Tate rested one hand on the mantelpiece and stared deep into the flames. He was worried what effect the arrival of Donna Macintyre would have on his plans.

'I was asking you, what's the score?' Anton urged.

'There's to be no changes to the details we discussed earlier. Just remember what I told you. As soon as Gilfeather comes out of the woodwork, in your own inimitable way, you will tell Macintyre that Gilfeather is the real father of his kid. If Macintyre runs true to form that should be the end of Gilfeather. All I'll have to do is tidy things up. That should keep you happy enough to concentrate on business. OK?'

'It'll be worth the wait,' Anton grinned.

'You'll be needing this.' Tate produced a ticket for the benefit from the inside pocket of his suit jacket and pushed it along the mantelpiece.

They discussed the finer details over another round of drinks before Anton took his leave in plenty of time to get ready for the function. He had gone over and over the whole scenario in his mind, looking for a flaw, but he had to admit that the wily chief superintendent seemed to have come up with the perfect way to satisfy everyone. Pity about the kid though, he thought. He seemed all right.

Steve Munro was getting toey. Jimmy hadn't let him out of his sight since he got back from Shane's the night before, and here it was way past the time when they should've left for wherever it was Jimmy intended taking him. All he had managed to get out of Jimmy was that they were going for a drive some time in the afternoon, to catch up with Donna. The screams he'd heard after he'd been dropped into the Thames were still fresh in his mind, depriving him of the nerve to argue. Jimmy's mood didn't help. Not since he'd called Parkhurst Prison and discovered that Archie Kemp, doing solitary, was beyond his reach.

'I'll kill that little bastard Mick. Honest to god.' Jimmy pushed aside the curtain in the bay window and looked out into the street.

'It's your own stupit fault,' Old Davey smirked. 'I wouldn't trust that halfwit with a push bike, never mind a motor. You've only yourself to blame.'

Agnes stopped ironing and put her hands on her hips. 'Hey you, mister. That's enough of that. Yer talking about yer own flesh and blood there, yeh know.'

Old Davey laughed. 'That's how come I know he's a fucken halfwit.'

'Don't build yersel up, mister, yer too bloody stupit to be a halfwit.'

Not sure of what Agnes and Old Davey had been saying Munro went over to the window and said softly, 'If I'd known you were going to have trouble arranging transport I would have suggested we hire a car on my expense account. I could probably arrange it with a phone call or two.' After Jimmy turned and looked disdainfully at him he added, 'Or if it's not too far, Scotland for instance, I'm sure I could stretch to a taxi.'

Jimmy was about to ask him why he hadn't opened his mouth sooner when the sound of a car horn drew his attention back to the street. 'For Christ sake come and have a look at this, would you? The bold Mick's cadged a motor from the British Museum.'

Old Davey, trying to see what all the fuss was about, squeezed in between Agnes and Munro. Seeing his youngest son grinning up at him from behind the wheel of an ancient, red Morris Minor mailvan, he said, 'In my day you would've been a millionaire if you had one of those.'

'In your day you would've been a postman if you'd had one of those, yeh edjit,' Agnes laughed.

Before he'd had a chance to get a whiff of the lingering stench from the old van's day job, that of ferrying fish around the market, Jimmy had decided to take Munro up on his offer. 'Looks like you're up for a taxi there, mate,' he told the American, and steered him towards the door. As he stepped out the front door to patches of clear blue sky and a pavement still wet from the afternoon's showers the phone ringing in the inside pocket of his suit jacket startled him once again. 'This fucken thing always frightens the shite out of me,' he said to Munro and took himself off to the side. He was gripped with anticipation when he heard the voice of Dermot Mulholland on the other end of the line. 'Dermot. The man himself,' he said. 'I was wondering where you'd gotten to.'

'Why didn't you tell me you'd already caught up with the one you were looking for? You could've saved me a lot of fucking around.'

'What're you talking about?' Jimmy braced himself for the news.

'You'd better watch yourself, Jimmy son. I don't think you're very popular in some quarters.'

Picturing the glint in Dermot's eyes Jimmy responded, 'Dermot, do us a favour, pal.'

'You didn't do too bad a job for somebody who doesn't seem to know what I'm talking about.'

'Dermot. What fucken language are you talking?'

'Does the name Eddie Simpson ring a bell?'

'That cunt.'

'I'll take that as a yes.'

'So what's the score with him then?'

'That's for you to find out Jimmy. I only asked you if the name Eddie Simpson rang a bell. Far be it from me to put ideas in your head.'

'Dermot. For fuck sake.'

'It turns out your man was in the market for a certain product. I thought you must've found that out. Although, come to think of it, the only way you could've found out was through my source, and he never mentioned it to me.'

'What source is this?'

'Now now, Jimmy. Don't be asking any silly questions. Just content yourself with the knowledge that it's a very reliable source. The same source that told me that your man's in a sorry state over in the Queen Alexandra Hospital in Victoria.'

'You're a toff, Dermot. As soon as I get this squared away, me and you are going to get ourselves blootered. I'm paying.'

'May the road rise to meet you Jimmy.'

'The same to you.'

Jimmy hung up and turned to Munro. 'Right, pal. Me and you are off on a wee sortie.'

Munro followed Jimmy to the pavement's edge, ready to join him in making a run for the taxi rank opposite. He saw Jimmy hesitate, as if he'd forgotten something, and start walking towards the house.

'Whistle that taxi while I go and get something, will yeh?' Jimmy hurried up the stairs and into the house, leaving the front door open. As he walked through the parlour on his way to the kitchenette Agnes looked up in surprise and said, 'I thought you were away.'

Old Davey, not one to miss an opening, said, 'Away with the fairies, heh, heh.'

Ignoring them, Jimmy went to the old chipped mug on the shelf above the sink and slipped the bone-handled razor into his pocket beside the mobile phone. By the time he reached the front door on his way out the taxi was pulling up at the kerb. Urging Munro into the back seat ahead of him, he told the driver. 'Victoria. Vauxhall Bridge Road.'

'Is it safe to ask where we're going yet?' Munro looked sideways at Jimmy, drew his head back and raised his eyebrows.

'Aye. No bother. Ask away.'

'Well? Where are we going?'

'Visiting. We're going visiting, pal. Then we're going on to find Donna and Corrie.'

'Anybody I know?' Munro had the distinct impression that he wasn't going to get a straight answer.

'Not somebody you'd recognise.' Jimmy smiled at his own joke and leaned forward to issue instructions to the driver. 'As soon as you cross the bridge turn into John Islip Street and drop us off at the Queen Alexandra Hospital. It's on your right, just past the Tate Gallery. You got that?'

'That's Westminster,' said the driver.

'Pardon?' Detecting a note of sarcasm Jimmy cocked an ear.

'I said, that's Westminster. You told me Victoria.'

If the driver had been anywhere other than behind the wheel of a car Jimmy would've slapped him to the ground. 'Hey you, mister. Just drive the motor and keep your fucken yapper shut, yah cunt.'

The driver made the turn into John Islip Street and pulled into the kerb. 'Out,' he said. 'Before I call the police.'

Raging, Jimmy stormed from the taxi and, before Munro had a chance to move, pulled the driver out onto the street and dragged him along the ground, shaking him like a rag doll. Climbing into the taxi he wound down the window and told the shocked driver, 'Phone your depot and tell them Jimmy Macintyre borrowed one of your taxis.' After a moment's pause he added, 'Forget it. I'll do it myself.' Pulling the mobile phone from his pocket he, calmer now, craned out the window and dialled the number written on the door.

'Put me through to Jackie. If he's still the manager there?' Jimmy told the despatcher and waited. 'Is that you, Jackie? Aye. It's me, Jimmy Macintyre. Aye. I'm all right. Of course I'm out, but eh, Jackie, shut up a minute. You'll need to do something about this new driver of yours. What's he done? He's a cheeky cunt, that's what he is. Nah fuck it. I haven't got time. I'll drive the fucker myself. What? Keep the meter running? You're as bad as this cunt. Keep that up and I'll take the taxi off you.' Hanging up he turned to Munro, who had heard every word, and said, 'Where to, sir?'

By the time they reached the hospital, further along the road, Munro, subjected to a terrifying ride of crunching gears and near misses, thought he was in danger of being admitted as a patient. As soon as Jimmy alighted from the vehicle Munro climbed behind the wheel and said, 'If there's any more driving to be done, I think I'd better be the one to do it.'

'Suit yourself, but make sure you keep the meter running. I want to see how much we're going to save.'

A man of extremes, thought Munro as he watched Jimmy mount the hospital steps. He'd seen a man reacting, in a heartbeat, with swift and uncompromising brutality, as if it was his born right. Like a black knight. He also saw a man, after the event, who was witty, charming and cordial. There and then he wondered if there was any hope for him.

At the enquiry counter Jimmy smiled at the attendant, glad that she was young and female. This always brought out the best in him. 'I'm here to see my brother,' he said, intending to short-circuit the usual question asked of those arriving outside visiting hours.

'What's the family name?' the girl replied, fingers poised above the computer keyboard.

Jimmy craned over the counter and said, 'Sinclair. Ehh, what am I saying – Simpson. Aye. Eddie sometimes calls himself Sinclair. He thinks it sounds dead posh.'

'It's all right Mr ... Simpson,' the girl grinned. 'He's in ward E8 on the second floor. Turn left when you come out of the lift.'

'Thanks, doll,' Jimmy winked.

To his annoyance Jimmy found that Eddie's room in ward E8 housed three other patients besides him. One look at Eddie, bandaged like an Arab in a sandstorm, told Jimmy that he wouldn't be calling out, though.

When Eddie Simpson saw Jimmy approach his eyes screamed in terror when the words failed him.

'Settle down, pal,' Jimmy said and drew the plastic

curtain around the bed. 'You'll do yourself an injury.' Eyes bulging, Eddie Simpson began to tremble.

'I'm going to do you a wee favour, Eddie. I'm not going to take this personal. I know what things are like in this business. You've got to do what you're told. No questions asked. I can appreciate that.' Jimmy waited for a response, a nod, anything, and continued. 'I won't bother asking you if you had anything to do with the bombing up in Archer Street. That would be an insult to my own intelligence. I'm only going to ask you who was behind it, and I'm only going to ask you the once.'

Eddie's eyes frantically darted left and right as he tried to shake his head.

Thinking that the recently ex-convict was attempting to answer in the negative Jimmy reached into his inside pocket and produced the razor, giving the impression that he was slightly peeved at having to follow through with his threat so soon.

In desperation Eddie raised his head off the pillow and angled his upper body towards the writing pad on the stainless steel cabinet beside the bed. Jimmy reached for the pad and handed it to him.

Eddie began to scribble, using the hand with the least bandaging. Jimmy put the razor away, thinking that the answer was a foregone conclusion. When the notepad was handed to him he looked at it and drew his head back in surprise. 'Archie Kemp? Never.'

Anticipating Jimmy's next question Eddie held out

a hand and beckoned for the return of the pad. By the time Jimmy asked, 'Why?' the answer was half-written.

Jimmy read, 'Archie didn't want to harm Donna. He told me to make sure she wasn't on the premises. Sorry about the other girl.'

'Fuck the other girl. Why did he do it? What was he thinking about?'

Eddie took his turn with the pad and handed it back to Jimmy, 'I think he must've wanted you to think it was Anton. It wasn't Anton. Believe me. I'd tell you.'

Jimmy swept the plastic curtain aside and stopped dead. After a moment's pause he turned and said, 'Can you hear the war drums, Eddie?'

When Donna went into the bathroom her hair was wrapped in a towel and she was wearing one of the house bathrobes. Shane was sitting on the toilet seat hunched over the foot resting on her knee and applying a fresh coat of varnish to her toenails.

'This is the life,' Donna beamed, allowing herself a moment's respite from her worries.

Shane swung her foot onto the floor and looked up in time to catch the melancholy look in Donna's eyes. At that moment there wasn't anything in the world she wouldn't have done for her. A smile was all she could offer.

'I'd better go first,' Shane said at length, and placed

her make-up bag on the bureau in front of the mirror. 'It takes me a bit longer than you.'

'Go ahead, love. I've got to dry my hair anyway.'

Donna came out of the bathroom just as Shane was applying the finishing touches to her make-up, brushing on a thick coat of gloss lipstick in between the lines she had so meticulously pencilled in. Donna couldn't help but whistle.

Shane held the straight black wig in the fist of her left hand and brushed it this way and that, experimenting with a number of styles. After shaking it to give it a more natural look she stooped to put it on and finished with a confident flick of her head. 'The dresses are hanging up in the wardrobe, if you're looking for them,' she said, patting the wig down at the sides.

'These are absolutely gorgeous.' Donna held up a dress in each hand and then modelled them against herself. 'Which one's mine?'

'Take your pick. They're both the same size.' Shane wasn't being as amicable as she was trying to make out. She had already gone through the process of trying to select a dress and couldn't make up her mind.

After several minutes of deliberation Donna selected the black, strapless number and draped it over the end of the double bed she'd claimed for herself and Corrie. 'You know,' she began. 'It's a bloody miracle you having two beautiful after-five dresses just hanging in the wardrobe like that, Shane.

I don't know what we would've done without them.'

'Enjoy them while you can. Because the next time you see them they'll be at the Wheatsheaf as part of my act.' Shane paused for a moment while she kept track of Donna in the mirror. Lowering her voice she continued, 'This Gilfeather geezer – do you think you'll have any difficulty recognising him after all these years? I mean, ten years is a long time in anyone's language. People do change, you know.'

Despite the accompanying trauma at the very mention of his name Donna threw her head back and laughed. 'Don't worry yourself about that sweetie. If I had any doubts about recognising him, his American accent would give him away.'

'You never said he was an American.'

'I never said a lot of things, but it doesn't alter the facts, does it?'

Shane nodded silently, thinking that she'd touched a nerve. With the dress in one hand and the stockings she'd just extracted from the packet draped over her wrist she excused herself to the added privacy of the en suite. When she emerged a good five minutes later she was wearing a low cut, turquoise evening dress with thin shoulder straps and matching high-heeled shoes. She looked a million dollars and Donna told her so. Shane returned the compliment.

'I'm sorry if I'm a bit hard to get on with at the moment, Shane. It's just that ...' Donna paused to compose herself. 'It's just that, barring a miracle, this is my last chance to find a compatible donor for

Corrie. The doctor told me last week that even if we ... Well, he told me we're nearly out of time.'

'I'm sure everything will be fine,' Shane said and placed a consoling hand on her friend's shoulder. When Donna failed to respond positively she added, 'Come on, we're not going to get a result if we hang around here.'

'Can you give me a couple of minutes to speak to Corrie? You know, in case something happens?'

'God, I don't believe you Donna. All of a sudden you've given up the ghost. Where's the fighting spirit that got you this far? Geez, you've only got to take one look at that boy out there if you're starting to wilt.'

'Who the fuck said anything about wilting?' Donna snapped. 'That little boy is my heart.'

'Ohh, very ladylike I'm sure.' Shane stood with one hand on her hip and mellowed Donna with her smile.

'Give me a minute.'

Corrie's eyes were glued to the television when Donna squeezed up next to him on the couch. Annoyed at the invasion on his space he frowned and turned to lodge a protest. He changed his mind the instant he set eyes on his mum. 'Mum, you look beautiful. Just like a fairy princess,' he told her.

If only we could guarantee a happy ending, Donna thought, stopping short of planting her lipstick imprint on his forehead. 'You've been a good little soldier for mummy, Corrie. I want you to know that mummy gets all her strength from you. I need you to promise me that you won't give up the fi – You have to promise me that you won't worry about anything.'

Puzzled, Corrie looked into his mother's eyes and said, 'Why should I start to worry, mummy? Daddy promised me he wouldn't let anything bad happen to me.'

'Why indeed, when you've got medicine like that?' Fighting back the tears Donna planted that kiss fair in the centre of his forehead.

'Yuk, where's the lipstick repellent?'

Looking herself up and down one last time Shane checked to see that everything was in its right place, with no telltale bulges. Satisfied, she pinned her shoulders back and entered the room smiling broadly. 'Come on, girl,' she urged. 'Let's get this show on the road.'

At the door Donna turned and blew Corrie another kiss. 'I might be bringing somebody up to see you later so make sure you wear your good pyjamas, like a good boy.'

TWENTY-SIX

The first hint of the enormity of the occasion dawned on Donna and Shane when they were joined at the lift by some elegant ladies accompanied by distinguished men in dinner suits. But the real magnitude of the gala was brought home to them when the lift door opened on the ground floor and exposed them to a foyer full of milling guests, half of whom were vying for position close to the array of television cameras panning the immediate vicinity, while the other half, in an attempt to be as inconspicuous as possible, were doing the complete opposite. All were in high spirits and contributing to the general air of excitement.

'Shit, have a look at this, would you,' Shane whispered, holding her hand over her mouth. 'This is a regular who's who if ever I saw one. God look, there's what's-his-name from the telly.'

Donna made no attempt to respond to her friend's obvious excitement and continued scanning the area, looking for Gilfeather. The disappointment on concluding that he was yet to show failed to diminish the anticipation in her eyes.

'See somebody you recognise?' Shane asked mischievously.

Donna's eyes went up. 'The odd one or two,' she replied grinning.

'But not who you're looking for?'

'Not yet.'

'Is it just me, or are we getting our fair share of looks?' Self-consciously Shane glanced down at her perfectly flat crotch.

'No more than anybody else,' Donna assured her and helped herself to a glass of champagne from a passing tray.

'You're sure it's not me? God, I'd be mortified.'

'Nah. They always have a good gawk at these dos.' Donna answered half-heartedly and continued scanning the foyer, paying particular attention to the new arrivals.

Grinning mischievously Shane popped her face in front of Donna's and said, 'Any sign of him?'

'Nope.' Donna, with Shane at her heels, moved to a position near the front entrance and focused on those making their way up the red-carpeted steps, slowed by a television camera near the vast double doors.

Chief Superintendent Tate dodged around the delighted couple being greeted by the nightly news television interviewer, flashing her best on-camera smile, and blended with the crowd.

Shocked, Donna recognised him immediately and turned her face away. 'Christ, Shane,' she whispered. 'Has he spotted me?'

'Well, if whoever it is you're talking about hasn't spotted you by now he soon will,' Shane continued covertly scanning the foyer. 'Unless you stop your carrying on.'

Donna took her powder compact from her purse and, dabbing at her nose, used the tiny mirror to focus on the policeman making his way through the crowd. She was horrified when she saw him walk straight past Anton Winters without as much as a second look. 'Fucking shit,' she said and snapped the compact shut. Except that Tate was fatter, greyer and uglier and looked as if he'd aged two years for every one, she had no trouble recognising him. How could she forget? He'd been the star attraction in the diary.

'You all right?' said Shane.

Donna nodded in the affirmative but the look in her eyes said no. She acknowledged that it was too much of a coincidence for Tate to be in Brighton for any reason other than to be looking for Gilfeather.

'You don't look it.'

Distraught at the thought of Gilfeather making an appearance and fleeing the moment he saw the ranks of the opposition, Donna sustained herself with the knowledge that, up to now, he had managed to stay one step ahead.

'I think you're worrying for nothing, Donna. I'm sure Gilfeather'll show.' After a pause Shane added,

'It's your Jimmy I'd be worried about.'

'Thanks a lot.' Donna glanced to the heavens and began walking towards the ballroom with her invitation at the ready. On handing the invitation to one of several smiling ushers waiting to show the guests to their reserved tables she experienced an adrenalin rush like no other.

The ballroom's wide panoramic windows, which overlooked the sea, were draped with royal blue velvet curtains, the richness of which was greatly enhanced by the starkness of the white walls. Accordingly, a contrasting burgundy coloured carpet, where it could be seen in the aisles and in between the tables, boasted the hotel's anchor and crown insignia in gold. On the crisp, white tablecloths the silver service cutlery glistened and twinkled, reflecting the light from the grand chandeliers, which partly eclipsed the ornate gilding on the high-domed ceiling. At one end, above the stage, adding to the air of mystery and contributing to the general feeling of excitement and expectation charging the room, was a large banner with a black curtain covering it.

For a minute or two after sitting down at a table set for eight Shane, trying to drink in as much of the atmosphere as possible, gazed around the room unashamedly. Donna simply looked for Gilfeather.

'It looks like we've got the whole table to ourselves,' Shane said after a while, noting that the only movement in the ballroom was that of the waiting staff scurrying around the tables with the appetisers.

Donna paid her no heed. She had locked on to Anton and Tate watching her from tables at opposite ends of the dance floor. Faced with the enormity and futility of her cause, it was all she could do to keep from bursting into tears.

Shane reached out and patted her on the arm. 'Come on Donna, it'll be all right.'

On their respective tables Anton and Tate were not the most sparkling of company. Apart from waiting for Gilfeather to make his long-awaited appearance each was impatiently anticipating the overdue arrival of Jimmy Macintyre.

'You know Donna, I'm starting to think our host wants folks to notice us. We're not half sticking out like sore thumbs. The two of us sitting here on a big empty table. God, have a look at them, they could hardly miss us, could they?' Shane smiled, doing the best she could to keep Donna's spirits up. 'Hey Donna,' she added, leaning forward and smiling, 'when this is over, and Corrie's all better, we'll look back on this and laugh.'

'God. I hope you're right.'

From across the room Chief Superintendent Tate alternately drilled Donna with his eyes, picked at his smoked salmon or scrutinised the other guests, wondering if any among them had been summoned there for the same reason as himself, and he fingered the envelope containing Gilfeather's 'annual fee' he was carrying. He was still wondering when a drone of excited whispers accompanied the main lights being dimmed in the wake of an army of waiting staff sweeping through the ballroom, clearing tables. A spotlight trained dead centre of the darkened stage commanded complete silence as Jimmy Macintyre, accompanied by Munro, seized the opportunity to steal in under the cover of the subdued lighting.

Jimmy, dressed in his customary suit, and Munro in a sports jacket at least one size too small for him, were stopped by the hotel security before they took one step inside the ballroom. Munro automatically reached for his press-card, a ploy that usually worked. It dawned on him that he'd lost it, just as Jimmy took a security man to one side.

'Listen dynamite, do you realise who the fuck you're talking to?' Jimmy was confident that his reputation would gain him entry.

The doorman was a local lad, physically inept and little qualified to withstand intimidation. 'No sir,' he said.

In a moment of inspiration Jimmy winked and said, 'That's good, because we're working undercover. Me and Sergeant Munro there.' Unopposed he guided Munro into the ballroom and stood next to the wall, just inside the door.

As the spotlight played across to stage right, Donna thought the suspense would kill her. 'Christ,' she muttered under her breath and reached for Shane's hand under the table. Chief Superintendent Tate, in the absence of any contact by Gilfeather, could hear his heart pounding in anticipation under his shirt.

A voice boomed out as the spotlight trained on a deserted stage. 'Distinguished guests, ladies and gentlemen, allow me to introduce you to our host for this evening. The one and only Mr Dave Carson. What about a big round of applause?'

Donna held her hands over her face as the well-known television compere bounded onto the stage to the theme of his weeknight quiz show. She looked down at the table, gripping her temples with thumb and forefinger and shook her head disconsolately. 'I don't know how much more of this I can take,' she mumbled, eventually angling her eyes up at Shane and grimacing.

'Are we all having a good time?' the compere bellowed, striding across the front of the stage. 'Good, I'm glad to hear that,' he added, without waiting for a reply. 'It makes my job a lot more fun. Anyway, enough about that. Before we get on with the evening's entertainment it is my pleasure to welcome you here this evening on behalf of some very generous and civic-minded people.' The compere paused to reach into his inside pocket for his notes, prompting an enthusiastic round of applause.

Tate took the opportunity to feel again in his own inside pocket for the envelope containing the money.

'Ah, here we are.' Maintaining a broad smile for the benefit of the television cameras the compere began reading. 'Ladies and gentlemen. We all know why we're here. To raise money for the Blood Marrow Donor Registry. So, if you don't mind, I'll get the ball rolling with the first of tonight's pledges.

As I call your name would you be kind enough to make your way up to the stage. First we have the Right Honourable Bill Hutchinson, Minister for the Media and Communications. We'll hear more from Bill in due course. In the meantime, ladies and gentlemen, please put your hands together and give him a big round of applause.'

A lone spotlight focused on the confidently smiling cabinet minister and escorted him all the way to the stage. 'It's a great pleasure to be here,' he said in a broad Welsh accent and took a plain white envelope from the inside pocket of his jacket.

'Geez,' Donna said. 'Wasn't he Bill Hutchinson the reporter? Have a look at him now.'

Tate was thunderstruck when he heard Dave Carson call his name.

'Now, the last of our extremely generous benefactors I'd like to introduce tonight – Chief Superintendent Tate of the Metropolitan Police Force. Come on up, Chief Superintendent!'

Tate rose to his feet slowly, not quite comprehending. The compere gave him time to reach the stage before he read out the pledged amount. 'Ten thousand pounds. Phew. A lot of work must've gone in to collecting this tidy sum, Chief Superintendent?'

'There was a lot of people contributed to that, you might say,' said Tate, shifting awkwardly and shielding his eyes from the glaring light with his open hand. On the way to the stage, though bewildered and nervous, he had worked out what was going on, and had been forced to admire Gilfeather's ingenuity. The money was being handed over in full view of the public.

'You're very modest,' beamed the compere, holding Tate by the elbow, obviously singling him out for special attention. 'Without taking anything away from the generosity of the other benefactors assembled on stage, I think it is only fair to mention that you have pledged your support for this worthy cause on an annual basis.'

Seeing that Tate was completely stuck for words the compere excused him to the safety of the other men and women assembled on stage. 'Modesty forbids,' he told the audience and turned to bow at the line-up, his impromptu action encouraging another tumultuous round of applause.

At the back of the ballroom Jimmy fought the urge to shout an obscenity. Instead he muttered, 'Bullshit,' just loud enough for Munro to draw his head back and look at him.

'You know, I'm quite stunned,' continued the compere, diverting momentarily from the script. 'Ladies and gentlemen, you see before you on the stage people who have come a long way in life. Not only have they achieved success in their chosen field of endeavour, but each of them, let me tell you ladies and gentlemen, has attained far greater heights as a human being.' Pausing for effect the compere added, 'It shouldn't surprise us that people like this wish to share their good fortune. Just take a look at them.

Each of them, without a thought for personal gain or glory, have raised funds for this most deserving of causes.'

Keen to keep the momentum going the compere bowed his head solemnly and raised his hands to silence the crowd.

'Ladies and gentlemen, without further ado, it is my absolute pleasure to introduce you to Dr Brian Cullen, who, on behalf of the Bone Marrow Donor Registry, is here to accept the individual donations from our first batch of patrons. Ladies and gentlemen, I ask you to put your hands together again. Come on, let's shake this place to its foundations, why don't we?'

Directed by the compere, the Right Honourable Bill Hutchinson started a procession of awkwardly smiling individuals filing past the doctor. Dr Cullen graciously accepted an envelope from each of them and placed it on a silver platter held by a model hired for the occasion. When it was Tate's turn the compere moved in as the envelope was being handed over. 'Chief Superintendent Tate, congratulations once again on a fine effort. Now. For the benefit of the guests here tonight and the viewers at home, could you tell us briefly what motivated you to pledge your support on an annual basis? You never know, you might encourage others to join you. Wouldn't that be wonderful?'

The chief superintendent, normally no stranger to being interviewed by the media, had been making use of every second of what little time was available to come up with a feasible answer. Assuming the role of the dominant police officer, a persona never far from the surface, he added a modicum of humility for the benefit of the television cameras. 'It's a long story, Dave, one that would take me all night to tell. Let's just say that I'm no different to any of the other civic-minded people gathered here this evening who have combined their resources for the good of such a deserving cause as the Bone Marrow Donor Registry.' Tate smiled modestly and waited for the applause to die down. 'As far as raising the money is concerned, let me just say that there are a lot of generous people out there who are willing to put their hands in their pockets for a worthy cause. Those everyday people are the ones that deserve all the credit.' Under the circumstances, on such short notice, Tate thought that he handled the situation rather well. Especially since he'd had no clue as to what was going on until he'd been called to the stage.

'There you have it, ladies and gentlemen,' the compere said, turning to face the audience. 'You all heard me use the term, "modesty forbids". Well, without fear of contradiction I think we just witnessed the true meaning of the words. Wouldn't you agree, Dr Cullen?'

'An understatement if ever I heard one,' Dr Cullen said, rationalising that the chief superintendent's visit the day before had been part of the process by which the Bone Marrow Donor Registry had been selected as a perpetual beneficiary.

'Well spoken, Dr Cullen. But while we've got you to the microphone would you like to say a few words on behalf of the Blood Marrow Donor Registry? I'm sure our guests here tonight and the millions of viewers around the country would like to know a bit more about the kind of work you do.'

Dr Cullen cleared his throat. 'After tonight you are all well aware of the work some people are prepared to do in the name of a worthy cause. To them I offer my heartfelt thanks. But the story would only be half told if I didn't shed some light on the operations of the Blood Marrow Donor Registry and what its objectives are. After the great effort of everyone involved in tonight's activities, I've got no doubt that everyone will soon be aware of this great institution, and the good they do. Now, I've given this a great deal of thought, and rather than bore you with a whole set of facts and figures I decided to let actions speak louder than words. In this ballroom tonight is a woman whose nine-year-old son is dying of leukaemia.'

As the doctor swallowed hard and again cleared his throat Donna tilted her head towards the ceiling and shut her eyes in silent prayer. Shane moved around beside her and grasped her by the shoulders. At the back of the ballroom Jimmy's stoic expression masked the turmoil within.

Dr Cullen cleared his throat again and continued.

'For two years this young woman and her husband, with all our limited resources at their disposal, have been searching the world for the blood marrow donor that would save their son's life. Two long years of heartbreak and disappointment, the enormity of which you will grasp when I tell you that time is about to run out.'

The doctor stopped suddenly and looked to the compere for guidance.

'Ladies and gentlemen,' the compere began, after a hasty aside with Dr Cullen. 'If we could just have Mrs Donna Macintyre to the stage. Where are you, Donna? Come on ladies and gentlemen, what about a big round of applause?'

It was Shane who stood up first, attracting the pin-point accurate attention of the spotlight. 'Come on, Donna, your audience is waiting.'

Donna made her way to the stage in a trance. The only words to register with her were, that time is about to run out.

With the microphone in his hand Dr Cullen smiled, took her by the hand and turned her to face the audience. Then in an apparent change of heart he took her other hand and turned her to face him. 'Donna,' he said softly, but in a voice the microphone picked up, 'we've found a compatible donor for Corrie. One of the tissue tests proved to be a match.'

Donna would have crumpled to the floor in a heap had the doctor not immediately taken her in his arms.

As it was, she stared blankly over his shoulder, oblivious to all, even the countless flash lights.

To the backdrop of a standing ovation the compere stood to one side and allowed the media to milk the moment for all it was worth. 'This, ladies and gentlemen,' he said at length, 'is what it's all about.'

Jimmy watched his mesmerised wife being led from the stage with Dr Cullen. For the first time in his life he cast his eyes upwards and acknowledged the possible existence of a God.

He expected his wife to come straight back to the table and, with Munro in tow, made his way there, only to find that they had the table to themselves. Whatever was going on, he thought, paled into insignificance compared to what he'd just heard.

Backstage, caring hotel staff led Donna and Dr Cullen to a room reserved for visiting dignitaries and discreetly shut the door behind them. Donna desperately wanted to rush to Corrie and break the news, but first she had to have the answer to the question she was certain Corrie would ask first.

TWENTY-SEVEN

'I wanted to tell you as soon as I found out, Donna,' Dr Cullen said holding her at arm's length. 'But the donor insisted that we do it this way. I hope you're not annoyed with me? I know the pain every day brings.'

Donna shook her head slowly and tried to smile, her rapid blinking releasing twin wells of tears to track down the sides of her face. 'How could I ever be angry with you, doctor, when you've just answered all my prayers?'

'Believe me, Donna, I would love to take all the credit for that. But eh, I'm afraid that honour belongs to someone else. I'm only the bearer of good tidings.'

Donna's eyes widened in expectation. 'The donor. You're talking about the donor?'

'Indeed I am,' the doctor smiled.

'Dr Cullen, at this moment I love you dearly, but if you don't tell me, I swear –'

The doctor went to the door of the adjoining room

and rested his hand on the knob. 'I think that privilege belongs to the donor, don't you?' he said, and swung the door open. Donna couldn't believe her eyes. There smiling demurely, with her hands on her hips, was Shane.

'I think I'll leave you two alone,' the doctor said, rubbing his hands together and backing out of the room. 'There's probably one or two items you wish to discuss.'

After a moment of stunned silence Donna shrieked and rushed towards Shane, wrapping her arms around her. 'Steady on, girl,' Shane joked. 'I can't have you smudging my make-up.'

'You know, Shane,' Donna said when Shane at last managed to wiggle out of the bearhug of an embrace, 'for one horrible minute I was half-expecting to see Gilfeather standing there. I don't know what I must've been thinking.'

Chief Superintendent Tate, on the way back to his table, finished his third interview in a row, detoured specifically to make eye contact with Anton and discreetly nodded him towards the foyer. He had come out of this smelling of roses and the last thing he wanted was Anton Winters fucking things up.

'Listen Anton,' he said, steering him into a quiet corner. 'I haven't got time to talk, but there's been a change of plan. We've been stitched up by an expert. You saw what went on in there. It's left me with no room to manoeuvre. All we can do is get on with business. Do you understand what I'm saying? I want to leave things the way they are. If it's only going to cost us a few grand a year, I want to milk this for all it's worth.'

Anton looked off to the side and shook his head. 'What about Macintyre?' he said. 'What about our agreement?'

Tate gritted his teeth, jutted out his chin and grasped Anton firmly by the shoulders. 'For Christsake man, don't tell me I have to explain it to you?'

'I must be missing something.'

'Anton, listen to me. For some reason or other Gilfeather has decided to pass on the proceeds of his extortion to this – to this fucking charity.' The policeman paused for a moment, a puzzled look in his eye. 'You didn't think that I'd volunteered to donate the money? Surely.'

'Give us a bit of credit. I figured that much.'

'Then you'll have no trouble seeing what Gilfeather's up to. He got me to hand over the money in full view of the public.' Tate shook his head and laughed. 'You've got to give it to him. He's got me by the balls.'

'He hasn't got me by the balls.'

Tate's face darkened. 'He's got *us* by the balls. Anything happens to me and you wouldn't last five minutes. I'd see to that. No pally. Me and you are joined at the hip from here on in, whether you like it or not.'

An image of Archie Kemp talking down to him

flashed before Anton's eyes, enraging him. Under no circumstances was he prepared to be Tate's subordinate. Him nor anyone else. Not now. Not ever.

Mistaking Anton's silence for a backdown Tate continued, trying hard to contain his excitement. 'Like I said, I've come out of this smelling of roses. A good career move. And it won't do us any harm when it comes to business.'

Singlemindedly, Anton persisted. 'It's not going to stop me telling Macintyre who the father of his kid is. Nothing's going to deny me that. If Macintyre chooses to do something about it, that's got fuck all to do with us.'

'You're still not listening, are you? We can't risk it. I was under the impression that Gilfeather was going to show. Obviously he's not. The idea was to get the incriminating evidence off him, then give Macintyre the bad news and let him do the rest. If we do it your way, the material that he's using to blackmail us will still be out there, ready to come back and haunt us. No. My way we just go along quietly and bide our time. Christ. What's the worst thing that can happen? We have to hand over a paltry sum of money, to a good cause, once a year? I can raise that much legitimately, with a raffle and the likes. You know, in case my superiors start asking questions.' Tate paused and chuckled to himself. 'The clever bastard hasn't cost us much and he's made sure we're well compensated. Right enough. You've got to hand it to him.'

In the absence of the favourable response he'd anticipated Tate jabbed a finger directly at Anton's face. 'In other words, I won't allow you to say a word to Macintyre. Understand?'

Seething, Anton nodded in agreement. He understood all right, but he doubted that Tate did. This was personal. If Tate wasn't prepared to keep his side of the bargain then he had no alternative but to take matters into his own hands. 'I see what you mean,' he said, having no desire to show his hand. 'Business comes first.'

Tate breathed a sigh of relief and slapped Anton on the side of the shoulder. 'To business and a productive and profitable future,' he said, raising an imaginary glass.

Smiling like the Mona Lisa Anton reciprocated and wandered off in search of an appropriate place to think. The cocktail bar in the hotel foyer seemed as good a place as any.

As soon as Anton turned his back the smile vanished from Tate's face. With the feeling that Anton was now a total liability he returned to the ballroom in search of Jimmy Macintyre.

Jimmy, sitting with Munro, saw Tate manoeuvring his way around the tables towards him and thought about making himself scarce. He wanted to avoid anything that detracted from the exhilaration of the moment.

'Congratulations on the good news,' Tate said, offering his hand.

Ignoring the hand Jimmy got to his feet and said, 'There's always something happens to fuck things up.'

Tate ignored the barb and eased Jimmy to one side, out of Munro's earshot. Leaning closer he whispered, 'I thought I'd just cap your night off by telling you who was responsible for the fire bomb up in Archer Street, but if you're not interested, that's all right.' Tate turned and walked away, returning when he realised that Jimmy was making no attempt to stop him.

'Anything you've got to say is of fuck-all interest to me now,' Jimmy told him.

Eyes blinking, Tate picked at a slither of food trapped between his teeth. 'Suit yourself,' he said at length. 'I've got no hard evidence, so it looks like Anton gets away with it. Again.'

'Huh,' Jimmy laughed. 'You must take me for a right mug.' He chose not to divulge his information to the contrary, or elaborate on the fact that Anton's card was already marked, or that nothing was going to happen this night. Not now.

Tate fired a parting shot. 'Remember one thing, Jimmy. It's survival of the fittest in your caper. I'd watch my back if I was you.'

'I'm officially retired,' Jimmy called after him. 'Tell that to all the Mickey Mouse cunts. Tell them it's safe to come out to play again.'

'A friend of yours?' Munro said, raising an eyebrow.

Jimmy, keeping track of Tate all the way to his seat, felt as if he didn't have a care in the world. He was experiencing natural ripples of euphoria, better, he supposed, than that chemical-induced shite the junkies are used to. If only Donna was here to share it with him. 'I wonder where the fuck Donna and them are?'

'Maybe we should go look for them.' Munro smiled apologetically at the adjoining table, hoping they'd excuse Jimmy's continued use of the vernacular.

'Aye, come on. We're doing no good sitting here like a pair of edjits.'

Before Jimmy had a chance to move away from the table Munro leaned across and placed a restraining hand on his shoulder. 'Jimmy,' he said solemnly, 'I couldn't be happier for you.'

'Thanks, big man,' Jimmy answered with more than a hint of emotion. 'I hope you get a wee result yourself, before the night's out.'

Munro met with a determined resistance when he painstakingly explained to the concierge that he needed Donna's room number because Jimmy was the father of the young boy mentioned on stage. After a five pound note changed hands they were rewarded, not only with the room number, but a smiling escort all the way to the lift.

'If I'd known you were going to give that fiver away, I'd have kept the fucker,' Jimmy said. 'There's cheaper ways than that of getting information.'

From his position sitting up at the bar Anton spotted Jimmy and made a lunge for the lift, getting there in time to use his foot to stop the lift door from shutting. 'A word in your ear, Jimmy,' he smiled.

Jimmy's first reaction was to kick Anton's foot clear of the door. A pleasing enough notion under different circumstances, he thought. But presently at peace with the world, he said, 'Me and you have got no business, Anton. Not tonight.'

'I've got something interesting to tell you,' Anton persisted.

'You go on ahead,' Jimmy said to Munro and stepped out of the lift. Holding open the lift door, he added, 'Tell Donna I'll be up in a minute. Tell her everything's OK.'

Intending to retrieve the cigarettes and lighter abandoned when he chased after Jimmy, Anton led the way back to the bar.

Munro rode the lift up and hurried to room 507. When Donna answered the door on the first knock the smile she thought was indelible vanished from her face. 'Steve,' she said, 'what – what are you doing here?'

'I've come to share in your good fortune. Your husband shouldn't be too far behind me. He's down in the foyer talking to some gentleman. He said to tell you that he'd be up in a couple of minutes and that everything's OK.'

'Dad,' Corrie shouted and bolted for the door.

Feeling her knees go weak Donna shouted, 'Corrie, come back here this minute,' and made a lunge for him.

As Shane looked in from the bedroom, wondering

what all the noise was about, Munro gently stopped Corrie from squeezing past him and looked over at her. The blood drained from his face as he did a double take. Shocked, he stammered, 'Tommy? Tommy is that you?' Shane's strong physical likeness to his wife, in her younger days, was not only incredible, it was damning.

Donna, dumbfounded and thinking that her mind was playing tricks on her, loosened her grip on Corrie and moved to a position halfway between Munro and Shane. She blurted out, 'Gilfeather?'

One look at Munro, his face a chalk-white veil of utter astonishment, and Donna, her eyes pleading, turned to Shane for reassurance. Shane, embarrassed by having her father see her like this for the first time, smiled demurely and did nothing to refute the accusation. All three were momentarily speechless.

Corrie seized the opportunity to slip out of the room unnoticed and made his way to the stairs, thinking he'd get caught if he hung around and waited for the lift. At the bottom of the stairs he adjusted his baseball cap and peeked out into a foyer, all but deserted while the main course was being served.

Jimmy and Anton looked down when the boy squeezed in between them. 'Corrie, what the fu – wee son.' Jimmy scooped Corrie up in his arms and hugged him for all he was worth. 'What're you doing down here? Does your mammy know where you are?'

Corrie smiled at his father and cupped his cheeks

in both hands, making his lips pout as if he'd been sucking on a lemon.

'You're a rascal.' Jimmy sounded like a frog as he lowered his son to the ground and steered him to one side. Turning to Anton he said, 'I'll only be a minute.'

Anton smiled down at Corrie and reached out, too late to pat him on the shoulder. Corrie, paying him no regard, took Jimmy by the hand and tugged him towards the lift.

'Hey, hold your horses, wee man.' Jimmy lifted Corrie up onto a stool at the opposite end of the bar to where Anton was standing. 'Sit there a wee minute while I get rid of this geezer. What do you want to drink? A lemonade?'

'No. Hurry up, Dad. Mum's up in the room waiting.'

'Some result that, eh?' Jimmy put his arm around Corrie and gave him a gentle squeeze. 'What did I tell you? I told you I wouldn't let anything happen to you. I told you everything would end up all right, didn't I? Isn't that what I said?'

'Aunty Shane's going to be the donor, Dad. Mum told me.'

'Away!' Jimmy's chin dropped. 'Never? You're joking me? Aunty Shane, eh?'

Corrie nodded enthusiastically.

'All this time, right under our very noses!' Jimmy was truly amazed. 'Christ, we don't even know her last name. You wouldn't credit that, would you?'

'I think her last name might be Gilfeather,' said Corrie eagerly.

Jimmy laughed nervously. 'Where did you come up with that name? You must've overheard me and your ma talking. Is that where you heard it?'

'No,' said Corrie emphatically. 'That's what mum called Shane after Mr Munro showed up.'

'Are you sure you're not imagining things?'

'Nope. I remember thinking it was a funny name. A good name for a pigeon. Get it. They've both got feathers.'

'Well I'll be fucked,' Jimmy said, forgetting himself. 'It looks as if the bold Munro's got himself a bit of a result and all.'

'What was that you said dad?'

'Nah. Nothing. I was just thinking.' Jimmy looked over at Anton, intending to get rid of him.

Corrie inadvertently followed Jimmy's gaze. After the excitement of seeing his father he took a clear, uninterrupted look at the grinning Anton. Visibly shaken, he tugged at his father's sleeve until he stooped low enough for him to whisper directly in his ear.

'Umm, is that right now?' Jimmy said, squinting up in order to maintain eye contact with Anton. Corrie turned his back on Anton and frantically nodded his head.

Jimmy pointed him at the lift and sent him on his way with a gentle pat on the bottom. 'Off you go son, before the photographers get wind of you. Tell your ma I'll be up in a wee minute.' Turning and sauntering back to Anton he said, 'Now Anton, where were we?'

Anton squinted and looked around the foyer, nervous in case the chief superintendent made a return visit. 'You might want to hear this in private?' he said.

As usual, thinking in terms of wanting no witnesses Jimmy replied, 'Why don't we take a walk outside? That should be private enough for anybody.' Other than the provocative glint in his eyes Jimmy seemed very nonchalant.

No stranger to the ways of Jimmy Macintyre Anton sought the sanctuary of his room. The room in which he'd concealed, for emergency use only, a snubnosed Smith and Wesson. 'No need for that,' he said. 'My room's just as close and it's a whole lot more comfortable. Room 634.'

Jimmy thought for a moment. He wasn't keen to be seen getting into the lift with Anton. 'On you go,' he said. 'I'll be up in a minute. I don't want to push my luck being seen with a convicted felon. I don't want to end up back inside for nothing.'

Anton laughed and walked off towards the lift.

Jimmy entered the stairwell and took the stairs two at a time, stopping to catch his breath when he reached the sixth floor.

'You don't mess around, do you?' Anton stepped out of the lift, surprised to see Jimmy standing there waiting for him. 'What did you do. Take the other lift?'

'No. I thought you were in a hurry to get this over with,' Jimmy smirked, his breathing close to normal.

Recognising that particular tone in Jimmy's voice Anton glanced at him warily and headed along the deserted corridor, careful to remain abreast of him. On reaching the room he unlocked the door and took one step back.

In suite 507 things had reached crisis point. Munro was still coming to terms with the shock of learning that his long-lost son had surfaced as a woman. He was embarrassed, curious and stuck for words. Shane, for the first time in years, felt like a man being caught dressed as a woman. Worse. By his own father. She felt humiliated, ashamed and self-conscious. Donna, as much in need of answers as Munro, consoled herself with one thought only. At least Jimmy didn't have to learn Shane's true identity. She was about to alert the others to the danger and the safest course of action when, horrified, she suddenly remembered that Corrie had been in the room when it was revealed that Shane was in fact Gilfeather. 'Corrie,' she said sternly, 'did you understand any of what was said before you ran downstairs?'

Thinking that he was already in enough trouble for sneaking downstairs, Corrie shook his head vigorously.

Donna smiled and touched him on the cheek. 'That's OK. Mr Munro thought that Aunty Shane was somebody else.'

Shane and Munro caught the gist of what Donna had just said and anxiously awaited her approach. Donna steered them to one side and said, 'Whatever happens, not a word of this to Jimmy. As long as he doesn't know who you are, Shane, I think I can come up with something to sweet talk him. If I know him, for the time being, he'll probably be too happy to care.'

Their own agendas temporarily forgotten Munro and Shane eyed one another nervously. Munro voiced their concerns. 'Wouldn't it be better if we all got the hell out of here while you did your sweet talking? You know. Just in case?'

Donna thought for a moment and said, 'Nah. It'll be all right. You'll see. The only ones who know that you're Tom Gilfeather are standing in this room. Are either of you going to tell him?'

'Huh? Not me,' said Shane, speaking for both of them.

'Good. Now I know you two have got a lot to talk about, but Shane, before my Jimmy shows a face, would you mind telling me why you just didn't get tested and remain anonymous?'

Shane looked over at Corrie sitting watching television. 'I wanted to be near Corrie,' she said, adding quickly, 'As his aunty, of course. It was my prerogative.'

'How did you know about him? I mean, did you see the advertisement in the paper, or something? Why didn't you – ?'

'I often get the Chicago *Post*. Force of habit, I

suppose. When I saw your advertisement, naturally I decided to take a closer look. I recognised you right away and felt sorry for you, I had to find out more. It wasn't hard to land the gig at the Wheatsheaf. One audition was all it took. I found out what was going on all right, but unfortunately I'd already set the train in motion, with regards to Tate and the dirt book. I think you know enough about that story. All I did was redirect some of his ill-gotten gains to a better cause. Sorry for taking your diary, by the way. I couldn't help myself.'

'Where is it anyway?' Interrupted Donna.

'It's downstairs in the safe. I took it down earlier. If I don't collect it by twelve o'clock tomorrow, the manager has instructions to hand it over to the police. Clever eh?'

Jimmy stepped into the darkened room and looked beyond the French windows to the twinkling lights defining the foreshore below. He said. 'Nice view,' and stepped up to the full-length window.

'Fancy a drink?' Anton approached the mini-bar and glanced over at the armchair where the Smith and Wesson was hidden down the side of the seat.

The sea air wafted into the room the instant Jimmy slid open the French windows and stepped out onto the balcony. Proceeding cautiously over to the edge he gripped the stone balustrade as if his life depended on it and peered over the edge, just once. 'Christ of almighty,' he mumbled, and backed into the room thinking, Forget that.

'You're not too fond of heights I see, Jimmy,' Anton smirked, and handed him a glass.

Jimmy accepted the glass and manoeuvred until Anton was directly between him and the open window. 'Right, you were saying, Anton?'

Anton backed up to the armchair, sat down and grinned wickedly, ready to savour the moment.

Had it not been for that sickening sneer Jimmy would've heard him out. In a flash he threw the contents of his glass into Anton's face and leapt at him, gripping him by the throat with one hand and pummelling into his face with the other.

Gripping the hand that held his throat Anton, his face a mask of blood, slid his hand down the side of the cushion and groped for the revolver. As he touched the inlaid wood of the handle the armchair toppled over backwards, spilling him onto the floor, and the revolver beyond his reach.

Jimmy saw Anton reach for the gun and for a split second was undecided what to kick first. The instep of his right foot caught Anton flush on the face, deciding the matter, and flipped him over onto his back, unconscious. Not satisfied Jimmy hovered over him, his teeth clenched tight and bared like a wolf, and stamped his heel down until the defenceless man's face was pulp. Fearing he might have killed him, he backed away suddenly. Only because he had something to say.

He looked around the room for something to fill with water and ended up with a glass. The first swill over Anton's face produced a deep, guttural moan and washed away some of the blood. He then undid his zip and rained a steady stream of pee over Anton's face, filling his eyes and mouth, and forcing him to splutter awake. Anton spat out some teeth and tried unsuccessfully to focus with eyes closed tight as drums.

'Hey you mister. Can you hear me?' Jimmy held a foot on Anton's chest. 'You know what this is for, don't you? This is for my pigeons. You were spotted climbing over the back wall. My wee boy saw you.'

When Jimmy made reference to his son Anton, knowing that he was past the point of no return, tried to speak. A broken jaw and lips hideously swollen made his first attempt unsuccessful. Persisting, his grotesque face taunting and malevolent, he managed to croak out the words. 'Your son? That's the biggest joke in London. Everybody except you knows that Tom Gilfeather is the boy's father. If you don't believe me, why don't you do a DNA test. Stupid fucker.'

His eyes focused like a hawk's before the kill, Jimmy hesitated. Then the image of Munro returned, telling him Donna was searching for Gilfeather. Instinctively he brought his heel down on Anton's throat with all the force he could muster, again and again. Not satisfied with that he dragged him out onto the balcony and hoisted him up on the balustrade, leaving him dangling over the edge, the sea breeze blowing in his hair and his bulging, unseeing eyes staring at the pavement six floors below. His chest heaving, Jimmy gulped in air and marked time until he recuperated. One last, exerted push and Anton was over the edge.

Breathing easier, he sidestepped the pool of blood on the carpet and hurried for the stairs. Anton's words had reached in and torn out his soul. The mental torment increased as one morbid thought relayed to another, culminating in an all-engulfing anguish and an intangible, heartbreaking, physical pain. Not Corrie. Please God, no. Not my wee boy. Not my Donna. He wanted to cry but the tears wouldn't flow.

The door to suite 507 opened to him after he'd thumped it several times with the heel of his hand. He saw the nervous reticence in the smiles that greeted him change to that of shock. They saw a man covered in blood, wild-eyed, demented, tortured.

'Is your name Gilfeather?' Jimmy stood in the middle of the room and pointed directly at Shane. Shane backed away terrified and looked to Donna for help. Donna said, 'Jimmy, for goodness sake, Corrie's sitting there.'

Resolute, in the absence of the straight denial that he so badly craved, Jimmy advanced on Shane. Munro stepped in front of him and paid for it when a punch thrown from the hip knocked him sprawling to the floor. Donna threw herself at her husband, latching onto his arm. 'Shane's the donor, Jimmy. Shane's the donor,' she cried. Jimmy shook her off with a violent buck of the shoulder, heedless of her crashing into the wall backwards and slumping to the ground, where she remained perfectly still. Transfixed, and oblivious to Corrie's scream of terror as he ran to his mother's side, Jimmy grabbed Shane by the throat and backed her against the wall. In a lucid moment he said, 'Do you remember the time I saved you from Archie Kemp? The time I told him to leave you alone?'

In panic Shane nodded in the affirmative.

'Oh. So you do remember?' The heartache fanned out from the source and coursed through his body like an evil spell. A beaten man, he turned his back on Shane and bowed his head.

His shoulders heaving in time to the emerging sobs, Jimmy looked at Corrie cradling his mother in his arms and felt an emptiness where once he had known love. In one fluent motion he reached into his inside pocket for the bone-handled razor, flicked it open as he spun and raked it across Shane's throat, slitting it from ear to ear.

To the sound of her life's breath hissing and gurgling out, Shane had time to look down and see the gush of blood reach her waist before she collapsed on the floor in a spreading pool of red. Donna's ear-piercing scream brought Jimmy back to his senses. Looking down, he saw Corrie clutching him around the waist and weeping convulsively.

Through the sobs Jimmy heard 'Daddy ... Daddy ... Daddy!'